P. J. Womack

DARLING OF KINGS

Hayloft Publishing Ltd.

First published by Hayloft 2014

Hayloft Publishing Ltd, South Stainmore,
Kirkby Stephen, Cumbria, CA17 4DJ

tel: 017683 41568
email: books@hayloft.eu
web: www.hayloft.eu

Copyright © P. J. Womack, 2014

P. J. Womack has asserted her right to be identified
as the Author of this Work

ISBN 978-1-910237-02-1

This book is sold subject to the condition that it shall not, by way of
trade or otherwise, be lent, resold, hired out, or otherwise circulated
without the publisher's prior consent in any form of binding or
cover other than that in which is is published and without a similar
condition incuding this condition being imposed on the
subsequent purchaser.

A CIP catalogue record for this book is available
from the British Library

Papers used by Hayloft are natural, recyclable products made from
wood grown in sustainable forests. The manufacturing processes
conform to the environmental regulations of the country of origin.

Designed, printed and bound in the EU

This book is dedicated to Steenie

*'Darling of Kings, Patron of Arms,
Muses Protector, who from harms
Did shield professors of them twain,
Lies here by a base soldier slain.'*

Acknowledgements

I wish to thank my parents Ron and Kate Womack, for first imbuing me with a love for history; my son Peter, for all his support and patience, my dear friend and gossip Carol Dougherty, for sharing the adventure of writing this novel; my friends Pauline and Wayne Ashton and Nadine Martin, for their love and encouragement, and the late Peter Perry, for his kind assistance and belief in my writing. P. J. W.
April 2014

Prologue

Southwick House, South Sea near Portsmouth.
23rd August 1628

> *O Jonathan, laid low in death!*
> *I grieve for you, Jonathan my brother;*
> *Dear and delightful you were to me;*
> *Your love for me was wonderful,*
> *Surpassing the love of women.*
> I Samuel I: 25-26

Charles Stuart was kneeling at his morning devotions in the chapel at Southwick House, the home of Sir Daniel Norton, when the news was delivered: praying with all the fervour of his coldly passionate being that God would this time vouchsafe a victory and vindicate himself and Steenie in the eyes of Parliament and the country. Such was the intensity of his petitioning of the Almighty that at first he scarcely noticed the unwarranted intrusion into his communing with his God.

Sir John Hippisley walked forward hesitantly and then bowed low. As he straightened up Charles noted the haggard, strained features, and his attention sprang back.

'Your Majesty... forgive me... the Duke...'

Even before the words were uttered a paroxysm of fear squeezed the King's innards, but he only allowed a spasm to flit over his impassive features.

'Speak Sir John. What news of Buckingham?'

Hippisley moistened his lips and swallowed. 'Your Majesty, his Grace has been foully murdered; stabbed to death; he died almost immediately.'

The King was aware of the prayer book tumbling from his chaplain's hands; of the chapel seeming to strangely lurch, and of a sensation of falling; of being outside time. Summoning every ounce of strength of his prodigious will, he nodded then motioned for the chaplain to continue, unaware of the surprised glances exchanged by his host and Sir John.

'Continue,' he snapped, and the chaplain bent over and fumblingly retrieved the prayer book with shaking hands and resumed divine service.

Only the pallor and tightness of his skin betrayed a hint of what he suffered – eyes screwed up against the tears, hands balled so tightly that the nails dug into the palms and drew blood. Charles felt no physical pain, he was aware only that he must not allow himself to be seen to be any less than a king; a semi-divine being appointed by God, and above all human frailties, even now in the murder of the person he loved best in the world.

A life-time of suppressed and sublimated emotions carried him through. He intoned the responses as one in a dream (as surely this must be), then rose quickly from his knees, his only thought being that he must ensure the safety of the Duchess and that the ports must be closed. The rest could, must wait. The instructions were barked out as he walked so swiftly to his bedchamber that, despite his short stature, his courtiers almost had to run to keep pace with him.

At last the door was gained, was opened, as the roaring in his ears became a deafening crescendo; the constriction in his throat permitting no speech as he blindly waved his attendants out of the Royal Presence – no-one must witness this. The door had scarcely closed when grief at last overmastered and engulfed him, and he threw himself upon the bed in a torrent of passionate weeping, 'Steenie, Steenie, oh Steenie.'

Outside, the Gentlemen and Grooms of the Bed-Chamber stood

helplessly by, dazed and shocked, as they listened to their stricken Sovereign weep his heart out. None of them, even the older ones, had ever heard the King weep, not even at the deaths of his family; they would never hear it again.

'It's no use, my Lord; his Majesty will not open the door or allow any one inside. He still refuses all food and drink.'

Sir Edward Conway, Secretary of State, waved the young man away, and stood for a moment, gnawing his lip in perplexity. His repeated knockings at the King's door met with no response. There had been no contact with his Royal Master since the King had entered that sanctuary the previous day, nor was there any sound save the occasional muffled fresh outbursts of weeping. Conway felt no surprise at the extent of the King's grief, none at court and very few in England were unaware of the depth of his love for Buckingham – what had the Venetian Ambassador called the Duke? 'The King's inseparable spirit.'

Conway sighed and reluctantly walked away. A King without Buckingham – an England without Buckingham. It seemed impossible, unimaginable that the most powerful favourite ever known who many believed had ruled both King and country, and mayhap the old King also, was no more. Of his own feelings Conway was vaguely aware; he had served George Villiers, Duke of Buckingham for many years and had been equally infuriated and entranced by him – had loved him even, but his own grief must wait. There were more urgent considerations; those matters for which he had authority he had already arranged – for the detention and questioning of the assassin John Felton, and for the care of the Duke's body, which had already been embalmed and his heart buried at the nearby parish church of St. Thomas of Canterbury in Portsmouth. The Duchess, in the early stages of pregnancy, had been hastened to a nearby village in a state of total collapse.

Who now would rule the realm? Would there be another favourite? Conway doubted that; the King had cared for no one but the Duke; had listened to no advice save his. So who would assume the innumerable titles and positions which had been bestowed upon Buckingham? Would the King be reconciled to Parliament now that the chief reason for their enmity had been removed? Was his Majesty capable of ruling on his own even *with* Parliament? Listening yesterday to his King's wild and impassioned weeping he had even feared for his reason. And what of the great fleet waiting in Portsmouth harbour in readiness (of a sort) for another assault upon La Rochelle – waiting for Buckingham, its commander and High Admiral to join it on a death or glory mission, (or more failure and ignominy.) The fleet would wait in vain, for its commander had already embarked upon a more perilous journey and undertaking – to plead for mercy before the seat of God. Conway sighed again. So many questions, and while he pondered them a delirious country celebrated the death of the most hated man in England whilst their monarch sat alone in his chamber in black despair.

The next day the King finally emerged from his self-imposed exile, and those who beheld him were shocked at the devastation grief had wrought; his face was grey and etched with pain, the eyes puffy and bloodshot, and he looked far older than his 27 years. Yet despite the ravaged appearance his voice was tightly controlled and clipped; the speech impediment less marked. Although he shrank from the pain, Charles knew he must now hear the details of the murder; must take command. Sir Dudley Carleton, recently honoured with the title of Viscount Dorchester for his many years of faithful service, had been there and had witnessed the murder, and the King sent for him. Charles stood looking out of the window, face averted, as Dorchester recalled the appalling events; the same window where he had stood for over two hours anxiously awaiting Buckingham's arrival only a few days ago ('Oh Steenie').

He remained outwardly impassive as he heard of the violent rioting of sailors the previous day outside the home of the Duke's paymaster John Mason where Buckingham was staying, and of the Duke's coach being attacked; of the Duke's passing a restless night, and of his elation on hearing that La Rochelle had been relieved and there would be no need now for an expedition, dancing around the room in joy; how after breakfasting the Duke was rushing to the King with the good news ('Oh Steenie'), when he was intercepted by Sir Thomas Fryer and how, as he rose from a deep bow, John Felton had darted out from behind a curtain and plunged a knife deep within the Duke's breast with a blow so violent that Dorchester had heard his rib break, how Buckingham had uttered only the words 'villain! You have killed me,' had pulled the knife out and half-drawn his sword, had stumbled for a few paces after his assailant, and then fallen against a table, blood pouring from his wound and mouth. Moments later he was dead.

The King made no response as he heard the details of this horror but continued to stand gazing out of the window, and Dorchester's account came to a halt. There was silence for several minutes.

'And the murderer?'

'He escaped at first, running into the kitchen, but upon hearing shouting that a French man had murdered his Grace, he thought they were calling his name, and gave himself up. 'Tis strange that he could have escaped had he so wished, and none would have been the wiser.'

'It seems almost inconceivable to me that my foremost minister could be slain surrounded by attendants, guards and courtiers. There must have been a conspiracy.'

'It does seem to be a thing beyond belief your Majesty, but this Felton was a lieutenant in the army, and his uniform effected his admission into the house. The place was crowded; indeed many had not realised his Grace had been injured, and thought he had suffered a fit. It was only when they saw the blood that most people realised.'

'You have examined him?'

'I have your Majesty. He was taken first to the Governor's house under close guard; I had a difficult time extricating him from those who wished to slay him immediately. He says he fought at the Isle of Rhé and had been wounded, that he was owed money in back pay, and that he had a grievance against his Grace for having been passed over for promotion. Yet he claims the real motive for the murder was that he believes he carried out God's will.'

The King spun round.

'God's w-will?'

'Yes your Majesty. He is a fervent Puritan and followed the reports of the Grievances and Remonstrance of Parliament against the Duke. When he read that his Grace was accused of being the cause of all evils in the realm he resolved to rid both the country and your Majesty of that evil. He expected to be killed instantly, and had sewed a letter of explanation into the lining of his hat. He says he acted alone, and for love of God, his King and his country.'

'And you believe he had no accomplices?'

'I am not sure, Sire. He is still being examined.'

'I will have the truth. Let him be put to torture. Make preparations for Buckingham's body to be brought back to London in a manner which befits the esteem we held him in. He will be honoured with a state funeral, and you will order full mourning for the court.'

Dorchester bowed his assent. 'Your Majesty, I have taken the liberty of writing to inform the Queen of this tragedy.'

The King nodded, and turned back to the window; the interview was at an end. The truth was that, dazed and shaken, he could bear to hear no more, and while he longed for the relief of sobbing his pain out again, he would not allow himself that luxury, not yet at least. There was much to do, and the best way to honour his slain friend and the best remedy for his agony was work.

Work he did; within a fortnight his secretaries claimed he had despatched more business than had the Duke in three months, and had the King in the previous year. To ease his grief Charles determined he would pay the late Duke's considerable debts, and be a father to his children, a husband to his widow, and son and brother to his family. His memory would be cherished and enshrined within his heart; all matters would continue as Buckingham had wished, including the sending of the fleet to La Rochelle (for the rumour of the saving of that sad community was alas without foundation.) The King vowed he would devote his life to the memory of that dazzling, shining being, whom he doubted not was in heaven and with whom he would one happy day be reunited.

Though the incessant busyness produced a mind-numbing exhaustion, nothing could alter his anger and frustration at what he believed was the deliberate thwarting of his will; for John Felton was not tortured, it being said that this was unconstitutional, neither was the King allowed the consolation of giving his beloved Steenie the funeral and monument he desired for him; he was told that it was not safe for there to be such a display, there would be riots. Nor could he be allowed to erect a magnificent edifice while his father, the late King, lay in a shared grave. Instead the funeral of the most powerful man in England was quiet and subdued with few mourners; the coffin empty for fear of it being desecrated, Buckingham having been secretly interred the previous day. Seething with resentment, Charles could still honour the Duke by having him buried in the Abbey at Westminster; the first non-royal to be granted that privilege.

The King's anger was compounded by the celebrations held through-out the country, and Felton being held as a hero – the little David who had toppled Goliath. Charles was deeply hurt and offended, but his greatest rage was reserved for Parliament, and in particular for Sir John Eliot whose eloquent and impassioned attacks upon the Duke had so stirred and influenced the country that Felton had decided to resort to murder. Felton would be hanged, and Eliot would be punished; never again would Charles be inclined to look favourably upon Parliament, neither was the deep rift between himself and his people ever healed, for this was a king whose nature was not to forgive or to forget.

Weeks turned into months. Felton was hanged at Tyburn, repentant and begging for forgiveness which the Duchess of Buckingham granted. Charles, insulted and astounded that any would imagine that he could or should forgive, ordered the body to be hanged in chains at Portsmouth – no Christian burial for the assassin who had not only murdered his only friend and chief minister but had also killed a part of himself. He was informed that Felton had prayed for him and that he took a long time to die.

Those who had assumed that the King's relationship with Parliament would improve after the Duke's death were disappointed, neither did his Majesty favour any particular courtier, although it was noted that those friends, relatives and servants of Buckingham were always looked upon with kindness and generosity for the rest of his life. The agony in Charles's heart slowly crystallised into an aching void, eased only by endless work and by his vastly improved relationship with his French Queen, Henrietta Maria, known to the populace as Queen Mary.

Married over three years, from the start matters were stormy between them, for the young, frivolous, volatile and devoutly Catholic sister of King Louis XIII was used to a very different life in the royal court of France and was shocked and disappointed by her coldly unresponsive and apparently humourless young husband. Shocked too by the degree of his intimacy and reliance upon the dazzlingly handsome and ever-present Duke of Buckingham; the rows grew worse until neither could bear the presence of the other and they rarely shared a bed. Henrietta Maria could not pretend she felt grief or sorrow at the death of the man whom she had hated and considered her rival for her husband's affections, however, she had the sense to profess regret, and upon receiving Dorchester's letter informing her of the assassination she immediately set off to meet him.

At the sight of the King's agonised suffering her naturally affectionate nature yearned to comfort him. Comfort him she did, as the normally aloof and icily composed young man fell into her arms, sobbing unrestrainedly, and as she wept also, more in sympathy for his grief than at the death of the Duke, a bond was forged which continued to grow. She listened patiently while he talked incessantly about his 'martyr', of how the Duke had been unfairly blamed and misunderstood, of his beauty, goodness and devotion, of how no one could ever take his place and that he would miss him for ever and pray for him every day. The Queen, now able to be magnanimous, assured a delighted Charles that she prayed for Lord Buckingham also, and frequently visited with the Duchess whom she truly pitied. Encouraging the King to talk about the Duke tied him more closely to her for he had no such outlet with any other, and young as she was, she recognised that she now had the chance to claim her husband's heart, hitherto owned by the loathed Buckingham, and that if the King once began to love her, his nature was such that he would never turn away. Now she could become Queen indeed, and as time passed, to her surprise Henriette found herself growing to love her elegantly handsome husband, and their joy was profound on finding that she was at last with child.

On a cold December morning, the King retired to his private closet. Despite the ever present ache in his heart, Charles admitted that his spirits were lighter than they had been since that dreadful day, for the Queen's affection and tenderness toward him were ever more evident, and the news that he would have a child, and God willing an heir to the Stuart throne, filled him with gratitude, and he was deeply solicitous of his wife's care. How strange that the event which had caused him the greatest suffering he had ever known was proving to be reason for his present comfort, for he felt that his wife had saved his life; had rescued him from drowning in a hell of despair. If only he could have Steenie too then life would be paradise on earth.

At first Henriette's inhibited husband had been slow and reticent to respond to her demonstrations of affection, for it was only with Steenie that he had felt able to give and receive physical affection, though, unlike the late King his father, his strict code of morality forbade that he gave further expression to his attraction and love for Buckingham than fervent embracings, despite the rumours about the nature of their relationship. His young wife's obvious desire for him soon overcame his innate shyness and for the first time in his life Charles was free to give way to years of tightly-controlled and sublimated passion and to know the joy and pleasures of love-making.

A slow smile spread over the King's face as he thought of the forthcoming child; would it be appropriate to name him George? He looked up at the portrait of Buckingham hanging upon the wall near his bed and gazed again at those beloved features at which, in the absence of the original, he had stared devouringly so many times since August, even though the image was imprinted upon his heart. There he was in his physical perfection; the heart-shaped face, full lips, deep blue eyes and cascading chestnut curls which had captured the heart of his father King James, and those famously long, shapely legs.

'Oh Steenie,' he breathed and closed his eyes at the sharp stab of pain; even an heir and a happy marriage could not make up for his loss. Yet it had not always been so – it was hard to believe that there had once been a time when this irreplaceable man had not dominated his life, when he had not loved him but had actually hated him. The thought brought another smile to the King's face as he sat down and continued to look upon the likeness: the artist had admirably captured the mischievous expression in the eyes; a seductive smile played about the beautiful lips – he half expected the Duke to speak. He continued to gaze long and deeply as memories came tumbling back, unhindered and welcomed as the ghost of George Villiers, Duke of Buckingham beckoned him to remember and to never break faith with him.

Chapter One

Therefore my son first of all things, learn to know and love that God, whom-to you have a double obligation; first for that he made you a man; and next, for that he made you a little God to sit on his throne, and rule over other men.

James I from 'Basilikon Doron'

It was at Apethorpe Manor in Northamptonshire at the home of Sir Anthony Mildmay during the summer progress of 1614 that his Majesty King James I of England and the VI of Scotland had first caught sight of a face of such exquisite male beauty that his breath was almost snatched away, despite that he was well used to being surrounded by handsome young men, and that his current favourite, the Scottish Robert Carr, Earl of Somerset, was by his side.

On his return the talk was all of this beautiful young man who had gained the King's interest and therefore gained Somerset's enmity. George Villiers was the son of Sir George Villiers from Brooksby in Leicestershire by his second marriage to Mary Beaumont; an honourable gentleman from a minor gentry family. His father having died when he was thirteen, Villiers's ambitious and calculating mother had made two advantageous marriages, and perceiving that her second and favourite son was blessed with unusual good looks, grace and charm and not inclined to learning, she arranged for him to study in France to gain those skills necessary for a life at court. He returned after three years, an expert swordsman and rider and an incomparable dancer; a witty and delightful conversationalist with the glamour of French gloss in his suave, smooth manners and dress; in short, the perfect candidate for preferment at the decadent court of King James, and his mother viewed her handsome son with contentment.

At first it seemed that George would marry the daughter of the late Sir Roger Aston, who had been a Gentleman of the Bed Chamber and Master of the Wardrobe to the King, but her trustees had not viewed the prospects of the young man as keenly as had Ann Aston, insisting that he raise 100 marks as proof of his ability to afford to marry and keep a wife. Villiers declared he could not raise this sum, and although the besotted girl had told her suitor that she would marry him immediately without her guardians' permission, the marriage never took place. George was sorry but Mistress Aston's heart was not the first he had broken, nor the last, for although naturally good natured, he had inherited Mary Beaumont's ambition, and his sponsors Sir John Graham, a Gentleman of the King's Privy Chamber, his stepfather Sir Thomas Compton, and Sir Arthur Ingram envisaged a brighter future for this young man than being the husband of Ann Aston, and so he was persuaded not to think of marriage at so young an age but to cast his eyes upon the altogether more glittering prize of a life at court.

It was not by chance that the fateful meeting which was to alter the history of England occurred; George Villiers was the perfect person in the right place at the right time. King James's preference for good-looking young men was well known and had caused disquiet both in Scotland and now in England, not just for his morals, for although sodomy was disapproved of as a sin, it was well known that some men conducted secret affairs with male lovers; and had James also been discreet about his private life, it would have been tolerated better. The King, though, was immoderate in all things, it being said of him that, 'he loves indiscreetly and inadvisedly,' and he bestowed riches, titles and influence upon his favourites: he also openly bestowed affection; caressing and kissing them in full view of the court. However, the current favourite

Robert Carr's alliance with the powerful Catholic Howard family, with their pro-Spanish alliance stance, had caused real fear. So too had his increasing power and authority, for he was Secretary of State and only the previous month had become Lord Chamberlain.

The Protestant faction, spearheaded by George Abbot, Archbishop of Canterbury, and William Herbert, Earl of Pembroke, searched urgently for ways to counter the papist influence, and were handed the means by Somerset himself. James encouraged his favourites to marry, for women were no threat to him and he understood and approved of the need for a man to increase his wealth, position and the begetting of legitimate heirs through making advantageous alliances, (indeed the King had himself married and sired eight children).

So when his Robbie, then Viscount Rochester, fell in love with the beautiful Frances Howard, the King was only too delighted to facilitate the match. The fact that the lady was already married to the Earl of Essex was no matter, for Frances claimed that the marriage was unconsummated, though rumour maintained that she had herself caused this by the use of drugs, and so divorce proceedings began, including an 'examination' to ensure the lady was indeed still a virgin. It was also whispered that another woman was procured for this; for Frances and Rochester were already lovers. Despite the scandal, the marriage was lavishly celebrated, with the overjoyed King, who loved weddings and had paid for this one, drunkenly toasting the happiness of his sweet Robin, now Earl of Somerset, and his lovely wife.

Had Somerset had the wisdom to appreciate all he now had, future events might have been different, but years of royal favour had filled the favourite with arrogance and a mounting contempt for his maker, and now the Earl, encouraged by his wife, increasingly spent more time with Frances and less with the King, impatiently turning aside from his caresses and endearments and refusing to sleep with him. Furthermore there were increasingly violent rows, with Somerset even using language and threatening gestures towards his royal master which would have had any other man arrested, while an increasingly unhappy and frustrated King tried to mend matters with his beloved Robin. Abbott and Pembroke watched with intense interest, and perceiving their opportunity, looked around for the one weapon they knew could dislodge Somerset and his Catholic faction: a rival: he must be young, beautiful, Protestant and willing to obey them. In George Villiers they believed they had found exactly that.

Charles Stuart, heir to the throne, had not been on the royal progress; had been left behind despite his love of the hunt, but he heard of this young man; indeed it was impossible not to. In January 1615, Sir Peregrine Bertie, a member of the royal household, wrote to his brother that, 'the only news is of revels at court in all of which Mr Villiers was the principal actor,' while the chatty court chronicler John Chamberlain was telling Dudley Carleton, 'we speak of a masque this Christmas towards which the King gives £1500, the principle motive whereof is thought to be the gracing of young Villiers and to bring him on the stage.'

The King was so delighted with this performance that he had young Villiers repeat it; his eyes riveted by Villiers's dancing and the perfection of his face and body. George was brought to court and swiftly made Cup-Bearer to the King, a position which allowed him frequent access to the royal presence, and James often initiated conversation; his pleasure increasing upon finding that the young man was not only comely but charming and witty, and only too happy to talk about his experiences in France. He was clever too at impersonating the great personages he had met with, and the King laughed uproariously, pinching his cheek and telling him he was a 'droll bonnie lad', while Somerset silently seethed.

The presence of flamboyantly dressed, effeminately pretty young men had been a constant throughout the Prince's life, as was his father's kissing and stroking of his favourites; displaying more affection than he ever did to the lonely, reserved boy. The thought of yet such another neither pleased nor interested him, yet used as he was to male beauty, Charles never forgot his first sight of George Villiers; for such was the young man's physical perfection that it seemed that here in the flesh was the living image of those pagan gods about which he had read. Indeed his appearance caused such a stir that it seemed to be the main topic of conversation at court; moreover, he was generally acknowledged to be as inwardly beautiful as he was outwardly, with a sweetness of nature, impeccable manners and a desire to please which charmed most. Looking at this paragon who made the handsome Somerset appear plain by comparison, Charles was *not* charmed, but knew instinctively that the King, his father, would love him. The heir to the throne immediately hated him.

The Prince had been born in 1600 at Dunfermline Castle, the second son of the then James VI of Scotland and his wife Anne of Denmark. Despite the King's preferences for males, he had willingly married for the sake of the succession, telling the Scottish Privy Council that, 'as to my nature, God is my witness, I could have abstained for longer,' and later boasting that he had known no other woman than his wife, which caused no great surprise. At first James was delighted with his pretty, blonde, vivacious wife; his dear Anny, but the marriage soon soured and as he returned to the company of favourites it was said that, 'it is thought that this King is too much carried by young men that lie in his chamber and are his minions,' and whispers were heard that the Queen too took lovers, including the Earl of Moray who was savagely murdered in one of the internecine feuds of the Scottish nobility.

The day before the new Prince's birth had been marred for his mother by the ordering of the quartered remains of the Earl of Gowrie and his brother Alexander Ruthven, both involved in conspiracy, to be hung on gibbets, for there were rumours that the latter had been involved with the Queen. There was dark talk too that the young Prince, named Charles, and created Duke of Albany, was really the child of one Bedy, a Dane. What the King made of these rumours was not known, for he continued to protect Anne for whom he maintained a life-long affection even while he neglected her, and he accepted the child as his own, being unwilling to expose him to the pain he had himself suffered when being called the son of David Riccio; his mother's murdered secretary and close confidant. The thought of being called 'Jimmy Davidson' could still bring angry tears to King James's eyes even in later life.

The child was sickly and weak and he was swiftly baptised in case he died. Yet young Charles survived and was placed in the care of Alexander Seton, then Lord Fyvie, and his wife with whom he lived at Dunfermline Castle. His want of health remained a concern; for he was unable to speak well, his legs were weak and spindly and he was into his fourth year before he could walk unaided.

Charles did not see his royal parents frequently and so did not unduly miss them when his father left Scotland in April 1603 upon succeeding to the English throne. The Prince was sick of a fever at the time, and the Queen, who was heavily pregnant, stayed behind, and miscarried again; thus it was in June that she followed her husband with her eldest child Henry, and her daughter Elizabeth shortly followed. It was over a year later that Charles was judged well enough to travel to his new home, and now he had new guardians also, for he was placed into the care of Sir Robert Carey and his wife, who were keen to have the privilege, grants and influence which went with the upbringing of a royal prince, despite the dangers of his dying under their care. Nevertheless they were kind and had a warmly affectionate marriage and provided a calm and stable environment for the quiet, delicate little boy, who needed to be carried by an attendant when he was created Duke of York during the Twelfth Night celebrations of 1605.

King James viewed his youngest son with concern and perplexity, for the pale, silent child was strangely inhibited in his presence, as though aware of his father's disappointment.

'Can ye no walk no better yet?' he would continually ask, and his insistence on making Charles speak to him only resulted in his son being totally unable to produce any intelligible words for very fear: staring up at his father; his slightly protuberant hazel eyes huge in the pale, pointed face.

'Is he an idiot?' enquired the King of Sir Robert, who assured his

Majesty that the Prince was only thus because he was overwhelmed by his royal presence. Charles had Lady Carey to thank for refusing the King's suggestions that the cord under his tongue be cut to help him speak, and to have him put into iron boots. However they took their charge to one Edward Stutfeyld; 'an Artist for strengthening limbs, and straightening crooked bodies.' The King continued to demand constant updates on his son's progress, for although his eldest son and daughter Elizabeth were healthy and strong, he had lost too many children in infancy to view Charles with anything else than concern for his survival, and the King was to lose two more.

It would have been hard enough for any second son to compare favourably with the heir to the throne, Prince Henry, for he was everything that his less favoured brother was not; handsome, healthy and athletic, confident and studious; in short the model Prince. Charles was only too aware of the comparison, but he felt no jealousy for his glamorous older brother, just adoration and a fierce pride in him, and a total determination to emulate him in all things, including his style of dress, and when Henry and his household changed from wearing French fashions to Italian, Charles also changed immediately. Though he did not see Harry as often as he wished, for the Prince had his own household, he longed to join in with the games his brother and his companions played; trailing behind on his rickety little legs. His brother did not mean to be unkind, but frequently was, being impatient with his smaller, weaker and therefore boring younger brother, who poured out his love in affectionate letters, saying in one, 'I will send my pistols by Master Newton, I will give anything that I have to you; both my horses, and my books, and my pieces, and my cross bows, or anything that you would have. Good brother love me, and I shall ever love and serve you.'

Henry did not reply and Charles learnt early the lesson of swallowing his pain and feelings of inadequacy and loneliness. Both princes loved their pretty, vivacious sister, named after Queen Elizabeth, and looked forward to any time they could spend with her, although she and Henry preferred to be together and were devoted to one another.

Though Charles was small and weak, as he grew so did his determination, combined with an innate stubbornness, and slowly his legs became stronger. Each day he was on his horse, learning to ride well, to jump and tilt and becoming an accomplished horseman. Soon he hoped his father the King would allow him to ride in the hunts which occupied so much of his Majesty's time. He also played tennis and golf well and ran every day, and great was his joy and sense of achievement at being able and permitted to run with his brother. Yet the prince always remained short, with the bowed legs which he had inherited from James, despite questions about who had sired him, and this was a constant source of disappointment to him, resulting in him adopting a life-long characteristic quick manner of walking. Charles was equally determined to overcome the difficulties he found in speaking; practising for long, weary hours with pebbles in his mouth, which seemed to help not at all; and finding the careful formulating of words through in his head before speaking more helpful. Slowly his dogged persistence was rewarded, but he always retained a stammer, which became worse when he was under stress, and which contributed to his sense of isolation and frustration.

A similarly focused regime was brought to his studies, for Charles was determined to excel, believing this was one area where he could even surpass Henry and please his learned father, and the young prince applied himself diligently, learning Latin, Greek, French, Italian and some Spanish, mastering mathematics, and showing real enthusiasm for music, theology and particularly for paintings. He danced well and took pleasure in singing.

Charles's life continued uneventfully for several years. His admiration for his charismatic elder brother, whose investiture as Prince of Wales took place in 1610, knew no bounds, and he was gratified by Harry's lending him his horses and allowing him to use his stables. Yet sometimes Harry was not his sweet kind brother, as on the day which was seared into Charles's memory: both brothers were awaiting their father's pleasure while the Archbishop of Canterbury had an audience with the King in the next room. Henry walked over to a table upon which the Archbishop had placed his hat, picked it up, and eyeing Charles speculatively, he crossed over to where the small boy was sitting and placed it on his brother's head saying,

'When I am King I shall make you my Archbishop, for you're swotty enough for that position,' and seeing the look of hurt and confusion upon the child's face as the too-large hat fell over his eyes, he laughed and maliciously continued,

'And the long robe will cover up your ugly rickety legs.

The temper which lurked deep within and over which Charles was learning mastery rose unbidden at such cruel taunts and he jumped to his feet, snatching the hat off his head and trampling it under foot.

'I hate you! I hate you! I will never be your friend again!' he wept in impotent fury as he was taken out of the room, still screaming.

Charles was punished for such unprincely behaviour and had to stammer out an abject apology to his father and his Grace, and to Henry who graciously accepted his brother's genuinely guilty confession. He wrote a letter to the King thanking him for showing him his fault and then forgiving it; adding, 'although I cannot love and honour your Majesty more than I did, yet this shall leave me hereafter not to be so foolish.'

As the Prince of Wales grew older he began to regard his father with a more critical eye, for Henry was increasingly disapproving of what he perceived as the decadence and moral degeneracy of the court and of the influence and presence of his father's favourites. He disliked Robert Carr intensely, resenting James's devotion to the effeminately dressed young man who occupied the place he and his family should have had in the King's heart.

'There will be no lewd and degenerate minions or catamites in my court when I am King; no man shall rule me,' he declared to close companions.

The Prince shared his father's devout Protestant beliefs, but there the similarity ended, for he was abstemious, sombre in dress, austere and frugal; no curled and perfumed hair, whitened skin or bejewelled doublet for this prince of the realm; already frown marks were stamped upon his broad forehead; his demeanour proud and aloof yet gracious. Such was his dislike of the coarse language and profanities which were often heard at court (and particularly from his father), that he had boxes placed in his houses and anyone who swore was compelled to pay forfeit for the benefit of the poor. Henry's household pointedly excluded all Catholics, and he surrounded himself with soldiers, spending much of his day improving his military prowess. Over the years the rift widened as the differences in the two households became more marked; the pleasure-loving, learned and pacifist King, and the upright, earnest, warlike young heir. Charles looked upon his brother with respect and pride and a determination to follow his example, for this was how a prince should behave. Such impressions had a profound effect upon his developing personality.

It was perhaps not surprising that popular support grew around this splendid prince whose character, piety and military leanings gave such hopes for a glorious future reign. Nor was it surprising that the King, ever suspicious and insecure by nature, viewed Henry's popularity with growing jealousy, and began to fear the rising sun would supplant himself in his people's affections. His ambivalence towards his son and heir (which he felt towards all his family) resulted in his playing off his two sons against each other. He became prone to lecturing Henry, and one day, standing Charles in front of him, told the Prince of Wales that he was idle and that his brother's diligence put him to shame, and if he did not look to it he would leave his crown to Charles. James knew that Henry was far from idle and that he would never make good his threat, but this was a way of keeping the Prince in check.

For Charles these increasing occasions were a source of great tension and ambiguity; for though he craved his father's approval he did not wish it at the cost of seeing his adored brother humiliated, and he hurried after Harry to clumsily attempt to express his sorrow only to be rebuffed by an angry, 'oh run back to your books little Archbishop; it is all you are good for.'

Had Charles been of a different character then might the King's ploys have had more effect, with the younger vying with the elder, but to James's second son such a thing was unthinkable; his temperament and James's training on the nature of kingship were such that he could never condone any attempt to undermine his brother: for Charles was as clear in his mind of what was due to Henry as his future King as he was to his father, and of his role as second son. Nonetheless, such altercations left him miserable and confused as to what was expected of him.

The conflict between the King and Prince of Wales was sometimes expressed in public, as in the time when the pair were hunting near Royston: feeling Henry was not sufficiently enthusiastic, James reprimanded him, at which the Prince angrily moved his cane to strike his father, but succeeded in controlling his temper, and galloped away, with most of the hunting party following him, much to James's fury.

As the King and his heir became increasingly distant, James allowed Charles to spend more time at court and by his side, allowing him to entertain visiting dignitaries. The boy was thrilled by this, particularly enjoying being able to prove his hard-earned skills in riding during hunts and at the tilt (abilities which came so easily to Henry), but he lived with the constant fear that he would not live up to his father's expectations, and indeed the royal temper frequently flared, so that Charles carried the ever-present dread of being found to be inadequate. His efforts to deal with this resulted in a tightly-maintained control of body, mind and emotions which made him appear cold and reserved. Charles was not cold; indeed the intensity of his emotions sometimes frightened him, and made him all the more determined to master them.

As Charles approached his eleventh year the hitherto orderly and uneventful life which the young prince had lived came to an abrupt end, commencing with his removal from Lady Cary's secure and comfortable household. Now the young Duke's household was harsher and predominantly male. His new guardians did not get on and the atmosphere was tense and uncomfortable for the sensitive boy. Shortly after, the body of his grandmother, Mary Queen of Scots, was removed from where she lay in Peterborough Church and interred in the splendid tomb her son King James caused to be erected in the Collegiate Church of St. Peter, Westminster, and Charles was much affected by the sight of the hearse's progression through the dark: torches accompanying and lighting the way of the tragic Queen who had loved and reigned so unwisely and who had lost both her throne and her head.

The Prince was equally affected by the news that his dear sister Elizabeth was to be married to Frederick, Elector Palatine of the Rhine, and leader of the Protestant Union. The bridegroom arrived in England in October 1612, and the young couple fell in love at first sight, remaining devoted for life. Despite his sorrow at the prospect of losing his sister and the difference it would make in his own life; Charles shared the Princess's joy, and was delighted by the handsome Frederick's kindness and interest toward himself, to which he shyly responded. All would have seemed perfect had it not been for Harry's ill health; the Prince bravely joined in with the betrothal celebrations, refusing to accept his rapidly worsening condition and doggedly pushing himself with constant vigorous exercise, hoping by his strenuous efforts to throw off his sickness. He hoped in vain, for he was soon dangerously ill and despite all the desperate efforts of the royal doctors and the impassioned prayers of his demented parents, Henry Frederick Stuart, Prince of Wales, the glory and pride of England, died in a coma, aged eighteen. Charles was now the heir to the throne.

Chapter Two

What a delicious heaven it is for a man to be in a prince's favour! Oh sweet God! Oh fortune! Oh all the best of life! What should I think, what say, what do? To be a favourite, a minion!
John Marston 'The Malcontent.'

'All eyes are upon you, men look upon your worthy brother in your princely self; holding you the true inheritor of his virtues as of his fortunes.' So wrote Sir Robert Dallington in a dedication to the new heir. Charles desired nothing more than to fulfil these aspirations but was filled with doubt and anxieties. The aftermath of Henry's death had been a nightmare, for the King, stunned by grief and terrified by the reminder of his own mortality, had not even visited his dying son, and had been too distraught to take charge of the funeral preparations, so it fell to the young Prince, not yet twelve years old, to devote himself to the harrowing arrangements: the opening of and embalming of the once vigorous young body, the lying in state in the black-draped chamber at St James's Palace tended night and day by servants, and four weeks later he walked on foot as chief mourner in the funeral cortege of the brother he had idolised.

Charles was also given the responsibility for his sister's wedding which Henry's untimely death had delayed, and on Valentine's Day the two sixteen year olds married. For two months they remained in England and spent most of their time with Charles who found his fondness for Frederick growing. Then suddenly they were gone. Charles never saw his sister again.

The months following were bleak indeed as the young Prince attempted to come to terms with his grief and with the loss of the people he loved most, for although he had been aware of the death of siblings, he had rarely seen them and had felt merely a sad poignancy that he would never know or play with them. The enormity of the realisation of his new role was overwhelming, and he fell ill. It was the lowest point in his young life; his only solace was his absolute faith in God who had seen fit to call him to such trials, and the affectionate letters he received from Elizabeth. He had never felt so alone.

Over the years Charles devoted himself to fulfilling all his obligations and pleasing his unpleasable father with a grim and dogged determination. He loved James but was terrified of him; admired his learning and respected his God-given authority as monarch but could not approve of him. As Charles gravely gazed upon his father, seeing the undignified shambling gait, the bouts of laughter and the maudlin weeping, the drunken fumbling of and kissing of his favourite Robert Carr, and hearing the crude speech, he inwardly shuddered and became even more reserved, hugging his feelings to himself. Often as he lay awake at night he would remember his dead brother's disapproval of their father's unkingly behaviour, and hear again Harry's disparaging words about Robert Carr whom he had detested; 'there shall be no such degenerate minions in court when I am King. I shall be ruled by none.'

He vowed inwardly again that he would honour his brother, and live in a manner which would make him proud. Such thoughts also caused him guilt. The paradox between Divine authority and James's sottish, boorish behaviour seemed irreconcilable, yet he was driven by the desire to please the King and his unhappy mother while remaining true to his own ideals and principles and to the brother who appeared to be even more the epitome of princely perfection now that he was in heaven. He found such a desire was impossible to achieve.

Unlike with the elder son there was no conflict with the King nor was he a focus for popular support, and while this was a relief for James, Charles's lack of assertiveness irritated him, and he refused to give him any real responsibilities or allow him any influence. While courtiers and ambassadors noted the Prince's sober dress and demeanour, they also noted the King's disappointment that God had deprived him of his eldest son (even though he had been jealous of him), and left him with this one (ah the ways of providence were unfathomable!) For all Charles's emulation of his dead brother, he was not Henry. There were rumours of his suffering from 'green sickness,' a malady which usually afflicted adolescent girls, and talk that he was sterile and girlish. He blushed like a maiden if he heard scandalous conversation or swearing. In all he was not much more respected or visible as heir apparent than he had been to those conspirators who had plotted to blow up King, heir and Parliament in 1605; they had planned to capture Princess Elizabeth and make her Queen, and had only later realised that there was another royal prince.

The young man's relationship with his mother Queen Anne had steadily grown closer over time, and he frequently visited her. She and his father had not lived together for many years and she lived a life of extravagant frivolity. Prone to depression and increasingly poor health, Anne would sometimes castigate the King who had over the years given his heart and body to male favourites instead of his lawful wife, and hearing such loud denunciations, her son felt deeply uncomfortable but understood her anger and pain. After all, he too had been ousted by a cuckoo from his rightful place in his father's heart.

Regarding Carr as he did, it was no surprise that the thirteen year old Charles looked upon the new, yet more dazzling cuckoo, and detested George Villiers on sight.

In 1615 Robert Carr, Earl of Somerset was implicated in the horrific murder of his former friend and confidant (some would say he was more), Sir Thomas Overbury while the latter was imprisoned in the Tower for refusing to accept a post abroad. The King had been jealous and resentful of the clever favourite of his favourite and his intimacy with his Robin; for James cared not that Carr had relationships with women, nor that he married, but would countenance no male rivals. Thus when Overbury's formerly beloved friend and master married Frances Howard, whom Overbury bitterly called 'the whore', the cause of the rupture in their friendship was having Sir Thomas poisoned. When the appalling facts became known, both the Earl and Countess of Somerset were put on trial during which Frances confessed her guilt, but her husband obdurately maintained his innocence. No matter; both were found guilty and sentenced to death, but the King had mercy upon his former lover and the sentence was commuted to imprisonment. Somerset was saved, but the life he had so enjoyed was destroyed; so too was the marriage to the woman whom he ever after believed had ruined him.

Now Villiers's rise was unimpeded, and James heaped titles and wealth upon him. In an astonishingly short time the boy from Leicestershire had been knighted, become Gentleman of the Bed-Chamber, Master of the Horse, Knight of the Garter, Viscount Villiers and Baron Whaddon. In January 1617 he was created Earl of Buckingham and the next month became the youngest member of the Privy Council. This privilege was repeated when the Scottish Privy Council admitted him as a member; an honour never previously granted to any Englishman. He had also become the King's acknowledged favourite and a year after first meeting, the two had become lovers at Farnham Castle; some years later the young man writing to his King, 'all the way hither I entertained myself, your unworthy servant with this dispute, whether you loved me now better than at the time which I shall never forget at Farnham, where the bed's head could not be found between the master and his dog.'

King James was besotted and entranced with the young man whom he named 'Steenie', the Scottish diminutive for Stephen; for he said Villiers's beautiful features bore a close resemblance to the portrait in Whitehall of St. Stephen, whose face was said to be that of an angel. The King's angel had swiftly consolidated and developed his power and influence, deftly creating a system of patronage second to none. Cleverer and more able than his predecessor, the new favourite, though possessed of a genuinely charming and good-natured disposition, was capable of behaviour which belied the angelic features; he could be impetuous, over-confident, arrogant and soon angered. Moreover, he was determined to include his large and rapacious family in his good fortune, headed by his ambitious and domineering mother, Mary Compton, and he bestowed positions and wealth upon them. Under Mary's expert eye, he was particularly keen to arrange advantageous marriages for his kin, and that year saw the match of his elder brother John to the fourteen year old Frances Coke; an alliance which had caused scandal and unhappiness, and which would cause worse and he would have cause to regret.

It soon became apparent to George Abbot and those who had first brought Villiers to prominence as a challenge to Somerset's power, that they had badly misjudged the new favourite, now known as Buckingham, for behind the smiling, somewhat effeminate face and exquisite courtesy, lay an iron will and ambition to be ruled by none, and too late they realised that Buckingham was gaining more power and hold over the King than Robert Carr ever had, and moreover, the abilities to use it, for the young man learnt fast. While Buckingham remained outwardly eager to please, he was not afraid to oppose any that he thought thwarted his or his royal master's will, and now all the court and foreign ambassadors knew that the only access to the King was through his favourite.

To James, happier than he had ever been, Buckingham behaved with a combination of saucy, familiar insolence and abject servility which intoxicated the King, who was the 'dear Dad and Gossip' of his sweet Steenie whom he called his sweetheart and only child and wife. The recipient of such all-consuming adoration referred to himself as his Majesty's Dog and Slave, but it was clear to all that it was James who was enslaved.

It was clearer to none more than Charles, Prince of Wales, who heard his father repeatedly tell Buckingham of his love and need of him and of his being his only child; for the King would show more physical affection and love to the favourite in one day than he had ever shown to his son during his whole life. The King had unashamedly told a bemused Privy Council that he loved the Earl of Buckingham more than any; saying Christ had his John and he had his George. At sixteen the heir was still small and slight but had a dignity and elegance of his own; his pale face seldom smiled, but the features were pleasing if not yet handsome; the large, fine eyes thoughtful and observant. Sombre in dress, Charles was reserved, dutifully obedient to the King and painfully shy. The contrast between himself and the gorgeous, magnificent Earl of Buckingham who was ever extravagantly clad in expensive doublets which were drenched in jewels; his neck festooned with pearls, could not have been more marked. Buckingham looked every inch like a royal prince, but Charles had no desire to emulate him: he would not have debased himself to even try; Harry was still his role-model.

Yet there were times when even Charles's self-control broke and there were several occasions when he could not keep silent or resist retaliation. The previous year he had noticed a particularly valuable ring on the favourite's hand which he knew had been bestowed by his father. Jealous, the Prince asked to see it and tried it on his own slight finger; conveniently 'forgetting' to return it. Upon Buckingham requesting it the next day, Charles claimed he could not find it and was gratified to see a scowl upon the other's face. The Prince thought no more of it until he was commanded to the King's presence, whereupon James delivered such a tirade, his arm around Buckingham's shoulders, and forbidding him the royal presence until the ring was returned, that Charles could not hold back the tears. The ring was returned.

Then there was the occasion at Greenwich when the Prince was reluctantly accompanying his father and the favourite as they walked around one of the gardens, dawdling behind while James ambled in front, his arm around Buckingham, caressing his back and chestnut hair. The King sat down on a seat in a shady arbour near a beautiful fountain graced by a statue of Bacchus, and heaved a sigh of relief; his gouty legs were troubling him that day, and it was a cool, fragrant and pleasant spot. His eyes drank in his favourite's handsome face and lithe, slender body.

Charles saw that Buckingham had deliberately positioned himself where his royal master could appreciate his beauty and had adopted a suitably provocative pose to flirt with the King. The Prince stood awkwardly by, excluded. Seized by an impulse, he suddenly directed the fountain toward the hated rival, exulting at the astonished outburst from the soaked favourite; his carefully styled hair dripping.

'How dare you! Have you any idea how much this doublet cost?'

The laughter which rose was quickly stifled when the King, with more alacrity than his son could have believed, jumped to his feet, and grabbing him by his arm, his father roundly cursed Charles, striking him over and over until the shocked and terrified boy screamed aloud for mercy.

'Begone! Begone yeh misbegotten miscreant! Yeh have naught but a malicious and dogged disposition. If yeh ever cause my Steenie sich trouble or pain again, I'll pull down your breeks and whip your arse mysel.'

In view of such threats Charles did not dare defy his father when the King demanded shortly after that he play tennis with Buckingham. It was clear from the expression on his face that the idea did not appeal much to the favourite either, but he was keen to appear obedient to the royal will, and so the two young men entered the little Open Tennis Court beside the tiltyard at Whitehall Palace in silence. Tight-lipped and garbed in a tennis suit of taffety, Charles was determined he would not allow the favourite to beat him, and indeed Buckingham was surprised that his Royal Highness showed such surprising ability, despite his lack of height and slight figure. Surprised indeed and annoyed by his opponent winning several games in what he had assumed would be a quick and easy match so he could return to more enjoyable activities, (the luscious charms of Lady Elizabeth Danvers, who was watching the match, awaiting him), Buckingham's mind was only half on the match while he continually glanced over at Lady Danvers's provocatively displayed breasts which he imagined shortly caressing and kissing.

Several other spectators joined her, and whilst the favourite's tall, athletic figure attracted much attention and admiration, so did the dogged persistence of the Prince, and it was clear that John Webb's coaching of the royal heir had been worth the twenty pounds he had received. As the match became a contest of wills between the two, Buckingham stopped his smiling and posturing to please the crowd which had been drawn by the on court battle, becoming increasingly frustrated and anxious to appear at his best, and when another call went against him, he furiously contested it. The Prince would not yield one iota and his air of cold disdain irritated the favourite beyond bearing. After several minutes of heated argument, Buckingham lost his temper.

'This is intolerable! I am being deliberately penalised. If my opponent had been any but yourself I would have already won the match.'

'I am sorry if your lack of talent is causing you distress, my Lord. Of course you are correct: normally by now you would have won because your opponents always allow you to. However, you will find that I am of a different mettle, notwithstanding your great favour with his M-Majesty.'

It was the first time Buckingham had been deliberately crossed by the Prince, and he was furious. The long slender legs strode swiftly towards Charles; rage contorting the still beautiful features, his racket raised menacingly. Despite the shock, Charles was determined to retain control and dignity: *he* was the heir to the throne, not this parvenu. He would stand his ground.

'What Sir, would you raise your hand to your Prince in violence?'

The favourite hesitated, racket still raised: the icy calm of the Prince recalled him to the dangers of his actions. He spun round on his heels, and marched off, throwing the racket to the ground. Now Charles's anger was roused; Buckingham's disrespect was beyond belief.

'You will not turn your back upon your P-Prince, nor leave my presence without my permission. Return at once!'

'Kiss my arse,' was the sharp rejoinder.

Humiliation flooded through Charles. He barely heard the gasps and titters from the spectators. His face flushed then became deathly white with fury; he felt foolish and impotent.

'His Majesty shall b-be informed of this outrage.'

'Assuredly he shall!' came the reply as Buckingham bowed his regrets to Lady Danvers. The pleasures of her bedchamber must wait; he knew he must immediately put his side of the incident to James, for he was aware of how far he had breached protocol and the seriousness of his words and actions.

Shortly after Buckingham was by the King's side, relating the story to his dear Dad, and professing great sorrow. James laughed heartily at hearing his favourite's words, for he had a crude streak in his nature, (had he not said during his progress to England in 1603, when tired by the relentless demands of his people wanting to see their new King that if they wished to see more of him then he would pull his breeches down and they could see his arse?)

'Aye you are a naughty boy Steenie to talk thus to the Prince, but I doubt not that yeh had reason, for I confess I am often out of patience with him.'

His favourite, greatly relieved, leaned close to his master; slipping his arm caressingly around James's neck he nuzzled it, whispering seductively,

'Indeed I have been a naughty dog, and naughty dogs should be punished. I am entirely at your Majesty's mercy and insist you take out your displeasure on my body tonight.'

There were no repercussions.

Yet the increasing violence between Steenie and the heir worried the King, and he was desirous that they should be friends. Over the next few months both the Prince and favourite were careful to avoid any further confrontation and treated each other with a wary and enforced civility. Buckingham, realising how important this was to James, determined that he would make overtures to the Prince, albeit ones which meant nothing to him. However, this was nothing new, for his role as favourite necessitated him being friendly and charming to those he disliked. Yet Buckingham did not particularly dislike the Prince; he was simply of no importance to him, and the King's contemptuous attitude towards his son did not encourage his favourite to win the favour of one whom he believed to be dull, boring and of little consequence, despite advice from Sir Francis Bacon, Lord Keeper of the Great Seal, that he would be unwise not to cultivate the young man who would be king next. Buckingham had ignored him with the confidence of youth which assumed he had little to learn from the experienced and wily elder statesman; now he would ignore him no longer.

By the summer of 1618 the relationship between the two was genuinely friendly if not yet affectionate, for Charles was becoming reconciled to the fact that the only way to be more acceptable to the King was to come to terms with Villiers' central place in his father's life. The favourite, now Marquis of Buckingham, was equally desirous of gaining the friendship of the earnest young Prince, for he had become increasingly aware that James was ageing. Painfully afflicted by the gout, the King appeared old beyond his years and was often querulous and irritable. Fortunately his Steenie knew how to comfort and cheer him, and his Majesty still spent countless hours in the saddle enjoying the hunt, but only a fool would not look to the future. Buckingham was no fool.

Encouraged by Charles's more favourable attitude towards him, he resolved to woo the young Prince, certain of his ability to succeed, for who could resist him? The setting would be his newly purchased house at Wanstead where he would invite the King and Prince to a sumptuous feast in their honour and there he would lay siege to the young man's heart. The June day was auspiciously hot and sultry, the sky azure, and the festivities were held outdoors, set in an artificial wood planted like a palace in which the hall and presence chamber, bed-chamber, drawing-room, and cabinet were formed by drawing the hangings from one tree to another. The Marquis had spared no expense, and James, intoxicated both by the delight of the surroundings and the extravagant display of food, and by the amount of wine he had drunk, rose unsteadily to his feet to toast his beloved Steenie over and over. And not just Steenie, but also his family who were also invited, declaring that he desired to advance them above all others. 'I live to that end,' he repeated, raising his goblet to Lady Compton, Buckingham's mother, whose still handsome face smilingly dimpled as she inclined her head in gracious acknowledgment.

Charles was impressed despite himself at the faultless good taste exhibited by Buckingham; the setting, the furnishings and the food were all exquisite – all except the favourite's family; from the first the Prince had particularly disliked the Marquis's mother, finding her ill-bred and over familiar. That lady had attempted to engage him in conversation, and Charles, ever-mindful of correct protocol, had been displeased by such inappropriate informality and had dismissively brushed her aside, much to her chagrin. The mother of the favourite or no, he did not like her, and Charles never changed his mind but once about his first impressions of people. The exception to this rule was assiduous in his attentions to the Prince; pleasingly respectful, flatteringly desirous of his opinion on many subjects. As Charles basked in the radiance of the Marquis's smile; warm, golden and caressing as the sunlight which bathed the sumptuous hangings, he was aware of his former dislike of Buckingham thawing, and as the day wore on he was beginning to wonder how it was that he had ever thought ill of so charming a companion.

As the King contentedly continued to drink after eating his fill, a sleepy torpor stealing over him, Buckingham turned to the Prince.

'I wonder if your Highness would do me the honour of allowing me to show you the gardens? I have many plans and would be grateful for your advice.'

Delighted and amazed, Charles assented, while the Marquis addressed his royal master, whose head was nodding as he dozed.

'Your Majesty, I crave your permission to excuse myself and his Highness for a short time while I show the Prince around the gardens and gain the benefit of his expert opinion.'

The sleepy monarch opened his bleary eyes. 'I doubt yeh'll get much expert advice from yon, but you have my permission. Just dinnae be long Steenie; it's still hot and unhealthy to have too much sun.'

Buckingham kissed the royal hand, and the two bowed themselves from the King's presence. As he drew the Prince after him, the favourite exchanged a glance with his mother; he had confided his plans to her and asked that she would entertain the King in his absence, for unlike his son, James enjoyed Lady Compton's company. Hearing the Marquis speak of a walk, several others rose to join them. Charles felt disappointment and annoyance at their intrusion, but Buckingham was in command of the situation.

'Delightful and diverting as your conversation is, I must deprive myself of its pleasures this time; for I am determined to have his Highness to myself,' he told them.

The young men walked along a path in silence then entered through a weathered stone archway over which roses trailed, leading into an enclosed garden. The air was filled with fragrance; insects droning lazily in the summer warmth; the distant sounds of laughter from the guests occasionally reaching them.

'It was planted long ago and was fashionable then; I shall have it brought up to date, though it still has a real charm, do you not think?'

Buckingham stopped and bent over the flowers. 'I love the fragrance of roses; I will have lots of roses. I think heaven must be filled with their perfume.'

He straightened up and smiled at the Prince.

'I hope your Highness will forgive my importuning, but I will confess that I have longed to spend some time alone with you.'

Charles blinked, unsure what to say or think, and desperately afraid that his stammer would betray him and make him appear foolish. However, Buckingham, expert at reading the faces of others, pretended not to notice the young man's discomfort, and was desirous to put him at his ease.

'Your Highness, it is not in my nature to dissemble and to speak plain I must tell you that my conscience has long smote me concerning my behaviour toward you. I have been arrogant, petulant and disrespectful. It is my dearest wish that you will forgive me and accept my humble service. Please tell me it is not too late... could you ever look upon me kindly and forgive my faults?'

Whatever Charles had expected, it was not this; the powerful favourite confessing his faults and offering his service. He was stunned; no one had ever apologised to him before. He looked up at the man who had caused him such heartache, noting the high cheek bones in the delicately featured, heart-shaped face, the well-arched eyebrows over the knowing deep blue eyes fringed with long black lashes, the abundant chestnut hair gleaming in the sunlight, and the full lips curved in an exquisite smile. It was the first time he could recall deliberately looking full into his face, not snatching glances, and he felt dizzy. He thought out the words carefully before slowly responding.

'Indeed, my Lord, naught would make me happier, and I fear I must also apologise to you for some unseemly behaviour.' It never occurred to Charles that the heir to the throne need not apologise to any, least of all to the man who shared his father's bed and owned the King's heart.

He was rewarded by a smile of such surpassing sweetness that his heart was pierced with a hitherto unknown emotion which was both joy and pain.

'If it were not unseemly to contradict your Highness I would say the fault was all mine. Will you permit me to kiss your hand?'

Charles extended his slender hand and Buckingham brought it to his lips, murmuring, 'henceforth there shall be naught but the most cordial feelings betwixt us. And now my Prince let us walk further.'

Charles felt he was outside time, suspended in some magical realm: memories of faery-like beings and scenery from the masques he had watched in the Banqueting House came to his mind; and Buckingham? He was the most faery like of all: like some magnificent being, unearthly in his beauty; the light of the sun catching the precious jewels upon his green satin doublet and hat like points of fire. Charles moved as one under an enchantment through the translucent heat, and afterwards could recall little of the conversation; he was only aware of a growing joy and gratitude, and sorrow that only too soon this golden day must end. They wandered far and Buckingham led him into an orchard, and pointed to an open park area beyond which lay a forest where he would bring the King and Prince for hunting. He sat down upon the grass, his back against a tree, and looked up at the hesitant Charles.

'Will your Highness sit down a while? I am sorry there are no seats, but the grass is soft and dry.'

Though unused to such informality, Charles willingly sat beside him; nearby his servants slouched around, patiently awaiting their royal master. Buckingham began to speak about his plans to restore Wanstead House, of his interest in breeding horses, and how he intended to bring new breeds from abroad to improve the English stock. Looking shrewdly at the Prince, he told him how impressed he was with his prowess as a horseman, and his pleasure at watching him ride. Charles blushed; he was not used to compliments either; at least ones which meant anything.

The Marquis lay down on the luxuriant grass, stretching, and then rolled onto his stomach, removing his hat and pushing back the thick curls which had fallen over his eyes; gazing languorously at his companion and the Prince again felt a fierce stab of joy. Around them the air shimmered.

'Time to return, I fear his Majesty will be missing us,' Buckingham said, smiling.

Charles was surprised to find that the thought that it would be Steenie his father was missing and not himself no longer caused him any pain, and as he rose the Marquis proffered his arm, which Charles took, determined to hide the pleasure he felt at walking thus with his arm through that of the royal favourite's. Not since Harry's death had any shown him such attention; the physical sensation of close contact with another was intoxicating; overwhelming; he craved more. As they passed through the last garden, Buckingham leaned over and carefully plucked a white rose. He proffered it to the Prince, gazing into his eyes and murmuring, 'Accept this rose, my Prince and by its purity, know the depth of the devotion and faithfulness of thy Buckingham.'

Charles accepted it in wondering delight, his eyes shining and this time the favourite's smile was genuine.

Buckingham gently removed it from the Prince's fingers and deftly affixed it to his companion's dark doublet; as he bent over Charles could smell the fragrance from his hair, heady as any from the flowers in the garden. The favourite swiftly picked another rose, saying, 'I must have one too.'

The King was waiting, tired now with the chatter of Lady Compton, tired too with his surroundings, for he cared little for being outside, unless he was hunting. Missing his beloved Steenie, he was irritable, and seeing the young men walking arm in arm, smiling and united he exclaimed,

'Ah, here yeh are; festooned with flowers like two bonny wenches.'

The evening passed in a haze of happiness for the Prince and in his chamber that night he placed the wilting yet still fragrant rose between the covers of a book.

'I will keep it always,' he murmured, thinking over the events of this never to be forgotten feast. 'It was the feast of friends.'

It was like being re-born.

CHAPTER THREE

To Buckingham.
The King loves you, you him
Both love the same,
You love the king, he you
Both buck-in-game.
In game the King loves sport
Of sports the buck
Of all men you; and you
Solely for your look.
        Anonymous, circa 1620

The dark November morning cast no light through the curtains in the Bed Chamber of the Prince of Wales. He was already awake; an habitually early riser, Charles had woken sooner than usual, for this day he would dine and spend the whole day with Steenie. A smile suffused his thin face, and he rolled onto his side, hugging himself in happiness at the anticipated pleasure of the company of his best friend. Climbing out of the large, sumptuously covered bed, the Prince walked over to a small table, and unlocking an ornately carved silver casket, lined with velvet, he took out a pile of letters, wrapped in red ribbon. He would not call his attendants to dress and groom him just yet, he would re-read the letter he had received from Steenie the previous day, even though he knew the contents by heart, as he did all of the Marquis's letters.

Shivering, he pulled a gown around his thin shoulders; the chamber was cold, despite the fire which burned dully in the hearth. Reading by candle-light, Charles smiled; Buckingham wrote in an easy, unaffected manner to his 'dear young master,' and joy flooded his heart that he had such a friend. The once lonely and neglected Prince could scarcely believe that there was a time (and indeed a long time) when he had detested and feared Buckingham, and it was most wondrous that the one person of whom he had been so jealous was now his sole source of joy and happiness in the world. Moreover, his friendship with Buckingham had so pleased his father that Charles's relationship with the King was transformed; his Majesty had written to his son, 'I must confess to my comfort without flattery that in making your affections to follow and second thus your father's, you show what reverent love you carry towards me in your heart.'

Yet Charles was still unsure and hesitant in the King's presence, and was grateful to Steenie for his assistance in mediating on his behalf on the occasions when he had inadvertently offended his royal father. This help had been particularly appreciated concerning the blunder over his mother's will, for being informed by Buckingham that the King was furious with his son, the Prince had written, 'Steenie, there is none that know me so well as yourself,' and ending with telling him, 'I pray you to commend my most humble service to his Majesty, and tell him that I am very sorry to have done anything to offend him, and that I will be content to have any penance inflicted upon me so he will forgive me, although I had never a thought nor never shall have to displease him; yet I deserve to be punished for my ill fortune. So I rest, Your true, constant, loving friend.'

Steenie had smoothed it all out, delighting in his role, and so now the Prince was no longer the outsider, but a welcomed and accepted member of the Royal family of Steenie, Baby Charles and their dear Dad. The King was well pleased at the change in his son, all of which he attributed to the favourite's influence, and this change was noted and commented upon by the court. However, there were many who viewed the heir to the throne coming under the thrall of the increasingly powerful Marquis with surprise and some concern. Charles glanced up at a knock upon his door, and bade his Gentlemen to enter. He chose his clothes with care, for although still somewhat reserved in his dress, Buckingham had guided him there too. Looking at his reflection, Charles felt grateful that in the important area of appearance his dear Steenie had helped him be more fashionable and dress his hair more becomingly, for none had more knowledge in these matters than he. In truth, there was no area which had not come under the favourite's influence; Charles felt different and felt sure he looked different; perhaps even taller?

The subject of such adoration was still abed at his opulently furnished lodgings at Whitehall, overlooking the Privy garden. He was not asleep though, despite wishing to be, for his beautiful companion would allow him no rest.

'You will spend this day with the Prince? Again?'

'Yes again. I already told you this last night. Why do you need to bring it up now?'

'But you promised you would dine with me this day; you know I have arranged for the entertainment.'

Buckingham leaned over and kissed the pouting lips.

'This is the best entertainment you could give me.' And then seeing her scowl deepen, said, 'I promised you nothing; you assumed I would be there, but my first priority is to the King and Prince, and speaking of which, I must hurry.'

'I cannot see why you must spend so much time with his Highness; it is not long since you dreaded waiting upon him: dull and lifeless you called him,' she complained petulantly.

Buckingham turned to his lover, no longer smiling.

'That was before, and you will not speak so discourteously of my royal master. There, come, sweeting, do not scowl so or you will mar your pretty face with wrinkles.'

He swung his long legs out of the scented sheets; he was tired of her; tired of the incessant demands, the sulks when he would not devote more time to her. What had begun as an enjoyable diversion was rapidly losing its charm. The favourite had spoken truthfully when he said he had not promised; he was careful not to promise anything but skilled and pleasurable swyving to any of his many conquests, and he never spoke of love or marriage.

His latest amour glowered at him. 'And what, my Lord, am I supposed to do now pray?'

Her lover grinned, 'I suggest you catch up on the sleep I deprived you of last night.'

As he was dressed Buckingham too reflected on the change that five months had made to his relationship with the Prince; he no longer thought Charles boring or dull, or resented spending time with him; now he found himself looking forward to their meetings with a pleasure which, if it did not equal the Prince's intensity, rendered their time together sweetly agreeable. Strange that what had begun as the means to please the King and safeguard his own future should be fast becoming an important part of his life.

The Marquis was aware that he had few true friends; the penalty for the King's favour, with its attendant wealth and power; and he knew that many who professed to love him would be glad to see him topple; though the list of clients who owed him their loyalty and obedience as their patron was growing. Such was court life, and Buckingham had learnt to play its intricate and devious ways better than any, but it meant that the genuine friendship and affection of the Prince was all the more precious to him, and he recalled the pleasurable thrill he had felt the first time Charles had shyly addressed him as Steenie: no one else but his Majesty called him that name, and its exclusiveness enforced and emphasised their growing intimacy.

The Christmas festivities at court were the most enjoyable Charles had ever known, for Steenie was by his side, and the Prince lavished gifts upon his friend. So too did the King; dedicating a treatise on the Lord's Prayer to him, but the most valuable and coveted was his bestowing upon his young favourite the position of Lord High Admiral of the Navy. His illustrious predecessor Charles Howard, Earl of Nottingham was a tottering eighty year old, and James judged that in addition to his deriving the keenest pleasure from so honouring his beloved Steenie, the young man would bring to the role an energy and vigour, for his Majesty, pacifist that he was, was aware of the sad state of the fleet; corruption was rife, few ships were built and of those remaining many were unseaworthy. Buckingham's delight was shared only by the Prince and the Marquis's family and friends. The observant Venetian ambassador wrote to the Doge and senate that:

> *The King continues to show marks of special favour and liberality upon his prime Favourite Buckingham, who at present exercises favour and authority over all things. His Majesty has deposed the old admiral and substituted for him, with full powers, the Marquis of Buckingham, whose personal beauty and spirit together with the King's favour render him the chief authority in everything, and the entire Court obeys his will. All requests pass through him and without his favour it is most difficult to obtain anything or to reach the King's ear. I will leave no stone unturned with the Marquis of Buckingham, upon whom everything depends and upon whose wishes depends, being the sole dispenser of the royal actions. The appointment proves very unpalatable to many of the noblemen of the court, who resent seeing an inexperienced youth raised to such high rank without having merited it by any signal feat.*

The Twelfth Night Masque entitled *Masque of the Twelve Months* (the last ever performed there, as a fire shortly thereafter destroyed the Banqueting House) was written by George Chapman, for Ben Jonson was away from London. The Prince and Buckingham were the leading masquers, representing April and May, and although none could match the favourite's skill in dancing, Charles had a charming elegance which was most pleasing to the eye, and the King regarded the performance of his two boys with pleasure. Missing from the entertainment again was Queen Anne, despite the fact that performing in and watching masques had once been among her greatest pleasures. There had been much speculation regarding the sight of a great comet in the sky throughout the two previous months, with many claiming that it portended dire calamities and the death of princes, and Anne's worsening health was seen as proof of the virulent and pernicious influence of the comet. James had become increasingly exasperated, and was determined to counter any talk of God's judgment, referring to it as, 'Venus with a firebrand in her arse' and penning his own long verses, castigating any who dared to criticise the Lord's anointed.

Charles remembered well the previous year's Masque, *Pleasure Reconciled to Virtue*, for it was the first one in which he had led, and he had been anxious for it to be a success, spending countless hours practising. Unlike Buckingham and most of the performers, he had not enjoyed the rehearsals; determinedly forcing himself to remember and execute the intricate steps. The Masque had been written for the Queen, and the Prince was bitterly disappointed by her absence. He had waited nervously, dressed in a costume of a plaited white satin doublet, trimmed with gold and silver lace, upon which was placed a corset cut in the shape of the ancient Roman corselets; on his head he had worn a crown and tall white plumes, and a black mask had covered his pale face.

The other performers had been excitedly noisy; most had appeared in masques before. Nearby had lounged Jonson, who had written the Masque to demonstrate that under King James's beneficent rule, sensuous indulgence and strenuous virtue could now be reconciled, for Masques were far more than mere entertainment but had a serious purpose; through them the King was praised and presented as the bringer of order out of chaos. Some would say that in this Jonson rarely succeeded, for the acoustics in the hall were poor, the allegory and allusions often incomprehensible, and the court tended to talk throughout the performances. However, the sense of occasion and spectacle was undeniable, and owed much to Inigo Jones, the designer of the elaborate costumes, stunning scenery and effects upon which the success depended as much as it did on the writing and skill of the performers.

Charles had glanced over at Buckingham: despite the costume and mask, his height and grace had made him easily identifiable; relaxed and at ease, flirting with the giggling ladies and admiring their bare-breasted costumes. Acknowledged as the finest dancer in the realm, the favourite had no fears of failure; on the contrary, he had been looking forward to being able to display his superlative skills. The noise of the audience; (over 600 people crammed into the boxes,) had caused the Prince's stomach to contract, then the voices were hushed as the King had entered to the accompaniment of cornets and trumpets. All had seemed to go well; a large curtain dropped, painted to represent a tent of gold cloth with a broad fringe; the background of blue canvas, powdered all over with golden stars. This became the front arch of the stage, forming a drop scene, and on its being removed Mount Atlas appeared, whose enormous head was alone visible up aloft under the roof of the theatre; rolling up its eyes and moving itself.

The King, sitting under the canopy, had smiled at the appearance of Comus, the god of cheer, or the belly; curled hair bedecked with roses and flowers, drawn in triumph by four attendants with heads and javelins decorated with ivy, who sang before his Majesty. Another comical figure dressed in short red clothes staggered about, tankard in hand.

'Room, room! Make room for the bouncing belly,

First father of sauce, and deviser of jelly,' began the opening lines. The King enjoyed the mummery, laughing uproariously as Comus delivered his lines:

> *Beware of dealing with the belly; the belly will not be talked to, especially when he is full. There is no venturing upon Venter, he will blow you all up; he will thunder indeed, la, some in derision call him the father of farts.*

Then there had been the twelve Dancers' entrance, dramatically descending from above, the Prince forming the apex. As they elegantly landed they had bowed before the King and begun their performance, accompanied by the music of violins, and the audience watched in rapt attention as they were entertained by the most skilful and elegant ballets and dances. However, as their performance lengthened, some of the dancers became fatigued; the air, filled with the smoke from torches and lanterns and the sweat of the audience was stifling; their costumes hot and constricting.

As they began to lag, the King, impatient and restlessly tapping his chair with his fingers, had finally shouted, 'Why don't they dance? What did they make me come here for? Devil take you all, dance.'

Charles had thought his heart would fail him: the thought of being so humiliated in front of the King, court and foreign ambassadors who were sitting below his Majesty upon stools, was insupportable. But suddenly Buckingham had sprung forward, cutting a score of lofty and very minute capers, with so much grace and agility that, as the Venetian ambassador later commented, 'he not only appeased the ire of his angry lord, but rendered himself the admiration and delight of everybody.' The other masquers, thus encouraged, continued their performance with renewed vigour, and at the end of the Masque the Prince went in triumph and great relief to kiss his father's hands. The King had embraced and kissed him tenderly and then embraced and kissed his favourite, patting his face. As they changed their costumes, Charles had approached Buckingham and thanked him for his intervention; everyone knew the timely and stunning display had saved the Prince from disaster.

Buckingham had flashed that dazzling smile, and bowed low.

'It is my great pleasure and honour to serve you, your Highness. And may I congratulate you upon a resounding success; your grace and elegance is commented upon by all.'

Queen Anne had demanded that the Masque be repeated on Shrove Tuesday, for which Jonson wrote a new, humorous antimasque 'For the Honour of Wales.'

As he reflected upon last year, Charles was relieved that this year's performance was well received, and Buckingham had embraced him warmly, congratulating him upon its success, and whispering in his ear:

> *Sweet April, loved of all, yet will not love,*
> *Though Love's great godhead for his favour strove.*

His mother's absence saddened and worried Charles. Increasingly reclusive, the Queen's health was giving concern, and the Prince, Buckingham and even the King visited her at Hampton Palace, and there were unseemly discussions among the courtiers of the disposal of her lands and properties. However, it was clear to all except the Queen herself that she was swiftly failing, and when she moved to Denmark House, Charles was constantly by her side and he was with her when she died.

The Prince was deeply distressed at the loss of his mother, for in those awful days before he had Steenie as his friend, the Queen was the only one who seemed to care about him, referring to him as 'her little servant,' and Buckingham's genuine sympathy and kindness bound Charles to him yet more strongly. His father regretted the loss of his consort, who had ceased to be a wife to him except in name many years ago, but, as with Henry and his other dead children; he had resolutely refused to visit again once he knew she was dying, for James was terrified at the thought of death.

The funeral of the Queen of England was delayed longer than many thought seemly in the attempt to find adequate money for a state funeral. When it finally took place it was judged by some to be better than that of Prince Henry, but fell short of Queen Elizabeth's, and the chariot and six horses on which her effigy was drawn were acknowledged to be most remarkable. The dreary day ended tragically for the family of a Master Appleyard, a spectator, who was killed by the falling of a stone which formed part of the motto on Northampton House. As at his brother's funeral, Prince Charles was chief mourner; the King would not have attended had he been able, and now indeed there were great fears that he might shortly follow his wife to the grave. While at Newmarket he had been laid low by an agonising fit of the stone, and by the time he had settled at Theobalds he was seriously ill. Steenie was by his side, night and day, increasingly frightened by the King's worsening condition, and not only because of the uncertainty of his future, but because he truly loved the older man, who represented the father he had lost as a boy of thirteen, his royal master and patron, his lover and friend. James, convinced he was dying, settled his affairs, and commended Buckingham to his heir; charging the Prince to respect religion and the bishops. But the King did not die, and public thanksgivings were held at St. Paul's for his recovery.

At the end of May mourning for the Queen was cast aside and James was well enough to preside at the feast of St. George. Buckingham, more in favour than ever, received jewellery and lands belonging to the deceased queen. The following month the newly recovered monarch made his solemn entry into London, and it was commented upon that he was unusually courteous to those he met. He was gaily dressed, much to the consternation of two foreign ambassadors who were garbed in mourning and had come to pay their condolences. James, with a return of his usual acerbity, told them they were too late.

If the King's subjects had hoped that being almost called to heaven might cause their sovereign to revaluate his life, they were sadly mistaken. Though James had been badly frightened by being brushed by the wings of the angel of death, and had announced that he, 'promised not to betake himself so much to hunting and solitude in the future,' his resolve was soon forgotten and a week later found him hunting with Buckingham and the Prince at Eltham Park where he bathed his feet and legs in the steaming blood of a newly killed stag, for he had heard this would relieve the gout from which he still suffered. One courtier was heard to mutter that, 'the King loves swearing and hunting more than the church, and is ruled by a youth.' However, he totally denied such words after being arrested. Yet imprisonments did little to halt such talk.

Verses abounded too commenting upon the nature of the King's relationship with Buckingham; even the title which James had bestowed upon his favourite had caused amusement; it being said that his Majesty had called him thus because he had a fondness for the word 'Buck' with its reference to the pleasures of the hunt, and perhaps other pleasures. When a new ship was named 'Buckingham's Entrance' after its young High Admiral, it was swiftly changed after being the subject of many ribald and bawdy comments.

None were more relieved at the King's recovery than Buckingham, worried that a change of reign might mean a change in favour, for he was not yet certain enough of the young Prince's affection to be sure he would not fall, and he was only too aware of the whispering in corridors and behind his back and the speculative looks. His position as favourite had not gone unchallenged, for in the same way that he had been brought forward as a rival to Somerset and his allies, the powerful, pro-Spanish Howards, there had been a recent attempt by that family to protect their dominant position at court which the Marquis threatened.

The challenge had come early in that year in the goodly form of handsome young William Monson, who was dressed with care, his hair curled and perfumed, his skin washed daily with posset-curd in order to match Buckingham's translucent complexion. The rival took every opportunity to attract the King's attention; coyly giving sly glances with fluttering lashes, and wanton gesturing and posturing. Such was his persistence that he became a subject of derision, and James banished him from court. Steenie's relief was profound, and his royal master had been at pains to reassure him that he loved him only and he had naught to fear.

Buckingham *had* feared, for although it was true that Monson was not his match for beauty, charm and intelligence, yet James *had* looked, and more than once; for the Marquis had intercepted several appreciative glances, which had encouraged his rival to even more provocative displays. Steenie's fears seemed well-founded, for there was talk that the King was secretly arranging for the return of Monson to court, and even in May he was informed that some were still hoping that there would be a new favourite. Buckingham knew there would be more attempts, particularly as the years passed and he grew older, though thankfully his beauty increased rather than diminished. What a comfort it was that he now had the Prince's affection and confidence.

Even after James had recovered and Buckingham was safe, he still felt insecure. The stress of constant watching at the King's sick-bed, sleepless nights and the fear of the future took its toll, and the Marquis fell ill, for despite his youth and usual vigour, Steenie was highly-strung and prone to nervous prostration if subjected to worry and stress.

Now it was the turn of James to anxiously watch at his favourite's bed-side, holding the thin hand and wiping the clammy brow; snapping angrily at the doctors when there was no improvement; for he had little faith in their ministrations and physic. There could be no greater testament to the King's devotion than that his love for Steenie was greater than his dread of sickness; James had been saddened at the death of his wife but her loss had not greatly impacted his life, and despite idly noting that young Monson had a shapely arse, the King knew no one could ever replace his sweet Dog and Gossip, and he shook with fear at the thought of losing the young man who was the love of his life and who had brought such joy and pleasure to his existence.

Also at the bed-side was the Prince; his emotions were more closely guarded than his father's, but no less intense; the thought that he might lose Steenie as he had lost Harry was unbearable. His devotion was noted at court; Sir Edward Harwood writing to Dudley Carleton that the Marquis was as great a favourite with the Prince as he was with his father. Buckingham later thought that it was worth the pain and weakness to know the depth of Charles's regard for him; for after several days his fever had broken, and at last Doctor Mayerne had pronounced him out of danger. He had woken to find Charles sitting forlorn and pale by his side, and upon Buckingham croaking his name, the Prince had fallen on his knees beside the bed and wept.

CHAPTER FOUR

Come, offer up your daughters and fair wives,
No trentall nor dirge
will open good King James
his eyes,
But sacrifice to St. George
     From *As I went to Walsingham*

Buckingham sat in his mother's luxurious apartments at the Gatehouse at Whitehall Palace, known as the Porch; it was situated at the opposite end of King Street to the more ornate Holbein Gate, and opened out of the Cockpit into the Street. Mary was the first person to have dwelt there, and had insisted on considerable building and decorating in order to make the lodgings sufficiently grand for her. Thus she was ideally placed for being in the thick of court life, for Mary prided herself on her importance, particularly since she had been created Countess of Buckingham. Steenie's sister, Susan Feilding, was with them.

'And so his Majesty still desires you to marry? Well it is a goodly state for a man, and as I have told you George, it would be a great shame for you to be so blessed and favoured by the King if there is no one for you to pass your titles and wealth onto.'

Buckingham assented, but was still unsure how he felt about it. Now aged 27, he had at first assumed that his position as favourite precluded marriage, but James believed a man should marry and beget heirs, and since the previous year he had become increasingly keen for Steenie to choose a suitable wife. That naturally meant a wealthy heiress, and when it had become known that the King wished his favourite to marry, there was a flurry of excitement in the court as wealthy courtiers with daughters of marriageable age scrambled to push them forward, but the only one Buckingham had been tempted by was Lady Diana Cecil, the niece of Lady Hatton, already related to the Villiers family by her daughter's marriage to the favourite's brother. That lady invited the Marquis to a lavish feast, hoping that he would cast his eyes upon her niece. Buckingham did cast his eyes upon her and was impressed; beautiful the lady was, but not rich enough, and Steenie regretfully looked elsewhere.

'You were right to refuse Lady Hatton's niece, she is not near as great an heiress as you deserve, but I cannot say that I am surprised, for there is no end to that person's ambition; it is not enough for her daughter to be married to your brother, no, now she would have her niece married to my son the favourite!'

Buckingham met his sister's eyes and they both smiled, thinking the same, that their mother had conveniently forgotten that Lady Hatton's desperate attempts to extricate her daughter from an unwanted marriage had caused scandal and landed her in trouble with the King.

Mary warmed to her theme. 'You're the most important man in the country George. The most important and wealthiest man in the realm deserves to be married to the wealthiest heiress in the realm, and that is Lady Katherine Manners.'

'The Earl of Rutland's daughter? Surely she is but a young maid.'

'Her age matters not, but her wealth and her father's position do. And I am sure she is of an age to marry.'

Her son looked thoughtful. He knew the Earl of Rutland, and had accompanied the King on several occasions to hunt at Belvoir Castle. Indeed; the Villiers family had known the wealthy landowners, their imposing castle set high upon a hill, when they had lived at Brooksby in Leicestershire, and the previous Earl, Roger Manners, had been kind enough to leave some of his hunting hounds to Sir William Villiers in his will. When the ambitious

Mary had married her third husband, Sir Thomas Compton, she had begun a deliberate campaign to ingratiate herself with her powerful neighbours.

Sir Thomas's brother, Lord William Compton, later Earl of Northampton, was an intimate at Belvoir Castle, the seat of the Earls of Rutland, frequently dining there and accompanying the 5th Earl Roger Manners and his brother Francis at hunting, and over the next few years Mary had continued to work hard at developing links with the noble family at Belvoir; sending frequent gifts of artichokes, apples, cucumbers, larks, veal and lamb. Sir Thomas and Lady Compton had also provided a cook for the funeral arrangements for Earl Roger in 1612. Their cultivation of their powerful neighbours continued with Roger's successor, his brother Francis; sending rabbits for the King's visit in 1614, and giving frequent gifts of food.

The Earl had one daughter, Katherine, by his first wife, and two sons by his second, but one had died, and the other was sickly.

'I have seen the daughter once or twice when visiting with the King, but cannot recall what she looks like; at any rate I judged her scarce worth a second look.'

'It is true she is no beauty, but that is of no importance, she would bring great wealth, lands and connections. And it is thought her young brother is like to die, and then she will be Rutland's only heir,' observed his mother shrewdly.

'Mayhap, but the family are Catholics, and his Majesty will never permit me to marry a papist.'

The subject of religion was a sore point, for though Steenie accepted the Protestant teachings, even if he did not much live by them, the Countess had leanings toward the Catholic faith, and had not the sense to realise that her openly avowed interest caused her son embarrassment and was one more reason for him to be hated by enemies who needed no reason. Yet when Buckingham tentatively broached this prospective match, James was all in favour, 'but she mun change her religion; I'll no have my Steenie marry a heretic.'

Negotiations commenced; James commanded his chaplain John Williams to use his considerable powers of persuasion to show the errors of the Roman Catholic Church to Rutland and Katherine, but progress was slow; Francis Manners was most reluctant for his only daughter to marry the favourite, for not only was he adamant that she would not renounce her faith, he did not trust the charming Buckingham. Despite the undoubted influence he would gain by being allied to the most powerful man in the realm, Rutland could not bear the thought of Katherine sharing the bed of a man who shared the bed of the King, and had such a lewd and lascivious reputation. Moreover, the demands for the dowry were outrageous. The Earl was not pleased to be approached by Buckingham's mother, who as usual took it upon herself to conduct the arrangements, and whom he had first known when she was merely the wife of Sir George Villiers; he found the arrogance and greed of this upstart family sickening and was affronted at Mary's condescending attitude; as though he and his daughter should be grateful for the great Buckingham desiring her hand. The nobleman withdrew from the negotiations, and it was now Buckingham's turn to be affronted.

However, the Earl had reckoned without the determination and cunning of the Countess of Buckingham and his own daughter. Katherine Manner's mother, Frances Knyvett, had died when Kate was very young, and though her father had remarried, (some said unhappily) to another heiress, Cecily Tufton, and sired two sons, he was deeply attached to his only daughter, whose mournful, large, dark eyes and long nosed face resembled his own rather than her fair, pretty mother. Not yet sixteen, Katherine had known only a sheltered, pampered existence, and was used to getting what she wanted; and Katherine wanted Buckingham. She had heard talk of the King's favourite and his fabled good looks, and upon first meeting him she immediately thought that he resembled a chivalrous Knight from the stories she so loved. The Earl had stiffly introduced his daughter to Buckingham, who gallantly bowed over her hand, lightly kissing it and making some pleasantry.

Katherine's father noted the girl's heightened colour and stammering response with displeasure and some apprehension; as a frequent visitor to court and a member of the House of Lords, he had heard the scurrilous verses about the favourite, of how he had prostituted his beautiful body to enslave the King, and that no woman was safe from his advances. He need not have worried; the young girl had not been in any danger from the Marquis's attentions, for she was plain, and Buckingham was only attracted to beauty.

The favourite had immediately forgotten about Katherine until his mother had suggested her as a suitable wife, but the young girl had not forgotten, and had continued to dream and fantasise about him; desperate to catch any snippets of information and constantly importuning her father to invite the King and Marquis to visit Belvoir again. Francis did not share her enthusiasm, for previous royal visits had made considerable inroads into his fortune, and he did not crave Buckingham's company. When her father and stepmother reluctantly told her of the proposed match, Katherine felt faint with joy and disbelief; eating little and sleeping even less. To be sure, she was somewhat discomfited by being told that the price for gaining the man she already loved was the renouncing of her religion, but with the innocence and confidence of youth, she was sure her father would find a way so that she could keep both her faith and Buckingham, for she was devoted to both. When Rutland gently told her that the price was too high, and she must let go all hope of being the Marquis's wife, Katherine had raged and wept, refusing to eat and telling her concerned father that if she could not have Buckingham then her life was over.

Manners had discussed the matter with his wife.

'He is her first love and her heart is tender; the pain will soon pass. Perhaps we could send her away for a visit to relatives for a while?'

The Earl was not so sure, and was aware that he had displeased the King; it would not do to make an enemy of Buckingham. It was not just this marriage business which so pressed upon his mind, for his one remaining son, Francis, seemed to become sicker by the day, and for all that he had the best medical attention that money could buy, there was no improvement. There was talk of witchcraft; it being commonly said that three local women, Joan Flowers and her daughters Margaret and Philippa, formerly household servants, had bewitched his children in revenge for being dismissed from his service, vowing that the Earl and his Lady would have no more children. Katherine had become ill for a time, and then the heir and Rutland had become reluctantly convinced that his family had indeed been the victims of wicked practise and sorcery. The women were arrested and tried at Lincoln Assizes, and in March 1619 the two daughters were hanged; their mother having already died. Yet the deaths of their tormentors had availed naught; Francis remained dangerously ill, and was dead within ten months. There were no more children born to the Earl and the Countess.

Frequently away in London, Rutland had assumed that Katherine's infatuation for Buckingham had subsided and that she had accepted that the match was at an end. However, he was wrong, for his daughter was writing letters to the man she was determined to marry; and receiving some in return, (though to be sure, nowhere near as many as she had written and nowhere near as loving). Buckingham's mother too had written to her, assuring her that as in her heart she was herself a convert to the Catholic faith, she understood Katherine's struggle, as did her son, and that she already thought of her as her dear daughter.

Returning home early in the winter of 1619, the Earl surprised Katherine as she wrote another letter to the Marquis; scrawling page after page, telling him of her love and yearning for him in her childish, unformed hand. So engrossed was she that she did not hear her father's quiet knock at the door of her closet, or hear his approach. Only when he spoke her name did she become aware of his presence, and sprang up, pushing the letter under some papers and knocking over the quill onto the floor in her haste.

'Father... I thought you still in London,' she stammered in

confusion, her sallow cheeks stained crimson.

'My business concluded sooner than I had anticipated.'

His curiosity aroused by her obvious discomfort and guilty behaviour, he asked, 'Who were you writing to, daughter?'

Katherine was not quick witted, and could think of no other excuse than to say, 'No one in particular.'

'Indeed. Then I am certain you will permit me to read your charming correspondence to no-one.'

Katherine's burning cheeks now turned white with fear; she began to tremble.

'It is personal... just foolish things.'

'No doubt. You must have written very foolish things indeed to hide it from me, which I saw you do. Surely you cannot be too ashamed to show your father.'

'I am ashamed of nothing I have written, but I beg you will respect my privacy.'

The Earl was aware of his daughter's stubborn character; no doubt he had spoilt her, but she was the living reminder of his first wife, whom he had truly loved, and though there was no physical resemblance, even her wilfulness reminded him of her mother. He was not in the habit of reading his daughter's letters, but a horrible suspicion was forming itself in his mind.

'Kate, I wish to see the letter. I am certain you will not refuse my request.'

Then, as the girl stood silent and unresponsive, he continued, exasperated and becoming angry, 'Surely there can be nothing so personal that you would be afraid for your father to read? Give me the letter Katherine.'

'I do not wish to, my Lord.'

Now thoroughly worried, Rutland reached over to Katherine's desk, and rummaged underneath to where she had hidden the letter; disturbing other papers. Pulling it out, he read the cause of his daughter's disobedience.

'Good God, child! What is this?'

The Earl had known Katherine was attached to the Marquis, but had not realised the strength of her feelings for him. He was horrified; not only that his beloved daughter had deliberately deceived him and was involved with Buckingham behind his back when he had thought all was at an end, but of the content of her letter; her words held no restraint or prudence, pouring out all her passion, her determination to marry him, her desperation to know his lips and arms, and even worse, her resolve to give up her religion if that was the only way she could be his wife. She had seriously compromised herself: small wonder she had not wished to show him it.

He was deeply shocked. 'How long has this been going on?'

'A while,' Katherine was still trembling, but determined to hold her ground.

'And has my Lord of Buckingham replied to your letters?'

'Yes, he feels the same way I do. He loves me. He wishes to marry me.'

'Show me his letters.' Again there was no response, and her father picked up the other letters which were upon her desk. There were several from Buckingham, and two from his mother. Rutland read them in silence; he felt ashamed that his daughter had played so easily into the Villiers' hands: the tone and content from Buckingham were vastly different from Katherine's: while courteous and friendly, there was little of love, still less of passion, and even though the scoundrel wrote of his wish for the negotiations for the match to proceed, it was clear to the Earl that Buckingham was more attracted by Katherine's wealth than by herself.

Looking at the daughter he so loved, he could not but note her lack of any beauty, and of how unformed and thin was her figure. He had seen the sort of women at court that Buckingham associated with; the sort he admired. He closed his eyes, sick with fear.

'Daughter, your deceit causes me more pain than I can express. Surely I do not deserve such treatment at the hands of one I have ever cherished and treated with naught but love and kindness?'

His obvious distress caused tears to spring to his daughter's eyes, for although blinded by her passion for Buckingham, she loved her father dearly.

'I owe you more than I can ever say, but father, if you had not been so determined to end the marriage negotiations, then I would have had no need to resort to this.'

Rutland gently took her tiny hands within his own.

'Kate, you are little more than a child and totally innocent of the ways of court and of men. I understand your feelings for my Lord of Buckingham; he is most handsome and charming and I well remember my love for your mother, but oh daughter, this man is not for you.'

Katherine snatched her hands out of his. 'Why? Why do you hate him? Is it because he is powerful? Everyone says it would be an advantageous alliance.'

'Indeed they do, but for Buckingham, not for us. I do not hate him, but I know things about him that you, thank God, do not.'

'What things? Oh I know he is envied because of his wealth and position, and because the King loves him.'

'The King does indeed love him. Kate, there are certain matters which I cannot bring myself to speak of, but the Marquis is known to be of an impure and unchaste disposition.'

Anger flashed over Katherine's face. 'I cannot and will not believe that! I cannot believe that he is not as beautiful inside as he is outside. The King calls him his angel!'

'Ah yes, his angel. Kate, I beg you to trust me. This is your first love...'

'My only love!'

'So you think. But you will love again and to a man more worthy of you. In a few years' time when you are happily married to a man who loves you equally and who stays by your side, you will bless me for my refusal.'

'Never! I will never marry if it is not to my Lord Buckingham. I would sooner go to a nunnery.'

Rutland's face was grave. 'Better a nunnery than a marriage which will cause you naught but sorrow. Katherine, I know that in your short life I have refused you little, and mayhap had I done so then this would be less painful for us both, but as your father you owe me your obedience. I now claim that obedience and demand that you swear by the Blessed Virgin that you will give up all correspondence with Buckingham, return his letters and those of the Countess, and write a letter which I will dictate, informing my Lord that there is to be no other contact. Will you so swear?'

The girl's large dark eyes sparkled with tears. 'I cannot! You may as well ask me to give up my life!'

Then, seeing her father's inexorable expression, she flung herself upon her knees, sobbing hysterically, and begging him to be merciful.

'Merciful! If only you knew! Do you think you are the only person who has ever loved?'

The Earl's eyes were also filled with tears; was this then his punishment from God for his rebellion against Queen Elizabeth those many years ago? His two sons dead, and now to lose his daughter to such a life that the mere thought of it made him shudder. He pulled Katherine up from her knees and took her into his arms; stroking the disordered hair and kissing the wet cheeks. Within moments his doublet was soaked from her tears.

'Kate, you know how I love you; I would give my very life to protect you, but now I see that in order to protect you I must expose you to shameful matters of which an innocent maiden should know naught ; matters which I have sought to shield you from. Do you know the true reason for Buckingham's favour with the King?'

Katherine frowned, puzzled. 'His Majesty loves his sweet presence, his handsome face. He calls him his son, his friend.'

'He also calls him his dog, I... cannot bring myself to speak in detail, but I have seen the King embrace and kiss Buckingham as a man kisses a woman. There is common talk, terrible talk Katherine, of what takes place within the King's private bedchamber. And besides, the Marquis is renowned for having many mistresses. Do you wish to have your pure marriage bed defiled by his debaucheries? '

His daughter could not imagine what her father meant about the King and Buckingham, nor could he tell her, but she understood the rest.

'I know my Lord has had others. He is too handsome not to have. Indeed he has freely confessed this to me, but assures me he will be faithful when we are married.'

Rutland realised he would have to be brutal though he shrank from inflicting pain.

'Buckingham does *not* love you. He wishes to marry your wealth and connections, but once you have given him heirs, you will not see him. Forgive me, Kate, but he loves only beautiful women.'

Despite his frustration with his daughter, Rutland could not but admire her simple dignity.

'I am sadly aware of my want of beauty, but my Lord of Buckingham says he finds my difference to the ladies at court to be one of my attractions, and the Countess has already warned me that you would try to turn me against him.'

'Damn his eyes!' Rutland was stunned; the Marquis had prepared her for every objection. 'Enough! I require your promise.'

'Forgive me, my Lord, but I cannot. I would prefer to die than live without him.'

'He will break your heart, and you will break mine.'

'Whether he breaks my heart or no, I will never renounce him.'

'And so you would imperil your immortal soul for a mere man? Think daughter!'

'I trust in the mercy of God, that he who gave his only son would understand that though I claim to renounce my faith, that in my heart I will always be a Catholic.'

'Then you are resolved?'

'Forgive me, father, but I am.'

'So be it, then so am I. You will remain here in your chamber, and I will write straightway to Buckingham. I will also be interrogating the servants to find out who has been involved in this deception. And I will take these with me,' he snapped, preventing

Katherine from taking back the precious keep-sakes. He strode out to the sounds of his daughter's weeping.

The early spring flowers brought a welcome contrast to the grey sky and the stark, bare, skeletal branches of the trees over which the cawing crows circled and wheeled; it had been another harsh winter, and there were but few buds upon the trees. Buckingham clutched his velvet cloak more tightly around him; soon the church walk would be beautified and brightened by tulips and forget-me-nots, and he thought again that summer could not come too soon. Still cold, he walked briskly across the gardens of Goadby Hall in Leicestershire to the small church of St. Denys which backed onto it. He was spending a few days with his family, away from the incessant demands and intrigues of court; his mother wished to invite some of their former acquaintances to dine with them, and doubtless wished to overwhelm them with her grandeur and show off her stunning son, the King's favourite.

The dower house held many memories for him, including a visit from the King when he had first come to favour. The saddest was of returning there from Billesdon where he attended school, after the death of his father, for the home he had known at nearby Brooksby was now inherited by his step brother, William Villiers; his father's eldest son by his first wife, Audrey Saunders. The favourite had included Sir William and all his father's five children from that marriage in his own good fortune, and he would see some of them the next day. Buckingham had visited with his former tutor at Billesdon, Anthony Cade; a clever, godly and enlightened man, who recognising that young Villiers was no scholar, had not attempted to force him to become something that he would never be by brutalising him, as was often the way. Buckingham had showed his gratitude and affection by introducing Cade to the King and procuring for him the living of Grafton Underwood which he held as well as Billesdon.

The little church was even colder than outside; the air mustily sour, mingled with the aroma of candles; he heard the murmur of voices, the rector was busy in the vestry. The Marquis of Buckingham knelt quietly and prayed. This small church had witnessed many significant events in the lives of his family. Here were the monuments to many of his kin, both Villiers and Beaumont; his father, Sir George Villiers, had been interred in the family crypt one sad, bleak January day in 1606, and his grandmother Anne Beaumont had joined him exactly seven years later. Lying there too was his tiny brother Samuel, his parents' first-born son, who had died aged seven weeks in July 1590.

Buckingham recalled with a wry smile his mother's second marriage at this church, a mere six months after the death of his father, to the octogenarian Sir William Reyner. Recalled too the outraged expressions upon the faces of the tottering groom's horrified family, who saw the possibility of losing the wealthy inheritance they had long assumed was theirs should this covetous, ambitious woman, who had ensnared her elderly husband by allurements and provocations, give him a male heir. Happily for them, their fears had not come to pass; for Sir William, who had only lived another five months, was soon disabused of the notion that his new wife had married him for love, and had left her nothing in his will. A happier occasion had been the advantageous wedding the following April of his beloved sister Susan to William Feilding; a marriage which had proved to be unusually happy and fertile.

Buckingham wondered if his father was aware of his son's great fortune and of his wife Mary being a countess; did the dead know of the doings of their loved ones, or were they beyond all such concerns in heaven? He suddenly wished he knew more of such matters. He had a simple faith, (at least Anthony Cade had succeeded in instilling within him a firm belief in the Protestant religion) and he hoped that God would be merciful to him when he died and forgive his many sins, but most of the time he did not listen to the involved and lengthy sermons delivered with such passion in the royal chapel, unlike the King who liked to debate theology and whose knowledge was prodigious. James's favourite preferred to smile and wink at nearby attractive ladies; imagining them naked (although in most cases he did not need to imagine). The idea of eschewing the pleasures of the flesh was incomprehensible to him; even had he possessed a lesser libido.

The thought entered his mind unbidden that his father might know of how he had first gained the royal favour and what that royal favour actually involved. He felt uncomfortable with the idea. His mother knew; oh yes, Mary knew what her beautiful son had been called upon to do to earn the title marquis; what he continued to do so that she could be a countess, her other sons viscounts and her vast family have positions and wealth lavished upon them. Mary knew the cost of parading and prostituting her sweet George in front of a King who loved young men: had encouraged and nagged him incessantly to do whatever the King demanded; still nagged him. Her son was aware of her character; of how she was despised and detested, and how his patronage and favouring of his family had damaged his reputation beyond repair. Yet despite this, he loved Mary deeply, and was devoted to his family and loyal to his friends. Buckingham pushed the thought away, or tried to. Sodomy was such an ugly word; an ugly word for an ugly deed most would say, but he could not associate those words with actions which were at heart borne of love and need. Most of the time such thoughts did not concern him, but one time when he had overheard some particularly explicit and condemnatory comments, he had broached the subject with the King.

'Sodomy? It is a fearful wicked act, and those who commit it deserve to burn. But fear not sweetheart,' (for he saw Steenie's shocked expression), 'we have naught to fear, for sodomites are godless, papist sorcerers. You are my sweet wife and child, and I your husband and Dad.'

Buckingham felt unusually depressed; perhaps the atmosphere of the gloomy, dank church was pervading his spirits; he hoped he was not sickening for some infirmity. Steenie rose from his knees, and the Rector John White hastened over, bowing low and expressing his pleasure at the presence of the great marquis in his little church. For a moment Buckingham considered confiding in him; of asking for his prayers and guidance, but quickly decided against it, for though the Rector had been at Goadby since 1613, and Buckingham had attended his services after returning from France, he felt no bond with him. Perhaps he should open his heart to Anthony Cade, but immediately he knew that he could not do that either, (had there not been fumbled gropings in the night in the bed Buckingham had shared with a fellow pupil?) On reflection he decided to wait until his return to court and mayhap speak to his chaplain. Until then he would push away such disturbing assaults upon his conscience, and doubted not that he would succeed – he usually did.

Earlier that day, Buckingham had shown his mother the Earl of Rutland's short and formal letter requesting (nay demanding) that he would no longer write to his daughter and reaffirming that the match was at an end. He had written a cold and indignant reply; really the pride of this man was beyond bearing. He also showed her Katherine's final scribbled and tear-stained note which she had smuggled to him without her father's knowledge, telling him of the calamitous events, and that if he would but send word, she would escape the Earl's tyranny and marry him even if she was disinherited. Buckingham wrote back immediately telling her to do no such thing: she must obey and honour her father; a plain wife with no fortune was the last thing he wanted.

'So there's an end to the business. It's no great loss.'

His mother looked at him impatiently.

'How can you say so? There is none other with her wealth, and now that her brother is dead she is Rutland's sole heir, in addition to her inheritance and land through her mother.'

'That is true, but her father refuses me, and I will not beg!'

Mary was thoughtful; she had ensnared three wealthy husbands, and was experienced and clever in such matters.

'Perhaps there is another way. We will use what we have; Lady Katherine is deeply in love with you, and desperate to marry you.'

'She is, but her father loves me not, nor I him.'

'Three days hence I will call upon the Countess, for I know

Rutland is in Leicester this week, and I will prevail upon her to allow Lady Katherine to dine with me. You will also be dining with me.'

'Three days hence I must return to the King; he will allow me to remain here no longer.'

'Of course. You will be at Whitehall, and so will I and my guest, for although the Countess will think I mean to dine here, we will journey to London, and while there it will be too far to return before nightfall; Lady Katherine must needs spend the night under my roof, and so, my dear Buckingham, must you.'

'I am not sure; if this became known it would cause a great scandal; Katherine would be ruined.'

'I am depending on it becoming known; we shall then bargain with the two things Rutland holds most dear: his daughter, and his family honour. He *must* then agree to the marriage.'

Her son was not easy to convince, for although he was not in love with Katherine Manners, he had no wish to see her harmed in any way. Buckingham's heart was tenderer than his mother's, and he preferred to be open and truthful in his dealings; yet Mary persuaded him that he was doing the little heiress the greatest kindness, and he finally agreed.

Though the Countess of Rutland had been dismayed to receive a letter from the Countess of Buckingham announcing a visit now that she was at Goadby, she could think of no polite way to refuse it, despite her dislike of her. Nor could she withstand the invitation for her step-daughter to return with her for a meal, or Katherine's earnest pleading that she be allowed to go. The Countess saw Katherine leave with a happier face than for many a day, but her heart was heavy; she was sure her husband would be displeased, and was glad that he would be away until the following day, by which time Kate would also be home. She felt sure she could persuade the girl that it might be wise not to mention it.

Katherine's heart was lighter than it had been for many a day, and she prattled happily to the Countess as the carriage trundled through the Leicestershire countryside. The effects of enclosure had greatly impacted that landscape; now the fields were fenced around to keep in the sheep which were so important a part of the landowners' wealth, and to keep out the local folk who could no longer farm the fields nor pasture their beasts on common land. The Villiers had made much of their money from enclosing the land around Brooksby, to such a degree that the village, already decimated by plague, had all but disappeared. Sitting next to her prospective daughter-in-law, Mary was oblivious to the hardship experienced by the villagers, nor had she taken much notice of the riots which had broken out in response to this suffering back in 1607 which had been led by a tinker known as Captain Pouch. However, she had been perturbed when the unrest had reached Leicester; a curfew had been imposed in the city and a gibbet which had been erected as a warning had been pulled down.

At first Katherine was too busy talking to the Countess of Buckingham, noting the resemblance in her features to the face which haunted her every waking moment and listening to her speak of her son, to realise how long the journey was taking. She never heard the howls of the filth-encrusted vagrant, incarcerated in the stocks of a small village, who was being pelted with excrement and rotting food by jeering locals, but at last, upon commenting that she had not realised how far it was to Goadby Marwood, Mary had turned to her, and said smilingly,

'Assuredly it is not far, but as I said, we are going to my lodgings at Whitehall, and that is indeed a prodigious distance.'

Katherine was silenced; she knew Mary had not mentioned going to London, and that her step-mother would never have allowed it had she known. She looked at this handsome, over dressed woman, her hard face powdered and rouged, who could lie so easily, and felt a shiver of fear; she was very young and felt suddenly vulnerable.

Noting her silence, Mary was at pains to reassure her; 'while we are there I hope you will be content if a certain person calls upon us.'

'The Marquis?' Katherine gasped, her sallow cheeks flushing.

'The very same, my dear. Indeed, when he heard that I was to have the pleasure of your company, he was aflame to see you. Of course, had we been at Goadby then it would not have been possible, for his duties had required his return to court,' she added.

Their progress through a village came to a halt, and Kate glanced out. A piglet had been let loose by some local lads, who were laughing heartily as the perspiring, cursing owner chased after the squealing beast. Some of the villagers touched their hats out of respect at the sight of the grand coach and accompanying grooms. Mary took advantage of the delay to gloss over the awkwardness by commenting that it was a disgrace that such behaviour should occur, and the boys should be flogged. She need not have worried, the fear of her father's anger was as nothing to Katherine; all she could think of was that she would see her dear Lord again; see him and... she dared think no further.

The scheme worked as well as Mary had hoped. Her son had arrived at the Gatehouse, and at the very sight of him, resplendent in rose coloured satins, hair curled and love-locked, Katherine lost all thought of the father who loved her. Though Buckingham's image was in her mind every moment, she was reminded once more of the powerful effect his presence had upon her; she ate little, hungrily feasting upon his face and upon his every word, while he was his entertaining and confident self; all smiles and attention. The Countess sat quietly and observed with satisfaction. Shortly after the meal, she pleaded an indisposition, and said she must lie down for an hour or so to recover. For Katherine it seemed that time was standing still; she had never known such happiness.

Suddenly, Buckingham exclaimed, 'I must depart; forgive my detaining you till such a late hour Lady Katherine – the sweet pleasure of your company has so entranced me that I had not noted the passage of the hours.'

However, as he bade good night to his mother, Mary begged him to stay, saying she felt unwell, and besides the night was too far gone for him to repair to his own lodgings, (a mere few minutes' walk away,) to which Buckingham gallantly agreed.

Katherine lay in bed, her heart beating so loud she was sure he must hear it; for his chamber was not far. He must hear it and read its message; every beat proclaimed her love. At the knock on the door she trembled even more, and as Buckingham entered her chamber and bowed low, he saw the great and proud Earl of Rutland's daughter, a willing victim.

'Lady Katherine, I come to wish you a sweet repose, and to thank you for the pleasure you have afforded me by your charming companionship.'

He crossed over to the bed, and lifted her hand to his lips. He felt the trembling, and knew that he could take her if he wished. Sitting on the edge of the bed, he bent over and kissed her gently. It was Katherine's first kiss and she never forgot its sweetness. Clasping her in his arms, Buckingham kissed her again, more insistently, and her mouth opened to him. Murmuring her name, he stroked her hair, kissed her neck, his hands moved over the small breasts, feeling the hardness of the nipples. Straightening up, the favourite saw the adoring eyes, the look of desire upon her face, but he also saw the sixteen-year-old's youthful innocence, and this recalled him to himself.

'God's blood, she is but a child,' he thought. 'I cannot do it; I will not take her bud.'

To Katherine's dismay her suitor backed away from her. She reached out and grabbed his hand.

'My Lord, have I offended you?' Buckingham kissed her hand again, this time with genuine affection.

'No sweet Kate, but I have offended and gone beyond the bounds of propriety. I beg your forgiveness.'

Katherine was torn by pleasure that he had addressed her as Kate, and the desire to keep him with her. She suddenly cared nothing for the strict morality of her parents, of her church; nothing seemed to matter but this man.

'I must leave now. I respect you too much to do otherwise.'

His actions rendered him even more perfect in her eyes, and confirmed to her the unfairness of her father's opinion of him.

The next morning his mother asked, 'Well?'

Her son was not surprised; she had always assumed a right to know even his most intimate secrets.

'Lady Katherine will leave your home in the same state she entered it,' he answered, kissing her cheek as he left to go to the King. Mary was amazed – not many virgins would have remained so after a night under the same roof as Buckingham.

Katherine was bitterly disappointed by her lover's early departure. She had lain awake most of the night, desperately willing him to return to her bed, and afraid that he might do so. Now the thought of what she must say to her parents suddenly presented itself. 'Please holy Virgin, let me be home before my father.'

Her prayers went unanswered. The Earl had returned home early the next morning and was almost speechless with anger and disbelief that his wife had allowed Katherine to go with that dreadful woman. Horrified at her blunder, his wife had wept. 'She said she would return before nightfall.'

Servants were immediately despatched to Goadby only to be told that the Countess of Buckingham was not there, and was now at Whitehall. When Rutland was told, he sank onto a chair in despair; his daughter was ruined. Buckingham had out-manoeuvred him. When Katherine returned with her maid, she was not allowed into the house, nor would her father receive her. He had but one question, delivered through a servant. Had she seen the Marquis of Buckingham, and on hearing that she had, the servant returned and told her that his Lordship required to know if the Marquis had stayed the night. Katherine knew she had no choice but to answer truthfully. Rutland ordered his shocked and bewildered daughter from the castle and informed her she must stay with her Uncle Lord Knyvett.

The incensed Earl wrote a bitter, curt letter to the man he presumed had seduced his daughter, informing the Marquis that he was now honour-bound to immediately marry she whom he had ever advised to avoid the occasion of ill, though now he was sadly certain that she had ignored that advice, and saying that although she deserved not so great a care from a father whom she so little esteemed, yet he must preserve her honour if it were with the hazard of his life. He would not receive Katherine again unless Buckingham had committed himself to marry her.

Now it was Buckingham's turn to be insulted, and he replied in kind.

'I can delay no longer of declaring unto you how unkindly I take your harsh usage of me and your own daughter, which has wrought this effect in me, that, since you esteem so little of my friendship and her honour, I must now, contrary to my former resolution, leave off the pursuit of that alliance any more, putting it in your free choice to bestow her elsewhere to your best comfort; for, whose fortune it shall ever be to have her, I will constantly profess that she never received any blemish in her honour but that which came by your own tongue.'

The favourite informed the King of his decision, and his incredulous mother. Mary's pleadings and tears did not shake his resolve, nor did Katherine's. The court, fascinated and delighted with this salacious scandal, noted Buckingham's deliberate snubbing of the proud Rutland at the St. George's Day Feast; refusing to dance or speak with him. The Earl, visibly aged with grief and the fear of the stain of dishonour, beset with the daily letters from Katherine begging his forgiveness, and the importuning of his wife, was compelled to crave his Majesty's intervention with his favourite. Buckingham at last graciously relented, but now the dowry demanded was far higher and the amount was doubled. Rutland, cheated and betrayed, had no choice but to agree; he was beaten.

On 16th May the Marquis of Buckingham married with the Lady Katherine Manners in the private chapel at Lumley House near Tower Hill, in a simple ceremony conducted by John Williams. In view of the circumstances there were no lavish celebrations, and the wedding was attended only by the King and Earl. At the meal afterwards the poet Sir Henry Goodere celebrated the union in verse in his *Epithalamium to my Lord of Buckingham:*

Here Venus stirs no flames nor Cupid guides thy lines,
But modest Hymen shakes his torch and chaste Lucina shines.
We wish a son whose smile
Whose beauty may proclaim him thine,
Who may answer to our hopes and strictly may combine
The happy height of Villiers' race with noble Rutland's line.

Rutland sat grim faced. He would never forgive Buckingham. The King, who ever took a great interest in weddings and particularly in the marriage bed, informed his favourite to stay in bed next morning, when he would visit with Steenie and his wife. This was accompanied by a letter:

My only sweet and dear child,

Thy dear Dad sends thee his blessing this morning and also to his daughter. The Lord of Heaven send you a sweet and blithe wakening, all kinds of comfort in your sanctified bed, and bless the fruits thereof that I may have sweet bedchamber boys to play me with, and this is my daily prayer, sweet heart. When thou rises, keep thee from importunities of people that may trouble thy mind, that at meeting I may see thy white teeth shine upon me, and so bear me comfortable in my journey. And so God bless thee, hoping thou will not forget to read over my former letter.

James R.

After wedding and bedding his young wife, Buckingham blithely kissed her cheek, and left her for several days while he went hunting with the King. Seeing the hurt upon her face, her father did not have the heart to say that he had told her so.

Chapter Five

But this I scorn, that one so basely born
Should by his sovereign's favour grow so pert,
And riot it with the treasure of the realm
While soldiers mutiny for want of pay.
　　　　　Christopher Marlowe, *Edward the Second.*

Sir Francis Godwin, Member of Parliament for Buckinghamshire, stamped his feet noisily, and banged his gloved hands together. His face was mottled and pinched with the bitter January wind; his breath steaming.

'God's teeth! It is cold enough to shrivel a man's stones and freeze off his pintle.'

'Aye,' agreed his companion, Sir William Fleetwood, 'Tis cold enough.'

The Thames, the usual thoroughfare for journeying to Whitehall, was frozen over, the biting winds driving the ice with such violence that in some places it was piled up like huge rocks, assuming the likenesses of strange, disturbing sculptures. Few but the most aged could remember the time in the old Queen's reign when the river had last been twice frozen over in one winter. The watermen were loud in their complaints of the loss of their trade, but some tradesmen saw the means to profit from the severity of the winter, and set up stalls upon the thick ice to ply their wares; selling mutton pies, roast ox and ale.

Equally keen to experience the novelty were rosy-cheeked, snotty-nosed boys who kicked pigs' bladders around in a frenzy of excitement, and raced up and down the frozen river. Others took to the ice to shoot at marks, while attempting to ignore the cold which gnawed at their nipped fingers and bit their frozen feet.

'I hear that the King will return to court next week for the opening of Parliament,' said Sir William, for whom the activities upon the ice held no interest.

Sir Francis grimaced. 'If he can tear himself away from his hunting at Theobalds with Buckingham and the Prince.'

'His Majesty is wondrous fond of the chase; the weather would have to be severe indeed to prevent him from his daily hunting, that or his gout too painful.'

'The King cares for naught but the hunt, unless it is for his butt slave's arse.'

Sir William flinched at such coarseness and glanced around nervously. 'Have a care, sir, men have been imprisoned for saying less.'

'It makes it no less true.'

His companion was uneasy and cast around for a less dangerous subject. 'I trust your wife and family keep in good health?'

'Tolerable, I thank you. My brother tells me that there is to be complaint made about monopolies in this session of Parliament, and that Kit Villiers and Sir Edward Villiers are implicated. There is talk too against Buckingham, and Sir Francis Bacon.'

Fleetwood looked as though this conversation was little better to his liking, and saying that the weather was too inclement to tarry, he bade a hasty farewell. Despite both men representing Buckinghamshire in the Commons, Sir William was keen to distance himself in every way, for Godwin could be a dangerous acquaintance.

Secluded from such mutterings, Charles and Buckingham were most interested in the recall of Parliament, the first for seven years. The King's previous interactions had not always been happy, and the last one had sat a mere eight weeks. No lover of Parliament, about which he had once expressed surprise that his ancestors should have permitted such an institution to come into existence, James had written to his eldest son to 'hold no parliaments but for the necessity of new laws which would be seldom,' but the crisis in Bohemia concerning his daughter and her husband had compelled him to summon that august body to raise funds to assist them. In the March of the previous year Archduke Ferdinand of Styria had become the Holy Roman Emperor and King of Bohemia. Two months later he was expelled from the throne, and the Bohemian nobility offered the crown to Fredrick Elector Palatinate, married to James's daughter, Elizabeth. Frederick had written to the King, asking for his advice and Elizabeth to Buckingham, urging him to support their claim. However, his Majesty was not convinced that this would keep the throne of Bohemia Protestant, saying, 'What hath religion to do to decrown a king? Leave the opinion to the devil and to the Jesuits, authors of it and brands of sedition. For may subjects rebel against their prince in quarrel of religion? Christ came into the world to teach subjects obedience to the king, and not rebellion.'

Frederick accepted the throne, much to the discontent of his father-in-law, and the birth of another son – named Rupert and proclaimed as Duke of Lusatia – further enhanced the popularity of the royal couple. There was widespread rejoicing at the news of a Protestant king on the Bohemian throne and an English queen, and a great upsurge of feeling against Spain, resulting in a call for action against that country, heard on the street and even in the pulpit, where the Archbishop of Canterbury spoke out that Roman Catholic power was about to be toppled. Yet Frederick's reign was short-lived; within months the Spanish general Spinola, acting in the name of the Emperor, had moved his forces into the Palatinate, taking over the prized territory of the left Palatinate on the left bank of the Rhine, and in July 30,000 troops under the command of Count von Tilly marched into Bohemia. Facing this army alone, in November of 1620 Frederick suffered a crippling defeat at the battle of White Mountain, outside Prague. Now refugees, the royal family fled to The Hague; writing impassioned letters to the King of England for aid.

On hearing of his daughter's plight, James had shut himself in his chamber, and even refused to hunt, but he could not favour war; Frederick had ignored his advice and brought this calamity upon himself, nor could he could approve of the deposing of monarchs, even Catholic ones. Moreover, the thought of England being embroiled in a bloody war filled James with horror, and he would not risk the loss of friendship and the marriage treaty with Spain. Yet his heart was filled with sorrow at the plight of his beloved Bessie, and on reading the letters of his small grandson Prince Frederick Henry asking for help, the King wept.

Charles and Buckingham shared the general shock and outrage. The Prince, who had not seen his sister for seven years, retained fond memories of Elizabeth and her husband, and he spent many hours discussing the crisis with Steenie, re-reading the desperate pleas for assistance from the brother whom she claimed she loved 'more than all the world.' Charles volunteered to lead a glorious campaign, accompanied by Buckingham, to rescue the fair English queen from the papist ogre, yet he would not oppose his father, and qualified his offer to fight by saying he would only go if the King would give him leave. James dismissed him impatiently, snapping that he would agree to no such thing.

While still firmly supportive of the King's foreign policy regarding the Spanish match, the favourite's role began to subtly change; he was now courted and exhorted to influence the King's policy, and in the Privy Council there was now a pro-war faction, headed by Buckingham, who drew the Prince after him. Buckingham tried, but his power over James was never as great as was believed; it became generally assumed that he encouraged the King to maintain his Spanish alliance, and his friendly attitude to Gondomar, the wily Spanish ambassador, caused many to accuse him of being a crypto-Spanish spy.

Buckingham's first experience of Parliament was not one on which he looked back with any pleasure. On Tuesday the 30th of January King James had made his way on horseback in solemn procession to the House of Lords to declare the session open and was carried in a chair from the church to the Parliament House. His Majesty said he would speak but briefly, since he found his former speeches had been turned against him, but did in fact speak for over the hour. James had not abetted his son-in-law's claim to the Crown of Bohemia, but claimed he had spent immense sums in defending the Palatinate, and in embassies, and would spend his own and his son's blood in the cause, thus he trusted that his people 'would not be wanting, this cause being the cause of religion and the inheritance of my grandchildren.'

The King required £200,000 simply to set out an army, but the Commons only granted two subsidies, as a 'present of love.' Despite voting inadequate subsidies, the House, led by the irascible Sir Edward Coke, called for war, for the enforcement of anti-Catholic laws and demanded that the Prince of Wales should marry a Protestant.

Worse, far worse was to come. The use of patents had greatly increased throughout James's reign, providing the King with a much needed source of revenue and the means of rewarding royal servants and courtiers. Ever a contentious issue; the Members of Parliament now turned their attention to scrutinising monopolies and patents. There was a request made concerning Sir Giles Mompesson that the King would acquaint the House of Commons with the money he had received on account of the patent for inns, and that he would also advise them to proceed in the discovery of grievances. Mompesson appealed to Buckingham, a kinsman through Sir Edward Villiers, for help, swearing that he was innocent of the charges of raising extortionate sums under his monopoly for licensing inns.

Shortly afterwards his arrest was ordered, but Mompesson evaded capture by climbing out of a window and escaped to the continent. Outraged, the Commons now focused its full fury onto the favourite, seen as the source of all court corruption and the greatest monopolist of them all, who had procured wealth from the royal treasury, sold patents, and gained positions for himself, his kin and clients by seducing and dominating the King. Buckingham was seen as the power behind the throne; the reason for the King's reluctance for war, the friend of Spain and a concealed papist. He was a parvenu, an upstart, a night-grown mushroom with naught to recommend him but his outstanding beauty, grace and charm. Verses were written commenting on the fears of his influence, calling him the King*s* 'white-faced boy,' while James was personified as Jove who 'with Ganymede lies playing.'

Perceiving that they now had the opportunity to topple the hated and feared favourite, the Commons followed up with another attack on the patent for a monopoly of manufacture of gold and silver thread in which Buckingham's half-brother Sir Edward Villiers and brother Kit were involved.

'Monopolists and projectors are bloodsuckers of the kingdom and vipers of the commonwealth. Let no man's greatness daunt us, for the more we do to great men, the more we prevent in future these mischiefs,' thundered Sir Edward Giles to rapturous applause.

Now seriously concerned that his favourite might be attacked, the King intervened, going to the House of Lords, and giving a long and impassioned speech defending the Marquis, and thus warning his enemies to not press home their attack. Yet James also made clear his concern for justice.

'My Lords, my desire is that you look on Buckingham as he was when he came to me, as poor George Villiers; and if he prove not himself a white crow, he shall be called a black one,' said the King.

While relieved that his royal master was defending him, Buckingham was still unnerved by the King's words. He threw himself down upon his knees before James.

'Sir, if I cannot clear myself of any aspersion or imputation cast upon me, I am contented to abide your Majesty's censure and be called the Black Crow.'

The Marquis had been shocked at the strength of the feeling against him, cushioned by the adulation of the King, Prince and of his family, sycophantic clients and obsequious courtiers, he simply had no idea he was so unpopular. He was profoundly stunned.

'A good day's work, my Lord, but only a beginning,' commented Sir Francis Godwin to Sir William Fleetwood as they left the chamber.

'Will the King sacrifice Buckingham, think you?'

'There are some who think so. If his Majesty disowns him, then Buckingham will fall, and many with him. God grant it may be so.'

Headed by Coke, the Commons investigation now switched its attention to Buckingham's protégé, the Lord Chancellor, Sir Francis Bacon, but recently created Viscount St. Alban. He was accused of taking bribes and there were moves to impeach him. Ill and worried, Bacon wrote to Buckingham protesting his innocence and appealing for assistance, but to no avail, for the King had decided to sacrifice him, hoping that the Commons' hunger would then be sated and his favourite safe, and that such a gesture of consenting to the overthrow of such an influential servant of the crown would demonstrate his commitment to reform. The Marquis was truly sorry and regretted being unable to protect a man whom he regarded as his friend and mentor and of possessing great abilities. However, the evidence was damning, and both he and the King became somewhat jumpy when there was talk of Bacon standing trial for sodomy, for the Lord Chancellor's sexual preferences were as well known as the King's. Buckingham persuaded him it was in his best interest to give in without a trial, and Bacon was sentenced to £40,000, imprisoned in the Tower and barred from ever holding office or sitting in Parliament again. Buckingham alone was the only member of the House to refuse to vote against the Lord Chancellor.

The Prince had at first viewed the recall of Parliament with great interest, and had attended the Upper House daily, noting Sir Edward Coke's clever and learned discourses, laughing at his stories, and sitting upon several committees. He had even supported the investigations against monopolies. However, when he perceived that the mood of the Commons was bent upon discrediting Steenie, he was as shocked and unprepared as was his friend.

Charles had been at pains to support and comfort the favourite and the two were frequently to be seen walking in the Privy garden or Privy gallery; arms entwined around each other, their heads close together.

'All those barbed comments were aimed at me Charles; they seek to topple me by discrediting me.'

'Do not be discomfited, Steenie, they are envious of his Majesty's favour and affection for you.'

'Of that I am certain, but I will confess that I am not always as certain that the King will protect me.'

'How can you doubt it? You stand as high in my father's good opinions as ever. And there is none who can bring evidence of corruption against you.'

'I warrant that will not prevent them from trying, and that shitten hearted villain Coke is expert at twisting words, and influences the other members with his great learning. The King could not be seen to condone perceived wrong doing. Do you know that I have been called the only author of all grievances and oppressions – *me*!'

'He will never turn against you, do not fear!'

'I pray he will not, but he did not protect Somerset.'

'That was entirely different – the Earl was implicated in murder. There is simply no comparison!'

'There was not one good word about all my hard work and reforms in the navy, despite the King speaking on it. Not one word – his Majesty might as well have not spoken.'

'But he *did* speak, and the House heard him, even if they chose not to acknowledge it.'

Seeing that Buckingham was still concerned, Charles turned to face him, his hands reaching up to hold the taller man's shoulders.

'The King will not abandon you Steenie. But even if he did, I will not! There is nothing that anyone could say or do which would alter my love for you, nor can any misfortune take away our mutual constant affection.' Buckingham placed his hand over the Prince's and squeezed it tight.

Charles shortly had the opportunity to prove his loyalty during another outburst against Buckingham regarding his treatment of Sir Henry Yelverton, and was outraged as Yelverton claimed the favourite had assumed royal powers, comparing him to Hugh Despenser, the favourite of Edward II. The allusion to sodomy was not lost on any in the House and caused outrage. The Prince jumped to his feet, eyes blazing and white faced with anger.

'I will not s-sit here and hear my father's government to be so paralleled and scandalised. If you have aught to say against my Lord Buckingham then leave it till later.'

'Indeed, your Highness. Let Sir Henry Yelverton stick to the point,' agreed the Lord Treasurer Mandeville.

Buckingham stood up, his face pale but calm.

'Not so, let him proceed. He that will seek to stop him is more my enemy than his,' he said proudly.

But Yelverton had said enough, more than enough. His words took him to the Tower, for upon hearing them, James immediately perceived the point, and shrewdly commented, 'If Buckingham be Spenser than I must be Edward.'

Yelverton was ordered by the House to pay a fine of 5,000 marks to the Marquis of Buckingham, and to make a formal submission to him. The favourite remitted the fine, and received Yelverton's thanks and gratitude. He had survived the campaign to topple him, and proved Parliament-proof. Yet he had learnt much from this brush with disaster; henceforth he would never allow himself to be so vulnerable and unprepared. As for the Prince – he had experienced his first Parliament – had seen it at work and did not like what he had seen; his father was right.

'Your letters, my Lady.'

Katherine Villiers, Marchioness of Buckingham, sitting quietly in her closet, dropped her embroidery and darted forward eagerly to take the post – would there at last be a letter from her Lord? She leafed impatiently through them – some bills, one from her stepmother, another from a friend – not until later would these hold any interest for her. Yes! Her heart leapt at the sight of the familiar spiky writing, and she found her hands shaking as she tore open the letter, scanning quickly, desperate to learn if her husband would soon be with her. No. He regretted that business at court prevented his leaving. He trusted she was well, and that all the alterations in the house and park were progressing apace. He thanked her for all her letters, and was her faithful servant.

Katherine sat down, the letter fluttering onto her lap. She had been planning a walk in the gardens, beautiful in the autumn warmth, but now she cared for nothing. She lifted the paper again and re-read it. It did not take long, there were but a few lines, and those hurriedly scribbled, certainly not in his 'legible hand.' Katherine had written Buckingham letter after letter, describing in detail how she passed her days, the progress of the restoration, and thanking him for his kindness, his goodness to her; pouring out her love and adoration of he who had made her the happiest of women. Happiest? Certainly he was kind, none kinder; she had lovely homes, beautiful gowns, the costliest jewels, there was no end to the violet sugar cakes and expensive sweetmeats she enjoyed nibbling or the delicacies of almonds, orange chips, red sugar aloes, damsons and cherries, and as much of the equally costly white and canary wine, muscadet, port and claret as she could wish, although she drank but little. Yes her Lord was kind, and lavished upon his young wife everything she could have desired, everything, that was, except that which she most craved: himself. Katherine counted the lines; ten. Ten short lines, which would have taken – what? Five minutes of his precious time.

'He is busy, I must not be unjust,' she told herself, seeking to lessen the pain. Yes he was busy, none busier, but not too busy to attend the King and the Prince, or to go hunting and hawking. Not too busy to wait upon other women, not too busy to enjoy lavish feasts and banquets.

They had moved into their new home of Burley-on-the-Hill in May. Buckingham was determined to buy it from the Countess of Bedford whose debts of £50,000 had necessitated her regretfully parting with her inheritance. ('And she will soon be not the only one to have such vast debts,' Katherine's father had warned her, for in the year since they had married, the spending had been prodigious.) No matter, what he wanted he must have, and so £6,000 of her dowry had gone towards the cost, and he smilingly dismissed her concerns with a wave of his elegant hand, and, 'Oh I have sold Wanstead and some other properties. Why do you bother yourself with such matters, does the house not please you?'

Indeed it did please her, for it was in Rutland, and only thirteen miles from his childhood home of Brooksby, and near enough to Belvoir for her to visit with her family frequently. Buckingham had known the great estate since boyhood – what a pleasure it was for him to now own it! Of course it must be improved and rebuilt, the gardens remodelled and modernised, the interiors ripped out, lavishly decorated and filled with treasures – all must reflect the house of the greatest man in the realm.

Two months after moving in, Buckingham had arranged a lavish and costly entertainment for the King and Prince. Everything must be the very best, and so the music was written by Nicholas Lanier, a most fashionable composer, and *The Masque of the Gypsies,* was written by Ben Jonson. The other guests included the numerous Villiers' family, and members of the Manners' family and friends. The Masque delighted the King, who listened with smiling face and tear-filled eyes as his beloved Steenie, in his role as the first gypsy, expressed his gratitude to his royal master. Even the favourite's ragged costume and darkened face could not detract from his beauty and grace.

> *Myself a gypsy here do shine*
> *Yet are you maker, sir, of mine*
> *And may your goodness ever find*
> *In me, whom you have made, a mind*
> *As thankful as your own is large.*

Three days later it was repeated at Belvoir. After a magnificent banquet the King rose, and toasted the health of his favourite, debating who loved him most in all the world, and concluding that it was himself. Deeply moved, James then read some verses he had composed in honour of the occasion, declaring that they should be engraved in marble and set up as a perpetual memory of his visit. The King ended with his hope of 'a smiling boy within a while', for Katherine was with child, and her husband, and his mother had no doubts that she carried his heir.

'He must be called James, and the King will be his god-father,' exclaimed Buckingham.

'The first of many sons,' Mary nodded emphatically. Yet no one was more delighted than James, who was sure it would be a bonnie lad, just like his sweet Steenie. Buckingham was in a frenzy of happiness during the royal visit: relieved at having outsmarted his enemies, he laughed, smiled, and danced, at pains to include all in his joy; showing his guests around Burley and telling of his plans for improvements, of what grandeur his son would inherit. The favourite had cause to be content with his newest house and the magnificence displayed both outside and within which reflected his own.

His large household, worthy of a king, had performed their duties impeccably, and few would have been aware of the vast amount of work required to provide the lavish banquet for their noble master and his royal guest. In the bake-house, pantry, cellar, boiling house and pastry yard, the all-male staff laboured from morn till evening. The massive kitchens were a hive of activity as the cooks, wearing short, white linen aprons, bustled under the strict and knowledgeable eye of the master cook, attending to vast copper and brass cooking pots, and to the sizzling roasts skewered onto the cob-irons over the huge fireplaces; their hot juices spitting into the dripping pan beneath. Young scullions longingly sniffed the delicious aroma of dishes and delicacies which they would never taste, and were cuffed over the head when they got in the way.

Later, when the banquet was done and their master and his

guests were replete with food and wine, they would begin the seemingly endless washing and scouring of pots, pans and spits in cauldrons mounted upon iron trivets, the sweat trickling into their sleepy eyes, and their hands sore from the hot water and alkaline lye made from wood ashes. Only when all the work was finally ended, at least for a few hours, could the lads join the rest of the kitchen staff to ravenously devour their own meal.

Kate had not been surprised that James was so besotted; never had her husband looked more handsome. To his wife he was his usual kind self, but his attention was reserved for the King and Prince. There was no disguising the admiration in Charles's eyes, and watching the two young men together, she felt a stab of jealousy, for she recognised in the reserved and grave young man a different kind of rival for her lord's affections. James treated her with a friendly affability; fond and foolish Kate was no competition for his sweet gossip's heart, and would provide Steenie with the heirs upon which the King longed to lavish wealth. Yet when she caught the Prince's eyes upon her, there was no warmth, and Katherine knew that he did not like her because she was Buckingham's wife and shared his bed (sometimes). Only when his gaze rested upon her husband did those cold eyes light up; ablaze with emotion. Kate resented the King's hold over her husband, but she feared the Prince's.

Katherine had hardly been able to disguise her impatience for the visit to end; she was weary of smiling, of talking, of non-stop frenetic activity, of talk of Buckingham's heir; she felt tired and sickly, and wanted the King and his son and the Villiers to go and leave her dear lord to herself. Go they did, however, her dear lord went with them. She had not seen him since, despite her daily importuning of him to inform her when she would be so fortunate as to see him again.

Yet even before when they had lived at Whitehall she had rarely seen him, so much of his time was taken with business (and pleasure) and many of his nights spent away. In Katherine's dreams she had imagined her life with Buckingham, had expected him constantly at her side, that they would be inseparable, that he would leave his courtier's life, but these were a child's dreams and the reality was that it was the Prince with whom he was inseparable, and that when he wasn't with his Highness then he was with the King. Katherine did not wish to share her dazzling husband with anyone, but it was soon clear that she was not the highest on her husband's list of priorities. There were frequent arguments; Katherine was used to her own way and would not suffer in silence. At first her husband would laugh, playfully teasing her about her tantrums. He could not take her seriously. He was eleven years older than she and to him she was 'my poor little wife', a silly, sweet child to be petted and humoured. Buckingham was fond of Katherine, and genuinely wished her to be happy, but as the rows and tears intensified, he became irritated by her incessant demands.

'I am not your pet lap-dog Madam, and it would behove you well to realise the obedience you owe me. Have I not given you everything you have asked for, and more?'

'Everything but your time. I wish you with me; no woman ever loved a man as I love you.'

'Then for God's sake leave me be, for you will never tie me down.'

'Where are you going? Which woman is it now? I know you are not faithful,' she raged at him.

'I go to the King. I owe everything to his Majesty; my place is by his side, and my duty is to please him. I cannot comprehend how you thought it could be otherwise. You must accept and be at peace with this or you will never be happy,' her husband told her.

Please James he certainly did. Katherine watched as the King caressed and fondled his favourite, his hands incessantly stroking his hair, his face, the tightly clad buttocks. She saw no hint of distaste, for Buckingham returned the King's kisses and affection.

Yet even then she pushed away her fears, and refused to entertain any doubts about what transpired in the King's bedchamber – it was common for men to display their friendship through embracing and kisses, was it not? She had Lady Purbeck to thank for enlightening her.

Frances Villiers, married to the Marquis's older brother John, made it clear that she was visiting on sufferance, that she had no liking for the wife of her detested brother-in-law, and even less for the rest of the Villiers clan. Cold and proud, Frances would sit silent and aloof until the time of departure, and Katherine found the visits as great a trial as they were for her sister-in-law, for she could not like anyone who had no love for her lord. The two young women were the same age, but there the similarities ended. Frances was beautiful with fair lustrous hair, moon-pale skin and exquisite features; her loveliness emphasising the plainness of Katherine's long horse-face. It was only when Katherine learnt of the cruel way she had been forced into a marriage with a man she loathed that she began to feel some warmth towards her.

Frances's father, Sir Edward Coke, ambitious to regain power, had arranged the match with Buckingham and his mother, and the King had given his permission. However, Frances could not consent to marriage with a man she found unattractive and dull. John Villiers had inherited none of his mother's good looks, and the only similarity to his brother the favourite was the name they shared. Moreover, he was increasingly prone to black depressions and unstable behaviour. The young girl's mother, the redoubtable Lady Elizabeth Hatton, of proud and noble stock, would not agree either, and when she found that her husband, whom she detested and lived apart from, was adamant that their daughter must marry Buckingham's brother, she resorted to stealing her away and hiding her at the home of a friend.

Sir Edward had pursued them, accompanied by servants and his sons, all armed to the teeth. The door was knocked down and the terrified girl dragged from her hiding place upstairs and carried off, her mother in hot pursuit behind. These scandalous doings were a great source of comedy and entertainment at court. Less amusing were the dark tales which surfaced of Coke's mistreatment of his daughter, it being said that he had the girl tied to a bed-post and whipped, until the naked, delicate skin of her thin back was running with blood. Frances gave in.

Kate truly pitied her; she could not imagine what it must be like to be so abused by one's own father, and put into the bed of a man one could not love. She knew Rutland would never have treated her so, and felt a sudden rush of gratitude to the father who truly loved her and who had always wanted the best for her. Katherine had met Sir Edward Coke, and would not have liked the old man with his sharp little eyes and clever face even had she not been informed of his less than complimentary opinion of herself. Frances's hatred of the Countess of Buckingham was frightening in its intensity. She detested the whole Villiers' clan, but she no longer hated her husband, who followed her every move with dog-like adoration. No, she could not hate him, for he adored her and was kind, but she could not love him and submitted to his embraces with gritted teeth and closed eyes. Frances pitied him, for his melancholia increased, and when the black humours were upon him he would weep and fall upon his knees before Frances, begging her to love him.

Frances's dislike of her mother and sister-in-law Susan were reciprocated. Mary seemed to take a cruel delight in taunting her daughter Purbeck, and was ever glancing at her slight figure for signs of pregnancy.

'Still no child yet? After four years I would have expected at least two and another on the way. I was with child within a month of marrying, and I presented my lord with a child every year thereafter.'

The cold blue eyes regarded Katherine speculatively.

'We hope for better things from you, daughter. Do not be over long in giving my dear son an heir.'

Katherine flushed darkly, and mumbled, 'It is my dearest wish.' Seeing her embarrassment, Frances turned on the Countess.

'Then I should instruct your dear son to spend more time at home.'

Mary's brows contracted, her lips sucked in. 'Buckingham

knows his duty – both to the King and to his family.'

'Indeed he does,' spat Frances scornfully, turning away.

Katherine tried to smooth matters over. How she hated these all too frequent altercations, so different from her former peaceful and gentle life at Belvoir.

When the two women became more friendly Frances had asked Katherine how she could bear to be touched by a man who shared the King's bed, and on hearing Kate's reply that she took no account of untrue and salacious gossip which was the result of mere envy, the other had laughed bitterly.

'Oh Kate! What a little fool you are! How ignorant you are and how innocent! I cannot believe you have been married to Buckingham a year and yet know not how he came to be favourite. Do you not know why the King calls Steenie his dog? It is because he takes him as a dog takes a bitch.'

Katherine jumped to her feet, her hands at her mouth, horrified. 'I will not listen to your lies! I will not.'

'You have said you pity me, and with good reason, but I pity you more, for your lips must be sullied by those lips that kiss the King's, aye and kiss more than his lips. And the worst of it is that you love him. Even though I have been cursed by marrying a Villiers, at least I thank God that I have married the ugly brother whom the King does not want.'

'You will leave this house now Madam, and not return unless you admit that you have lied,' Katherine told her as she swept out of the room.

Frances did return, but although she asked Kate's forgiveness for having wounded her, she could not retract her words. She did not need to, for Katherine now knew the truth.

The winter of 1622 threatened to be as severe as its predecessor, but did not prevent the Christmas festivities at court being more lavish than ever. The Twelfth Night masque named *The Masque of Augers* written by Ben Jonson, was performed in the new Banqueting House, though it was still not fully completed. The severity of the King's gout delayed the performance by a week of the Prince's masque entitled *Time vindicated to himself and his honours*, in which Charles dramatically descended in disguise from the ceiling in a cloud. James was vastly pleased with his new Banqueting House, and its creator, Inigo Jones, was in great favour. There was a great hall on the first floor, linking with the King's privy gallery and private lodgings, and underneath an arched bricked grotto, covered with shells and with a little fountain, where his Majesty entertained his favourite and others with private amusements, and where it was said that wine flowed as freely as the water in the fountain. Topical as ever, Jonson had composed a rhyme for the opening of the King's grotto, (termed a cellar)

> *Since, Bacchus, thou art father*
> *Of Wines, to thee the rather*
> *We dedicate this Cellar,*
> *Where now, thou art made Dweller.*

The King returned to his beloved Theobalds in January, where it was thought he would stay until Easter. One day after dinner, riding on horseback, his horse stumbled, casting him into the frozen river, where he stuck head down in the ice with only his boots sticking out. Sir Richard Young leapt off his horse, and risking his own life, went into the water and lifted the King out. Spluttering and shocked, James returned to Theobalds and was placed into a warm bed, taking no ill from his accident, which caused much amusement when related.

Unusually, Buckingham had not been with the King at the time and was at first seriously concerned, but on learning that James had taken no hurt save the loss of his dignity, he laughed heartily at the description of the King's legs and boots waggling about in the ice.

'God's wounds,' he exclaimed, wiping his eyes.' My poor old Dad! I thank God he is unharmed, but upon my soul I should like to have seen it!'

The French Ambassador, the Comte de Tillières's comments were typically more acerbic, observing that the only ill effect of the immersion was that it had put so much water into his Majesty's wine.

Throughout Katherine's pregnancy the Villiers family had been assiduous in their care of her, in particular her mother-in-law who dictated what she must do, must not do, what she must eat, when she must rest. Katherine was grateful but was well aware that it was not herself that was the focus of attention, but the heir she carried in her belly. She became restive under such constant surveillance, but Mary's interference was as nothing to the King's, whose knowledge and expertise now included pregnancy and child-birth. Buckingham had fondly shown her one of James's doting letters (one that was fit for her eyes).

> *My only sweet and dear child,*
> *The Lord of Heaven bless thee this morning and thy wife my daughter, and the sweet little thing that is in her belly. I pray thee, as thou lovest me, make her precisely observe these rules; let her never go in a coach upon the street, nor never go fast in it; let your mother keep all hasty news from coming to her ears; let her not eat too much fruit, and hasten her out of London after we are gone. If thou be back by four in the afternoon, it will be good time. And prepare thee to be a guard to me for keeping my back unbroken with business before my going to the progress. And thus God send me a joyful and happy meeting with my sweet Steenie this evening.   James R.*

'How kind is his Majesty! And he has engaged to pay for your lying in – a vast amount I warrant. I will be sure to tell him how honoured and grateful you are for his care, and that you promise faithfully to follow all his advice,' said Buckingham, pecking Katherine's cheek, as he turned to go.

'Do you leave now my Lord? I had hoped I would have the pleasure of your company this evening, my father dines here.'

'You read the letter; his Majesty expects me soon, and you will have the Earl and my mother and sister to amuse you.'

'But when will you return?'

'I know not. Nay do not sulk, you know my time is not my own.'

'Your husband has the affairs of the realm to occupy him. You must not expect him to sit at your feet all the livelong day,' admonished the Countess, his mother.

'Promise me you will write straightway.'

'Of course I will, my dear.'

But of course he did not. The months slowly passed. Buckingham bought Wallingford House, for although the favourite still maintained his apartments at Whitehall, a man with a wife and a family needed larger accommodation, and this one was perfectly situated, overlooking St. James's Park and near to the Tilt yard. It scarcely needed to be mentioned that it must be redecorated and refurbished, and Katherine wearily viewed the never-ending procession of work men with their clumping feet and noisy chatter. Her head throbbed with the noise; she felt choked with the dust. She was now near her time, and longed for the quiet of Burley, with its clean, wholesome air, but her husband was adamant that his son must be born here in London. Katherine was apprehensive of the child birth ahead of her, and was genuinely grateful for once of Mary's sensible, encouraging words, and those of Buckingham's fertile sister Susan.

'Indeed it does hurt somewhat, but not more than you can bear, and when you hold your son in your arms, and see the pleasure on my brother's face, I promise that the pain will be soon forgot.'

It was on Susan's advice that Katherine sought the ministrations of the King's physician, Doctor Theodore Mayerne for advice regarding the birthing. He recommended that in her ninth month she anoint her pudenda with an unguent morning and night which included such ingredients as water of stag's head, confection of Alkermes of Montpellier, finger bones, crocus martis corallines,

Cretan dittany and even the dried testicles of horses. On smelling this concoction, Buckingham was glad he had an excuse not to share his wife's bed.

At the end of March, Kate's pains came upon her, and on being informed, the King hastened to Wallingford House, anxious as any father, and indeed, more anxious than the real father, and certainly showing more interest and care than he had in the birth of his own children. Upon receiving messages from him for the tenth time, Katherine managed to send the answer that the labour progressed well, and thanked his Majesty for his care of her. At the fifteenth she wished with all her heart that he would go away. At the twentieth she was in no state to either respond or care.

After a long and difficult labour, the Marchioness of Buckingham was delivered of her first child. It was a daughter.

Chapter Six

Heaven bless King James our joy,
And Charles his baby. Great George our brave viceroy
And his fair Lady.
Old Beldame Buckingham, with her Lord Keeper
She loves the fucking game
He's her cunt creeper.
These be they go so gay,
In court and city,
Yet no man cares for them,
Is not this a pity.

Anonymous, 1623.

The small figure astride the powerful white charger thundered down the course at the tilt yard, the sun glinting on his gold and silver armour, the crowds enthusiastically applauding. No hint remained now of the sickly child with the spindly, rickety legs who had not walked until he was four.

'S'blood, his Highness rides well!' exclaimed Philip Herbert, Earl of Montgomery.

'He does indeed,' Buckingham replied, clapping louder than any. The Marquis and Montgomery had not fared so well, having little success in all the courses they made.

As he watched, Buckingham was aware of a growing pride and respect for the young heir to the throne. This was *his* friend. As the Prince dismounted, the favourite loped over to him and pulled him into a warm embrace, kissing his cheeks.

'Well done! Well done indeed, my Prince! Your skill bested us all and put us to shame.'

Charles flushed with pleasure; he had received scant praise in his life, and to receive it from Steenie whom he so admired was heady indeed. He had been determined to prove worthy of the people's acclaim, of the King's approbation, but mostly of his friend's approval. Despite being the Prince of Wales, part of Charles would always feel that he was still the runt of the family.

Later in private Steenie continued the same theme, an arm slung affectionately around the Prince's neck.

'I swear there was none other to touch you. No doubt that fat booby Lando will even now be panting back to his apartments to write to the Doge about the skill of England's Prince.'

Buckingham did not flatter, for he spoke what he truly felt. Long gone was the impatience and resentment at being forced to devote himself to Charles; now the devotion was real and he was proud to be known as his friend and confidant.

Charles's high standing continued the next morning when he beat Buckingham for the first time at tennis, winning £100 in a bet. Steenie was surprised though not as surprised as the Prince himself.

'Well played, Charles. Once more may I proffer my congratulations, despite that you have deprived me of the money I had hoped to gamble this evening at cards.'

'You need not give the money Steenie, if you need it,' Charles replied apologetically.

Buckingham threw back his chestnut curls and laughed, his eyes dancing in merriment.

'But of course I will pay you! And this time I promise I will not have the temerity to lift my racket to your Highness!'

Buckingham felt no resentment at being beaten by the Prince; he was touched by Charles's delight and developing skills, particularly when he was aware that he was the chief reason for the Prince's growing confidence.

'Dear Baby Charles! How sweet was his pleasure, and only he would feel real sorrow at beating me!' he reflected, as he left the tennis courts, whistling jauntily. For a brief second he considered returning to Wallingford House, considered it but then rejected it, having an altogether more enjoyable alternative in mind. The favourite turned towards his apartments; thinking again how glad he was that he had retained these. He washed in scented water but scarcely heard the chatter of his barber as he shaved him, curled his golden beard and moustache and arranged his hair. Usually such conversation afforded him much amusement but today he was impatient for the ministrations to end, for his mind was focused upon a diversion of a different sort, the thought of which flooded him with desire.

Later, dressed in a beaded green doublet, a ribboned garter below the shapely knee, clad in matching green hose, a plush cloak of a deeper hue with embroidered edges thrown over his shoulders, feet clad in silken rosetted slippers, his hat adorned with a feather and large jewel, and carrying leathern, perfumed gloves, Buckingham set out to Essex House, the home of Lucy, Viscountess Doncaster. He was admitted immediately, but there were little preliminaries, and five minutes later the costly green doublet was on the floor of the lady's chamber.

The affair had begun over two years ago, and the fact that Lady Doncaster still held Buckingham's interest was as much a reflection on her lively wit and personality as it was upon her considerable beauty. Lucy Percy, the daughter of Henry Percy, Earl of Northumberland, had married James Hay against her father's will in 1617. As wilful as she was lovely, Lucy had fallen deeply in love with the Scottish Hay, more than twice her age and a former King's favourite; within three months of the marriage she was with child, but the infant son died two weeks after birth, and Lucy never became pregnant again.

Her besotted husband, created Viscount Doncaster and well provided for by the King, (who ever retained an affection for his former favourites provided they had the sense to graciously step aside without making a fuss when the next young man came along), loved her too well to care, and he already had a son from his first marriage. Lucy had been insupportable when Doncaster had been sent abroad to Germany as ambassador; weeping inconsolably that she could not live without him for long, and accompanying him to Gravesend, tearfully waving his ship out of sight. The young wife had counted the days till her husband's return, devouring his letters and writing daily. Then Buckingham smiled at her.

Whilst acknowledging her beauty, and thinking that Hay would be fortunate in his marriage bed, the favourite had not at first taken much notice of Doncaster's wife. He had been involved with the Countess of Salisbury and there were others only too eager to catch his eye. Perhaps that was the real secret of the affair which was to last the rest of Buckingham's life, for Lucy had shown him scant attention, and certainly no inclination to flirt, giving him his due respect but naught else. The Marquis was curious – despite his outstanding good looks, he was not overly vain, but was acquainted with the chambers of many of the attractive ladies at court, indeed he had bedded most of them, but they soon bored him. Lady Doncaster was well aware of the favourite's charms, and equally aware of his reputation, but had determined that she would not contribute to the names on the long list, to be seduced and then discarded. Besides, she loved her husband and was content with her life.

It was during a masque that Lucy and Buckingham first spent time together, dancing for a large part of the evening, much to the pique of several of the court lovelies, who regarded her monopolising of the favourite with displeasure. The two were well matched, both in their beauty and in the skill of their dancing, and Buckingham found himself increasingly engrossed by his partner; admiring the red, sensual lips, and the creamy skin of her full breasts, daringly displayed. Later, while dining, he was equally impressed by her conversation; Lucy was knowledgeable, witty and amusing, and by the time the masque ended in the early morning, Buckingham knew that he wanted her. Normally under such circumstances he would not have retired alone to his own chambers, and he was disappointed when the Viscountess bade him a very definite farewell: disappointed but intrigued. Lucy had slept little the rest of that night. She had not expected to be so attracted to Buckingham, to find him so fascinating and agreeable. Tossing restlessly, she thought of her husband, so far away, for until this night, her first and last thoughts had been of him, but try as she might, Lucy was disturbed to find that it was only Buckingham's face she could see.

The following day she had received a note from the Marquis, thanking her for her company the previous evening, and asking if he could call upon her. Lucy's first inclination was to immediately agree, but then she decided differently – no, let him wait. She sent a carefully worded reply, thanking his Lordship for his kindness, but informing him that as her dear Lord was abroad she thought it improper to receive him, being mindful of her reputation and also of his, for was he not about to marry the Earl of Rutland's daughter? Her admirer was initially surprised and annoyed at receiving the refusal – his first ever, but then he laughed. Lucy had cleverly gambled on his interest but had read him correctly, Buckingham was now committed to the chase.

It was conducted over two delicious months. The rules were understood implicitly by both protagonists and by the end, Buckingham was as much the quarry as was the lady. For the Marquis the game was an exciting and novel experience, until this time a woman would tumble into his bed as soon as he looked at her, even before, and he found himself thinking of Lucy more often than he was usually wont to do. Their courtship was spiced with meetings, planned and unexpected, with written notes and deliberately provocative word-play, and their frequent partnerings at dances heightened the smouldering atmosphere between them.

Lucy teased, tempted and then rebuffed him, knowing exactly how far she could go to increase and prolong his hunger of her, and Buckingham was hooked, wanting her as he had never wanted a woman before. The outcome was inevitable, and both knew it, for their eyes betrayed their desire. Their passion was finally consummated one evening during the Christmas festivities. As ever the dancing was but a preliminary to their flirtation; the air crackled between them.

'I swear your beauty outshines the moon and stars,' Buckingham told her.

'Did you just say the same to your last partner? I noticed she was very flushed at your attentions,' Lucy returned archly.

'I said little to her and what I did say I cannot recall, for all I could think of was being close to you. Beauteous Madam, you know well my passion for you; how long will you continue to refuse me?'

'My Lord, you also know well what my answer must be. I am married and love my husband, as befits a wife, and you have other paramours to distract you.'

'Doncaster is the only man of whom I have ever been jealous; I cannot bear to think of you in his bed. Lucy! I swear my need of you bemaddens me! I promise your husband will prosper if you will give yourself to me, and I will have no other but you.'

His partner smiled, 'I do not believe you capable of being faithful, my dear Buckingham, and the eyes of all the women at court are upon us, envying and hating me. You have your pick of them; I pray you will accept that we can only be friends.'

'Friends I already have, friends ride together, dine together, play cards together. I have altogether different plans for you.'

'And what exactly are your plans, my Lord?'

Buckingham told her, whispering, silken voiced, in her ear.

'How disagreeably hot it is in here. I fear I shall faint if I dance any further.'

'Then I insist that you must not so risk yourself. Will you permit me to accompany you to somewhere quieter, where you can recover yourself?'

Buckingham and the Viscountess left the crowded hall swiftly, ascending into a gallery; around which stood a few spectators watching the dance, and the couple walked further on to where there were several secluded alcoves, fronted by ornately carved pillars. Buckingham pulled Lucy into one: he was not prepared to wait any longer; the chase ended here. She was instantly in his arms, kissing him with equal intensity, her tongue entwined in his. Enflamed with a desire which blocked out all rational thought, they gave no heed that they might be discovered; his hands were tugging impatiently at her tightly laced bodice, his mouth on the voluptuous breasts; she could not have stopped him had she wished. She did not wish to, for all thought of her husband was now obliterated, all that remained was her utter need of Buckingham. Pushing her against the wall, her lover pulled up the layers of her voluminous gown and they at last gave in to the passion which they had so long held in check. They were seen and heard, and by the next day it was common knowledge at court that Lucy Hay was Buckingham's mistress.

James Hay, Viscount Doncaster, had returned home in January 1620, impatient to see his beloved wife. He had been away longer than he had either anticipated or wished, and the Comte de Tillieres wrote to Paris that the favourite had deliberately delayed his return in order to consummate his love for Doncaster's wife. The Viscount had noticed that Lucy's letters, once so frequent and filled with endearments, were arriving less and less, and were no longer so tender. He was puzzled as to the cause, but it was only when he had been with her for several hours that he became genuinely alarmed. His wife seemed cold and distant, disinterested in anything he said, and he was hurt that she did not even seem affected by his having been ill.

Even worse was her disinclination for his love making. The first few nights she had pleaded an indisposition and he loved her too well to force her. However, after a week he was irritable and worried, and when he sought answers, Lucy claimed that naught ailed her, and she knew not to what her Lord alluded. Hay drew her to him and looking full into her eyes, asked her if she still loved him. His wife told him that she did, but that night, when he finally had to insist upon his marital rights, he knew the truth: there was no warmth, no fire – the Viscountess submitted to his caresses but she no longer enjoyed them, for her desire was for another man, and

Doncaster was compelled to admit the painful truth that his Lucy no longer loved him.

He did not have long to find out the reason. Speaking with Sir George Goring, his friend and the cousin of his first wife, the cuckolded husband could not contain his anger.

'So I am the last to know! Everyone at court knew, even the ambassadors! God damn his eyes! I am not sure which is worse to bear, the pitying looks, or the sneers! And I must accept it, must dissemble, must smile and make low legs and kiss the hand of that cozening, vile-hearted villain who pretends to be my friend but who swives my wife!'

Goring was truly sorry for his distress, but did not know how to lessen it. 'He will tire of her, he always does, and then she will realise her foolishness.'

'It will never be the same betwixt us, never! When I look at her now, I see *him*, when she consents for me to lie with her, all I can think of is that *he* has been between her legs. A pox on him, I wish the black-hearted bastard dead and in hell!'

'Hush, my Lord. I understand your anger, most of the husbands in court do, but he is still the favourite and could ruin you if he wished.'

'I will ask the King if I can return abroad. I cannot tarry here.'

'That might be best,' his friend replied soothingly, 'I am sure Buckingham will arrange it for you.'

'Of that I am in no doubt,' Doncaster snapped.

Lucy had seen his pain and had regretted it, but was powerless before the passion she felt for her lover. Not long since she had admired her husband's good looks and stylish clothes, for next to the favourite, Doncaster was the most flamboyantly dressed man at court. But now, she viewed him differently, as she scrutinised him she saw an ageing man, his face lined, the eyes pouched and puffy, and his dress seemed ridiculous and foolish, no longer disguising the thickening figure. No, Lucy no longer loved him, but did she love Buckingham? At first she thought so. She cared for nothing but being with him; his skilled and sensual lovemaking had awoken in her an equal passion, and for a long time their lusts were insatiable. Yet later, she realised that it was simply that – lust, not love. On reflection she realised that she was glad, for Buckingham was a painful person to love; the King, the Prince, his wife and his innumerable discarded mistresses were proof of that, and she did not need his love. Lucy did not want him with her constantly but only in bed; what she wanted from her lover was precisely what he gave her – exquisite pleasure and power at court.

Moreover, she was well aware that Buckingham did not love her either. She doubted if he could truly love a woman, but she bound him to her precisely because she did not love him and therefore made no demands upon him except those in bed which he was more than delighted and equipped to fulfil. Lucy was clever and perceptive enough to know that if she ever became needy then she would lose him, and she had no intention of giving up her role as the favourite's primary mistress. Altogether it was a most satisfactory arrangement.

Doncaster remained at court and swallowed the bile of betrayal, as he was expected to, and as his rival had promised, his acquiescence was rewarded. In September of that year he was created Earl of Carlisle. The Carlisles frequently dined with the Buckinghams, occasions which the favourite's wife detested, and on one such evening the Marquis was taken ill at supper, needing to retire to a bed at Essex House. The thought briefly passed through Buckingham's mind that Carlisle might have had him poisoned, but thankfully he was recovered enough by the next day to re-join the festivities, and the truth was that the Earl was too ambitious to risk losing Buckingham's patronage, and besides he now had the attentions of the wife of the French ambassador to help heal his wounded pride.

Katherine had not been married to Buckingham long before she realised that the Viscountess Doncaster remained her husband's lover, despite his protestations that the affair had ended before their wedding. Kate had instantly hated her, recognising her beauty and poise, and her confident easy way of conversing with the Marquis. Constantly watching her husband's every move, she intercepted the expressions of interest which were exchanged, the fleeting smiles, the raising of the eyebrow. Katherine missed nothing and seethed. Sometimes, naked in bed, the sweat cooling after their exertions, Buckingham would tell Lucy of his wife's jealousy, of her accusations. His mistress was sympathetic, but was astute enough never to criticise her. Wife or no, Lucy knew Katherine was no threat to her, and learning that Buckingham's wife was inhibited and shy in the marital bed, she smiled to herself: the favourite had not married for love, but for a wealthy alliance, and for the begetting of heirs; she need have no fear of being supplanted, and if Katherine wept her heart out over her handsome husband's infidelities, then so much the worse for her. She was a little fool. Lucy had sometimes wished that she was the favourite's wife, certainly she looked a far more suitable partner than the plain little creature he had chosen; still, death and second marriages were commonplace, and then who knew what might happen?

On learning of Kate's pregnancy Lucy was wise enough to profess her delight; her only regret was her own continuing barrenness – though in view of her frequent coupling with Buckingham, perhaps it was fortunate. It was to his credit that Buckingham expressed more disappointment over the child being a girl to his mistress than to his wife, and when Kate contracted smallpox, the Marquis was desperately worried, for Kate's mother had died of the same disease, and for a while Lucy hardly saw him, though she often sent word privately, assuring him of her prayers for the safety of both wife and child. Only to herself did Lucy acknowledge that it would be most opportune if the Marchioness fled this vale of tears, for her own husband was not young and was often indisposed. However, Kate recovered though her face was scabbed and marked with the pocks, and upon seeing her reflection, she wept tears of weakness and bitterness.

'You must not distress yourself, daughter. Your lord does not love you for your looks. You must regain your strength and health, and we will pray that God will grant you a fine boy by this time next year,' the Countess of Buckingham told her. Mary had not been as kind as her son about the birth of his daughter, nor as kind as the King. Kate had been much affected by James's gentleness and care, telling her not to worry herself, for this was merely a practice run, and he doubted not that her daughter would be a great comfort to her.

Buckingham had peered bemusedly at the tiny wailing creature; he was not sure how to react. The King had forbade him entering Katherine's sick chamber, for fear that he also might contract small-pox, and Buckingham had reluctantly agreed, for he knew that it would be potentially disastrous for him if he lost his beauty.

'Well, it is clear that she favours the Manners family rather than the Villiers,' the Countess later commented. 'However, there is time for her to become pretty.'

'She will be loved whether she favours the Manners or Villiers, and she is already pretty, and like to be a great beauty,' replied her son. He lied, for it was clear that the ailing, puling infant was far from pretty, but he would not allow his mother to upset Katherine, who smiled her thanks through tear-filled eyes.

The Countess's poor opinion of her granddaughter was modified by her being named Mary after herself, which was soon abbreviated to Mall. As if to reward her father for his belief in her, Mall gradually grew in looks and strength, and Mary was soon telling all who would listen (and those who would not) that her sweet little Mall very much resembled her father, having his chestnut curls, blue eyes and dimpling smile. Moreover, she also had his sunny and winning disposition, and it was not long before Buckingham was devoted to his small child, and never regretted once that she was not a boy. He had no doubts that sons would swiftly follow.

It was well that at least his daughter pleased him, Buckingham commented to the Prince, for God knew his other kin caused him to be beset with perplexities. He had known for some time that his mother inclined toward popery, and although he had tried on divers occasions to warn her of the inadvisability of this course, she had not heeded him, and he had no real interest or knowledge to debate theology with her. Buckingham was therefore displeased but not altogether surprised when he was informed that she had outwardly made a confession of her faith, though not as displeased as the King, who took it as a personal affront, and after attempting to wean her back to the Protestant church through the interventions of such worthies as Doctor White and Doctor Laud, he banished her from court. However, the gossip continued, for it was rumoured that, long since estranged from her third husband, Sir Thomas Compton, the Countess of Buckingham was involved with the Lord Keeper, John Williams.

The favourite was even more concerned about his brother John, Viscount Purbeck, whose depressions had now progressed to severe mental illness, and there were long periods when he was out of control and unaware of anyone save his wife Frances. Buckingham loved John deeply and was anguished at his increasing bouts of madness, spending large amounts of money on doctors who attempted to treat him. Finally he had John brought to Wallingford House, against his brother's will, so that he could be sure he was being adequately cared for.

The favourite had been dining with the Prince when he had received disturbing news from Katherine. He had hastened home to be informed that Purbeck had broken out of his chambers, and had beat at the glass windows at the front of the house with his bare and bloodied fists, crying out to the people that passed that he was a Catholic and would spend his blood in the cause. Entering John's darkened room, Buckingham's heart was filled with pity at the sight of the desolate, dull-eyed, apathetic figure slumped over the chair. Kneeling before his brother, he had lifted the torn, bandaged hands, and gently kissed them. John had looked up with the hurt eyes of a wounded animal, and recognising him, had said, 'George, forgive me.' Buckingham put his arms around the wasted form and the brothers both wept long and hard.

John's wife, Frances, Lady Purbeck, vowing that she could live no longer with her husband, made petition to the King for maintenance, and Buckingham agreed to pay her, yet he did so with a bad grace; he was having his sister-in-law watched for proof of adultery with Sir Robert Howard. The affair appeared to be common knowledge, but so far the couple had been prudent enough not to be caught. Buckingham's anger burnt within him when he thought of her, and of his poor, demented brother. He had besought John to disown her, but perceiving that such talk only contributed to Purbeck's agitation, he had left off. However, once he had evidence, then the whore would feel the full extent of his wrath. The favourite was not by nature vindictive, but he would never forgive Frances for the slur she had brought upon his family's honour, but most of all he could not forgive her for hurting the husband who loved her and sought to protect her, and he was convinced she had exacerbated his insanity. Well, she would be protected no longer, and despite John's pleas, the slut would be divorced and imprisoned. No, he was not vindictive, but when his family were concerned, Buckingham made an implacable enemy.

Not all the Marquis's concerns were unpleasant, for he had acquired another two houses. York House, a grand mansion situated on the Strand, had belonged to the disgraced Viscount St. Albans, and he was most reluctant to part with it, only agreeing when he thought it would restore his favour with the King. The favourite was delighted, but was less pleased when he was informed of the poor state it was in, and how much it would cost to be brought up to the standards he expected.

His other new home was New Hall at Chelmsford in Essex, a palatial residence built for Henry VIII. Buckingham and his mother had viewed it in June, and as he gazed upon it, the favourite knew he must have it, despite the vast amount of money he would need to spend upon it, and despite his financial advisors beseeching him to make urgent cut-backs in his expenditure. Buckingham never regretted buying New Hall, for of all his houses, this was the one he truly loved; surrounded by parks and woods, it was away from court and all its demands, but near enough that he could journey there easily.

'We shall stay here often. We shall be happy and none will be allowed here save those I love,' the Marquis murmured to the Prince, his face alight with joy.

The Countess of Buckingham had not been long banished from court before James allowed her back.

'The King would have been kinder towards his favourite had he kept her away,' observed the Comte de Tillieres.

The unlikely truth was that the ageing king had developed a fondness for the countess and for her daughter Susan, Countess of Denbigh, for they were his beloved Steenie's family and so they became his family, and now they must be constantly with him at table and in his carriage, and not only they, but all his numerous kin were welcome at court, and it was often commented upon that it was passing strange that the King who was well known for his dislike of both women and children, and had seen but little of his own, now allowed the family of his favourite to swarm all over the palace. As Buckingham's wife, Katherine had a special place and he must have his 'sweet little grandchild, ma bonny Mall' around him constantly, playing with and dandling the child upon his knee.

Buckingham was touched and amused at the sight of the King of England gossiping contentedly with his mother and exchanging remedies, for James was often in great pain with gout, and had little faith in physic, but trusted Mary's knowledge of country lore. The countess had some little experience but a vast amount of confidence in her own abilities. No matter how severe the gout, the King was determined to hunt, and now the favourite's women must also accompany them, James referring to them as 'the cunts', which bawdy term Buckingham also used, for both were men of their time and regarded women with scant respect.

Charles had little time and even less respect for his father's female entourage and it took all his deep affection for Steenie to accept their permanent presence at court. From morning until night they were there, and the Prince would cringe as he heard the strident, ringing tones of the Countess of Buckingham holding forth on all subjects, the majority of which she knew little or nothing about. Charles was civil, but he could not be friendly and recoiled from her. He welcomed Steenie's over-familiarity but would not tolerate it from his dreadful mother.

'Dear God, the woman is appalling. She behaves as if she is now queen in my mother's place,' he thought, but he would never say as much to Steenie. His friend could guess though, and would often smile apologetically; his mother increasingly embarrassed even he.

The Prince was cold towards the marchioness, for although she was nobly born, he was bitterly jealous of her, and his dislike was exacerbated by Katherine's demands upon his friend's time. Charles felt no surprise that Steenie's wife loved her husband so passionately – he expected as much, but her constant mewling after him, the incessant letters, tears and reproaches irritated him beyond words, and he was relieved that the favourite seemed to concur, except that he was genuinely fond of his wife. The Prince could not understand why, and was always greatly pleased when Kate was packed off to Burley. The general opinion of the Villiers family was even less complimentary, nor did the King escape severe censure.

'I believe this is but further evidence of the King's desperate infirmity of mind. Although formerly his Majesty did not care much for the conversation of ladies, now he daily becomes more like an old woman himself,' observed the Comte de Tillieres to the Venetian ambassador exasperatedly, as they had waited for over three hours to be received by the King, only to be finally informed that his Majesty had gone out in his carriage with the Countess of Buckingham and her daughters.

'True my Lord, it appears to me that there are many in this land who fear his Majesty is but the dupe and puppet of Spain. Indeed, all good sentiments are clearly dead in the King; he is too blinded in disordered self-love and in the wish for quiet and pleasure, too agitated by constant mistrust of everyone, tyrannized over by perpetual fear for his life, tenacious of his authority as against the Parliament and jealous of his son's obedience,' replied his companion.

'Undoubtedly. I fear this is a King devoted to his own nothingness, for a flask of wine is dearer to him than his own kingdom, and he is hated and despised by the people. He cannot utter a thing without the Spanish ambassador, Gondomar, knowing, who is undoubtedly more minutely and profoundly advised than his Majesty.'

'The King no longer has any interest in his own policies, but cares only for pleasure. I think his mind deteriorates as quickly as his body fails. Yet he continues to keep the Prince in the background and denies him authority. I wonder the heir can tolerate such treatment.'

'Hmph! His Highness fears his father, and will not stand up to him. Even his friendship with the royal favourite has not given him sufficient confidence to go against the old man.'

'Well, my Lord, I doubt not that you have other matters to attend to, and we have wasted an afternoon waiting upon a king who does not wish to see us. In future I suggest we address ourselves to the Marquis of Buckingham, and wait upon him; for it appears that all business is accomplished through him.'

'I agree. Buckingham's favour has increased to such an extent that some believe he has bewitched the King. I bid you a good day my Lord.'

William Herbert, Earl of Pembroke apprised the handsome young man standing before him with a critical eye, as if he were assessing the merits of a young horse he was considering buying.

'Yes, I think he might do – he might very well do,' he murmured, thoughtfully stroking his beard.

The youth glanced at Lionel Cranfield, Earl of Middlesex and Lord High Treasurer of England, his brother-in-law and benefactor, anxious to see his response. Cranfield smiled broadly.

'I am delighted you think so, my Lord.' He turned to the boy, 'You may leave us Arthur, his Lordship and I have matters to discuss.'

The young man bowed and withdrew.

Pembroke's hard eyes narrowed, 'You believe that the King will grant your request for him to be admitted as Groom of the Bed-Chamber?'

'I do, his Majesty knows full well what my obedience cost me, and besides, he will assume that he is favouring Buckingham's family.'

Yes, reflected Cranfield grimly. His obedience had cost his acceptance of marriage to a woman who had neither beauty, charm nor fortune. All she had to commend her was the Villiers blood, being niece to the Countess of Buckingham. Cranfield, a widower, had been pressurised to marry Anne Brett when his heart was engaged elsewhere, and he had so disliked her that he had appealed to the King. Buckingham had explained his actions, saying that he had never intended to thrust his kinswoman upon him, but only commended the match to him from no other ground than but upon the great desire to have him for his friend and ally.

The marriage had gone ahead, but James was determined to reward his servant for his obedience and had appointed Cranfield to the Privy Council, and allowed him to keep all the considerable profits he made as Master of the Wardrobe. There was talk that his wife was involved with Thomas Howard, the Earl of Arundel, but her husband dismissed such a notion; she was too plain to tempt any man.

The new Lady Cranfield's younger brother appeared to have inherited his sister's share of good looks, and the thought came to Buckingham's enemies that the youth might be used as a rival to topple him. The marquis had survived the attacks of his enemies through Parliament, but could a handsome, new face at court prove a more serious threat? Pembroke and Middlesex thought so. The two men were allied through their fear of Buckingham's ever-increasing power and had watched his growing influence over the heir to the throne with disquiet. Pembroke had no particular liking for his fellow conspirator, regarding him as an upstart and overly ambitious, and that ambition had been well rewarded by both the King and Buckingham, for Middlesex was clever and resourceful, had worked with the favourite on overhauling and reforming public services and had been appointed Chief Commissioner of the Navy. Like his patron, Cranfield craved power, and his desire for further wealth and position had led to a gradual distancing between the two men. Pembroke reflected wryly that it was ironic that Buckingham might have given the Lord Treasurer the means to overthrow him, and if that were the case, then Middlesex's power would then also need to be curbed. Ah well – first to rid the country of the detested Villiers.

'How amusing it would be for the King's favour to alight upon the young man as a result of his being Buckingham's cousin,' smiled Pembroke.

'Indeed my Lord, I confess that I would derive great pleasure from Buckingham being toppled as a result of enforcing this marriage upon me,' Cranfield purred.

Pembroke gave a short laugh, 'So once again I find myself resorting to using the King's weakness for young men to bring down the current favourite. It seems but yesterday that I was bringing forward young Villiers. God's Blood! Who would have thought that such a pretty, docile youth could have turned out to be more powerful and dangerous than Somerset ever was! Well, I pray Brett will prove more amenable and less intelligent.'

'Your Lordship may depend upon it.'

'I *do* depend upon it, and so must you, for Buckingham would make a dangerous enemy. Young Brett need have no abilities except to simper and smile at the King and allow himself to be pawed and slobbered – indeed, it is vital that he has no other talents: God forbid we should inflict another such as Buckingham upon ourselves!'

Early in the year it was bruited that there was a new favourite, and the rumours gained strength when the King bestowed the place of Groom of the Bedchamber upon Arthur Brett as Cranfield had gambled. Soon the court was abuzz. When the Countess of Buckingham heard of it, that lady immediately addressed herself to her son.

'Of course I am certain there can be no substance to these rumours, my dear George, but it is as well to stop them before they go any further. I shall speak to the King straightway.'

'I pray you will do no such thing! Your concern is natural, but his Majesty will not tolerate your interference.'

'Interference! When have I interfered in any of your affairs! I am sure that I know well my duty before God as a woman to interfere in state business! I cannot comprehend how you could accuse me of such behaviour.'

Had the matter been less disconcerting Buckingham would have found his mother's outrage amusing, but he was only too aware of what was being whispered around the corridors and chambers of the court.

'Calm yourself Madam. I intended no disrespect, only that this is something that I alone must discuss with the King.'

'Then I recommend you do so with all alacrity, for it is most grievesome for me to think that I may have caused you harm by putting that silly boy Arthur before the King.'

'I know full well who is responsible for this plot to push forward my cousin.'

'Indeed, Cranfield. And how he and my niece can bear to primp and push their own kin forward in such a manner is a thing beyond my belief! I shall speak to them both, indeed I shall!'

'I beg you will not, I will deal with this matter myself. And now, dear mother, I must attend the King.'

Mary looked hard at her son, as if calculating in her own mind whether his beauty had begun to fade.

'Well, I praise God that you are as handsome as ever, though mayhap somewhat lean. I shall have some delicacies sent over for you. Thankfully you look younger than your years – doubtless you have inherited this from me, not your father. Perhaps you should spend more time attending the King than the Prince, George, and not give your cousin the opportunity to sneak into the King's bedchamber.'

'I thought you were encouraging me to cultivate his friendship as the next King.'

'Well, there is no need for you to continue to do so for you have gained his love. Now you must retain the King's! I trust you still sleep with his Majesty often and do all which is required to please him.'

Mary's son sighed, rubbing his hand wearily over his eyes, he felt tired beyond words, 'I will do everything required, and now I must leave you.' Buckingham kissed his mother's hand, and turned to depart.

'I pray you will advise the King to banish your cousin, George. I do not wish to awaken one morning to the news that you have been imprisoned, or worse. For my own part, I declare that I shall not receive them again, and I shall retire now to pray.'

'I am sure that will be best,' Buckingham told her.

'And be sure to eat more.'

After changing his clothing, and curling and perfuming his hair, Buckingham thoughtfully regarded his image in the looking glass. He was now in his thirtieth year and was relieved that he could detect no decline in his beauty, but his mother was right, he was lean, his appetite had been poor of late, the result of his worrying over this situation and over John. James had been as loving as ever, but his favourite was aware that the King had looked appreciatively at that wanton Brett, and more than once. Yes, Mary was also right that he must find a way of removing his rival from court, but then there would always be others. Thank God that Charles's love for him was not based primarily on a fair face and shapely arse.

It was unfortunate that he came across young Brett on his way to attend the King, and he was immediately infuriated by the insolent smirk on the ingle's face.

'Get you gone!' he ordered Brett's companions, who seeing the anger on Buckingham's face, scurried swiftly away, leaving their friend to face his kinsman alone. Buckingham's temper was well-known and feared.

'Can I help you my Lord?'

'Help *me*? I am the one who has helped *you* and your family, and am rewarded by your treachery. So you think you can take my position? Take the King's love from me?'

'No my Lord, I would never think such a thing.'

'No? I see you wiggle your prick-struck arse, smiling and taking every opportunity to flaunt yourself in front of the King.'

The young man retreated, shocked by his cousin's fury. Buckingham grabbed him by his ruff, tearing it, and slammed him against a pillar.

'You've been told that you can be the next favourite, but I tell you that I'll see you dead before I'll see you in the royal bed!'

Terrified, Brett dropped to his knees and tremblingly attempted to kiss Buckingham's hand. Suddenly, Buckingham saw a scene in his mind's eye, eight years previously, when, in this same building, he had knelt before the current favourite, Somerset, and besought his patronage. The Earl had told him he'd have none of him and would sooner break his neck. He had pitied Somerset then, pitied him as only a man whose star is in the ascendant can pity one whose time is coming to an end. Sweet Jesu, was he now in the same position?

'Get out of my sight; henceforth I no longer regard you as my kin, look for no more favours at my hand,' he snapped, kicking out at the still kneeling and shaking young man, who scuttled out of his presence, relieved to escape.

Half an hour later Buckingham was on his way to the Prince's apartments, after a stormy confrontation with the King. His anger and hurt were such that he had accused James of unfaithfulness, storming out of the royal presence without permission and leaving the King profoundly shocked and shaken at his sweet Steenie's gossip threatening him. Charles had looked up brightly as Buckingham walked into his chamber unannounced. His friend's informality and lack of decorum, while offending others, always delighted him, and he was on the point of saying he was happy to have the unexpected pleasure of his company again so soon, when he saw Buckingham's white, strained face.

'Steenie, what is it? What has happened? Are you ill?'

Buckingham attempted to tell him, but could not, the tears choking him. Tenderly, the younger man took him in his arms and stroked his hair, while Buckingham sobbed out his incoherent story. It did not occur to the Prince that his friend's passionate and violent outburst towards the King had been in any way at fault.

'Sweetheart, do not distress yourself! It will come to naught, my father loves you too well. There is none can take your place, Steenie, none.' Buckingham spent that night with the Prince.

By the end of the year the Venetian ambassador, Alvise Valaresso, was writing to the Doge and Senate that,

> *the quarrel I reported between the King and the favourite was true. The latter took offence at some show of favour by the King to a young gentleman of the chamber, cousin of the Marquis. However, matters have quieted down and the Marquis seems more in favour than ever, and now has under seal a fresh gift from the King worth some 20,000 crowns a year. Yet some who observed the fate of the earlier favourite Somerset think that his Majesty's favour is like the summer sky, from which, when quite serene, a thunderbolt sometimes falls unexpectedly.*

A month later Lionel Cranfield, Lord Treasurer, thought it prudent to send Arthur Brett to France to put the Marquis out of jealousy. The King, increasingly in pain, had more to concern him than the gossip and rumours about a new favourite. The truth was that he had thought Brett a comely enough lad, for despite increasing age and infirmity, he was still susceptible to handsome young men, but Buckingham's enemies had totally misread him: his love for Steenie was rooted in more than mere passion. Buckingham was the bedrock of his existence, and as he became older, sicker and less interested in politics, the King's need of, and dependence upon, his favourite increased rather than declined. The situation was markedly different from eight years earlier, and Pembroke and Middlesex had badly misjudged the situation. Buckingham had survived again, but Cranfield was a marked man.

Public opinion remained strongly in favour of action to aid the King's daughter and her husband, and to restore the Palatinate. As the Spanish match became increasingly unpopular, even James, disconnected as he was from his people, could not but be aware of the murmuring and discontent. More and more time passed yet the marriage seemed no nearer, and he became increasingly anxious – it was vitally important to his pacifist policy that England was allied with Spain.

Buckingham and the Prince, still fully supportive of the King's policy, talked often of Elizabeth's plight, and of the endless delays in the marriage negotiations. The previous year Charles had considered the possibility of going in person to the Spanish court, but as negotiations appeared to proceed, there had seemed no need. Then there were ever more setbacks and with no end in sight, the favourite, ever impatient, was increasingly fretful.

'A pox on these cursed interminable talks! What else remains to be said? If the match comes to naught then I shall be blamed. How can we be certain that the Spanish negotiate in good faith or simply to keep the King from intervening on the Continent?'

'Our ambassador the Earl of Bristol has assured me that there is either sincere intention of giving my father and myself full satisfaction, both in the business of the match and of the Palatinate or they are the falsest people upon the earth.'

'Well it's my opinion that Bristol has been over long in Spain. He's too easy on them, and his reports are like himself: all wind and no substance, they tell us nothing. At this rate you will be thirty years of age and not wed! There must be a way to move the business forward.'

'I have also been thinking this. How much easier it would be if we were able to speak directly, face to face.'

Buckingham jumped to his feet, and crossed over to where Charles was sitting, grabbing him by the shoulders.

'Yes! That is the solution! We must go in person to Madrid, you and I! We could cut through all the nonsense and have the marriage treaty signed before Bristol had time to deliver yet another windy speech. I warrant we'd have the Infanta in England and wedded and bedded before the end of the summer!'

The Prince looked startled. Although originally his idea, it had been more a grand, romantic gesture than an actual plan.

'I am not sure Steenie, perhaps it would be better to leave it to skilled negotiators.'

'If you wait for them then your pizzle will drop off from old age and lack of use, Charles! No, it is an excellent idea. I don't know why we have not done it sooner! And then we could be sure about the truth of what is being said. Enough time has been wasted, and I doubt not that you are eager to see the Infanta's beauty with your own eyes, eh?'

'My father will never agree to it, Steenie.'

'Oh he will profess himself disinclined, but if we prepare ourselves with cogent reasons then I think he can be persuaded.'

'I do not know how we could persuade him,' said the Prince, suddenly fearful of the thought of his father's wrath. Buckingham walked over to a table, picked up a sweetmeat and nibbled it thoughtfully.

'We must make him think it is *his* idea; use his own reasoning and way of arguing, then congratulate him on his skilled assessment of the situation. With any luck he will order us to Spain himself!'

Charles laughed, 'Then I will leave that part to you. I fear I will become anxious and begin to stammer, and that always irritates him. But do you think it is really prudent to go ourselves to Spain?'

'To hell and Halifax with prudence and diplomacy, prudence will not gain you a warm marriage bed! No, there has been enough prudence and talk, action is now called for.'

The two young men continued to discuss the matter long into the night, and by the time Buckingham took his leave, they had decided on how to approach the King the next day.

'Excellent! I doubt not that you may expect a merry meeting with your beloved, who will be so overwhelmed by the sudden appearance of her handsome suitor, which she will liken as manna from heaven, that she will be as eager as yourself to marry.'

'I trust you are right Steenie.'

'But of course I am right! How could it be otherwise? And so, my dear young master, it is decided: we shall go ourselves for the daughter of Spain!'

Chapter Seven

Carlos Estuardo soy
Que, scindo Amor mi guia,
El cielo d'Espana voy,
Per ver mi Estrella Maria.

Charles Stuart am I
Love has guided me far,
To the heaven of Spain
And Maria, my star.

                      Song composed by Lope de Vega, 1623.

'More delays, and never any plain answers to our questions! Here is another letter from Dad demanding our return,' exclaimed Buckingham, gnawing his finger in irritation.

'We must reply straightway to reassure him,' the Prince replied.

'Reassure him about what? We should be home by now – the fleet is ready to embark to bring us and the Infanta to England. Instead what have we accomplished? Naught but to engage in endless, endless talks and accede to more and more demands. I tell you Charles, these Spanish seek to make fools of us; you, Dad and I, and I trust Olivares not one whit. Well, by God, they will find we are not the men to be duped or taken in by their papist schemes.'

Charles sought to soothe his friend, but the truth was that he was also seriously concerned. What had started out as an exhilarating adventure was turning into a nightmare. It had all begun so well – the two young men had humbly besought the King with well-rehearsed speeches and impassioned pleas to allow them to depart secretly to Spain to woo the Infanta and conduct the negotiations in person, bringing back the Prince's bride to England. As they had anticipated, James was shocked and most reluctant, but they had gradually worn his resistance down, for their dear Dad found it difficult to refuse them aught, and Steenie was handsomely at his most persuasive and eloquent. However, after passing a sleepless night, James changed his mind and tearfully told his sweet boys that he had repented of giving his permission and could not allow them to go into danger. Furious, the favourite had berated his royal lover, saying that if he went back upon his word then his promises would be ever worthless. The King called in Sir Francis Cottington, an experienced diplomat who had been consul at Seville and an English agent at the Spanish court, for his opinion.

'Baby Charles and Steenie have a great mind to go by post into Spain to fetch the Infanta. What think ye of the journey?'

Cottington was staggered, and his face reflected his shock.

'I confess your Majesty that I can but think ill of it. Such a venture can only end badly. It must undo years of careful diplomacy, but worse of all is that it would deliver the Prince and heir to the throne as hostage to any demands the Spanish might choose to make,' he eventually answered.

James collapsed in tears, throwing himself upon his bed and weeping passionately. 'I knew it. If you go I will be undone. Will ye both break my heart? If any mischance occurs it will be the death of me.'

Buckingham had rounded on Cottington angrily, and for a while the Prince feared that his father would forbid him to leave, but the King could not withstand the combination of consistent pressure and the favourite's honeyed words and loving pleas, and so it was on Tuesday, 18 February 1623, that the Marquis of Buckingham and the Prince of Wales had left New Hall, disguised by large beards and hoods drawn over their faces, and adopting the names of Thomas and John Smith, brothers. Carrying £1,000 in gold, and bills of £20,000, they were accompanied only by Sir Richard Graham, Buckingham's Gentleman of the Horse, and had arranged to meet at Dover a reluctant Cottington and Endymion Porter, a Groom of Charles's bedchamber, and a close friend of the Marquis's. Porter had Spanish relatives and had been brought up in that country as a page in the household of the powerful favourite Olivares and was married to Buckingham's half-niece.

It had all seemed immensely amusing, and the two young men had burst into laughter at the sight of themselves in their disguises.

'Greetings my dear brother Tom,' exclaimed Buckingham.

'I thought *you* were Tom – I'm John I think.'

'Are you?'

'I am not sure now.'

'Faith, nor am I!' said his friend, roaring with laughter and slapping the Prince upon his back.

As the royal favourite galloped off in fine spirits with his best friend, his mind bent only on the adventure ahead, he gave scant thought to the ageing and bereft king he had left behind. James had written to him shortly before he had left court for New Hall.

My only sweet and dear child,
I am now so miserable a coward, as I do nothing but weep and mourn, for I protest to God I rode this afternoon without speaking to anybody and the tears trickling down my cheeks, as now they do that I can scarcely see to write. But alas, what shall I do at our parting?

They rode swiftly to Gravesend, where, on crossing the Thames, the Prince's beard fell off, to their great merriment. Having forgotten to bring any small change, they were forced to pay the ferry man with a gold piece, who regarded the theatrically garbed men doubtfully. Thinking they were intending to cross to France to settle an account in a duel, he raised the town officers, whereupon they had to swiftly escape. The fact that the Prince and Buckingham kept forgetting whether they were Tom or Jack did nothing to alleviate suspicions, but seemed to them most droll. Then near Rochester they observed a cavalcade approach, which as ill luck would have it, was of the ambassador of the Holy Roman Emperor, en route to London, and so to avoid them, they leapt over hedges and ditches and crossed by fields to escape detection.

Yet more excitement followed, for a message had been sent by Sir Lewis Lewkenor, who accompanied the ambassador, to arrest the three suspicious characters for their outlandish behaviour, thus at Canterbury Buckingham was forced to reveal his true identity, pulling off his beard with a dramatic flourish and thinking swiftly of a plausible excuse. He told the Mayor that he was on a secret visit to the fleet as Lord Admiral.

Again at Dover they were stopped, causing Buckingham to later comment that it was wondrous fortunate that they ever left the shores of the realm at all. There they were met by Cottington and Porter, who had arranged for a ship to carry them across the Narrow Seas. Setting sail at six in the morning, the adventurers had a stormy eight hour crossing, during which both the Prince and Buckingham were extremely seasick. However, on arrival at Boulogne, they were in excellent spirits once more, and rode three posts to Montreuil, where they were again almost detected, for two German gentlemen commented upon their likenesses to the Prince and Marquis, having apparently seen them at Newmarket, but Dick Graham succeeded in convincing them of how unlikely a thing it would be for them to be there. Buckingham was so impressed by his acting skills that he promised to recruit him into the next masque.

Three days after their departure, the bold knights had reached Paris, where they bought peri-wigs, and spent the first day in looking around the city, having secured lodgings above a post house at the sign of Grand-Cerf in the Rue St. Jacques. The favourite was relieved to reach there without further incident, being much wearied, and in some discomfort at having had seven falls. The Prince had no falls at all, and was in a state of great excitement. There they wrote to the King to recount their adventures.

Dear Dad and Gossip,
We are sure, before this, you have longed to have some news

from your boys, but before this time we have not been able to send it to you, and we do it with this confidence that you will be as glad to read it as we to write, though it be now our best entertainment.

This day we went, he and I alone, to a periwig-maker, where we disguised ourselves so artificially that we adventured to see the King, and then we saw the Queen Mother at dinner. I am sure now you fear we shall be discovered, but do not fright yourself for I warrant you the contrary. And finding this might be done with safety, we had a great tickling to add it to the history of our adventures.

Tomorrow, which will be Sunday, we will be (God willing) up so early, that we make no question but to reach Orleans, and so every day after we mean to be gaining something, till we reach Madrid. I have nothing more to say, but to recommend my poor little wife and daughter to your care and that you will bestow your blessing upon,

Your humble and obedient son and servant,
   Charles,
Your humble slave and dog,
   Steenie.

That evening the Queen's chamberlain procured them good seats at a rehearsal of a masque, and there they saw the Queen of France, whom they gazed upon with no little interest, she being the sister of the Prince's intended wife. Also performing was the little Princess Henriette Marie but the two young men scarcely noticed her.

Being eager to reach Spain, they departed the next morn, taking beds at simple inns along the route, and bought local homespun coats, and thus they covered 60 arse-chafing miles a day. As it was the season of Lent, meat was not served in any inn, but when near Bayonne, the weary and hungry group came across a herd of goats, Dick Graham suggested sneaking up upon a kid, thereby procuring a more satisfying repast. However, the animal would not yield to the honour of providing a tasty meal for the noble travellers, whereupon he and Buckingham chased it around a haystack, and would have in no wise caught it, had not Charles, after watching with great amusement and much laughter, finally shot it.

Galloping across the border to elude the French frontier officials, the two wrote to the anxious King, 'On Friday last we arrived here at five o'clock at night both in perfect health.'

At home the news of the Prince of Wales's and Marquis's departure was greeted with disbelief, then with mounting fear and unrest, not only at the thought that the Prince might shortly bring back a Spanish, Catholic bride to be England's next queen but of what might befall the heir to the throne. James reacted to criticism by penning verses to applaud his son's and favourite's actions.

Other verses were less complimentary in their assessment of the madcap Prince of Wales, and his father;

> *For Buckingham his Spouse is gone,*
> *And left his widowed king alone,*
> *With sack and grief upblown.*

As James had predicted, Buckingham was blamed. The King wrote innumerable letters to his 'sweet boys and dear venturous knights, worthy to be put in a new romance,' already desperate for them to return. Had he been aware of the risks his sweet boys ran, he would have trembled yet more, for at an inn, at St. Augustine, ten miles north of Madrid, Charles became involved in an altercation with two Spanish soldiers over the respective merits of English and Spanish ladies, which almost ended in a duel.

Finally in the evening of 7 March, the two adventurers arrived at the house of the British ambassador, where Buckingham sought entrance. The Earl of Bristol was dumbfounded to find the English stranger who called himself Thomas Smith dramatically throw off his beard and hat to reveal the features of George Villiers, the Marquis of Buckingham. He was even more so to hear the bone-weary but elated favourite inform him that the Prince of Wales was waiting outside. Bristol had heard rumours of the journey, but discounted it as nonsense. However, the Spanish King, Philip IV, and his favourite and chief minister the Count of Olivares, had known of their presence within an hour of their arrival.

The heroes' welcome accorded to the English heir to the throne and the King's favourite was all the young men could have desired, and boded well for the accomplishment of their task: when Buckingham's old friend Count Gondomar met with the Prince, he fell upon his face crying, *Nunc Dimittis*, the King was polite and friendly, Olivares was helpful and encouraging, and the brothers Smith were feted and entertained by the Spanish court, given exquisite gifts and their vanity pandered to as much as they could have desired. Excited crowds thronged the streets, enjoying the fireworks and torchlight processions, and shouting, 'Viva! Viva! El Principe de Galles,' jostling for a glimpse of the elegant Prince of Great Britain and the magnificent, glittering English favourite, dressed as resplendently as any prince, and shimmering with jewels. Everywhere was heard the song that Lope de Vega had composed in honour of the occasion, for the Spanish were much taken with the youthful heir to the English throne and impressed with the bravery of his journey, and they confessed there was never Princess courted with more gallantry.

Charles's impatience to see his bride was stretched to the limit on learning that a meeting could not be arranged at this time of Lent, as the Infanta was with her priest and confessor much of the day, however as a gesture of goodwill, her suitor would be afforded a glimpse when she took her afternoon ride in the royal coach. So it was that the Prince caught sight briefly of the woman for whom he had risked so much, and seeing the blush which stained her cheeks, he was thrilled, and assured by Buckingham that this betokened a sure and certain sign that the lady was overcome by love.

'Do you truly think so Steenie? Did you see her? Is she not the loveliest woman you have ever cast eyes upon?'

Steenie had probably seen her more clearly than Charles, for less hindered by propriety than the Prince, he had poked his head out of the window as their coaches had passed each other, and stared. It did not occur to him that the lady's blushes were caused by his flagrant and insulting flouting of decorum. His first thought was that the artist who had painted the Infanta's likeness which Charles so cherished deserved to be flogged, for he had greatly exaggerated her beauty. To be sure, her hair and skin were fair, but her heavy features were rendered less pleasing by the jutting Habsburg chin and fleshy lips, and Buckingham knew she would not tempt him. He was relieved, however, that Charles was still entranced, for the favourite reflected that his Prince had no experience with women and was easily pleased.

'The Infanta's skin is as fair as reported,' he answered truthfully, and then, glancing at his companion's wrapt expression, he laughed. 'Never fear, my dearest Carlos, we shall soon have the lady in your bed!' he smiled, patting the Prince's knee affectionately.

'I swear I am all impatience until I can speak with her directly,' the Prince told him, his eyes shining.

'I doubt not that she is as eager as yourself,' replied the favourite.

However, Buckingham could not have been more mistaken in his assessment, for the devoutly Catholic Infanta Maria was filled with horror at the thought of marrying a heretic, and had privately confessed to her brother that she would sooner take the veil. In private she wept bitterly and prayed for the strength to undergo her martyrdom. Her gallant lover's patience was sorely tried, for despite constant requests for a private audience with the lady, no definite answer was given, and all that occurred was a meeting attended by the King and the lady's innumerable attendants, where the Prince was instructed what to say and even what to wear. 'What gross impertinence to treat a Prince of the blood royal of the House of Stuart thus!' Buckingham had muttered. When Charles followed his friend's advice and refused to follow these instructions, and spoke freely, the entire court rose and left, to the great shock and chagrin of their English guests.

There were compensations – much time was spent in the pleasurable pursuits of hunting and taking picnics in the hills with the King and his courtiers, and Buckingham watched proudly as Charles distinguished himself in the tilt-yard. There were also masques, and bull fights, but the young men were particularly affected by the magnificent collections of paintings and sculptures they saw. Fired by the desire to have a similarly dazzling collection at home, they acquired many of them, including several portraits by Titian, and a work by Corregio entitled 'St John the Baptist' and 'Jupiter and Antiope,' which the King gave to his delighted prospective brother-in-law. The Prince sat for a portrait by an artist named Velasquez, paying one thousand escudos for the sketch, which he sent as a gift to the Infanta, who received it impassively and never looked at it again.

However, even such pleasures stalled, and both chafed at the innumerable delays. Even worse was to come, for it appeared that the Spanish courts, and indeed the entire country, were convinced that the real reason that Charles had come secretly was because he wished to convert to Catholicism. Buckingham had first been made aware of this during a meeting with Count Olivares, who assured him that when the Prince openly embraced the true faith, then the negotiations would proceed with alacrity.

'My Lord, I am filled with amazement. We have come here to conclude a bargain already made, not to embark upon new conditions,' returned Buckingham, shocked and perplexed.

'Indeed, it is I who am surprised, for it is generally believed that both his Highness and yourself are here to avow your allegiance to the Holy Catholic Church, which we cannot conceive but his Highness intended upon his resolution for this journey,' replied Olivares, with a frown.

'Me? Whatever could have made you assume aught so unlikely?' exclaimed Buckingham, aghast.

'I have been assured that your Excellency is very open and favourable to the true faith, and your mother and brother... are they not converts?'

The Marquis inwardly cursed his mother: he had warned her that her openly Papist ways would harm him. Buckingham had no doubt that the Spaniards had heard of the criticism levelled at him that he was a secret Catholic. Drawing himself up to his full height, the English favourite gravely regarded his Spanish counterpart.

'Sir, I assure you with the utmost seriousness that at no time have either his Highness or myself ever considered abandoning the Protestant faith into which we were born, and in which we shall die.'

Olivares bowed. 'Of course, we shall respect your wishes, however... one can always pray.'

'Pray until your knees drop off, my Lord, but I must tell you plain that if you strike any more upon that string, you will mar all the harmony.'

Buckingham stormed into the Prince's presence in a fury.

'Steenie?' His friend recounted his conversation with Olivares, and Charles reacted even more strongly, for he was a devout Protestant, and both feared such news reaching the King's ears. James had written a firm letter to his sweet gossip when his favourite had suggested that the match might be speedily concluded if he would but acknowledge the Pope Chief Head under Christ. To Buckingham this was merely an expediency which meant or mattered little, but the King, learned theologian that he was, knew full well the implications.

'I am sure ye would not have me renounce my religion for all the world. I am not a Monsieur who can shift his religion as easily as he can shift his shirt when he comes in from tennis,' he had written.

'What can have persuaded them of so unlikely a matter?' asked the Prince.

Buckingham admitted what Olivares had said about his family, seeing Charles's face tighten – he was not unaware of his Highness's dislike of his kin, and here was another reason for that animosity.

'I doubt not Gondomar has played his part in providing this nonsensical gossip, well, by God, I shall straightway disabuse him of such a notion. Fear not, my dear young master, I am certain I convinced Olivares that they could not be more wrong.'

However, Buckingham had not convinced anyone, for Olivares had reported their meeting to King Philip and both assumed that the Marquis's disavowal was mere play acting. It was impossible for them to conceive of any other reason for the English Prince to steal away incognito to their country. Moreover, Philip had sworn to his dying father that he would not give way on any religious concessions, no matter how small. The Prince of Britain would either embrace Catholicism or he would never embrace his sister. A campaign thus began to convince and facilitate the conversion of both their English guests. They were invited to hear sermons expounding Roman doctrine, and shown Popish pictures. At the Carmelite monastery of San Geronimo, Buckingham had endured a four hour presentation on the nature of truth by Father Francisco de Jesus, but after another lecture which the Prince did his best to refute, Buckingham could take no more, leaping up, he threw his hat, diamonds and all, upon the floor, and kicked it. 'Enough!' he cried. Offended, the priests withdrew.

Couriers were kept busy carrying innumerable letters back and forth to England, and Buckingham lost patience with the vast amount of correspondence that was required of him. There were letters almost daily from the King and from Buckingham's wife, who wrote incessantly of how much she missed him, and like James, lived only for his return. Buckingham was touched by Katherine's affection, but her cloying and demanding letters also wearied him, for there were reproaches amongst the assurances of love. He wrote back daily to the King and less frequently to Kate, running out of things to say, but was advised by Cottington to write long letters, for that gentleman assured him that his wife would be happy with the smallest titbits. He was correct.

I humbly thank you that you were pleased to write so many letters to me, which was so great a comfort to me that you cannot imagine, for I protest to God I have had a grievous time of this our grievous absence, for I am sure it has been so to me, and my heart has felt enough, more than I hope it shall ever do again, and I pray God release me quickly out of it by your speedy coming hither again to her that does dearly love you as ever woman did man, and if everybody did love you but a quarter so well, you were the happiest man that were born, but that is impossible.

Kate was visited frequently by her father the Earl of Rutland, who had shared the general sense of horror at the Prince's and Buckingham's madcap journey, but Rutland was not shocked. He no longer felt any sense of surprise at the actions of his son-in-law, and privately blamed him for the whole escapade. The Earl was concerned at his daughter's grief over her husband's absence, for she took no interest in anything else except little Mall, and was severely disappointed when she found she was not with child – knowing the importance of providing an heir. Gradually news filtered back of Buckingham's affairs with other women in Madrid, and Rutland was anxious enough to desert his habitual reticence, and wrote in a forthright manner to his daughter's husband.

My Lord, you are in a hot country and should therefore take great care unto yourself of your behaviour with women. If you court ladies of honour you will be in danger of poisoning or killing, and if you desire whores you will be in danger of burning, therefore, good my Lord, take heed.

Buckingham contemptuously dismissed his letter and ignored his advice, as he did his mother's. He was not a man to refuse his pleasures when they were offered, and offer the Spanish ladies did, enamoured by the tall and handsome Englishman's fair skin and blue eyes. However, there were some letters which caused him concern, amongst the innumerable ones requesting his favour, and vowing undying devotion, there were warnings of dangers at home, where his enemies continued their efforts to undermine him, notably Lionel Cranfield, Earl of Middlesex. Equally disturbing was the news about his brother John, who had deteriorated to such a degree that he had been removed from Kate's care at Wallingford House, and taken forcibly out of London to the country on the King's orders to be kept under the care of Sir John Hippisley. Susan Denbigh, his beloved sister, was also unwell and depressed after a miscarriage. Normally a lively and affectionate correspondent, she had written to tell her brother of how sad she had been to receive what she had thought an unusually formal and reserved letter from him, calling her Madam, and signing himself as her honourable servant, but then she had realised that this was a letter written to Katherine, and that he had mixed them up.

'Damn!' thought Buckingham, praying he had not also mixed up his mistress Lady Carlisle's letter with Kate's.

Meanwhile in England preparations to receive the Infanta preceded with a vast deal more alacrity than did the marriage negotiations. At St. James's Palace extensions were being made, rooms were being lavishly redecorated and furnished, and Inigo Jones had designed a chapel for the new Princess's use, though the King could not resist saying that they were making a temple for the devil. The fleet lay idly at anchor at Dover, ready to sail to Spain under the command of the Earl of Rutland, a sumptuously furnished cabin awaited the presence of the Prince of Wales's bride. The King was cautious about revealing much of the contents of his sweet boys' letters, and had to angrily upbraid the Marquis of Hamilton for leaning over his shoulder in an attempt to read the latest missive. James longed for their return, writing with an affection and desire every bit as strong as Katherine Buckingham's.

The King spent all his time with Steenie's family, taking comfort in the presence of his kin, and ever seeking to find the likeness of his beloved in their features. He delighted in little Mall, now over a year old, constantly quizzing Kate as to whether she was with child, and on finally realising that she was not, James's disappointment was as severe as her own. The besotted king wore a miniature of Buckingham next to his heart, and he spent long hours sighing over it and re-reading Steenie's lively, droll letters. He had scarcely batted an eye when he read his favourite's demands for yet more jewels, and of finer quality than had hitherto been sent. They must outdo the Spanish in the extravagance and splendour of their gifts, and the King's sweet boy gave fair warning that he would send no more exotic beasts if James did not, demanding that he 'look to it,' and ending by writing, 'I kiss your dirty hands.'

Buckingham had written affectionate, informative letters to his dear Dad and gossip, but he and Charles were careful not to give the whole picture of what was really the situation, and that even the naturally optimistic favourite feared that they were losing control of the business. The Earl of Bristol, with his vast experience of affairs and of the Court, was excluded from the negotiations which until recently had been his sole concern and responsibility, and was bitterly offended and not a little concerned that the match was now being conducted chiefly by Buckingham, inexperienced, and ill born for great affairs.

Moreover, popular opinion was now turning against James's golden boy. There was some distaste taken at him by the Spanish king who was heard to say that he would treat no more with him, but only with the ambassadors, and there were bitter complaints about his arrogant, high-handed manner, and he was called a broken and violent minister. Olivares was sent to the Prince to speak with him concerning the Lord Marquis forgetting himself so far as to intimate a dislike for the slowness of the negotiations, and Olivares told Charles that the Lord Marquis must consider better how great a Prince the King of Spain was, when he came to speak in his presence. Both the Prince and Buckingham were greatly affronted.

Rumours abounded about the English favourite's scandalous

whoring. It was even said that he had attempted to seduce the Count of Olivares's wife and that Bristol and the Count had sent a notorious stew to an arranged assignation instead, from whom Buckingham caught the pox. Steenie had laughed when he heard this piece of gossip, merely commenting that only beauty attracted him, and the Countess was old and ugly. Nevertheless, the story followed him for the rest of his life. More damaging were the reports of his behaviour with the Prince. The reserved Spanish court was genuinely scandalised by Buckingham's familiarity with the English heir to the throne, looking askance as he strolled around with his arm around the Prince's neck or waist, or lolled against him when sitting, one long leg dangling over the arm of the chair.

They watched in shocked disbelief at the displays of open affection, in which Buckingham slapped his Highness's back and addressed him by fond and foolish nick-names, embracing and kissing him warmly. Nor could they countenance the favourite sharing Charles's bed, or entering the Prince's rooms unannounced and half-naked, scratching his back-side, his sitting at table with him without his breeches, and removing his hat in his presence. Even Buckingham's disrespectful and inappropriate conversations about his wife were seized upon and endlessly criticised. He often made light of Katherine's conversion to Protestantism, attributing it merely to lechery while laughingly pointing at his privy member and claiming that lust was more persuasive than any amount of sermons. Nor was this mere affectation, for the favourite, whose own religious convictions, while genuine, never ran as deep as did those of his wife, proudly believed that Kate had chosen him above her own God.

Charles's and Buckingham's joy at hearing that the Pope had granted a dispensation was much tempered by the increased conditions, which not only greatly dismayed them but also caused consternation when known at home, one writer noting, 'It is said there be jewels gone from the Tower to Spain of £600,000 worth. God send us our chiefest Jewel especially safe and well, every way, back again unto us. God send us our Prince home again.'

Buckingham accused the Spaniards of deceiving them in an underhand way, and angrily declared that his Highness would leave, declaring that the Count had broken his word, as they were expecting the dispensation, and not additions to the articles, after which the whole business remained practically suspended for four days. It was becoming clear to Buckingham that what he had idly assumed would be a relatively simple business, swiftly accomplished, was increasingly beset with difficulties. The dispensation was, as he told the King, 'clogged with conditions,' and he knew that Parliament would never repeal the recusancy laws against Catholics.

It was now that the favourite began to consider whether it might be more provident to return home, despite their extreme reluctance, but yet again they were swayed by promises dangled by Olivares. Buckingham was honoured by James by his creating him Earl of Coventry and Duke of Buckingham, the first non-royal to be granted the title since the wars of the roses. The King had long desired to advance his beloved Steenie further, but Buckingham, well aware of what his enemies would make of this, had refused. But now it occurred to him that this would give him the prestige he needed, by making clear the extent of his royal master's approval and faith in him, and might well facilitate the negotiations.

As the months passed, Buckingham's threats that he would leave were received with barely concealed pleasure, for he was now held to be a serious hindrance to the negotiations, it being said that the Spanish would prefer to throw their Princess down a well than entrust her to the Duke. Bristol was sufficiently alarmed to risk writing to the King to inform him of what his favourite was really up to:

May it please your most Excellent Majesty,
Ever since I have had the misfortune to differ from his Grace the Duke of Buckingham, I have been treated worse than a dog, yet I have never allowed resentment to get the better of myself, and have been, if possible, more respectful than before. The truth is, that this king and his ministers are

> *grown to have so high a dislike of my lord Duke of Buckingham, and on the one side to judge him to have so much power with your Majesty and the Prince, and on the other side to be so ill affected to them and their affairs, that unless your Majesty be pleased in your wisdom either to find some other means of reconciliation, or else to let them see and be assured that it shall no way be in my Lord of Buckingham's power to make the Infanta's life less happy unto her, or any way to cross and embroil the affairs betwixt your Majesties and your kingdoms.*

Buckingham was however, not so green or careless of his King and Prince's honour as Bristol assumed. He had some skills in diplomacy and cared desperately that the marriage be accomplished, believing that he was obeying James's wishes and commands. When it was suggested that the Duke should return to England while the Prince remained, Steenie was horrified. He knew well what reception he would receive from his King and country if he left the youthful heir to the throne alone and at the mercy of the Spanish King, his ministers, and his priests, a virtual hostage.

Charles was still reluctant to leave, clinging stubbornly to the belief that a lasting agreement could be reached, and Olivares had smilingly made very clear to Buckingham that his master King Philip could not possibly allow his dear English brother to depart just yet, for the love he bore him and his desire of coming to a better arrangement in this business urged him to beg his Highness to refrain from taking any resolution in opposition to the plans which had been proposed. It took all Buckingham's will power not to strike the sallow, sardonic face. He understood the real meaning behind the suave, smooth words – the Duke would be allowed to leave, but not the Prince.

'I will never leave his Highness!' the favourite exclaimed. 'The Prince is dearer to me than mine own life – naught but death shall separate us!'

Olivares bowed. 'Such touching devotion!' he murmured. 'The Prince is indeed blessed to have so loyal and faithful a servant.'

So be it, thought the Spanish minister, if Buckingham remained then it seemed unlikely that Charles would convert, for the Duke had forbade any more attempts to persuade the English heir to embrace Catholicism, and if he did not convert, then there would be no marriage. He would simply see to it that the demands made became impossible for the English to accept.

Charles had still not spoken to the Infanta without her ever-present entourage, and he was seething with resentment and impatience, though few beside the Duke would have known, for the Prince did not wear his emotions in full view for all to see, unlike his hot-headed and volatile friend. However, Steenie had thought of a way of by-passing the formality and traditions of the Spanish court: it was well known that the lady daily took the air in a secluded garden surrounded by a high wall, and so to the Casa del Campo behind the Royal Palace did Buckingham and Charles secretly hasten, taking Endymion Porter with them.

The Prince looked up at the wall uncertainly. 'Are you certain this is a good idea Steenie?'

'I can think of no other way in which you will be able to speak with the Infanta privately, and so, my brave Carlos, up you go.'

The Duke bent his back to help the short prince climb up the wall. Charles accepted the lift up, but then stopped. 'What should I say?'

'Tell her that you braved all the dangers of the journey from England for one glimpse of her beauteous face – which is all you will glimpse if you do not hurry and climb this wall.'

'But what if I forget what to say? Or what if I stammer? She will think me a fool.'

'It matters not. Just fall upon your knees and declare your love by speaking what is in your heart, and do it quickly, my back is breaking with your weight.'

'Perhaps you should come with me.'

'No! Now go – your bride awaits you!'

Charles scrambled up the weathered brick, and then disappeared over the top. There was silence for a moment – Buckingham and Porter looked at each other – the Duke hoped the Prince had not fallen. Then there came a shrill, protracted scream from the other side of the wall, and excited shouting. In alarm Buckingham began to scale the wall hurriedly, if anyone had harmed his adored Charles then Spanish blood would flow in this land. At the top of the wall he looked down into the garden and saw the Infanta, white with shock, huddling against her attendant for protection, and the grim-faced Prince striding silently towards a small gate in the wall, while behind him an elderly courtier followed, his wild gesticulations accompanied by a torrent of words which the Duke could not understand, though the meaning was only too clear.

Charles marched hastily through the gate, and continued past his companions. The three Englishmen said nothing, Buckingham and Porter waiting until their Prince was ready to divulge the details. Buckingham looked quizzically at his friend, an eye-brow crooked.

'She screamed out as soon as she saw me. I ran towards her to explain, but could not remember the words. Her governor begged me to leave, he said it was an outrage upon her honour, that if I did not go he would pay for it with his life.'

'Did the silly wench think you were intending to rape her?'

'She was very frightened, and hid behind her attendants.'

Buckingham snorted. 'A good tumble would much benefit her, I think. Why so coy?'

'It is the way of the Spanish court, your Grace,' explained Porter.

'Then give me our English court and English wenches any time,' rejoined the Duke.

Seeing Charles's crestfallen face, he put his arm around the slight shoulders and squeezed him tight.

'I have never felt such shame, Steenie. If this gets out then all the court will hold me in contempt.'

Buckingham had himself felt inclined to laugh at the sheer farce of the situation, and would certainly have done so had it happened to himself, but instead he answered, 'If any one does then I swear they will pay for it.'

Shortly afterwards King Philip informed the Prince and Duke that the marriage could not take place earlier than September, and that his sister must remain in Spain for a year after the ceremony, within which time all the penal laws in England against Catholics must be relaxed, and an oath sworn by King James, the Prince and council that they would never be reimposed, together with the full assent of Parliament. Should his Highness wish to stay in Spain for another year, then he might have possession of his wife sooner.

Buckingham flew into a violent rage, his anger blazing forth: not a man to restrain his expressions, he declared that it was all a plot to mock and betray them, and never had he known such duplicity. He and Olivares exchanged stinging remarks, the Count replying sharply and upbraiding Buckingham, saying it would have been better for carrying the affair to a successful issue if he had never meddled with it, but had allowed the Earl of Bristol to guide the business, as he had done up to that time. The Prince subsequently remonstrated so bitterly that he could not restrain his tears. Now all pretence of friendship between the English and Spanish favourites evaporated, and Buckingham, ever frank, was vociferous in his condemnation of Olivares, telling him that he was two-faced, and that there was no honesty in Spain. Olivares accused Buckingham of being an enemy to the marriage and of negotiating with the French ambassador, the two were forced apart on the point of duelling. Now there was such bad feeling between the two men, that for some days they did not speak to each other.

Charles and Buckingham realised that they must be completely truthful with James, and dispatched Cottington with the full sad, sorry story. The King was distraught and overcome with horror upon hearing what a situation Baby Charles and sweet dog Steenie found themselves in, writing that the news had,

...struken me dead, I fear it shall very much shorten my days. Come speedily away, give over all treaty. But as for my advice and directions that ye crave in case they will not alter their decree, it is, in a word, to come speedily away if ye can get leave, and give over all treaty, and this I speak without respect of any security they can give you, except ye never look to see your old Dad again, whom I fear ye shall never see, if ye see him not before winter. Alas, I now repent me sore that I ever suffered you to go away. I care for match nor nothing, so I may once more have you in my arms again. God grant it! God grant it! Amen! Amen! Amen! I protest ye shall be as heartily welcome as if ye had done all things ye went for, so that I may once have you in my arms again. And so God bless you both, my only sweet son and my best sweet servant, and let me hear from you quickly with all speed, as ye love my life. And so God send you a happy and joyful meeting in the arms of your dear Dad.

'What think you of the Infanta's beauty?' Charles quietly asked Buckingham one evening, as they sat in a large window seat overlooking a fine knot garden. Many of the English retinue were nearby occupying their time in gambling at cards, some stretched out sleeping, some drinking and engaged in conversation. Others were laughing at the comic antics of Archie Armstrong, the English court jester whom James had sent over to amuse his son and favourite – both wished he had not, for he was generally disliked. The Duke sipped his wine thoughtfully.

'Well?'

'The lady's skin is very fine.'

'Yes, but what else?'

'Her hair is of a pleasing colour.'

'And?'

The Duke shrugged, 'And her hands are said to be most elegant, though I cannot vouch for that as we have not been near enough to see them.'

Charles made a grimace of impatience. 'Apart from her complexion, hair and hands, what think you of the lady?'

His friend took another sip of wine. 'I am not sure what you would have me say,' he answered cautiously.

'I would have you speak truly. Tell me upon your love for me what you think of my bride.'

Looking the Prince full in the eyes, Buckingham leaned closer and answered in a low, urgent voice.

'Very well, as you conjure me upon my love for you, then I will speak what is on my heart. I like not the lady, neither do I like this court nor this land, and... I like not this marriage.'

Charles leaned yet closer to the Duke and whispered, 'Neither do I.'

A delighted smile spread across Buckingham's handsome features. 'You do not? You no longer regard her as the loveliest maid you have ever seen?'

'No. Do you?'

'God's truth, no! I never did! I want us home and out of this misbegotten match.'

'As do I.'

'God be praised!' Buckingham leaped to his feet and danced around the room in joy. His companions looked up from their game of cards and laughed. Archie immediately cavorted around in a parody.

'Steenie, have you lost your senses?' asked the Prince in wonder.

Buckingham sat down again, grasping Charles's hands. 'No, my Prince. I have finally come to them, as I think have you.'

Leaning close, their heads touching, the Duke spoke in whispers. 'I am of the opinion that this frozen virgin hath no great liking either for this marriage, for I have ne'er seen a woman behave in so cold a manner, and Porter has told me that he had the report yester e'en that she has said she will not marry a heretic, and would rather take the veil. I believe that you have had a lucky escape my sweet Charles, for I strongly suspect you would find little warmth or passion in the marital bed, and fear she might consent to the marriage, and then straightway enter a convent.'

'I see now that we have been deceived all along, and what I took for chaste and modest demeanour is merely overwhelming and offensive pride. You saw it before I did, Steenie, I should have listened to you earlier; henceforth I will always rely upon and trust your advice.'

'Then we must think very carefully of our strategy. How do we extricate ourselves from this alliance with honour? And how do we persuade these Papist cullions to allow you to leave their dung-infested land?'

'I have thought on this long and hard. It appears to me that they will only permit my departure if I concede to their demands.'

'But you cannot! Dad would never agree, nor would Parliament!'

'True, but an agreement made need not be necessarily kept.'

Buckingham looked baffled. 'You mean... what?'

Charles glanced around to ensure he could not be overheard – the room was noisy again with laughter at Archie Armstrong's continuing antics.

'Be silent!' Buckingham thundered.

The little man scowled, and bowed, thrusting out his tongue as the Duke turned his back. The jester's behaviour was increasingly insolent, even daring to censure the conduct of the expedition to Buckingham's face. The favourite had declared he would have him hanged, to which the jester replied that 'dukes had often been hanged for insolence but never fools for talking.'

Buckingham turned back to the Prince, his face now serious.

'Come,' he beckoned, slipping his arm through Charles's and drawing him into a private chamber. They sat again and resumed their conversation.

'We agree to all their demands, but when we are safely home we repudiate them all. God knows we have reason enough.'

The Duke was stunned. This was a side of Charles he had not hitherto seen, nor was it a ploy he would have himself thought of, for even Buckingham's enemies could not accuse him of underhand dealings: the Duke was painfully honest if he had been displeased or offended.

'My dear young master! I am most impressed! I confess I did not believe you capable of such subterfuge! But what of the King?'

Charles flushed. 'It is not dishonesty Steenie. I would not compromise my own integrity, nor would I offend against my conscience. If the Spanish had treated with us in a fair and honest manner as befits honourable men, then we would not be forced into this position. The blame lies with them, and I shall explain the situation carefully to my father.'

The Duke smiled, 'I know Dad will be relieved to have us home, though not more relieved than myself. God! How I detest this country! And you are in the right of it, we have been treated shamefully, particularly by that fleering, shitten-mouthed Olivares. I am proud of you my Prince, and I am sure the King will be.'

Charles smiled faintly. 'I trust he will be, Steenie.'

'Then we play the Spanish at their own game! Excellent! Here is to dissembling.' Buckingham raised his glass.

'Here is to dissembling,' and the Prince drank deeply.

Charles wrote to James outlining their strategy, and urged him to pretend to accept the terms of the marriage settlement, assuring him that the oath to swear that Parliament would revoke all the penal laws against the Papists in three years need not necessarily be considered binding because if he thought he might do it in that time and if he did his best but it did not take effect, then he would not have broken his word. The Prince told King Philip that he was prepared to accede to his proposals, which came as not as much a surprise for them as Charles had expected, for they had been intercepting and reading his letters. Therefore the Spanish increased their demands once more. The Prince again accepted.

Thus the sweltering summer dragged on. The entertainments and masques became sporadic, for the intolerable heat made any activity unpleasant, and the professions of friendship were now as barren as the arid Spanish landscape. Buckingham did not even pretend to be friendly – disgusted by the lies and deception, he was cold and distant, and found that not even the Spanish women held any attraction for him. Instead he spent every moment with the Prince for whom he had gained a real respect. He was impressed and surprised by Charles's skills in the art of dissimulation, there was no doubt that the Prince could match any Spanish dissembling. Accustomed by a life-time of repressed emotions and naturally reserved, Charles could disguise his feelings and found this form of negotiation came easily to him, and once he perceived what might be accomplished by duplicity, he continued to use it throughout his life.

The Duke reflected that it was well that his friend had this ability, for there was no doubt that he did not possess it, and he found himself increasingly irritable, edgy and feeling unwell. He longed for home and the lush, English summer, for New Hall, for his dear Dad, for his little daughter. His desire to be gone was exacerbated by finding that his wife Katherine had been ill, and for a time he feared that this was God's punishment upon him for his constant infidelity. He confessed to Kate, who had heard the tales anyway, and told her that if she was ill then he would come home. Buckingham was greatly relieved to hear that she was much recovered, for though he had never been in love with his wife, he nevertheless cared deeply for her. In another long letter the Duchess wrote,

Dear heart, I hope you make no doubt of that which has been cause of all my illness, for never creature has felt more grief than I have since your going. And where you say it is too great a punishment for a greater offender than you hope you are, dear heart, how severe God had been pleased to have dealt with me, it had been for my sins and not yours, for truly you are so good a man, that, but for one sin, you are not so great an offender, only your loving other women so well. But I hope God has forgiven you, and I am sure you will not commit the like again. And God hath laid a great affliction on me by this grievous absence; and I trust God will send me life, and Mall too, that you shall enjoy us both.

I hope I shall bring you many more, for I am sure God will bless us both for your sake, and I cannot express the infinite affection I bear you, but for God's sake, believe me, there was never woman loved man as I do you. I have felt enough for this absence, more than ever I shall do again, I hope.

Buckingham wrote again to his wife, encouraging her to be merry, for he was disturbed and somewhat irritated that she had made herself ill by grieving for him. He had enough to worry about in Madrid.

James formally accepted the Spanish terms, in the face of fierce opposition, and Rutland was finally ordered to set sail, but even then there more delays. The Pope died and the marriage could not proceed until the new Pope gave his approval, and Philip would not agree to the Infanta leaving before spring. Meanwhile, the tensions between the Prince's entourage and the Spanish intensified, and Charles feared that violence might occur. The stifling heat was unbearable, the country was full of Catholics and damnably foreign. There was little to do but drink and play at cards and tables, and one servant declared that he had never believed in purgatory until he had seen Madrid in mid-August.

There was an unfortunate incident at the King's house, where the Lords Carlisle and Denbigh were lodged. Denbigh was taking a pipe of tobacco late one night, on a balcony which hung over the king's garden. He blew down the ashes, which falling upon some parched, combustible matter, began to flame and spread. Disaster was averted by the prompt action of Master Davis, Carlisle's barber, who leaped down from a great height and quenched it.

Finally, the English tempers snapped when Sir Edmund Verney struck a priest in the face for attempting to convert a dying page boy, culminating in a fight between the local populace and the Prince's retinue. It was clearly time to depart, and Charles finally agreed to terms which he had no intention of honouring and signed the marriage contract. Bonfires filled the horizon in Madrid in celebration of the betrothal, but now the Spanish were as keen to see their English guests depart as were their visitors, but this was delayed by Buckingham's illness, which some attributed to the pox, but was in reality a fever brought on by the stress of the last few months. Charles watched over him anxiously and the Duke wrote to the King,

> *Sir, I have been the willinger to let your son play the Secretary at this time of little need, that you may thereby see the extraordinary care he has of me, for which I will not entreat you not to love him the worse, nor him who threatens you, that when he once gets hold of your bedpost again, never to quit it.*

At last Buckingham felt recovered enough to travel, and delightedly told James,

> *Sir, my heart and very soul dances for joy, for the change will be no less than to leap from trouble to ease, from sadness to mirth, nay from hell to heaven. I cannot now think of giving thanks for friend, wife, or child. My thoughts are only bent of having my dear Dad and master's legs soon in mine arms, which sweet Jesus grant me, and your Majesty all health and happiness.*

Protestations of love and friendship were exchanged alongside magnificent gifts, but, unlike Charles, Buckingham could not bring himself to pretend, saying to Count Olivares, 'I tell you very frankly that I shall never be a friend to your Excellency.'

On 17 September a subdued John and Thomas Smith sailed to England, landing at Portsmouth on 5 October, where they were met by the sight of bonfires blazing in celebration that the heir to the throne was returned safely. Again the young men were filled with zeal for their mission, but it was no longer to bring the Spanish princess home, but to break the Spanish alliance.

CHAPTER EIGHT

There are in this state three sorts of men. The party of the Papists which hate you. The party of the Protestants, including those they call Puritans, whose love is yet but green towards you, and particular great persons, which are most of them reconciled enemies, or discontented friends: and you must think there are a great many that will magnify you and make use of you for the breaking of the match or putting the realm into a war, which after will return to their old bias. For particulars, it is good to carry yourself fair, but neither to trust too far nor to apply too much but keep a good distance, and to play your own game, showing yourself to have, as the bee hath, both of the honey and of the sting.

Sir Francis Bacon to the Duke of Buckingham, November 1623.

The crowded hall in the Banqueting House at the Palace of Whitehall reverberated with the roar of applause: throughout the room the distinguished members of the House of Lords and the House of Commons were upon their feet, clapping enthusiastically, many cheering and stamping. George, Duke of Buckingham, bowed elegantly, acknowledging their thanks and praise. Apparelled in his parliamentary and ducal robes and garter, his handsome face flushed, his eyes sparkling; the myriad lights of the candelabras reflecting upon his jewels, the Duke appeared in regal glory as he accepted the accolades of the most powerful men in England. His eyes flickered across the room to the end of the long table where sat the Prince of Wales, and the two exchanged a warm smile.

King James had opened Parliament on the 19 February 1624, and five days later at two in the afternoon the members of both Houses had assembled to hear the royal favourite address them on the proceedings in Spain. The Duke was brought into the chamber between the Chamberlain, the Earl of Oxon, and the Lord Steward of the Household, the Earl of Cambridge and placed on the Earls' bench at his rightful place. Then at the Prince's request the Duke gave a long, masterfully crafted speech covering the whole of the negotiations betwixt the two nations during the previous decade, interspersed with extracts of letters read by the Lord Keeper Williams, at his command: in which the duplicity of Spain and her chief minister the Count of Olivares were laid open. Buckingham revealed that he himself had been informed by that very person that the primary Spanish design was to convert his Highness to their Papist religion.

'Shameful, I say! Shameful!' cried Sir Francis Godwin excitedly, jumping to his feet; unable to keep silent at this example of Spanish perfidy.

'No popery!' shouted another, and around the chamber these sentiments were echoed.

Gratified, Buckingham had continued, his earnest, fair face enhancing the impact of the story he wove, as he told the noble Houses of the Earl of Bristol's dealings with himself and how Bristol had contended against him, ever taking the part of the Spanish, and that these people never intended either match or restitution of the Palatinate and wished his Highness at home again.

'And by this time the bravest Prince in Europe is accounted cheap and vulgar in the court of Spain, so that they will scarce bestow a visit upon him,' cried the Duke, to groans of outrage.

Then Buckingham delivered his trump card, indicating to the Lord Keeper to read the letter written in King Philip's own hand to Olivares, which stated clearly that his father's intent was to never marry his sister the Infanta Donna Maria with the Prince of Wales.

Pausing for effect, and so that the full impact of the extent of Spanish treachery could be savoured, his audience now at fever pitch, the favourite waited until the room was silent before exclaiming in ringing tones, 'My Lords and Gentlemen, I must now put to you the question: in view of all the evidence presented here today, do the Houses judge that his Majesty should remain bound by his treaties with Spain? Or, with these treaties set aside, whether his Majesty is best to trust to his own strength, and to stand upon his own feet? If the bringing of darkness to light deserves any thanks, your Lordships and Gentlemen owe it, and must wholly ascribe it, to the Prince his Highness. I thank you.' The Duke sat down to tumultuous and deafening applause.

'Well said, your Grace, well said,' cried Sir Francis Godwin.

'Spoken like a true Englishman.'

'We'll have none of this Papist alliance.'

As Buckingham left the chamber, he was surrounded by smiling faces. It seemed everyone wished to shake his hand and congratulate him. 'Never any man deserved better of his King and country,' Sir Edward Coke told him, 'you are the saviour of the country.'

Such praise and adulation was intoxicating. The young man regarded himself as a true patriot, and to hear such words from men who had accused and vilified him in the proceeding Parliament three years ago was heady indeed – he craved more. Buckingham clambered into the Prince's carriage, and Charles drew him into his arms.

'It was a triumph, Steenie, a triumph! All men speak well of you! There can be no doubt that both Houses will recommend breaking off the treaties,' proclaimed the Prince exultantly. Yes, reflected the Duke as a sudden chill ran through him, it was a triumph, but what of the King?

St George on horseback's prestige grew yet higher when it was learned that the Spanish ambassadors had complained to James about Buckingham's speech, saying he deserved to lose his head for such disrespect to the Spanish king. It was the culmination of his popularity which had begun the moment he had landed in Portsmouth, for he was believed to be responsible for saving the Prince from Papism and bringing him safely home.

Everywhere there had been demonstrations of public joy. In the streets tables were spread with all manner of provisions, setting out whole hogheads of wine and butts of sack, and bonfires blazed. There was a solemn service in St. Paul's, where the singing of a new anthem was specially observed entitled, 'When shall I come out of Egypt and the house of Jacob from among the barbarous people?' Ballads were sung, and verses written in favour of the Duke, once reviled and detested as the King's upstart catamite and Ganymede, but now the darling of his country.

The two conquering heroes rode swiftly to Royston to the King, and James, seeing their arrival through the window where he had watched for many a long hour, shambled down the stairs to receive them. The Prince and the Duke dropped down on their knees, the King fell upon their necks and they all wept unrestrainedly.

'Oh ma boys, ma boys,' sobbed the ecstatic King.

For a short time after the return it seemed to many as if all was exactly as it had been before their journey and it was noted that the embraces and familiarities between the King, the Prince, and Buckingham were just the same as though they had not been an hour absent, for they spent most of their hours with his Majesty with the same freedom, liberty and kindness as they were wont. However, in reality everything was changed, and ill health had not numbed the King's astuteness. After the first few blissful days, he found that his sweet boys were markedly different. There was a maturity and confidence in Charles that had been entirely absent before, outwardly indicated by his growing a beard. Now the Prince moved and spoke in a manner which befitted the heir to the throne. It was not long before this was commented upon.

'He is grown a fine gentleman and beyond all expectation I had of him when I saw him last, which was not these seven years, and, indeed, I think he never looked nor became himself better in all his life,' was one observation.

Yet, it was also abundantly clear that the time in Madrid had solidified his relationship with the favourite: before they went they were close friends, now they were inseparable, and as close as brothers – closer, for Prince Harry had never been as dear nor so loving as was Buckingham to the Prince.

> *All have observed a different demeanour and new confidence in the Prince, and indeed the King has found much has changed since his son and favourite were last home, for the friendship and intimacy twixt the two is even more marked. This has caused some discontent among those at court, who fear the results of such an alliance, and his Majesty appears to already feel the lessening of the Duke's affections toward him, wherein he perceives it has been bestowed upon his son,* wrote the Venetian ambassador to the Doge and senate.

The Prince had at first accepted that it was his duty to the King, to his God and to his country to agree to the match with the Infanta, and only later had he persuaded himself that he was in love with her. It was a young and inexperienced man's fantasy, fuelled by Charles's romantic nature and by the reports of her beauty and desire to be his wife. The reality had proved to be very different – the Infanta was not so fair as he had at first thought, nor did she desire the marriage. He had been duped and humiliated. The heir had returned home disillusioned and ready to give over being in love, for now there was only room in his heart for one object of adoration and love, and that was Steenie who was more beautiful than the Spanish princess, admirable in every way, and moreover, he returned the Prince's affection.

Not only had Charles's love for and dependence upon the Duke vastly increased, but Buckingham's attitude towards the heir to the throne had undergone a transformation. Though the days of tolerating the Prince merely to please his father had long since gone, now the favourite desired his company as he desired none other, relishing their time together. They were rarely apart, neither could bear the absence of the other for long, and when with James, the King's sweet gossip found himself impatient for the Prince's company, eager to share new thoughts, new discoveries, to show his treasures and to forge their strategies and plans.

It had come as a surprise to the Duke that he could receive anything other than favour and wealth from his courting of the royal heir, but in the cultivated and upright young man, Buckingham recognised attributes which neither he nor the King possessed but that he wished to emulate. Slowly and subtly the Duke was being as influenced by the Prince as Charles was by him. Though vastly different in looks and temperament, the two young men changed and moulded each other, gaining from their intense friendship a source of satisfaction which they found nowhere else. Steenie now felt somewhat uncomfortable at the bawdy, coarse jokes and comments which spiced his conversations with James when in the Prince's presence, and more than once, on being drawn away by the King to spend time in private, he had cast a wistful look over his shoulder.

The truth was that, for the first time in his life, George Villiers, Duke of Buckingham, had found someone whom he truly admired and by whom he needed to be admired; in his charmed existence there had been few who had commanded such admiration and respect and this formed a powerful hold over him. The time in Madrid had altered his satisfaction with being the King's servant, however favoured, and had given birth to the desire to exceed the confines of the role he had hitherto played as favourite. Proteanlike, Buckingham possessed the ability to mould himself into whatever he had felt the King and Prince had desired him to be. Now his behaviour and demeanour with each were markedly different – with both he was familiar and loving, but there was no trace of insolence towards the Prince who had gained his respect, particularly in Madrid. Though the King loved him still and had lavished wealth and positions upon him as on no other before him, he was conscious that James would never allow him to be more than his favourite, his handsome gossip, lover and servant with restricted responsibilities. But the glittering, exquisite young man was content no longer to be confined to the role that his Dad had created for him, and although the chains that bound him to the King were forged of gold, yet for all that, they were still chains, and now they chafed.

Only with Charles could he be more than a royal favourite, for Charles needed and wanted, not a servant, but an equal, and Buckingham effortlessly glided into that new role. The Steenie of old was transforming. His ties to the King were slowly unravelling while the Prince beckoned him forward to the future which the two young men dreamed of creating together: a future where Spain was the enemy, not an ally, and where Buckingham was the chief minister; an England which was very different from that governed by 'the wisest fool in Christendom.' This was the England that Charles and Buckingham envisaged, and James and his old, pacifist policies had no part in it. Gradually there was an almost imperceptible change in his relations with the King; a distance crept between them, and though the Duke was affectionate and solicitous of James's health and comfort, the King knew what he could scarcely bear to acknowledge, Steenie had given his heart to the Prince.

Such knowledge was hard enough to bear, but there was more, far more for the ageing, sick king to contend with, for his boys now wanted the treaty with Spain, the cornerstone of his foreign policy for so long, to be broken. James was profoundly shocked when his hitherto subservient and timid son told him that he would have none of the marriage, for the Spaniards had deceived him, and would continue to do so if he allowed them.

Yet physically feeble as he was, James would not hand over the reins of government to either his son or his favourite, and both knew that they would have to tread a careful and perilous path to achieve their aim of a total break with Spain and war with that country. The Prince made his intentions very clear, giving away the heavy gold bowl which had been a gift to him from the Queen of Spain to a footman, and when the Infanta sent sweets over for him, he gave them away to another servant. Likewise, a gift from the Spanish ambassadors of three cartloads of delicacies was dismissed, and Cottington was commanded to distribute them to the poor.

At the end of October Buckingham called a meeting of a select group of the Privy Council to inform them of events in Madrid, and to attempt to gain support for breaking the treaty and declaring war. Several such sessions followed, chaired by the Prince, but to their disappointment, only a few were in agreement with them, including the Earl of Carlisle and Sir Edward Conway; several were non-committal, but the Lord Treasurer, Lionel Cranfield, Earl of Middlesex and others were vehemently opposed.

'It is my belief that your Highness is honour bound to marry the Infanta,' said Cranfield. 'Did you not tell us that you had signed the marriage agreement in Madrid?'

Charles rounded on him angrily. 'I advise you, sir, to stick to matters of money, of which you presumably have some knowledge and not talk of honour to a gentleman.'

The Duke was furious at the lack of support, striding up and down the council chamber and berating those who opposed them. Later the Prince and Duke spoke in private.

'By God, that went not as well as we had anticipated. I cannot believe the intransigence of Middlesex,' said Buckingham, frowning.

'I did think we would have had more support Steenie.'

'They did not seem to comprehend that if Habsburg expansion is not stopped now, then they will dominate all Europe, and we will be at their mercy. It's vital that we begin preparations for war now, and that we win Dutch support; we badly need their naval power. And we must persuade the King to recall Parliament, at least there we may be certain that there will be support against Spain.'

'My father is most reluctant, and he remembers that in the last sessions you were attacked and denounced.'

Buckingham snorted. 'That was then. Matters are vastly different now, I am beloved by the people and both Houses, or at least by many of them.'

'We also need the support of your enemies Steenie. I think it would be provident to have Lord Saye and Sele restored to favour, however Pembroke and Williams remain.'

'Leave them to me, but Middlesex will prove more of a problem, I fear.'

'The man is an insolent and vulgar upstart,' said Charles.

Buckingham agreed, 'but he is also clever and dangerous.'

The favourite and Prince's continuous efforts to persuade the committee-council to recommend that the King summon Parliament proved successful, as were Buckingham's efforts at reconciliation with the Earls of Oxford and Southampton, and even Pembroke and Williams. However, Lionel Cranfield, Earl of Middlesex, proved impervious to the famous Buckingham charm. Most reluctantly James issued the writs summoning a new Parliament, but he was miserable, desperately hoping that there could still be a chance of salvaging the marriage settlement. Shortly afterwards the Earl of Bristol was recalled from Madrid to answer charges for his conduct. But now the Spanish became equally keen for the alliance to be concluded, and the King was told that his daughter the Infanta was busy learning English, and a magnificent trousseau had been prepared for her.

Buckingham and Charles were dismissive, and kept up the relentless pressure upon the King, but then to James's delight, in January the Spanish ambassadors informed him with joy in their hearts that King Philip had offered to send his sister to England in March. Moreover he had agreed to surrender the lower Palatinate in August and work for the recovery of the Upper Palatinate, terms which not long since would have pleased and satisfied both the

Duke and Prince; it looked as though the alliance might be on again. On hearing this, both young men were stunned, and Buckingham retired to his bed.

Later that day the Prince sought an audience with his father. 'Notwithstanding your Majesty's pleasure at this news, I have no confidence that these promises mean aught, for both myself and Steenie have personally experienced their slippery and treacherous ways. Therefore, I pray your Majesty will give me leave to insist that I will hear neither of friendship nor alliance with Spain – I will never marry the Infanta, and regard her country and her brother as the enemy of England and Christendom.'

James regarded him in horror. 'Will ye have me go to war in my old age and break with Spain?' he asked wearily, tears in his eyes.

'I am willing to take up arms against them myself, if your Majesty will give me leave,' was his son's reply.

Looking at the stern, upright figure before him, face impassive, his manner unyielding, James could scarcely recognise him. The timid young man who had quailed before his father's temper was no more.

Parliament was opened, and Buckingham was extolled. Both Houses agreed to petition the King to break off negotiations with Spain, and Charles and Buckingham were optimistic that Parliament would be favourable for voting adequate supplies to finance the war. The Duke was asked to arrange an audience with his Majesty that they might proffer their advice, but James refused. The Spanish ambassadors had privately been in contact with him and yet again he had changed his mind, and was now in favour of renewing negotiations. Charles and the Duke were aghast. The King's vacillations were scrutinised and commented upon, the Venetian ambassador, Alvise Valaresso, saying, 'His Majesty seems practically lost. He comes to various decisions and inclines to his usual negotiations; he does not care to fall in with the wishes of his son-in-law and the favourite. He now protests, now weeps, but finally gives in.'

Early in the New Year the Duke had received an urgent message from his mother that she desired to speak with him on a matter of great importance to their family. The Countess bustled in accompanied by Buckingham's sister Susan, Countess Denbigh.

'My dear son,' Mary began without preamble, after greeting him. 'I fear I bring you news which will distress you, and indeed will cause distress to all our kin. I confess that I have not slept at all last night, nor will I until this dreadful business is dealt with.'

'What dreadful business?' asked the Duke, levelly.

'Your brother Purbeck's wife is with child!'

Buckingham was now all attention. 'You are certain?'

'Oh yes, there is no doubt of it,' replied his mother.

The Duke glanced at his sister for confirmation, who nodded. Buckingham leaned forward. He did not need to be told how serious this was; for it was most unlikely that the child was his brother's, no, he doubted not that it was her lover's, Robert Howard. Nor did he need to be told that if this child was a son and accepted by John, and he himself had no male heir, then the child could inherit his titles and wealth. Despite that he needed not to be told, nonetheless, Mary insisted on holding forth at length.

'Yes, yes, just so, there can be no doubt of the parentage,' he said, attempting to stem the tide of his mother's outrage. 'Well, we have her now. I will have proceedings brought against her immediately – she will be tried for adultery.'

There was a silence, and Mary exchanged a look with her daughter. Buckingham knew his mother well. 'What? There is more?' he demanded.

'Well, my dear George, there is no doubt that this brat is the fruit of her lust with Howard, but, well, she may claim that the child is her husband's.'

'However could she claim that? They have not been together in months.'

There was another silence. Buckingham grew impatient. 'Well? There is obviously something you need to tell me and I beg you will do so with all alacrity. I am to meet with his Highness shortly.'

The Countess opened her mouth to speak, but Susan grasped her hand, and said quickly, 'There was a time, just once, when John escaped his confines and found her... I know not how... when his whereabouts were discovered again, they were together.'

'Good God! Are you telling me that he lay with her?'

'No, of course not, but doubtless she will claim he did so.'

Buckingham rose, and walked over to the window to help him gain mastery of his temper.

'So he escaped? How? When? And you did not think it worthwhile informing me of this? What were you both thinking of? Anything could have happened to him!'

'We did not wish to worry you, my dear. You have so many cares and have been indisposed, and he was soon back in our care and no harm done.'

'No harm done? No, none at all other than that he might have gotten his wife with child!'

'But he did not, I am certain of it.'

'How do you know? You were not there.'

Mary was now flustered, even she quaked when confronted by her son's anger. 'Your brother is not capable of such an act, he is insufficient. Indeed, I am not convinced that the marriage was ever properly consummated.'

'And you know that for certain, do you? My dear Madam, forgive me, but I doubt that even your omniscience extends to what does or does not go on in the marital bed,' responded her son, scathingly. 'Well,' he continued, 'what is done is done, or not done, according to you. I will instigate immediate proceedings, and we must hope that Lady Purbeck will not claim her by-blow is her husband's and now if you ladies will excuse me...'

Susan rose hastily, anxious to be gone, but the Countess of Buckingham lingered.

'George, there is another matter pertaining to this business concerning which I would speak with you, and I will not detain you long.'

Buckingham nodded, and kissed his sister farewell. After she had left, Mary began. 'My dearest son, you must forgive my importuning of you, but I doubt not you know it is only with your best interests at heart that I ever speak.'

Buckingham could not prevent his eyebrows from rising, but kept silent. He just wanted this to be over.

More confident now, his mother continued, 'It is with a mother's love that I am compelled to say that which I would prefer not to say, and that is that this frightful business with Purbeck's wife would not be so serious had you sons or even one son of your own. Yes, my dear, I am aware that this is not a pleasant subject for either of us,' she hastened on, noting her son's impatient frown, 'but the fact is that you have been married four years and there is but one child to show for it, and yes I know you will say that you were away in Madrid, but you were home a year before that and have been back several months now. I had hoped that after all this time there would be several little children for me to love, and that Mall would have sweet brothers to play with, but... now my son, I pray you will give me leave to finish... I know Kate is plain compared to some others at court we could mention... yes, you know to whom I refer, and if you take your pleasures exclusively elsewhere, you will never be the father of fine boys.'

Her son looked up in relief as the door opened and the Prince entered.

'Ah, Steenie, I was becoming concerned,' Charles bestowed an affectionate smile upon his friend, and merely acknowledged the Countess's curtsey with an inclination of his head, and a cool, 'Madam.'

The Duke rose and said abruptly, 'I thank you mother for your ever kind concern into all the aspects of my life. Allow me to kiss your hands, for now I really must leave you.'

As she left her son's chambers, somewhat more hurriedly than she would have liked, the Countess thought, 'Really, his Highness is so cold and proud, and George becomes more ill tempered by the day. Whatever has happened to my sweet boy? I must speak with him about assuming godly patience. I blame the Prince's influence.' She had thought to remind him again of the common belief that if a child was conceived when a man was in his cups then it was more likely to be a girl, but even she knew when to keep silent.

The Duke entered his brother's chamber. John was on his knees, eyes closed, fervently praying. Buckingham glanced at the attendant.

'His Lordship has been like that this the past hour, your Grace,' he told him.

Buckingham walked over to John and said quietly, 'John, my dearest brother, it is your brother George. I would speak with you on an important matter.'

Purbeck continued to pray, and Buckingham repeated his words.

'Pray with me George.'

Surprised, the Duke knelt beside his brother, but kept silent. After several minutes, he began again, 'Jack, it grieves my heart to speak of this. You know that your wife is with child, and you must realise that it is not yours, but is her lover's Robert Howard.'

There was the faintest flicker over Purbeck's face, but he continued to pray.

Buckingham tried again, 'Dear brother, I am aware of your love and forbearance toward your wife, but she has cast your love and kindness in your face again and again. Now she brings shame and disgrace upon your name and upon our family – you can ignore it no longer – *I* can ignore it no longer.'

Purbeck continued his impassioned prayers to the Virgin and the saints, the Duke sighed deeply and rose. He hesitated a moment, his eyes wet with unshed tears.

'Jack,' he said gently, 'I have started proceedings against Lady Purbeck for adultery. She will be found guilty.'

Again there was a flicker over his brother's features, but otherwise there was no reaction, just the interminable muttering.

Buckingham turned round and walked swiftly out of the chamber, the tears now coursing down his cheeks.

The next day he was surprised to find a note delivered from Purbeck, begging him to meet with him as soon as possible. This time John was not praying, but walking restlessly around the room. On seeing Buckingham, he ran forward, and throwing himself upon his knees, beseeched him not to prosecute his wife.

'I love her! Be merciful! I believe the child is mine – a gift from the Almighty. But I will never divorce her! I beg you George, be merciful!'

Buckingham gently prised his brother's hands from his legs, attempting to calm him, but he could not give the reassurance John craved. On the contrary he was determined to ruin the faithless whore – even had she begged him herself, he would not have relented, for where his family were concerned the Duke had no pity.

Buckingham and Charles now resolved to tackle James face to face, and the following morning the Duke was up betimes and galloped to the Palace of Theobalds in the cold spring morning, dreading the confrontation. His mother, wife and sister were staying with the King, and were delighted to see him.

'My dearest George! This is indeed an unexpected pleasure,' exclaimed the Countess of Buckingham, as her son kissed the King's hands and was embraced by him. 'We were only just now lamenting the sad want of your presence, and here you are to make us all merry!'

Buckingham smiled, and kissed his family, reflecting that it was unlikely to be a merry meeting with the King.

'Steenie, we will hunt this afternoon if the weather is kind. Ah, there was a day, and not long since, when your old Dad would have cared little for rain or shine, but now alas, my sad want of health plagues me.'

'Is your Majesty still troubled by the gout? I am most grieved to hear you are so indisposed.'

'I am still lame in my left leg, and look how my fingers swell.'

The Duke lifted the gnarled, grubby hand, and kissed it with affection, for all his opposition of the King's policy, he still loved him dearly.

'Have not your doctors been able to provide any effective relief?'

'They? Pah! You ken well my thoughts on doctors and physic, sweetheart, but the sight of your bonny face is better medicine than any a doctor can give – you have been gone too long from my side.'

'I have sent for some herbs which I will have made up. I am certain your Majesty will find they are most efficacious,' interrupted the Countess of Buckingham, listening in to the conversation.

'I thank you, mother, for your care of his Majesty, particularly as I fear I cannot stay long here, but must return to Whitehall on important business,' said the Duke swiftly.

A torrent of disappointed exclamations greeted his words.

'But you have only just arrived, my Lord! Surely you can stay at least one night?' cried Katherine.

'No Kate, I cannot, but I will sup with you and then return to Whitehall this afternoon,' her husband told her, relenting a little at her sadness. 'However, first I crave some private speech with you, Sir,' and he drew the King away, James leaning heavily on his arm.

'So Steenie, you will not even stay one night with your Dad? What is your important business which must drag you away so soon?'

'It is *your* business that I am about, Dad. I have promised your son, the Prince, that I will soon return.'

The King's face darkened at the mention of Charles.

'Aye, you will not tarry here when yon Baby Charles calls, ye must off, off to his side!'

Buckingham was nettled by his words. 'Both his Highness and myself spend ourselves in your Majesty's service, and God knows there is need, for when our backs are turned, then those sly Spanish vipers endeavour to turn you again to Spain!'

'They have no love for *you,* Steenie!'

'Nor I for any of them. I have seen through their double-dealing.'

166

'They inform me that your behaviour caused great offence in Madrid.'

'*My* behaviour?'

'Aye, your whoring, and your temper, and your mocking of their ways and their religion. I am told your over familiarity with the Prince caused great scandal. Now, what sort of over familiarity would that be?'

Aware that the King had developed a jealousy of his son, the Duke answered carefully.

'I consider myself most fortunate in having gained Baby Charles's friendship and trust, and am grateful to your Majesty that you first brought us together.'

'Friendship is it? Naked in his chamber, openly kissing and fondling him, sharing his bed?'

Buckingham knew that James was asking him if he and the Prince were lovers, and his cheeks reddened. The wily old King noted the blush and took it as an admission of guilt.

'Aye, aye, I see how it is! As soon as you take my boy away you're working your charms on him to mould him to your will.'

'I doubt that your Majesty sees accurately how this or any other matter is,' responded Buckingham coldly. 'The Prince is my dearest friend, closer to me than my own brothers, and if I did share his bed 'twas to comfort each other in our sadness and grief at being apart from your Majesty.'

'They say that you are the chief reason there was no marriage settlement,' said the King, changing to another subject.

'I opposed them only when I realised their duplicity, when Olivares told me they expected the Prince to convert. I have told you all this.'

'The word is that Philip wished for Bristol to continue the negotiations, and they say that had he done so then the Infanta would now be in England.'

'Then I praise God that I had the courage and love for my country and king to behave as I did!' Buckingham exploded. 'I regret nothing I did or said, and I resent your Majesty even giving voice to such opinions! I wear myself out in your service, to be told that you listen to lies and vile calumny from these Popish vermin!

'You wear yourself out pursuing your *own* policies and schemes, you and Baby Charles! All those meetings and discussions behind my back – deceitful, Steenie, deceitful! Don't think I don't know it! My eyes may be old and dulled but I can see that you look more to the rising sun than to me, your maker!'

Now furious, the favourite exclaimed, 'Your Majesty is both unjust and mistaken! I came here to beseech you once more to finally put an end to the Spanish treaty, which I have importuned you to do since I returned from Spain, and I must speak plain Sir, and tell you that it is not myself who has been deceitful, but your Majesty, by allowing these shitten-mouthed Spanish cullions access to your presence – they laugh at your gullibility. They laugh at *you*.'

James stood up, his face a mask of fury, shaking his fist in the Duke's face. 'I'll listen no more to your crude, catonic words! You're an ingrate, a faithless ingrate – away with ye! I'll listen no more!'

Buckingham rose also, his face white and pained. 'Then I will not inflict my ungrateful and faithless presence upon your Majesty any longer, but will return to his Highness, as obviously you believe I take pleasure only in his company.'

Bowing low, he strode out of the room, stopping briefly to recover himself before bidding his family farewell. He wiped a trembling hand over his brow, a film of sweat covered his pale skin. He was shaken and appalled by the row, and felt sick to his stomach. The next day his black mood had not lifted, and he wrote to the King,

> *Dear Dad and Gossip,*
> *Notwithstanding this unfavourable interpretation I find made of a thankful and loyal heart, in calling my words crude, catonic words, in obedience to your commands I will tell the House of Parliament that you, having taken such a*

fierce rheum and cough as, not knowing how you will be this night, you are not yet able to appoint them a day of hearing. But I will forbear to tell them that notwithstanding your cold, you were able to speak with the King of Spain's instruments, though not with your own subjects.

There was no response from James, but he knew that the King was still meeting with the Spanish ambassadors. Buckingham longed to go to him and be reconciled. His heart ached at the rift between them, but he dreaded a repetition of their last time together, and so he wrote again, begging the King to look favourably upon Parliament's response, and to cease his vacillating, telling him, 'so long as you waver between the Spaniards and your subjects, to make your advantage of both, you are sure to do neither.' The Duke continued,

I should for my own contentment (though I am sure I do you some service here, and would be able, if you would deal heartily and openly with me, to do more,) wait upon you oftener; but that you go two ways, and myself only one, it occasions so many disputes, that till you be once resolved, I think it is of more comfort and ease to you and safer for me that I now abide away. For to be of your opinion would be flattery, and not to speak humbly mine own opinion would be treachery. Therefore I will at this time with all the industry of my mind serve you here and pray for the good success of that and the lengthening of your days, with all the affections of this soul that will live and die a lover of you.

Buckingham felt dispirited and unwell, and was let blood. He had never recovered fully from his illness in Spain. He took himself to New Hall, usually his favourite house cheered and invigorated him, but even walks in the newly ordered gardens and the sight of the bright spring flowers, bravely tossing their heads in the cool breeze, did nothing to raise his spirits; he was chilled by the winds, and chilled in his heart. Sleep evaded him, and he missed the Prince, whom they had both decided should stay at court to monitor events. The Duke had even more to concern him, for aware of the coldness betwixt the favourite and the King, Middlesex had sent for his brother-in-law Arthur Brett to return from France. The young man was soon at court, smiling and handsome, deliberately and provocatively dressed in French fashions, which it was well known the King liked. Buckingham had caught sight of him once, and scowled at him, deliberately ignoring his cousin's low bow. The possibility that James's love for him might be dying caused him great pain and anxiety. Despite his intimacy with Charles, the old man was still very dear to him.

After a few days the Duke could stand no more and returned, determined to be reconciled with James. After intense discussions with Charles, they decided that Buckingham would stay at Theobalds with the King, ensuring that neither the Spanish nor Brett were allowed access to him, while Charles would continue pushing for support for war with Spain. James received his favourite with pleasure and affection; he had also been miserable at their separation, and Buckingham was determined to avoid all contentious talk, and so basked in the King's pleasure at having his sweet Steenie gossip to himself. However, a visit from the Prince, in which James saw the delight with which the young men greeted each other, provoked a jealous outburst, and being informed that all men spoke well of the heir, the King reproved him for making himself too popular, to which the Prince replied that he would always behave as an honourable man.

James worked himself into one of his ungovernable rages, in which he accused his son of stealing his only love, and both the Duke and Prince regretfully decided that it was best for Charles to cut short his stay, while Buckingham placated and amused his royal master. The uncertainty both of the outcome of his and Charles's anti-Spanish policies, and the uncertainty of James's temper took its toll on the favourite, for he was increasingly unwell.

The King's state of mind occasioned as much gossip as his poor health, and the Comte de Tillières commented, 'The King descends deeper and deeper into folly every day, sometimes swearing and calling upon God, heaven and the angels, at other times weeping, then laughing, and finally pretending illness in order to play upon the pity of those who urge him to generous actions, and to show them that sickness renders him incapable of deciding anything, demanding only repose and indeed, the tomb.'

It was recognised that the Duke and Prince trod a perilous path. Their anti-Habsburg strategy to which they were committed was not certain to succeed, and again there were whispers of Buckingham losing his favour. He still had many enemies, and was not confident that if the King turned back to Spain that James would protect him as he had done three years earlier, and even the Prince might not be able to save him. The spectre of the former favourite, Somerset, haunted him.

The Venetian ambassador Alvise Valaresso noted in his journal that,

there is certainly much to be feared that these two young men, without good advisers and without supporting props, may come off badly in opposing the obstinate will of a very crafty King and the powerful arts of the most sagacious Spaniards. The King has remained at Newmarket, Buckingham staying with him like a sentinel. Many think that he is losing favour.

'It will never happen to you Steenie,' Charles reassured him. 'The King loves you. *I* love you, and even if you were taken to the Tower, I would be by your side. Fear not, sweetheart.' But the Duke recalled James's words of only a few months previously, that if his favourite ever dared say he was more master than the King, he would cut off his beautiful head.

Charles was single-minded in his pursuit of the success of their policy: seeming to gain confidence and inner strength with each day; unlike his beloved friend, the Prince was not of a nervous or excitable disposition, and was rarely ill. At last it appeared that their planning and persistence had paid off, for James suddenly capitulated, though not without tears and many deep sighs, and finally agreed to break the Spanish treaty. Though their sovereign wept, the country went wild with joy, and Buckingham and Charles were the heroes of the hour. Buckingham rode to Chatham to inspect the fleet, and was shocked at the perilous state of his Majesty's navy, few ships were sea-worthy. He summoned a committee of both Houses in the painted room at Whitehall to find ways and means of raising money to fit out new ships of war, promising 15,000 pounds of his own money.

Yet even now, Buckingham was not secure. He had reports that James was bestowing his smiles upon Arthur Brett, encouraged by Middlesex and the Earl of Arundel, and he was horrified to find that the King had met with Padre Maestro, who had been sent by the Spanish King with yet another proposition. Realising that there was no possibility of resuming negotiations unless Buckingham was permanently silenced, another secret meeting had taken place where the Spaniards went determined to incriminate the Duke. Despite the vigilance of the favourite and the Prince, the Spanish ambassador, Don Carlos Coloma, managed to slip the King a secret note, requesting a private interview with his chaplain Don Francisco de Carondelet. On All Fool's day, while the Duke and Prince attended the House of Lords, Carondelet was led to James's privy chamber, while others stood guard outside. He told James that Buckingham intended to shut him away in one of his country houses, leaving him to his sports, while he took over the direction of the government himself.

'The Duke has reconciled himself to all the popular men of the state and drawn them forth out of prisons, restraints and confinements. He has openly bragged of your Majesty's submission to his will, and revealed in the Upper and Lower Houses very secret proceedings taken upon your Majesty's oath. If your Majesty wishes to preserve your authority intact, I beseech you to take action immediately by cutting off so dangerous and ungrateful an affector of greatness and popularity as is the Duke,' Carondelet told him, persuasively.

The King was deeply concerned by the skilful accusations. 'I find it difficult to believe that Buckingham is in truth affecting popularity, but confess that I have had good cause to suspect him of late, and I fear the extent of his influence over the Prince. When my Baby set out for Spain he was as well affected to that nation as heart could desire, and as well-disposed as any son in Europe, but now he is strangely carried away with rash and youthful counsels and follows the humour of Buckingham, who has I know not how many devils within him since that journey.'

'I am most grieved to hear this your Majesty, but sad as it is to relate, I have already given my humble opinion that it is only because of the Duke's anger against the Count of Olivares, and personal pique, that our two nations are not already permanently united.'

Then the Spaniard added, knowing of the King's jealousy of his favourite's intimacy with his son, 'And, all the world knows that his Highness was as much in love with the Infanta Maria as it is possible for a young man to be, that is before the Duke worked his undoubted charms upon him to draw him away, desiring that none should have influence or access to the Prince save himself. Indeed, I personally experienced many occasions when I could not enter his Highness's chamber, for my Lord of Buckingham was in a state of undress, and it would not have been seemly. Of course I am sure that his entire engrossing of the Prince was merely high-spirited, youthful exuberance, and that his Highness is blameless. However, I fear I must inform your Majesty that it is commonly said abroad that Great Britain is no longer governed by a monarchy, but by a triumvirate, of which his Grace the Duke is the chief, his Highness the Prince the second, and alas, your Majesty the last of all.'

Carondelet left the King's presence feeling satisfied that his objectives had been accomplished. Relations between the King and Duke remained outwardly cordial but James was cool. The accusations against his favourite worked upon his mind, and he brooded long and hard, watching his favourite and son with suspicion, noticing every smile between them, every quiet conversation. The Spanish ambassadors were invited for a further audience, and seeing the ground already laid, moved in for the kill. The Duke, Injosa told James, had broken off the match in order to marry his daughter to the Elector Frederick's son, and intended to keep Charles bound to himself and unmarried, and thus the throne would pass to the Palatine, and when Frederick died, Mary Villiers would be Queen of England. It was a measure of the distance between himself and Steenie that James would even listen to such words, let alone countenance them. Wasting no time, eager to press home their advantage, now Inojosa told the horrified king that he had absolute proof that Buckingham was planning to force James to abdicate in favour of Charles, who was completely under his sway. Thus, Buckingham would be the ruler of England. The King was left shaken and stunned. He was still haunted by terrible memories of his youth in Scotland when he had been abducted more than once by men whom he had loved and trusted.

On St. George's Day James prepared to leave St. James's Palace for Windsor for the traditional Garter ceremonies, accompanied by Charles and Buckingham. The King and Prince entered into the coach, but as the Duke followed, James raised his hand, 'Nay Steenie, I cannae bear that you sit near me – you mun stay away.'

Buckingham was staggered, 'What is it your Majesty? Have I offended you?'

'Ah, Steenie, Steenie – would you kill me?'

The King burst into passionate weeping. 'I am the unhappiest man alive! To be treated with such cruelty and forsaken by those who are most dear to me!'

'But what have I done? What can be laid to my charge that I could offend so gracious a master?' cried Buckingham, now seriously frightened.

'I know it all Steenie! All your treacherous schemes and plans to assume power and marry Mall to the Elector's son!'

The Duke knelt before his royal master, tears in his eyes. 'Your Majesty, Dad! I swear by the name of my saviour that there is not one word of truth in any of these allegations! Where are my accusers? Let them come forth and accuse me to my face. Let there be a full investigation to uncover who has sought to harm me with such malicious and cruel lies. I beseech you to command this, nay I demand it!'

Charles, as shocked as his friend, joined his voice to the Duke's, imploring the King to allow Buckingham into the coach.

'Silence, you disobedient and ungrateful child! I'll no have him anywhere near you, to corrupt you with his wicked and pernicious ways!'

The King signalled to the driver to move off, and in disbelief the Duke looked up to see James, his face averted, weeping into his hands and the Prince's white, shocked face, gazing back at him. The royal coach lurched away, leaving the Duke of Buckingham, the most powerful man in the realm, kneeling in the dirt. Around him stood servants and courtiers, silent and unsure of what to do, transfixed at the enormity of the scene they had witnessed. Buckingham stood up. He was scarcely aware of how he reached Wallingford House. Katherine ran towards him, delighted at his unexpected return, but then she saw his face.

'My Lord? What ails you? Are you ill?'

Her husband shook his head. 'No one is to disturb me. No one.'

On reaching his chamber, Buckingham cast himself upon his bed, shaking from head to foot as one with an ague, his eyes fixed unseeing upon the ceiling. He lay there unmoving as the light slowly faded, and then he turned onto his side and wept his heart out. That which he had feared had happened: it was over. His reign as royal favourite was over. It felt like death.

CHAPTER NINE

I cannot content myself without sending you this present, praying God that I may have a joyful and comfortable meeting with you and that we may make at this Christmas a new marriage ever to be kept hereafter; for God so love me, as I desire only to live in this world for your sake, and that I had rather live banished in any part of the earth with you than live a sorrowful widow's life without you. And so God bless you, my sweet child and wife, and grant that ye may ever be a comfort to your dear Dad and husband.

King James to the Duke of Buckingham, December 1624.

The kindly rays of the June sun beamed down upon the Duke of Buckingham's head, and he removed his hat as if to receive its blessing, leaning back against the rusticated seat. He closed his eyes, sighing contentedly; the balmy air gently played with his glossy curls, echoing his sigh, and brushed his face as though bestowing a lover's tender caress. The scent of early summer flowers was intoxicating, and as he opened his eyes, he took in the beauty of the colours, and the perfection of the garden's designs. The soporific, drowsy drone of insects gradually lulled him to sleep and for a while he dozed, only waking when he was brought his letters – several from the King and Prince, and others from his family.

The Duke smiled, but felt too weary to immediately read them, besides there was now no sense of urgency or panic, no sense of anything much really, except a deep sense of peace and well-being, which he had not known for many a long month. The terror and fear of the last month had fled, and he felt strangely disconnected to them, as if those dreadful events had occurred to someone else. This particular seat, situated in a secluded and pretty arbour and entwined by fragrant flowers was Buckingham's favourite spot at New Hall, and he had frequently repaired to it during the weeks since he had retired there to convalesce. At first he had lain in cool sheets scented with the dried petals from the rose gardens, and then had enjoyed sitting quietly in one of the deep mullion windows which graced the south front of the house, leaning against vast damask cushions, and covered by an embroidered quilt. Too weak and listless to read, he had looked out upon the lovely knot garden with great pleasure. Indeed, the whole of New Hall pleased him, even though Inigo Jones's alterations were not yet complete, and he thought the wide sweeping staircase particularly fine, even more so now that he need not be carried up and down it.

For a while his present seat was the furthest walk that the Duke could manage, but as his strength had gradually returned, he had begun to wander around his estate, some parts but newly planted, and had found everywhere a source of delight and wonderment. For this he had chiefly his head gardener, John Tradescant to thank, formerly the late Robert Cecil, Earl of Salisbury's gardener, and the designer of the gardens at Theobalds and Hatfield House. Buckingham liked the man, and enjoyed their talks and the planning of his gardens and park here and at Burley and York House, and although he had but little knowledge, the Duke had a good eye, and was willing to accept Tradescant's experience of what was required to make the most fashionable and stunning displays.

Above all, Buckingham loved trees, and a vast amount of money had been spent on obtaining supplies. The King had over a thousand oak trees sent from his woods in Kent, an equal amount of walnut trees had been bought from the Earl of Northumberland, and Tradescant had visited the Low Countries during the spring to obtain more. Then there were the countless apple and pear trees for the orchards, and Buckingham's particular favourite, the cherry tree. He had spent many hours in silent contemplation of the exquisite, delicate blossoms, marvelling at their perfection and drinking in their beauty, finding healing for his weary body and disordered mind. Buckingham had also employed Mountain Jennings, the King's gardener at Theobalds, and Robert Phippes and Richard Harris in his gardens and park, and the Dutch inventor Cornelis Drebbel to design the magnificent fountains here at New Hall and at York House. The Duke sighed again, yawning and stretching his long legs before he picked up the letters and prepared to read them. Doubtless the Prince would be confirming his visit to which his friend looked forward with pleasure, for he knew not how soon he would return to court.

'How shall I ever bear to leave here?' he murmured, looking around and reciting to himself a line from William Lawson's book on gardens, parts of which Jennings had read to him.

'What was paradise? But a garden of Trees and Herbs, full of pleasure and nothing there but delights.'

His quiet reverie was broken by the sound of running and a childish voice.

'Dad, Dad! Where are you, Dad?' Buckingham replaced his hat and stood up, laughing. His little daughter Mary came into sight, accompanied by the Duchess and the child's nurse. Seeing her father, the two year old rushed into his welcoming arms, and squealed in delight as he swung her around.

'Again! Again!' she demanded.

'Mall, remember that your father is but recently recovered from sickness,' reproved her mother, anxiously hurrying over to the Duke.

Buckingham laughed again, and sat Mall upon his knees, covering her little face with kisses. The child clasped her arms around his neck and nestled closer to her adored father. Kate sat down happily beside them, noting again the similarity between the two people she loved most in the world; the lustrous, chestnut curls, the sparkling, blue eyes; the sweet nature, and yes, even the sudden temper. And like her father, Mall loved to dance and particularly for her daddy to watch and applaud. Best of all was when he would dance with her, holding her tiny hand within his own, teaching her the steps, both of them laughing merrily at mistakes, while Kate would smile and clap. The Duke would always bow and kiss his daughter's dimpled hand, while she curtsied, before gathering her into his arms.

Smiling, and relishing this precious time with her beloved husband and daughter, Katherine reflected that these last few weeks had been the happiest she had ever spent with her lord – how strange that she had to thank a serious illness for her present contentment, and for Mall's, for the little girl idolised her glittering, magnificent father, for ever trailing around after him when he was at home, and plaintively asking when he would return during his all too frequent absences. Kate did not completely understand the events which had culminated in her husband almost dying from fever, and recalled with a shudder of horror those appalling hours, the despair of the near hysterical King and the terror-filled eyes of the Prince. Of her own grief and fear, no words could do justice, but she had known she would sooner die than lose him.

Glancing again at the handsome, still pale face, she breathed a silent prayer of thanks to the Holy Virgin for saving him. As soon as he was well enough to travel they had slowly repaired to New Hall, far from the intrigues of court and the importuning of suitors and clients, and where the beautiful gardens, now coming into their first summer glory, had worked their healing balm over the Duke's sick body and tormented mind. There was no doubt he had much benefited too from Kate's constant and loving ministrations, and from the charming, amusing affection of their little daughter. Never had Katherine spent so much time alone with her husband, and never had her lord been so sweetly considerate and gentle. Buckingham had ever been a kind and generous husband, but the fever had burned away his impatience and restlessness; gone too were the sudden outbursts of temper and the frenetic activity.

He had held her hand and thanked her for her love and care of him, saying he did not deserve so good a wife, even his love-making was less urgent and more loving and frequent, and Kate was in hopes that she might conceive, and give him the heir he so craved. Of course she did not always have her husband to herself. The King and Prince were frequent visitors, as were his mother and sister. Kate knew she must not be selfish – it was natural that such a man must be beloved by many, and she viewed the King's renewed love for her husband with equanimity. She could also tolerate the Countess, but the Prince was something different, and she was increasingly aware of his dislike of herself and all who were close to his Steenie. Seeing her lord so contented with his quiet life, Kate desperately wished that they could continue thus for ever, and that he would retire from court, away from the politics, and suitors, and enemies; away from Lady Carlisle and his other mistresses; and most of all away from the Prince; where they could live quietly and peacefully, with as many children as God would grant.

Hoping to enlist support, Katherine had broached the subject to Buckingham's mother, but to her disappointment the Countess had recoiled in horror.

'Retire from court? My dear, how could you even think of such a thing! Would you have him lose the King's favour?'

'I would have him well and happy as he is beginning to be now. This life agrees with him, and me,' Katherine added.

'He is but still recovering, and is not fully himself; but when he is, then you will find he will be all itching to return to court, and to his old ways.'

'His old ways almost killed him,' retorted Kate, sulkily.

'Aye, he has ever taken things too much to heart, and made himself ill as a result, but now there is no cause for him to be anxious, for he is secure in the King's affections, and in the Prince's.'

Noting her daughter-in-law's unhappy expression, Mary continued, 'You must realise that if he loses his Majesty's favour then he will lose everything – we will *all* lose everything – including yourself.'

'I would have everything I need, and most of all I would have my husband!'

'You foolish girl! And what if he lost his life – if his enemies prevailed against him? What then?'

'The King would never allow him to be hurt! Let there be another favourite! Let another carry his burdens! I care not, as long as my lord is away from court!' she cried.

The Countess regarded her steadily. '*You* may not care, but Buckingham will care! It would kill him to be replaced – do you know your own husband so little that you do not realise that he would die of grief – that he almost *did* die of grief?'

Katherine turned her head away, her eyes filled with tears. 'I only know that I cannot bear to go back to how it was, with the incessant clients, with his endless absences, and the scheming, his other women, and, and the Prince!'

Mary nodded, 'Aye, aye, I have seen that you find it hard. You thought to keep him to yourself, as a beautiful bird in a gilded cage, for no-one's pleasure but your own, but no one person can possess my son, even though they try; not yourself, nor the King, nor the Countess of Carlisle, not even his Highness. Buckingham will not be caged, and if you attempt it, then depend upon it, you will succeed only in breaking your own heart with unhappiness.'

As Katherine broke down and sobbed, the older woman relented, patting her arm.

'Come, my dear, you are married to the handsomest and most famous man in the realm, and are the envy of all women. Now dry your eyes, and do not let your lord see that you have been weeping. And I strongly advise you to attempt to gain the Prince's friendship, unlike his father he has no love for you.'

Despite that a part of her concerns were for her own and her family's future, the Countess knew her son better than did his wife, and as she surmised, the Duke had reacted badly to Kate's suggestions of his retirement, laughing at first in disbelief. Yet seeing him now so carefree and happy, she mentioned it again. Mall looked up and smiled.

'See, my lord, Mall would like her daddy home with us, would you not Mall?'

'Yes! Yes!' exclaimed the child.

A shadow passed over Buckingham's face. 'This is not a subject for discussion before our daughter, and besides, there is naught to discuss. And now my darling sweeting, off you go with your nurse, for I must attend to these letters, but first I will have a kiss.'

He bent down and drew his child to him. Mall bestowed half a dozen, and would only agree to leave upon receiving his promise that he would soon follow her into the house.

'And then we can dance!'

Buckingham laughed, 'Mayhap.'

Still smiling, he turned to the letters, nodding in satisfaction at the tender greetings from his royal master. 'His Majesty urges me to keep warm, and to avoid any more use of physic if I can help it. He says he has sent more gifts of fruit. Have they arrived?'

'Yes,' replied Kate. 'A whole load of melons, peaches, grapes and sugared beans.'

'How good he is! I must return indoors and thank him straightway.'

'Do you wish me to write for you again, dear heart?'

The Duke glanced at his wife warmly. 'My thanks, but no, sweetheart. I believe my strength is sufficient for me today.'

Buckingham rose, and taking Katherine's hand, they returned to the fine red bricked house. He wrote immediately to the King, thanking him for his gifts and care, continuing,

> *for so great a king to descend so low, as to his humblest slave and servant to communicate himself in such a style of such good fellowship, with expressions of more care than servants have of masters, than physicians have of their patients (which has largely appeared to me in sickness and in health) of more tenderness than fathers have of children, of more friendship than between equals, of more affection than between lovers in the best kind, man and wife; what can I return? Nothing but silence.*

Two days later Charles arrived, and he stood uncomfortably while Mall, after executing a careful curtsey, then demanded that his Highness sat and watched her dance. The bemused Prince did so, but was embarrassed as the child cried,

'Clap! Clap! You must clap and sing!'

Laughing, aware of his friend's awkwardness with children, the Duke gently picked his daughter up and took her out of the room, despite her complaints, while he and the Prince talked. Later, he drew him outside, where they could be alone, and where he could show him the gardens and park. Charles spoke with enthusiasm of all that had been accomplished there, and told the Duke of how he had admired the avenue of lime trees planted four deep on the mile length approach to the house, admitting that he had not noticed them previously, having been too concerned at Steenie's sickness. Arm in arm, the two friends passed through the knot gardens, and wandered towards the lily lake.

'Soon when I am stronger, we will hunt in the park; it is well stocked with deer, and we can go hawking. Perhaps tomorrow we will play tennis,' said the Duke.

Charles smiled, 'I think we may wait a little longer until we play tennis, Steenie.'

'Perhaps you are right, my Prince, but I do not wish you to be bored while you are here.'

'How could I possibly be bored when I am by your side?'

Buckingham smiled back, and squeezed Charles's arm affectionately.

'How lovely it is here,' said the Prince.

'Almost too lovely. Kate seeks to persuade me to retire from court and live here with her and Mall.'

Charles frowned. '*Retire?* Does she have any conception of what she asks? It took your near death to remind the King of how he loves and values you, and she would have you turn your back on him and throw his love and favour in his face? Turn your back on *me*?'

Buckingham smiled again. 'She does not know what she asks. Women can be such fools.'

'They are worse than fools; they are almost without any use at all.'

'Well I can think of one good use!' returned the other, grinning. He was aware of Charles's jealousy of his wife, and hers of him and of the King's for his son, but at the moment none of it seemed to matter. One blessed effect of his illness was that it had left him feeling curiously removed from all cares, suspended in a haze of calm and joy.

When they returned to the house, it took all the Prince's innate good-breeding and love for his friend to speak to the Duchess, but the next day when she was about to join them in a game of bowls, he was not able to prevent his face from registering his displeasure, and Katherine, looking at her husband, took the hint. After an hour, the Duke was becoming fatigued, and Charles, watching every expression, suggested they sit for a while in the rose garden. He gazed at his friend's face, noting the pallor despite his sitting out in the sunny weather, and the dark circles beneath the eyes. He hungrily drank in the beauty of the fine bones, even more chiselled since the illness, and he felt his heart pierced again with a love that was both joy and pain. The perfect alabaster features which ravished that heart resembled an angel's more than ever.

They spoke quietly of events at court, and their plans, and of the impeachment of Lionel Cranfield, the Earl of Middlesex on charges of financial corruption – the first man to be impeached for four hundred years. He was greatly disliked for his ambition and greed, but the King had been unhappy, telling the Duke, 'You're a fool Steenie, you're making a rod with which you'll be scourged yoursel'.'

And turning to his son he had said, 'You'll live to have your bellyful of Parliaments!'

James had made a speech in Cranfield's defence, but then had accepted the will of his favourite, his son and Parliament. Middlesex was found guilty. The Earl of Bristol was also in England and demanding a speedy trial, threatening to divulge the true events in Madrid.

Attuned to the Duke's every mood and move, Charles noticed

that his friend's eyes were beginning to close, and gently pulled his head onto his own shoulder. Buckingham fell into a deep sleep, and when he finally woke, saying, 'oh forgive me! You should have woken me,' the Prince kissed his tumbled hair, and helped him to his feet. Their arms around each other's waists, they slowly meandered back to the house, and when Kate saw them thus she remarked coldly, 'I was on the point of sending out to search for you my lord. I was concerned at how long you have been gone.'

The Prince regarded her with hauteur. 'Why should you be concerned Madam? *I* was with the Duke. Who could care for his comfort and safety better than I?'

It could not last of course. The King wanted him back at court. The Prince wanted him back at court, and he was needed to oversee the plans and policies which he and Charles had set in motion. The only people who did not want him back were his enemies, particularly the Spanish ambassadors, and Katherine.

The French ambassador d'Effiat wrote to the French King that,

The Duke of Buckingham has returned to court, though much discoloured and lean with sickness, fearing to stay away from court any longer, as is thought, for the plots of his enemies. Yet, from what I can see, his position is now as firm as it hath ever been, for King James will not countenance either the Spanish ambassador nor the would-be rival Brett, who have been banished from the royal presence, lest either cause upset to his favourite, for the King loves Buckingham so deeply that he lets him do what he likes and sees all things through his eyes, and the Prince looks upon him as the sole source of his happiness and contentment.

Viewing the affection which the King lavished upon him, it was difficult for those at court to believe that only two months previously they had been convinced that the Duke's astonishing reign as royal favourite was over.

The news of the assumed fall of the Duke of Buckingham had swept around the court like a whirlwind, and by the time it had reached the Lord Keeper John Williams, it was commonly believed that the toppled favourite had been arrested for treason and taken to the Tower. Williams was as shocked as any. Despite being formerly opposed to the break with Spain, and unsure of whether to continue to support Buckingham, what had decided him, like many another, was the Prince's obvious devotion to the Duke, that, and the fact that James was visibly failing, for more men than the Duke were now looking more to the rising sun than the past. The ambitious Keeper Williams therefore had cast his lot with the Prince and Duke. Now he was in danger of losing his place, and determined to act swiftly, he had succeeded in ascertaining enough of the true events to know that the Duke was at Wallingford House, though many claimed excitedly that his arrest was imminent. The Lord Keeper had been received by the Duchess, white-faced and terrified, clutching a crumpled, sodden handkerchief.

'My Lord will not see you. He refuses to see anyone, even myself. The lamps have not been lit and he will not speak, nor drink nor eat. The servants say he has fallen from favour, can you tell me what has happened?' she had pleaded.

'It is imperative that I see the Duke,' repeated the Keeper. Bowing to Katherine, he had spun on his heels, hurrying out of the room and up the grand stairway to Buckingham's apartments. Kate had hurried after him, her kerchief pressed to her mouth in fear. Williams did not hesitate, and after knocking at the Duke's bedchamber, he had entered without waiting for a reply. The room was almost in darkness. At first there was silence, then a low voice was heard.

'Who is there? I gave orders I was not to be disturbed.'

'It is the Lord Keeper, your Grace. I am here to offer my support and service.'

'I thank you Sir, but neither will avail me aught now, and the kindest service you can render me is to leave me in peace,' returned the weak and dispirited voice.

Williams had turned round to where Katherine stood whimpering, and ordered the servants to bring lights. As the darkness gradually receded, Williams saw Buckingham lying on his disordered bed, still fully dressed and in his boots. With a shock he had taken in the drained face and puffy eyes, and wondered for a moment if it really was the end. It was obvious that the Duke thought so – surely he had not given up?

'I thought you had come to arrest me,' Buckingham had murmured.

'Please God there will be no arrest, your Grace, and if you will act quickly, this sad day may yet be redeemed.'

'How so? His Majesty will have none of me,' said the Duke, his low voice devoid of emotion, as if nothing mattered any more.

'The King's moods are as changeable as the weather. Come, my Lord, this is not like you, to accept defeat without even putting up a fight. Leave your bed, and go straightway to his Majesty, plead your case before him with all the persuasiveness at your disposal.'

Still the Duke had not moved.

'Will great Buckingham allow the Spanish to say that they have vanquished him? Will you desert the Prince in his hour of need?'

Stung by the words, the Duke had sat up and pushed the tumbled hair out of his eyes.

'I do not think the King will allow me into his presence.'

'Mayhap no, but your situation will be no worse than it is now, and at least you will have received your doom standing upon your feet, as befits a great lord, and not lying on your bed, weeping like a jilted maid.'

'You are impertinent Sir! Do you speak to me thus because you believe in your heart that I am favourite no longer – that even now my cousin Brett takes my place?'

'No, your Grace, I speak out of my love for you, and because I am certain that there is every chance of overturning this set-back, but you *must* do it now!'

Buckingham had slowly risen; his expression quizzical.

'Now, your Grace, change your doublet and bathe your face; appear before the King in all your splendid beauty. Abase yourself, smile at him, use whatever means you need, but persuade him of your innocence, and turn his anger back to love.'

'And if Brett is already there?'

'Then hold your head high with pride, but know that over half the men at court sweat in very fear for the outcome of this meeting.'

'Including yourself?'

'Including myself.'

'Then God grant it will be a merry meeting.'

Williams had nodded, while muttering a fervent Amen.

Two hours later Buckingham had been at Windsor, and had requested permission to enter the King's presence, his arrival causing a ripple of whispers as all had waited to learn the fate of the greatest man in the realm. His heart and head pounding, the Duke had reflected how strange it seemed not to approach the King immediately without any announcement, confident of his welcome – strange and bitter. He had heard himself being announced, and then with a rush of relief so powerful and sweet that he felt he could scarce breathe, he'd heard the words of welcome that he had feared he would never again hear.

'Steenie? Here? Why does he wait outside? Bring him hither.'

Then he was being ushered into the royal presence. As he walked towards the King he saw the Prince, smiling in delight, and James, his face wreathed in smiles.

'Oh God, I could not bear to lose him,' had thought the young man, suddenly overwhelmed by love for his royal master.

He had planned carefully what he would say, but the intensity of his emotions would not allow him to speak, other than to say, 'Your Majesty...' before breaking down, and throwing himself at the King's feet, his arms embracing James's knees.

'Oh ma boy, ma Steenie!' wept the King.

Charles had risen, and had swiftly dismissed everyone in the room, leaving his father and friend alone, this reconciliation was for themselves only. That night Buckingham had slept contentedly in the King's arms.

Over the next few days Buckingham had felt that the memory of that terrible day must have been a nightmare, for it appeared that he was as much in favour as ever, and he was at pains to make clear to the King the depth of his affection and gratitude, swearing repeatedly that the allegations were false. Yet despite the warmth and that James professed himself satisfied that his Steenie was innocent, the Duke had been disturbed that the King was still proceeding with the investigation into the allegations against him.

'His Majesty still does not trust me. It will look as if he still believes I am guilty if this goes ahead,' he'd told the Prince moodily, his anxiety returning.

Charles had shaken his head, 'No Steenie, he does it to prove that he is confident of your innocence. My opinion is this, that you can incur no danger in this, but if you oppose the King's proceedings, that might make him suspect that you have spoken things that you are unwilling he should hear of, and I cannot think any man is so mad as to call his own head in question by lying about you, when all the world knows me to be your true friend. So my advice to you is that you do not oppose, or show yourself discontented at the King's course, for I think that it will be so far from doing you hurt, that it will make you trample under your feet those few poor rascals that are your enemies. Now, sweetheart, if you think I am mistaken in my judgment in this, tell me what I can do in this, or in anything else, to serve you, and then you shall see what all the world shall daily know more and more, that I am and ever will be, your loving, constant friend.'

Accepting the Prince's advice, Buckingham had returned to town with the King, but was unable to think of hunting, or entertainments or enjoying the early May sunshine, for by now he felt thoroughly unwell. He had retired again to Wallingford House, and taken to his bed, requesting his doctor. The sickness rapidly took hold, and Dr. Mayerne had informed the anxious king that his favourite was dangerously ill.

Both King and Prince hastened to Steenie's bedside, in despair that he might die. His suspicions now forgotten, James knelt upon his gouty old knees beside the man he had loved and favoured as none other, and raised his hands in the air, beseeching God to spare his Steenie, and afflict himself instead. More reserved in his grief, only Charles knew the extent of his own suffering, and he vowed that the Spaniards would pay for their actions and words, for he had no doubt that his beloved friend's illness was caused by the pain and anxiety he had suffered.

Slowly the Duke recovered, and now the King's joy knew no bounds. He showered his favourite with gifts, and on finding that Wallingford House was besieged with suitors for the Duke's favour, had ordered a guard placed around so that none might importune his sweet boy. The Spaniards, deeply disappointed that the Duke was in favour again and equally grieved at his surviving so serious an illness, claimed that the guard was necessary because Buckingham had gone off his head, like his brother, and this was without doubt the judgment of God. Others said it was because the King was about to arrest the Duke.

The young man himself had finally no fears, for never had the King been more loving or anxious to make amends, believing like his son, that his own conduct to the Duke had precipitated the illness which almost deprived them of him for ever, indeed, Charles had made very clear to his father the degree to which the King was to blame for Steenie's illness, and James had meekly concurred. There would be no more rifts between them, for James doubted not that another such would kill them both. There were no more rifts, and the next nine months were some of the happiest James had spent with Steenie for many a while, for neither were willing to risk another breach, with the attendant hurt and pain.

By mid-July the Duke was so much stronger that he paid his physicians off for their care of him in his illness, paying out in excess of £400. He celebrated his return to health and the renewal of his relations with the King by holding a magnificent feast at Burley-on-the-Hill, at which James was the guest of honour. It was clear to all that Buckingham was firmly back in favour, and that the King would tolerate no more attempts to dislodge him, neither would James now permit the Spanish Ambassador into his presence, saying that it would kill the Duke with grief.

So determined was the King that naught would upset his favourite that he had Buckingham's would-be rival, Arthur Brett, banished from court. However, the young man decided to hazard one last attempt to gain favour. He had been approached by William Coryton and Benjamin Valentine who suggested that he return to court, where he would be under the protection of the Lord Chamberlain, the Earl of Pembroke. Brett had approached Pembroke, but that wily nobleman, perceiving that the Prince was so much for the Duke, resolved to have no part in the plot. Without any support, and with his kinsman Middlesex having been toppled, Brett planned to take matters into his own hands, and had taken himself to Waltham Forest where the King was hunting, and upon seeing the King approach, he laid hold of his stirrup, begging to plead his case. But James would have none of him and was much offended at this, ordering the Earl of Warwick to forbid him coming into his presence, and later ordering his arrest.

Buckingham was now not only the undisputed favourite, but his power had never been greater: with the fall of Middlesex, and Lord Keeper Williams, Arundel and Secretary Calvert being dropped from the select committee which advised his Majesty on foreign policy, and the Earl of Bristol waiting to be called to trial, the Duke was now recognised as the unchallenged ruler of England. Only Pembroke remained of his enemies, and the Duke moved towards making peace with him.

The Spanish alliance smashed, his kingdom moving towards war with that country and his health increasingly worsening, James submitted to the will of his Steenie and accepted negotiations for a French match. The King, once compared to Solomon for his wisdom, was no longer in control of his realm. Prematurely aged, in constant pain, and still not recovered from the trauma of almost losing the young man whom he had loved as no other for the last decade and to whom he felt himself married. James was now content to spend his days in company with Buckingham's family, occasionally riding and hunting a little, if his health allowed him, but his dim eyes were ever searching for that bright, fair face which now encompassed the whole of his world.

Recognising his old master's increasing frailty, and equally anxious for naught to mar their love for one another, the Duke stayed by his side as much as his duties would permit, lying with the King at night, and soothing him in his sleeplessness. During his absences, Buckingham wrote affectionate, tender letters daily, thanking James for his goodness and favour, assuring him of his love, and telling him that,

> *I so naturally love your person, and adore all your other parts, which are more than ever one man ever had, that, were not only all your people, but all the world besides, set together on one side, and you alone on the other, I should, to obey and please you, displease, nay despise them all.*

None now dare stand against him; never had a favourite wielded such power, and it was abundantly clear that his influence over the son was as great as over the father. 'Infinite is the affection betwixt the Prince and him,' noted one observer.

Yet this intimacy was looked upon with anxiety and fear by many, particularly the Duke's enemies, who saw that 'he and the Prince agree as though they were but one.' A vigorous and strong Prince of Wales, pursuing an anti-Spanish policy was much welcomed, and even a joint alliance between favourite and Prince was acceptable, but many believed that Charles was the puppet of the Duke, and was dominated by him. There was also another concern, though this was whispered: Buckingham had first gained his place at court through his looks, and it was generally believed that his hold over James had been sexual. Charles was acknowledged to be of a very different disposition, being chaste and abstemious. However, there was no denying the Prince's passionate love for the Duke; could Buckingham have seduced and corrupted the youthful heir as he had seduced his father?

The subject of the nature of Steenie's relationship with the King had never been mentioned by the two young men, and for Charles it had long ceased to be of any consequence. However, one day came when the depth of their friendship enabled them to discuss it. Whilst there had been many verses written lauding and praising Buckingham's rescuing the Prince from the clutches of the Papist princess, he was still the subject of others of a more scurrilous nature. The Duke had offered money for information about the authors of such lewd and profane doggerel, but had been informed of one which was well known abroad, and whose author was beyond his reach, in France. The writer, one Theophile de Viau, had openly written what many believed about James and the Duke:

> *This learned King of England*
> *didn't he fuck Buckingham?*
> *I have neither blood nor rank*
> *to merit a marquis for a whore...*

Charles was outraged. 'This is sheer filth! How dare this damned cur write such wicked lies!'

'My dear young master, your concern for the King's honour does you naught but credit,' the Duke told the Prince.

'Thank you Steenie, naturally that does concern me, but in truth I was thinking more of your own honour, which this French miscreant besmirches with his lies and shitten mouth.'

The Duke was angered by the poem, but suddenly fearful of his friend's reaction. Was he really unaware that he had been his father's lover, and if so, would he turn against him if the truth was ever revealed? An overwhelming need to be honest with the Prince rose up within the Duke's heart, and although he feared that he might regret it, he could never control his impulses. For a moment he was silent.

'And if they were not lies?'

Charles looked up slowly from the paper, and a faint blush spread over his cheeks. Buckingham observed it, but could not take the words back. His heart pounding and cursing himself for a fool, he said, 'My Prince, my love for you is so deep that with you I cannot dissemble, and while it is ever my desire that you regard me as honourable and worthy of your respect, I must confess that while I am much concerned at such writings being spread around, I will not pretend that it is entirely false.'

The Prince looked down again at the paper, and his hand trembled. 'You *are* honourable and worthy of respect Steenie, no man more so. I am not unaware of the way in which my father loves you, yet I cannot blame you in this, for does not the Scriptures say that he that loves much hath much forgiven him? I find your honesty in so delicate a matter, which could have harmed you, to be yet further evidence of the greatness of your soul. For myself, I will ever be your faithful and loving friend.'

Overwhelmed with relief and gratitude, the Duke seized the Prince's hand and kissed it fervently.

'My life is your own.'

By the autumn of 1624 the negotiations for the match of the Prince of Wales with Henriette Marie the sister of King Louis of France, were well advanced. Buckingham and Charles had sent the Duke's close friend Henry Rich, Baron of Kensington as their ambassador, though James also dispatched the more experienced Carlisle to oversee the business. Reading Kensington's descriptions of the little princess, the Duke laughed.

'Kensington protests to God that she is a lovely, sweet young creature,' he read to the Prince, who pulled a face.

'Yes, well we have heard that before, have we not my dear Charles? I confess that I cannot recall what she looked like when we saw her in Paris, can you?'

'Not in the slightest. Was she there?'

'Her appearance matters little. It's the alliance with her brother that we need, and speaking of little, he also says that her growth is not very great but her shape is perfect.'

'Her growth not very great? I trust we can be sure that

Kensington is not attempting to marry me to a dwarf.'

His friend laughed again, 'Well to be sure, he tells me that he has begun an affair with the wife of the Duc de Chevreuse who is a notable beauty with a reputation for acquiring lovers. I will write back and remind him to keep his mind fixed more upon his Prince's needs than on the needs of his prick.'

Charles had little interest in the sexual affairs of others, indeed, there were whispers both at home and abroad that he well might turn out to be less than man, a rumour which both Kensington and Carlisle had been at pains to quash. Certainly the Prince approached these marriage negotiations in a very different frame of mind to the last. He was not in love, nor did he expect to be, indeed he doubted that he desired to be, for his observations of women were not complimentary. Marry he must, and soon, and he was of course in total agreement with Steenie's assessment of the situation. The chief architect of this alliance was Buckingham, and notwithstanding the extreme unpopularity of the Spanish match, the Duke had no compunction about committing the Prince to marriage with another Catholic princess. His rationale was simple – Spanish expansion must be stopped, and the best way was for England to ally herself with the power of France.

'For myself I do not care a fart for the friendship of the French, but as long as she is not disgustingly ugly and can bear children, then I will marry her, for you are right Steenie, that it is only through this alliance that we will recover the Palatinate for my poor sister, and if *these* negotiations fail, then Spain will laugh at us both.'

On November 10th England and France signed a treaty in Paris. Kensington was now elevated to the Earl of Holland, and a month later articles were agreed and signed at Cambridge by the King, the Prince, the Duke of Buckingham, and Secretary Conway. The King's hands were now too afflicted with arthritis for him to be able to sign the articles, and he had to use a stamp. The other members of the council were affronted at their exclusion, and on seeing the celebratory bonfires, were obliged to ask what the country was celebrating.

The Venetian ambassador commented with his usual perspicacity,

In this marriage treaty, Buckingham has shown how he has outgrown his former role as mere favourite, and is in effect now the chief minister in England, and the courts of Europe now take note that it is the Duke with whom they have to deal in their diplomacy with this country. Yet, while his Grace ends the year being the darling of King, Prince, and Parliament; his popularity may not last, for this marriage to the French Catholic princess is no more popular than that with the Catholic Spanish Infanta was, and I believe there will be widespread dismay at news of the same concessions being granted which were promised to the Spanish. It is likely that there will be a back-lash, which will catch the Duke, and may cause him some damage.

The Christmas festivities were muted by the King's poor health, and he remained at Cambridge, taking to his bed, and continually attended by Buckingham. The entertainment of his guests was left to the Prince, James only occasionally venturing forth from his chamber, not coming once to the chapel or even to any of the plays he so loved. The Twelfth Night Masque, another by Jonson, was postponed until 9th January. Sitting next to his dear old Dad, the Duke was concerned by the deterioration in the King's health. James had not been in favour of the French match, and did not trust the French, nor was he happy at the concessions to which he had been compelled to agree, of which most of his Privy Council were unaware, but he was now beyond resisting either his son or his favourite. Unable to even hunt, he was content to sit thus, a velvet coverlet over his knees, holding his sweet Steenie's hand.

'Can I do anything to make you more comfortable Dad?' asked Buckingham, gently tucking the cover around the King's legs.

James sighed, 'No, I thank you ma sweet boy, and I appreciate that yeh're here with me instead of dancing and celebrating.'

'Where else should I be, but by your side?' responded the other, simply.

James patted his face with his swollen, gouty hand. 'Ah, Steenie, I have loved you well. God knows a man never loved another more than I have you.'

The younger man held his hand tenderly, and placed it to his lips. 'No man e'er had so good a master.'

'Still so bonnie, still the face of an angel!' The King shook his head. 'It's a great sadness to me that all I have the strength to do is admire your beauty, at one time I'd have sat you on my knees and tumbled yeh!'

Buckingham laughed, seeking to amuse the King. 'Never fear, your Sowship, I warrant you and I will be honouring Dame Britannica Hollandia's establishment in Paris gardens with our presence ere long! Never have I seen such clean and accomplished courtesans, or such pleasant surroundings, either here or in France.'

'Aye, nor ones which cost so much! After all, a whore's a whore whatever she calls hersel' or her surroundings. Still, I'll no deny that I enjoyed watching ma lovely boy sport himsel' with the doxies.'

Buckingham grinned. 'I wish your Majesty could have seen the whores in Paris. Some could shoot out coins from their cunnies, I saw one nearly take a man's eye out!'

James laughed wheezily. 'There's no end to the mischief or trouble that come from whores, or the tricks devised to entrap a man, nor the filthy diseases emanating from them. You mun watch yersel' with women Steenie, for they'll do you no good. I thank God I have never favoured them.'

'Your Majesty is ever wise. What say you to a drive around the park? We can look at the deer even if we cannot yet hunt them, though I have no doubts that very soon you will be leading the chase after a lusty stag.'

The Duke had more to concern him than the King's failing health. His brother John's errant wife had given birth and on hearing the news that she was delivered of a son, the Duke cursed both she and her child. She was eventually discovered living in Cripplegate, and had named her boy Robert.

'Robert! The harlot has spirit, I'll grant her that!' said Buckingham incredulously.

'She names her bastard after her paramour to mock us,' replied his mother.

'Well I doubt that she will feel much like mocking when she is imprisoned,' the Duke replied.

Shortly afterwards Lady Purbeck contracted smallpox and her husband had again found her, and nursed her devotedly. Buckingham once more instigated proceedings, trusting that this time they would meet with more success, for both her lover Sir Robert Howard and she had refused to take the oath, and therefore could not be tried. Howard was taken to gaol, and Frances given to the care of Alderman Barkham, who treated her well and with kindness. Too well – for Frances escaped, and had but recently been discovered. Now the accusations would include witchcraft, for Buckingham had become convinced that his sister-in-law was plotting his family's destruction, and had proof of her procuring waxen images of himself.

The King's health continued to deteriorate, and by March he was at Theobalds when he was taken ill of a tertian ague, and it was soon clear that the illness was serious. Buckingham cancelled his plans to travel to France, where he was to stand as proxy for the Prince in the marriage to Henriette Marie, and he and Charles stayed constantly by James's bedside. Never an easy patient and unwilling to listen to his doctors, the King had at first tried to remedy the fever by holding his hands in cold water and drinking copious amounts of small beer, but when he continued to worsen, the favourite remembered a treatment from a Doctor Remington from Dunmow which he believed had helped him recover from his recent illness. He sent for the remedies and for his mother, knowing that his royal master was fond of her and might be more willing to accept treatment at her hands than those of his own doctors, despite their horror at this unorthodox treatment.

The Countess bustled into the sick chamber, replete with self-importance and confidence.

'Here is my mother, the Countess, Dad, and I have no doubt but that you will find these remedies more efficacious than physic,' Buckingham told the king.

The sick man looked up, and asked wearily, 'What is it?'

'Special herbal treatments which helped me when I was so ill. This plaister will draw the ill humours to itself, and so out of your body.'

'Aye, then do it, sweet boy, though I fear that my time is at hand, Steenie.'

'Do not say that Dad, we shall soon have you well and merry again.'

Mary affixed the plaisters to the King's wrists, and at first it seemed to afford some relief, but then James suffered another convulsion, and the doctors insisted that they were removed. Rallying, James asked for them to be applied again, and the countess moved forward to affix them.

'No, no! My Lord, I must beg that her ladyship desists!' cried Dr Craig.

'His Majesty requests it – and it afforded him some relief, which is more than did your physic,' responded Buckingham haughtily.

'His Majesty suffered a fit, your Grace! I beg you will desist! It may harm his Majesty!'

'It did *me* no harm and the King had already suffered several fits before it was administered.'

Craig looked at the Prince. 'Your Highness, I entreat you not to allow this – it is mere quackery.'

'You will obey the Duke, sir.'

Buckingham nodded at his mother, who deftly re-applied the plaisters and for a while the King drifted into sleep, seemingly feeling some relief, but after a half hour he awoke, struggling to breathe.

The physicians darted over. Doctor Hayes swiftly pulling the plaisters from the King's wrists, and attempting to settle him.

'I told your Lordship, look what your meddling has wrought!' spat Craig, his face furious.

'And your ministrations have been wondrous successful, have they not?' returned the Duke angrily.

As the night passed, James seemed to improve, and opened his eyes.

'Steenie?'

'Here I am, Dad. How fares my dear lord?'

'Ah Steenie, my throat pains me, and I am as weak as a new-born bairn.'

Buckingham thought of the julep which had so helped him when he could keep nothing on his stomach – a posset of milk, ale, hartshorn and marigold flowers, and mentioned this to his mother and the Prince.

'It will give his Majesty back his strength,' nodded the Countess, and the Duke sent his servant, Baker, to prepare it.

'Here, Dad, drink this, it will help you,' said Buckingham, holding the cup to James's crusted and trembling lips. The King took but a sip or two, but was reluctant to take more.

'Come, another sip,' the Duke urged.

The two doctors, Craig and Scot rushed over to the bedside, remonstrating violently. 'I must insist that you stop immediately, your Grace! We have not sanctioned this treatment – the effect on the King's weakened system could be as poison!'

'Poison? What does he say, Steenie?' mumbled the King, pushing the posset away. Craig immediately grabbed it.

'How dare you accuse me?' cried Buckingham, 'leave this room now, all of you! I swear sir, that if you do not remove your odious presence, then I will have you forcibly removed!' And to John Scot, he thundered, 'and I will throw you out of that window!'

The doctors withdrew with as much dignity as they could muster, but on turning, James's chief physician Dr. Eglisham told the Duke, 'This will be reported, my Lord Buckingham, and I am sorry that your Highness suffers yourself to be so led that many doubt whether you or his Grace is the Prince.'

'You are banished from court,' Charles told him curtly.

The King continued to weaken, suffering a stroke, and the Duke sat by his side, silent and sunk into a profound despair. Lord Keeper Williams and Archbishop Abbott were sent for and the King received the sacraments and made his confession of faith. On Sunday, 27th March James Stuart breathed his last.

Buckingham was prostrate with grief at the death of his royal master, weeping inconsolably as he recalled all that he owed James, and all that they had shared. His health still poor, having suffered a relapse in January, the Duke needed to be carried to his chambers in a chair. The new King shed no tears, but was concerned for his friend, and the two spent the first night of his reign together in Charles's bed chamber, returning to London in a coach as equals.

Buckingham knelt before the dignified young man who was now his sovereign, and swore his loyalty and allegiance.

The King raised him up, saying, 'Though you have lost a good master, you have gained another who loves you equally well. I solemnly swear that naught shall ever come 'twixt you and I, Steenie, nor shall anything part us. Our souls are knit together, yours and mine, and as David and Jonathan were known for the more than ordinary affection they bore each other, even so shall you and I be likewise known.'

Steenie took the slender, delicate fingers of his king and kissed them tenderly and lingeringly.

'I also swear that even death itself shall not separate us,' he murmured.

Neither was aware of the extent of the solemn pact they had sworn, the echoes of which would be felt throughout Europe. Neither remembered either the ultimate fate of Jonathan.

Chapter Ten

Of British Beasts the Buck is King
His Game and fame through Europe ring,
His horn exalted, keeps in awe
The lesser flocks; his Will's a Law.
Our Charlemagne takes much delight
In this great beast so fair in sight,
With his whole heart affects the same,
And loves too well Buck-King of Game.
                             Anonymous 1626.

King Charles looked across the room at the Duke of Buckingham and catching his eye, smiled warmly, how magnificent Steenie looked, no wonder Paris had gone wild over him. And this feast, given by Steenie at York House in celebration of his marriage, was everything he could possibly have expected from his beloved friend. Charles sipped his wine thoughtfully. He was never a big eater nor prone to drink much, and noticed with approval that his new wife did not appear to be either. He smiled at her, feeling pleased and in a good humour.

The King had met his bride at Dover and then they had travelled to Canterbury, where they had married according to the rites of the English church, a marriage having already being celebrated in Paris on May Day when the Duc de Chevreuse had stood proxy for Charles. Steenie had then journeyed to Paris to convey the new Queen of England home, though as it transpired, he had not accompanied her overseas to Dover, for he had been involved in business of his own, business of the heart. Charles confessed himself pleased with Henriette, and had been at pains to reassure his young wife, who had burst into tears, kissing her warmly and responding to her speech in French, as she spoke no English, though Charles doubted not that she would soon learn.

Relieved that she was not as small as he had feared, he had glanced down at her feet several times, until she had told him, 'Sir, I stand upon mine own feet. Thus high I am, and am neither higher nor lower.' Henriette reached to her husband's shoulders, a perfect height, it was thought, for a man who was himself only small.

Glancing shyly now at his tiny queen, Charles thought again that he was certainly not displeased with her appearance, for though she was no beauty, and had a sallow complexion and prominent teeth, he nevertheless admired her large sparkling black eyes. The young bride appeared to be quite amiable too, and despite that the journey to Canterbury had been marred by an incident when she had insisted that her governess Madame de St. Georges ride in the coach with them instead of the Duke's female relatives, and had sulked over his refusal, Charles was willing to overlook this, and was even willing to accept for the moment the vast entourage which had arrived with his wife.

The King and Queen, both dressed in green, had travelled through London by the royal barge rather than by coach, for the plague was most virulent once more, and the King had felt satisfied and proud to see the celebrations. As they passed through London Bridge to Whitehall they were encompassed on every side by cheering crowds in barges of honour, in wherries, standing in houses, on ships, and on each side of the shore. Fifty ships discharged their ordnance as their Majesties passed by, and the Tower did such a peel, that many in the crowd said they believed that the Queen could never have heard the like before. The bells had rung until midnight, the celebrations continuing till later on streets filled with bonfires.

'You s-see my dear, your people turn out to greet and welcome you,' Charles had told his wife.

Excited and pleased, Henriette had smiled back at him.

Charles turned to his bride, and said, 'there will be a masque and dancing later this evening, and the D-Duke will entertain us. I believe you saw him dance in Paris – he is most elegant is he n-not?'

Henriette looked over at Buckingham, his handsome face wreathed in smiles, laughing at some pleasantry. 'Yes, most elegant,' she answered, whilst thinking of how she disliked this gorgeously attired man.

It had not been so at first – like all the French court, the little Princess had heard of the incomparable Duke's fame, but naught had prepared any of them for the effect of the presence of the man himself – handsome beyond belief, dashingly gallant, and supremely confident, and his wardrobe! The whole of Paris was agog at the magnificence of his attire, the like of which had never been seen, not even upon the King; clad in a white velvet doublet shimmering with diamonds and precious stones, which scattered as he walked; jewels upon his person, jewels upon his cane, in his ear; dispensing largesse in copious amounts wherever he went; everyone even went mad for the hat he wore which was immediately copied and called 'the Boukinkan'.

It was no surprise that he outshone all at court, indeed outshone the very stars in the heavens, nor that women swooned and sighed at the mere sight of him, even the men could not deny his magnificence and splendour while they seethed in their jealousy. Henriette herself had at first succumbed to his charm, for she had never seen such a man before, and she blushed and stammered, gazing up into those wicked, azure eyes, trembling as he took her hand and kissed it, addressing her in perfect French. At first she had even guiltily half wished that the Duke was her betrothed, that was until she and the whole of the court observed his scandalous and unforgiveable behaviour toward her brother's wife, Queen Anne. From the first the Duke had made no attempt to disguise his admiration for the Queen, nor had she been able to hide the effect he had upon her.

The two had made an elegantly beautiful couple as they had

danced together, every eye upon them. None had watched them more closely than Anne's husband, King Louis and his cardinal, and the King had glowered sulkily at the sight of his wife, so unresponsive to himself, flirting and sweetly blushing as she smiled into the Duke's handsome face. His Majesty was all too aware of the comparison that all must make as the English man stood near, towering over him, glittering and glowing, self-assured and at ease, his white teeth adding a charm to a smile which was already almost irresistible. Louis smiled little, his double row of teeth caused him embarrassment.

Each day the famous Boukinkan had been cheered and watched by crowds when leaving his hotel, gasping at the sight of yet another gorgeous doublet and cape, dripping with jewels and embroidered with pearls. There were astonished murmurs when he appeared clad in purple satin – the colour of royalty, but this Duke looked and acted as regally as the king he represented. Yet his popularity turned to shocked disapproval as his conduct to the Queen became known; it was told that he had had the effrontery to make love to her whilst in a garden, and when the royal party had finally departed for England, the Duke had fallen upon his knees beside the Queen's coach, tears coursing down his face.

Henriette recalled with indignation how Boukinkan had turned back near Calais and left her, galloping back to Anne at Amiens on some pretext, entering her very bedchamber and kissing her hands and the coverlets upon the bed, whispering of his passion and desire, and refusing to leave. She could not forgive him for humiliating her dear brother, who had told her that he would never permit the Duke to enter his realm ever again, regardless of how well his sister's new husband thought of him.

At Boulogne Henriette and her party had been met by Buckingham's family, except his wife, who, she was informed by the Duke's insufferable mother, was with child. Henriette pitied her – she would never allow any man to treat herself with such contempt. And now she was being entertained by the Duke with a magnificence which would cause even a king to be proud, in a mansion which was as richly furnished as a palace, and with an extravagance that staggered even she who was used to the opulence of the French court. Upon meeting again, the Duke had spoken to her with scant regard for her rank, but she was astonished to see the familiarity with which he had greeted her husband, and equally perturbed to see the affection which her seemingly reserved and grave husband bestowed upon him. Buckingham, while attending to his guests, was very much aware of the King and Queen. His reunion with Charles had been sweetly affectionate, and the Duke could not resist alluding to the King's wedding night.

'It was a satisfactory outcome, Steenie, and went as well as could be expected,' Charles told him, colouring faintly.

'As well as expected!' thought the Duke, imagining the embarrassed fumbling and coupling of those two inexperienced virgins. Thank God Charles had been able to consummate the marriage. He had been rather anxious that his friend, unlike himself, apparently cold and indifferent to the opposite sex, might have proved insufficient. God! What a disaster that would have been! He had regretted that he had not been on hand to provide advice, (though he did not regret the cause) and indeed, the only reason that Buckingham was sure that Charles even knew what to do was because he had been there when James had in typically blunt fashion instructed him about 'the cod piece point', and what went where, saying, 'and if yeh have any questions, then ask yon Steenie, for he knows his way around a woman's body better than most!' Buckingham had bowed in amusement, as his companions laughed, but Charles had been mortified. The favourite thought that it was fortunate that the old king was not still alive to visit the newly wed couple in the morning and demand a detailed account of the night's activities.

The Duke had not been surprised to be informed that the King had not allowed any bawdy romping from those accompanying the royal couple to their bedchamber, and had bolted the doors, permitting only two members of his bedchamber to stay to undress him, after which the King had bolted them out also.

'I'll warrant you left your bride panting with passion for more of your caresses, eh?'

'I would like to think that I did my duty by my wife, and would hope that it was not too distasteful for her, though to be sure, I believe she did find it somewhat painful.'

Buckingham threw his head back and roared with laughter, slapping the King playfully on his back – his duty indeed!

'How I love you Charles! I doubt not that the Queen is counting the hours until you can retire again – though she must curb her impatience, for it will be late tonight when the feasting and dancing will end, and do not worry – the first time always hurts a little – it will be easier tonight. I trust my King enjoyed his bride? Does she please you?'

Charles was not in the least offended at the intimacy of his friend's questions. In a way it made him feel more of a man like other men, though he was still inhibited in discussing sexual matters, and was very much aware that few grooms were as virginal as their brides on their wedding night.

'It was not unpleasant, Steenie, but indeed, I did not expect it to be as special as many say, and will confess to you that I was somewhat concerned that I would appear foolish.'

'What? Worried that you wouldn't be able to gain access? Well, she *is* tiny,' laughed the Duke, but on noticing the King's concerned face he reassured him. 'But you have made a triumphal entrance into France, and claimed your territory! The first time is always the most difficult for the groom also, so now you have nothing to worry about.'

'I am sure *you* never have had anything to worry about, Steenie, with all your vast experience. And now I hear you have made conquest of the Queen of France's heart!'

Buckingham grinned. 'Ah, my dear young Master! Would that I had made conquest of more than her heart! Although I am still in hopes of that! Now *she* is a queen worth possessing. But her fleering fool of a husband has no liking for me, and in truth, I am glad

I have humiliated him, for both he and his cardinal have been singularly uncooperative in our talks on a joint policy against the Spanish.'

'Indeed, I was concerned to read of your difficulties, and look forward to speaking with you further on these matters.'

The thought that the Duke had not rendered the French king more willing to co-operate by making violent love to his wife simply never occurred to Charles, nor that his friend was in any way at fault – he was simply being Steenie, and therefore beyond reproach.

Sitting next to her husband at the feast, the Duchess of Buckingham looked frequently at the King and Queen, noting their smiles and their seeming pleasure in each other's company. Katherine was hopeful that the young couple would be happy, at least the Queen need have no fears of *her* husband ever straying. She sighed, thinking again of how relieved she was to have her own husband back home, despite the pain that tore her heart at the scandal surrounding his obsession with the French Queen.

'Take no note of it, men always speak ill of him out of jealousy,' her sister-in-law Susan had counselled her. Kate had smiled her thanks, but she knew, alas, that her husband's reputation was well deserved, but at least this latest amour was far away where he would soon forget her, and it was *she* who carried Buckingham's child. But to her dismay, the Duke talked of naught but 'his Queen' and of his determination to return to her. Of her beauty Katherine had no doubt, for even had her husband not spoken of it incessantly, there was a miniature of her that he wore upon his person, and he was equally open about writing and receiving letters. Kate had wept tears of bitterness, unable to hold them back when visited at Wallingford House by her father, who had listened grim-faced to his daughter's account of the latest outrage.

'He does not deny it – he is ever honest with me,' cried Kate.

'How honourable of him! It might have been kinder if he did not flaunt his infidelity in front of your face,' returned the Earl.

'He *is* kind! Always kind! But he speaks to me as if I am his sister, not his wife. As if I should be happy for him that he is in love with a queen.'

'We do not know the truth of the matter. I doubt that he did more than kiss the Queen's hands, and she was probably most affronted and displeased by his behaviour – at least I hope she was.'

'But she was not – she returns his love, and he will not rest until he has returned and made her truly his own!'

'How can you be sure she returns his love?'

'I have read her letters.'

'Surely he has not shown you her letters?'

Katherine nodded, her eyes brimming with tears.

Rutland rose, and walked over to the window, barely able to restrain his fury. After a few moments he sat down again by his daughter, and held her hand. 'Do not fret yourself, nor cause yourself to become ill. Buckingham will forget her when your child is born.'

The Earl did not believe his own words, but could not speak his true thoughts, that he wished his daughter would close her heart against her faithless husband, and again he wondered how it was that this man could have such an effect over those who loved him so unwisely – for it was clear that the new king was still in thrall to him, and now even the French Queen desired him. What was the secret of his power?

Sipping her wine, Katherine began to speak to the Duke about her wishes for the happiness of the King and Queen.

'How happy his Majesty looks, indeed I think I have never seen him so content. And the Queen, she is of such a perfect size for him, and appears so amiable that I believe that God has ordained them for each other, do you not think so, my lord?'

'Undoubtedly,' replied Buckingham, only half listening.

'I will pray daily that she will be a great comfort to his Majesty, and that they will be blessed soon with many healthy children, for there is no greater joy on earth than a happy marriage.'

'True, my dear,' returned her husband, glancing briefly at the Countess of Carlisle who was sitting nearby, and appreciating her beauty. That lady had been decidedly cool with him since she had heard the talk of his passion for Queen Anne.

Kate prattled on happily, while Buckingham smiled and agreed. 'And I believe they are already more than half in love with each other, for I have it on good authority from those who accompanied them to London that the King said his wife has the finest eyes he had ever seen and that he found everything about her enchanting, and the Queen said she thought her new husband most handsome, and was well disposed to love him even before she had arrived in England. Look at how they regard each other, as if none but they were in the room! Your mother says she doubts not that there will be a royal heir within the year! How wonderful it will be for both you and his Majesty to have a son. How happy I am for the King that at last he has found the perfect princess to love and bring him joy.'

Buckingham's eyes had glazed at Kate's ramblings, but at the last few words they suddenly cleared – his hand lifting wine to his lips froze.

'Will it not be a great blessing for the King and Queen to be in love?' asked Kate, and as he did not immediately reply, she continued, 'my lord? I said will it not be a great joy for him to be so settled and content after all his loneliness and sorrow?'

'Loneliness and sorrow? Whatever do you speak of, Madam? The King is neither lonely nor sad – he has *me*!'

'Assuredly – he has the fortune to have the most faithful friend that king or man could e'er possess, but naught can replace knowing the joys of marriage, for friendship betwixt man and man can never be the same as that which God has ordained betwixt husband and wife. And it will be of benefit to you, dear heart, for it will relieve the heavy burden upon yourself when the King does not need you as much.'

Buckingham turned and looked at his wife, unsure of whether she was really aware of what she was saying.

'And that being the case, you will have more time to spend at home with your family.'

Buckingham smiled coldly at Katherine. God, what a little fool! Did she really think he would prefer her company to the King's? He pushed his plate away, declining more wine, his appetite had suddenly gone, along with his good humour. He looked over at the royal couple, attempting to evaluate whether there was any danger that he might be replaced by the French chit. He was disconcerted to note that the King and Queen did indeed appear to be engrossed in each other. Charles was even smiling and obviously enjoying his wife's company, she laughing and beamingly animated. The favourite bit his lip in consternation, an icy cold seeping into his heart.

'How happy the King is! It must give your Grace such joy and satisfaction to know that you are the source of providing such felicity for his Majesty!' a silken voice whispered in his ear, and on turning round the Duke looked up at the knowing smile of Lady Carlisle, who had overheard some of Kate's words, and was astute enough to perceive that they had discomfited her lover.

It was perhaps fortunate that the masque and dancing which followed the feast preoccupied the favourite, but he took little pleasure in any of it, his eyes constantly upon the royal couple, and on watching them dance, his blood again ran cold.

'How well matched are his Majesty and the Queen,' commented Lady Carlisle, smiling archly, when she danced with the Duke, 'they dance like true lovers.'

It was undeniably true that the Queen danced well, and that the exercise and pleasure she derived from it lent colour and charm to her thin, sallow features and rendered her face quite pretty. Buckingham noted it – nothing escaped his attention, and his heart quailed when, after the dancing was finally over in the early hours of the morning, the King embraced him warmly and thanked him for one of the most enjoyable evenings he could e'er recall. The Duke bowed his acknowledgment and then watched in silence as Charles took his wife by the hand and escorted her to their apartments, where even Steenie was not wanted.

After seeing his guests depart, and bidding goodnight to those who were staying at York House, Buckingham had finally taken himself off to sleep alone, telling Katherine truthfully that he had a fearful headache, and felt indisposed and would disturb her sleep if he shared her bed. He lay wide awake, the flames from the fire casting strange and lurid shadows upon the walls, despite the luxurious warm covers and eiderdowns, he shivered violently as with an ague. Every word his wife had spoken, every word Lucy had spoken, every scene, every expression on Charles's face, was played over and over in his fevered mind. Could it be true? Could the French princess be the woman who finally awoke the King's latent passion? Could he fall in love with her, and so no longer need his Steenie? For so long Buckingham had been used to commanding Charles's heart, to being the most important person in his life, he had felt it was his by right – it had never occurred to him that this skinny, underdeveloped fifteen year old would or could replace him in the King's affections – even yesterday he would have laughed such a notion to scorn, but now... Could he bear to stand aside? Buckingham knew he could not, and it was not because he feared to lose his position as chief minister. He knew Charles would never deprive him of his wealth and position, no, it was not that.

Buckingham suddenly knew with a pain so powerful that he felt he could scarce breathe that what he felt was jealousy: for probably the first time in his pampered and privileged existence George Villiers knew what it was to feel jealous of another, and to fear that he might lose to another that which he most valued. Never before had he had any reason to feel thus. He had always had whatever and whomever he desired – was this what others had experienced when they had loved and lost him? It was misery! Abject misery! Buckingham knew then with startling clarity that the person he loved most in the world was Charles, his dear master, his beloved, sweet friend. The Duke's passion for Anne of Austria was engendered by lust – he desired her body, and he realised that he desired the pleasure of knowing that a queen was mad for him, as the old king had been mad for him, and he wanted the satisfaction of knowing that he could have the King of France's wife. He saw again the sweet, grave face of his greatest friend, the small, delicate form, the thin, bandy legs; the way Charles's face lit up when he saw him, and he ached with love and tenderness. Never had the favourite so appreciated that affection as now when he feared that the King might now look at his wife in that way. He recalled Kate's words that Charles had claimed that his wife had the finest eyes he had ever seen, and he hated her, for many and many a time Charles had told him that none, neither woman nor man, had so lovely eyes as he.

'I will have to leave court,' he told himself, 'I cannot stay and see her replace me in his heart. I could not bear it.'

The hours dragged by, and still the Duke lay awake in agony, imagining his beloved friend and his Queen naked in bed, discovering the joys of love. He dreaded the morning, when he would see the evidence for himself. Finally, unable to bear his own thoughts any more, Buckingham arose, feeling sick at heart and in body.

He need not have worried. The night of delights with which he had tortured himself by imagining was merely that – imaginings. Charles had got happily into bed with Henriette, both dressed in their nightgown and cap, and tentatively touched her arm. He was profoundly disappointed to feel his wife recoil, and trying again, had heard her say that she trusted that his Majesty would understand that she would prefer to sleep, for she was much fatigued.

'Of course,' he replied, trying to sound as though he did not care. Perhaps tomorrow she would be more responsive. But the Queen, while grimly accepting her conjugal duty, was not more responsive. Her inexperienced husband had not awoken her passions, and she made clear her distaste of his presence in her bed, sleeping with her back towards him at the opposite end of the bed. On the only occasion that he had shyly attempted to touch her tiny breasts, she had abruptly pushed his hand away with a definite, 'non!', and Charles was only permitted to lift her night gown sufficiently to allow him to perform the odious act, and that as quickly and quietly as possible. Many a night she refused him altogether, claiming it was some saint's feast or another and that her priests insisted upon her abjuring all pleasures of the flesh. Pleasures of the flesh! Charles had almost laughed at her words – he had known no such pleasure with his wife, and the experience was vastly different from Steenie's descriptions of sexual ecstasy. Humiliated, embarrassed and hurt, the young King withdrew from Henriette's bed and from her company.

'If she was *my* wife I would insist upon my marital rights more often!' Steenie told him.

'If she was *your* wife then I doubt that you would need to insist,' replied the King, glumly.

The coldness between husband and wife soon escalated into open hostility and centred on Henriette's Catholic faith. The young Queen had come to England intent upon the conversion of her heretic husband, for had not the Holy Father, when granting the dispensation to marry, told her that she was to be as the Frankish Princess Bertha, whose marriage to King Ethelbert had made way for the conversion of England? Henriette was determined to accept the challenge, and as her relationship with her husband deteriorated, the influence of her 28 priests increased and in particular that of her confessor, Father Berulle.

Charles's irritation with his wife's religious practices hardened into positive contempt, and almost every day furnished him with more reasons to dislike his French Queen and her retinues of messieurs, indeed he became convinced that they were all deliberately mocking not only himself but the Protestant faith. On one occasion the Queen and her ladies had laughed and frolicked noisily when a service was being held nearby. On another the King's chaplain was saying grace at dinner, when the Bishop of Mende began to say a Catholic grace in French; their competing voices became louder and louder until they were shouting at each other.

Charles left the table in silent anger.

The King's feeling of humiliation and sense of impotence over his wife's behaviour touched his old feelings of inadequacy, never far from the surface, causing the reserved young man to retaliate, and when the Queen's priests importuned him to have the chapel finished at St. James's, his answer was, that if the Queen's closet where they said mass was not large enough, let them have mass in the great chamber, and if the great chamber were not wide enough, they might use the garden, and if the garden would not serve their turn, then the park was the fittest place.

Henriette responded in kind: she refused to learn English and reacted in fury when she was told that she must have the Duke's female relatives as Ladies of her Bedchamber. She found the thought intolerable. It was bad enough that they were English, but that they were the relatives of the detested Boukinkan and would be for ever spying upon her, was not to be borne. When she heard that the group included Lady Carlisle, she was outraged, (though the Duke's wife, mother and sister would have agreed with her in this instance).

'What?' she shrieked, 'even his whore?'

Stubborn and self-willed, the young Queen had been petted and spoilt at the French court, and was possessed of a foul temper, prompting one observer to comment that, 'none but a Queen could have cast such a scowl!'

Charles poured out his heart to his only friend, who listened sympathetically, whilst secretly exulting. It was not that Buckingham wished to see his King unhappy, far from it; but he was utterly determined that none would supplant him in his master's affections. Unlike the situation with the previous King, when a new favourite would have meant an end to his power and position, the Duke knew that he was in no danger of losing the King's favour and would retain his pre-eminent position, but that was not enough. He must also remain pre-eminent in the King's heart and as far as he was concerned, the French match was merely a means to provide heirs to the throne and to cement a powerful alliance with France against Spain.

Buckingham was not vindictive, being more forgiving and tolerant than his master, but Henriette's character and her refusal to be ruled by him; indeed, her insolence and rudeness to himself and her husband caused him to heartily dislike her: very soon both regarded each other as rivals for the King's affection, and their dislike crystallised into enmity. The King unknowingly fuelled this hatred, for, disdaining to speak directly to his wife, he used Buckingham to convey messages, most of which were unpalatable to the lady, and which were delivered with such disrespect that Henriette was immediately antagonised. The Duke also took the opportunity to make his position of supremacy very clear, talking to her as if she was a silly little girl. He lectured her on her attitude to the King, on her behaviour, on her refusal to learn the language of her new home, even upon how she dressed.

The young Queen responded with unconcealed dislike and anger, telling Buckingham what she thought of him and his vile country, and then the favourite humbly reported her disagreeable words and unfortunate attitude to the King, who reacted with anger and sorrow that his dear friend and first minister should be thus abused. Soon the two households barely saw each other, residing in different palaces. Charles no longer yearned after his wife's attentions in bed, now both the thought and the lady herself repelled him. Buckingham, who was an expert at this type of marital arrangement, assured his master that this was for the best, and encouraged him to only visit with the Queen to fulfil his duty to his country.

While the King and Buckingham spent their days together, hunting, hawking, enjoying their art collections, discussing policy and in companiable intimacy, Henriette became ever more homesick and depressed, writing to her mother and brother of her unhappiness and laying the blame upon the Duke. She had no doubt that her husband's coldness to herself was largely the result of Boukinkan's pernicious influence; an influence which she could not but regard as evil and dangerous, and she confessed to those closest to her that she suspected the nature of that influence, for it was well known in France that the Duke had been the old King's catamite, and her fears were encouraged by her priests and by the gossip whispered by her ladies. Henriette was not unfamiliar with such matters, for her own brother Louis loved men as well as women, and their mother, the redoubtable Marie de Medici, had said that had her son not neglected his wife, then mayhap France would have an heir to the throne, and Anne might not have been so susceptible to the charms of that notorious womaniser the Duke of Buckingham.

Despite warnings from the Privy Council of the parlous state of the country's finances, Charles and Buckingham were determined to summon an immediate Parliament.

'It is high time to have subsidies granted for the maintaining of the war with Spain, and the fleet must go forth for that purpose this summer,' the King told his councillors.

That these subsidies would be promptly granted neither young man doubted, for had not that august body enthusiastically supported the Duke and the King, when Prince of Wales, during the late King's last Parliament?

When Parliament opened on 18th June there was much competition for seats, being a great interest in seeing the new monarch, dressed in his robes, and with the crown upon his head, despite being not yet crowned. After prayers, the young King hesitatingly began his speech from the throne by excusing his lack of eloquence and inability to spend much time in words, emphasising that he expected Parliament to continue the policies they had advocated in his father's reign; when they had encouraged the break with Madrid, and they must therefore now vote taxes to fight Spain and recover the Palatinate. This brief speech was followed by the Lord Keeper Williams speaking at length on the need for the subsidies, but no amount of money was mentioned, nor how it would be used and the Lower House was keener to speak of the dangers of popery and their discontent regarding the favourable treatment of recusants, which they did for twelve long days, until finally returning to the subject dearest to their King's heart.

Charles was utterly dumbfounded to be informed that only two subsidies worth £160,000 had been voted – woefully insufficient. And not only this, but the King was mortally affronted that the Commons had only voted him tonnage and poundage for a year, and not for life, which was usual, after which three quarters of the members hastily departed for their country estates out of fear of the plague which was killing more than 4,000 a week in London.

Deeply disappointed and offended, Charles ordered a recess on 4th of July until the beginning of the next month when the Houses were ordered to reassemble in plague-free Oxford. The Duke shared his master's surprise, not only at Parliament's unwillingness to grant the subsidies which they had both imagined were a foregone conclusion, but that his former popularity appeared to be waning; for now it was said that not only had the Duke rescued the King from a Papist marriage, but he had swiftly placed another Papist princess in the royal bed, and although this one was French and not a hated Spaniard, nevertheless a Catholic was a Catholic. Moreover, she was surrounded by a veritable army of priests, infiltrating and befouling the very court with their heretical practises.

There was talk again that Buckingham was a secret Papist, for were not most of his cursed family? That he remained the new King's favourite was another cause for grave concern, for this monarch allowed him unlimited power and authority, and would listen to no advice but his. Small surprise then that the Venetian ambassador noted that the King's passionate love for the Duke of Buckingham aroused great jealousy in all. There were even mutterings that 'twas no wonder that God had sent plague to the country as a judgment for sin.

By the time Parliament reassembled at Oxford the plague was already claiming lives in that city.

'It is an outrage sir, that his Majesty has dragged us all here,' exclaimed Sir Francis Godwin. 'I am too busy during this harvest time, and it is well known that this month is the most dangerous time for infections. I blame Buckingham. I doubt not that he believes that the members will so fear the plague that they will vote the taxes in their haste to escape.'

Hoping for a more successful outcome, the King told the members that he was grateful for the two subsidies already voted, but these were insufficient to send a fleet into battle, adding, 'you must yourselves decide which is greater, the danger of the sickness or the reputation of the kingdom, for myself I believe that the provision of further monies for the fleet should take precedence over all other considerations, for it were better that the navy should come home beaten by the enemy and half lost than not go out at all.' He continued that if the House agreed to vote the taxes, he undertook, on that royal word which he had never yet broken, nor given cause to mistrust, to call a Parliament in the winter to consider their grievances, and so demanded a speedy answer.

Buckingham himself confidently addressed both Houses with his usual charm and affability.

'By whose council was the Spanish matter undertaken if not by that of Parliament? His Majesty and myself have already furnished more monies than is required from the whole country. Put the sword into my master's hands and you shall name the enemy yourselves. If in my speaking unto you, my insufficiency has been harmful to the King, to the State, or to Christendom, I beg you will pardon me, for my intentions are pure,' he engagingly told them, but his words no longer had the same effect, for it was clear that the fleet was far from ready, and there was little support for a war which was as yet undeclared. Many of the members took the view that Parliament had *not* encouraged King James and his Majesty when he was Prince to break the Spanish treaty, nor had it pushed for war, but that his Majesty and the Duke had forced the issue. Neither was there much support for the Duke's view that an alliance with France was essential to England's security; for many believed that it would be more provident to concentrate on a sea war with Spain, if war they must have.

Now the extent of the Duke's slip from popularity became evident, for there were complaints about the abuses in the realm, complaints about the state of the treasury, complaints that the coasts of the realm were infested by pirates, while nothing was done. Then the floodgates were opened, and Buckingham was shocked to find himself named as the cause of all the country's miseries.

'His Grace is too near to his Majesty, his greatness and exorbitance are an offence to all, and his power and practice are both doubted and disliked,' thundered Sir Francis Seymour, as many applauded.

The shock experienced by the Duke was shared by the King, who had received the news of the proceedings with white-lipped anger, and at a meeting of the Privy Council at Woodstock he vented his displeasure.

'So *this* is the love my people have for me! *This* is the contempt in which I am held! After having committed myself to the policy which both Houses urged upon my father, and at the beginning of my reign with my honour at stake, I find myself betrayed and despised. No further subsidies voted for, and what I cannot e'er forgive or comprehend, my chief minister and friend about to be impeached for crimes no greater than giving loyal and devoted service to the crown, and for being loved by myself! This is insufferable, and I shall not suffer it – P-Parliament shall be dissolved forthwith!'

Williams, Lord Keeper, stood before the King, 'Your Majesty, I humbly urge you not to part in anger with your first Parliament, for if you do so then in due course your Majesty must needs summon another, and the next swarm will come out of the same hive.'

Buckingham agreed, kneeling before the King, and saying that he believed there was even now a way to clear his name and co-operate with Parliament. The sight of his beloved friend on his knees before him in humility caused Charles's indignation against those who had unjustly accused him to burn within him, and raising the Duke by the hand, the King told him, 'Your pleading and good nature reflect naught but credit upon you Steenie, but I will not have you treated thus by those who should be grateful to you, and who speak only through envy. Nor will I allow myself as Sovereign by the will of God to be trifled with and made a fool of – Parliament must learn that I will in n-no wise suffer disloyalty and disobedience – let them look to it. Parliament will be dissolved.'

It was soon well known that the King was on bad terms with his Queen, and equally well-known that he was on bad terms with his Parliament. Charles himself reflected to Steenie that it was a matter to him of much grief and not a little indignation that within so short a time of his succeeding to the throne he was so bedevilled with difficulties, being defied both by Parliament and by his wife.

The end of that year brought both joy and further dashed hopes – the Duke was on a diplomatic mission at The Hague in November when he received word that at long last he had a son and heir, whom he named Charles. It was well that he and the King had some tidings to cheer them, (it being commonly noted that his Majesty was as well pleased at the birth of his Grace's son, to whom he stood as godparent, as if the child was his own), for matters had not gone over well for Buckingham. Although the Treaty of The Hague had been signed by Denmark, Holland and England, the Duke was disturbed by Sweden and Venice's reluctance to join the anti-Habsburg alliance.

He was even more dismayed by France's hesitation, for were they not now allies and was not Charles now the brother of the French king? His dismay turned to affronted anger when he was informed that he would not be permitted to travel from The Hague to Paris; yet one more reason for Charles to dislike his wife. Neither had the Duke been successful in raising the finances so desperately needed for the war, for although he had pawned many of his own jewels, he was unable to pawn the crown jewels. The King roundly cursed the Parliament whose refusal to vote him supply had reduced him to such extremities and left him no option but to levy forced loans.

Upon Buckingham's return to England, he had been affectionately re-united with his royal master at Hampton Court, but their mutual delight was soon marred by the ill tidings that the expedition to Cadiz which they had seen depart in October with such high hopes, with instructions to sack and harass the enemy, had limped back home in ignominy and failure, the crew so full of sickness that they could scarce move the sails. They had not succeeded in forming a permanent blockade upon the Spanish coast, nor had they captured the Spanish treasure fleet upon which Charles and the Duke were depending, and the sick, half-starved, stinking and near naked remnants of the expedition arrived at west coast ports in their hundreds.

The whole expedition had been a fiasco – the ships were leaky and ill-prepared, many of the crews conscripted, above all the commanders, notably Sir Edward Cecil, appointed by the Duke, were inexperienced and indecisive. Despite all the money and time that Buckingham had spent, and despite his intentions that this glorious action would silence opposition and once more render him the darling of all, he was blamed for its failure. *He* was blamed, not the King, but Charles did not escape unscathed. He was now no longer viewed as 'Great Britain's Charlemagne' as he had been hailed at the beginning of his reign, a mere nine months earlier. One correspondent wrote,

You cannot believe the alteration that is in the opinion of the world touching his Majesty.

Charlemagne had been weighed in the balance, and had been found wanting by his people, his Parliament, his allies and by his wife.

CHAPTER ELEVEN

No distance of place, nor length of time, can make me slacken, much less diminish my love to you.
    King Charles to the Duke of Buckingham, 1627.

The Duke always builds upon the King's great affection for him, as his Majesty has protested that he would lose his crown and state rather than abandon him, but he judges badly in this as in everything else.
The Venetian ambassador to the Doge and senate, 1626.

On the cold, bright day of Thursday, 2 February 1626, Charles Stuart was crowned the lawful monarch of the three kingdoms of England, Scotland and Ireland. Unusually, the King had chosen to be dressed in white – the symbol of innocence – symbolising his marriage to his people, and was anointed with the sacramental oil made to his own formula. Only to Steenie had Charles opened his heart to speak of the importance of this day, delayed by the virulence of the plague, but even to his dearest friend he had been unable to fully convey the profound awe and significance in which he held his coronation.

A sacred and awesome trust and duty had been laid upon him by Almighty God. The hands which anointed him represented the hands of God, who had bestowed the power and authority upon him to rule his kingdom – he and he alone. As he sat upon the throne at the Abbey at Westminster, where the bodies of his father, mother and brother Harry lay, the crown was placed upon his head, and the young monarch had felt far more than its weight, for he felt the full weight of the responsibility entrusted to him: he would rule as a father to his people; a loving father but a firm one who would not hesitate to chastise or rebuke as necessary for the common good. He had spent much of the previous day in solitary prayer, humbly waiting upon the God he loved and trusted, petitioning the Almighty to bestow His favour and protection upon him and his realm and to endow him with the wisdom and strength to rule as a true prince of Christendom. Already the vastly different atmosphere at court had been noted and commented upon, for this King would not tolerate lewd and degenerate behaviour, and even Steenie had had to speak severely to his brother Kit Villiers regarding his drunken behaviour, making clear that unless he altered then he would be removed from his role as Gentleman of the Bedchamber.

Charles had besought God for a favourable outcome to his dealings with Parliament, praying for the ability to view them as ignorant and foolish children in need of guidance rather than rebellious and disloyal subjects. He had also most earnestly prayed for a reconciliation betwixt himself and his Queen, and that she would reconsider her refusal to attend the coronation. Henriette's determined avowal that she would neither be crowned nor even set foot in a church which she regarded as heretical had affected her husband more deeply than had any other of the many insults and humiliations. So shocked and upset was he after Buckingham had informed him of her Majesty's message, that he had gone personally to his wife, only to be refused admittance to her presence, even without the Duke, and it was only when he had demanded an audience as her King and lord that Henriette had permitted him access.

The Queen, flanked by her ladies and Father Pierre Berulle, was steadfast, and the King was told in no uncertain terms that even his offer of a private and curtained area in the church where she could watch the ceremony was not acceptable. Charles flinched at hearing the cold, proud refusal to compromise as though he had been struck, in truth a physical blow would have been less painful. On recognising the depth of his master's hurt and humiliation, Buckingham for once had been quiet and said little, even though he had not long since told the King that if his own wife would not obey him then how could he expect Parliament to? The favourite's anger burned at the insult the French chit had inflicted upon his dear friend and upon the country. His disgust and contempt increased yet more on being informed later that the Queen had stood at a window, looking on at the procession, while her ladies were seen openly frisking and dancing around the chamber.

The coronation was another opportunity for the King to demonstrate his continued favour and affection toward the Duke of Buckingham, who was appointed Lord High Constable for that day, and he had presented the King with the regalia upon bended knee, and as Master of the King's Horse, had the honour of putting on the King's spurs. It was also commented upon that as the royal party had alighted at Westminster Hall the Duke had stretched out his hand to assist the King up the stairs to the wooden platform; Charles had smiled warmly at him and putting his arm under his favourite's told him, 'I have more need to help you than you have to help me.'

Despite that the dangers of the plague had prevented the traditional parade through the city to the Abbey. The crowd, watching the pageant, cheered at the sight of their new monarch, and marvelled at the magnificence of the Duke of Buckingham, of which they had heard so much, but rarely seen. But, ever alert to portents and omens, there was a shiver of apprehension at the sight of the slight, youthful King clad in white, for was this not the symbol of martyrdom? Many would remember this day in the years to come. There was cause for more speculation a week later as Buckingham rode behind the King in procession to the state opening of Parliament when the bridle, with its plume of feathers, fell off the Duke's horse's head.

The news of Henriette's refusal to attend the coronation or be crowned was met with surprise and indignation, and merely confirmed the opinion of most of his Majesty's faithful Protestant subjects about their French Queen and her Catholic entourage. Another incident four days later reinforced the rift when an argument escalated into a serious row concerning where Henriette should stand to view her husband ride in state to the opening of Parliament. She had refused to watch from the Countess of Buckingham's apartments and a furious altercation ensued. With the flouting of his will and dignity and the insult rendered to his country ever in the King's mind, it seemed likely that the breach betwixt their Majesties would never be healed. For his own part, Charles believed that matters had gone too far for any meaningful reconciliation, and he no longer spoke to his wife, save when strictly necessary and those occasions frequently ended in disagreements, even to the extent of arguing about whether it rained or not.

He visited her bed but rarely, making clear that were it not for the duty incumbent upon him to beget an heir to his throne he would never willingly touch his wife again, such was his distaste of her. As relations between Charles and Henriette deteriorated, so the dislike between the Queen and the Duke intensified, and the rows between the two became increasingly violent and public. After a particular argument between the royal couple which had resulted in the King leaving his wife's bed, Buckingham had delivered a message to the Queen, and having been refused an audience with her, had entered her apartments anyway, ignoring the cries of outrage by her ladies and priests.

'Your Grace, this is simply not permitted! Her Majesty is indisposed! I beg that your Lordship will withdraw straightway!' exclaimed her confessor Father Berulle, placing himself in front of the door of Henriette's privy chamber.

The Duke regarded the small French man with scorn, his hands upon his hips, 'I am come sir, by command of his Majesty the King, and I *will* see the Queen. Kindly remove yourself.'

Berulle backed towards the door, spreading his arms out wide. 'No, no, my Lord! You may not enter the Queen's presence thus!

I beg you will leave until her Majesty agrees to see you at a more opportune time!'

'You forget to whom you speak sir! The only authority I recognise is that of the King, my royal master, and he commands me to speak with the Queen upon a personal matter to which *you* are not invited to listen.'

'It is not seemly that your Grace speaks upon the King's behalf on matters of a privy nature betwixt husband and wife.'

'I must tell you plain that I take your incessant interference ill, and it will be tolerated no longer.'

'It is well known that your Grace is the one who interferes and causes discord between those whom God has blessed in marriage.'

'How dare you address me thus, you cozening papistical rascal! Now remove your scurvy person or by God I swear I will lift you bodily out of my way!'

Berulle was thrust aside, still protesting loudly, and Buckingham threw open the door. Henriette and her ladies had been laughing and gossiping before they had heard the shouting, and there was a shocked intake of breath at such a breach of protocol. Mamie de St. Georges hurried forward, shielding her mistress.

'Your Grace of Buckingham, I must protest at this violation of the Queen's privacy.'

'Pray keep silence unless you are addressed Madam. I am here on the King's instructions to deliver a message to the Queen,' the Duke told her disdainfully. 'And as this message is of a privy nature I would request that you all leave.'

At this the ladies protested most vehemently, as did Berulle.

'Silence! You will all leave – *now.*'

'I will not leave her Majesty alone with your Grace – it is an outrage! I cannot believe that the King would knowingly permit this!'

'You will leave this room sir – either by the door or by that window – but you *will* leave and now – I will tolerate no more!'

Buckingham moved towards the priest, who, realising that the Duke was quite capable of making good his threat, scuttled out, exclaiming that he would inform his Majesty King Louis of the appalling treatment that his sister received, accompanied by Henriette's weeping ladies.

'How dare you behave so to a Princess of the House of Bourbon? I shall demand that you are imprisoned for your insolence and threats! To force your way into my presence and eject all my servants leaving me defenceless!'

Buckingham looked down at the pointed, furious face and laughed. 'You are merely a younger daughter of the late French King, and I can assure you Madam that your virtue, such as it is, is in no danger from me. You would hold no attractions for me even were you not married to my master.'

'No!' spat Henriette, 'a godly, devout woman would hold no attractions for you, but all the world knows of your preference for other men's wives, including my brother's. *And* of your other preferences!'

Buckingham frowned, 'I will no longer address your Majesty in French, but in the language of your country, as befits an English queen, though God knows you have neither the bearing nor the manners of a queen from any country.'

'Get out – leave my presence, or I will call the guards – you... you monster of depravity.'

The Duke laughed again. 'I will leave when I have delivered my message, and I will also add that your cold and unwomanly behaviour in the marital bed to the King your husband must stop – you were married only to provide this country with an heir to the throne, and you will do your duty.'

The Queen then rounded on him, in a passionate outburst of gabbled French, telling of her great detestation of him and all things English, and how the King's cruelty and his insolence to her were beyond bearing, and that she knew all England hated him and his influence over her husband, and that she prayed daily that he would be arrested for treason and executed.

Buckingham yawned lazily. 'If you wish to abuse me Madam then I suggest you do so in English, though perhaps you have not learnt to translate such foul language – I confess that I had not realised that the use of such descriptive oaths were part of the education of a princess of the House of Bourbon,' he told her coolly.

The enraged Queen snatched up a silver dish containing sweetmeats, and threw it at the Duke, narrowly missing him.

'You silly little girl. If you were my wife I would put you over my knee and spank you.'

Another missile sailed over his head. 'Madam, I must tell you that queens in this country have been executed for less!'

Henriette picked up a wine goblet, and seeing it, the Duke hastily retreated, escaping just in time as it smashed against the door. He walked swiftly out of the room, aware of feeling foolish in front of Berulle and the Queen's attendants. Shortly after he was telling the King of what had transpired: Charles had listened with horror to the outrage perpetrated upon his beloved Steenie, who had not only been assaulted by the Queen but abused and insulted by her rascally retinue. It could not continue. He was too angry to trust himself to speak to his wife that evening, but after a sleepless night the King had written a note to the Duke.

> *Steenie,*
> *I have received your letter by Dick Graham. This is my answer. I command you send all the French away tomorrow out of the town. If you can, by fair means (but stick not long in disputing,) otherwise force them away; driving them away like so many wild beasts, until you have shipped them, and so the devil go with them! Let me hear no answer but of the performance of my command. So I rest,*
> *Your faithful, constant, loving friend,*
> *Charles R.*

Charles had then informed the Privy Council of his decision, and sent for Henriette, but she refused to attend, pleading a toothache. 'So be it,' said the King shortly, and summoning the council members, they went to the Queen's apartments.

Entering unannounced, Charles stood silent for a moment,

watching his wife and her ladies dancing to the music of her favourite French musicians. Henriette suddenly saw her husband, and stopped in horror. His face told her everything she needed to know, and by his side, as ever, was the loathsome Boukinkan.

'Be silent and leave,' Charles told the musicians, who bowed and withdrew. Once more Madame de St. Georges hurried forward, her embroidery still in her hand, anxious to protect her mistress.

'I am pleased to see that your Majesty has recovered so quickly from your indisposition – truly a m-miracle cure! Steenie, you will deal with these people. Madam, you will come with me.'

The King took Henriette firmly by the hand and led her into her privy chamber. The Queen looked over her shoulder at Mamie in alarm, while Buckingham informed Madame de St. Georges and her ladies that they were all to depart from the kingdom, and would be taken straightway to Denmark House to leave for France as soon as could be arranged. At first Henriette could scarcely take in what her husband was telling her, despite that he spoke in her own language. She could not believe that he would really deprive her of virtually all her French household.

'That is not what was agreed when the marriage articles were signed, Sire. I do not think your Majesty would ever be party to any action which would not be honourable,' she told her husband, rallying all her courage.

'Matters have changed much since the agreement, and for your own good and the good of my realm I am determined that I will remove the baleful influence of your priests and all your women,' her husband responded.

'This is the Duke's doing – I entreat you Sir, do not proceed. I will be miserable beyond words.' Henriette protested, fighting a rising panic.

'This has naught to do with Buckingham. And it is not open to discussion.'

'But not Mamie! Not my dear Mamie!' she pleaded, tears spilling down her white cheeks.

'That lady is most certainly leaving – for I regard her as a mischief maker who has stirred my wife to unseemly b-behaviour and ungodly rebellion against myself.'

Henriette considered begging on her knees – surely he could not be so cruel, but seeing the King's icy calm she knew despairingly that this was not a man who would ever compromise or admit to being wrong. Hearing screams and shouting she rushed over to the window, and to her horror saw her ladies and servants and even her priests below in the courtyard being herded away, and there was Mamie de St. Georges, protesting loudly, her hat knocked off her head. The yeomen of the guard, directed by that devil Boukinkan, thrust them out of her lodgings, and locked the doors after them. Now all self-control forsook the Queen, and she screamed and hammered upon the windows with her tiny fists until the glass broke.

Appalled, Charles seized her shoulders and dragged her away, while she continued to scream, beside herself with grief and fear, her bloodied fists now pounding his chest.

'I hate you! I hate you! I will not stay in this country. I will return home to France and my brother will wage war on you and defeat you, and that pig Boukinkan will be hanged, and I will watch and dance!'

Guards quickly entered, and escorted the still weeping queen to her bedchamber. Henriette's English ladies were swiftly summoned and ordered to stay with her, and a doctor sent for. Buckingham returned from the courtyard, and on seeing his master's bloodied doublet and perspiring, tortured face he sprang forward in alarm.

'Good God! You are injured! Has the harridan harmed you?'

'No, no, it is not my blood, it is her own.' The King wiped his brow with a visibly shaking hand.

The two men retired to the King's lodgings, and the Duke poured them both a glass of wine.

'Sweet heavens, Steenie. I have never witnessed the like. She was as one possessed.'

'Mm I know – I observed her from the courtyard. Her retinue were fully as bad – the women howled and lamented as if they had been going to execution. Still, it is done, and a hearty good riddance!'

'The whole episode was utterly humiliating. I feel shamed by it. I doubt not that it is already all over the court.'

'I have no doubt either, but the shame was not in your behaviour but in the Queen's and her servants – I am certain that you will be much respected for your firm action.'

'I confess that I was most disturbed by the Queen's grief. It has never been my intention to hurt her, but to treat her with kindness.'

Buckingham shrugged, and took another sip. 'No husband has ever behaved with more patience and kindness toward a wife who has from the very start treated your Majesty with wilful disobedience, no doubt stemming from an obdurate and perverse disposition, which was most certainly encouraged by St. Georges and her priests. She will soon recover, leave her to her mummery and prayers.'

'I am sure you judge rightly Steenie,' replied the King.

Yet despite his words Charles remained miserable over the bungled affair, and Henriette, curled up on her bed, blamed Buckingham, and determined she would never speak to the Duke again.

On being informed that her father was come to Wallingford House, Katherine Duchess of Buckingham hurried downstairs to greet him. The Earl stood looking out of the window, his hands clasped behind his back, and upon hearing the door open, he swung round and smiled at his daughter.

'Dear father – what news?' asked his daughter anxiously, noticing his concerned face.

Rutland took her hand, 'Not good, I fear, my dear. They are determined to impeach Buckingham.'

Kate gasped, and knowing her fear and concern, her father would have eased her mind if he could, for she had cares enough already. Her baby son Charles failed to thrive and was ever fretful and sickly, despite all the money that the Duke spent on doctors, and the attacks on her dear lord had grieved and worried her.

Despite the King's assumption that Parliament had learnt its lesson from the last session when he had dissolved it, he was outraged and baffled to find that the Commons refused to vote supplies until there was an inquiry into their grievances. At first Buckingham had not been mentioned by name, though there was no doubt to whom was being referred, and in early March Charles sent an impatient message to the House that he required them to vote for the subsidies and told them, 'I would not have the House to question my servants, much less one that is so near to me.' Nothing daunted, Sir John Eliot continued his vitriolic attack on his former friend and patron, to which the King replied that he would be no less willing than his predecessors to redress their grievances but added, 'I see you aim specially at the Duke of Buckingham, and wonder what has so altered your affections towards him?'

The Commons ignored the King's warning, and a Committee for Evils, Causes and Remedies was appointed to prepare an indictment against the Duke. The strain began to tell on the favourite; deeply hurt and worried over the charges imputed to him, he fell ill. He had hoped to sway many of the members when he had addressed them to justify himself and explain his actions, but the old magic had gone and few were now favourably impressed merely by his handsome face and sweet affability.

'Gentlemen it is no time to pick quarrels one with another, we have enemies enough already, and therefore more necessary to be well united at home,' the Duke urged them. His pleas fell on deaf ears.

Katherine did not fully understand why her husband was being attacked so unfairly, and though Buckingham was at pains to downplay the seriousness of the charges, laughingly kissing her and telling her not to be affrighted, Kate recognised the signs of strain – the sleepless nights, the want of appetite and the frenetic restlessness and most tellingly the sickness which always betokened some impending disaster. She knew too how hurt and angry he was at what he saw as the betrayal of his friendship and patronage by John Eliot.

'After all the favours he has received at my hand. To turn against me thus in words of such envenomed enmity!' he raged.

Rutland had called each day, and endeavoured to answer his daughter's questions as truthfully as he could; for himself he was in no doubt but that the indictment was serious – serious for Buckingham and his daughter, serious for the King, serious for the country. And there was more to concern both King and Duke than his trial, for now the Earl of Bristol, finally determined to no longer obey the King's instructions to stay silent at his country estate, had applied to the House of Lords, and had been summoned by that body to appear before them, and now at long last Bristol had the opportunity to tell what he believed had really transpired in Madrid and to accuse the Duke of Buckingham.

Rutland feared that what he could say would prove very injurious to his daughter's husband, and the Earl was filled with foreboding for the future. The Venetian ambassador shared his thoughts, writing,

Recriminations continue between the Duke and Bristol, who accused the Duke of high treason. Before the Duke himself he brought forward many charges in matters of state and religion, as well as his vicious pleasures, especially in Spain. The Duke heard him quietly in complete silence and with self-command asked leave of the House to answer. He tried to persuade them of Bristol's ill-conduct, having perhaps spoken too boldly. He asked the House to punish the guilty, and if he were innocent to inflict a like punishment on the accuser. He excused his pleasures on the score of youth. He asked for silence at a distasteful matter, so as not to hurt his wife, saying that these things touched her and not others.

I visited the Duke of Buckingham. He responded to my offices with great respect. The pallor of his face betrays his deep uneasiness at the embarrassments in which he finds himself. He spoke of his affairs with temperate vigour, though he showed that his mind was tossed by a thousand agitations and about keeping the King to insist upon his authority in order to counteract the activities of the parliamentarians.

On the first day of the Duke's trial Kate had sat with tear-filled eyes as her father gently spoke of the proceedings. Buckingham had been indicted on eight long and complex charges, to which he had listened, sitting directly opposite his accusers, sometime with a shake of the head, sometime with a smile, though his colour changed several times as the charges were read, and only those who knew him well would have recognised that he was deeply affected; yet some said his attitude throughout was arrogant and proud, and Sir Dudley Digges opined that his Grace should be imprisoned, with which many of the House agreed.

'Arrested? But surely the King will not permit that?' exclaimed Kate, horrified.

'Do not be alarmed, daughter. I am certain his Majesty will never allow his favourite to be harmed.'

No indeed, and Rutland could not comprehend how the Commons could ever imagine that Charles would sacrifice his most beloved friend – his only friend. Did they not realise what manner of king they dealt with? Had the previous sessions taught them nothing? Had they not listened to the words he had spoken which made clear to all but the wilfully blind and deaf that the King was not capable of understanding the attacks on Buckingham as anything other than attacks upon himself and upon his royal prerogative? For Charles regarded himself and the Duke as one – his 'inseparable spirit' – to attack one was to attack both.

The next day the remaining three articles were presented, including the charge of poisoning his late Majesty King James, after which Sir John Eliot summed up, calling the Duke, 'the beast called by the ancients Stellionatus; a beast so blurred, so spotted, so full of foul lines, that they knew not what to make of it, and has consumed the revenues of the crown not only to satisfy his own lustful desires but the luxury of others, and by emptying the veins the blood should run in, he has cast the body of the kingdom in high consumption. The Duke is the canker which eats up the King's treasure, the moth which consumes all the goodness of the kingdom. His power is such that it can hardly be paralleled, except perhaps by that of Sejanus, the favourite of the Emperor Tiberius.'

On hearing these words Charles was at first too angry to speak, save remarking that if the Duke was Sejanus then doubtless he was Tiberius, but he could not allow such an insult to pass and he travelled by barge the next day from Whitehall to Westminster, with Buckingham, Rutland, Carlisle, Holland and Conway to address the Lords.

'I have been too remiss heretofore in punishing those insolent speeches that concerned myself, for that Buckingham, through his importunity, would not suffer me to take notice of them lest he might be thought to have set me on, and he might come on the forwarder to his trial, to approve his innocency,' the King told them, and shortly after Digges and Eliot were arrested and committed to the Tower.

The King's words had no effect, for the Upper House requested Buckingham's immediate imprisonment, but before it did so, it listened to another forceful and well-argued speech from the Duke, upon which the decision was made for a postponement of the request, and on 8th June the Duke presented a detailed reply to the charges. It was to no avail: his prosecutors listened stony faced. They had already decided that the Duke was guilty.

The day was sunny and warm when Rutland sought his daughter in the garden at Wallingford House, where she was enjoying the sweet fragrance of the flowers, and seeking to divert her tortured mind from events at nearby Westminster. The Earl sat down beside her, scooping up Mall and kissing her warm little cheek.

'You have news?' asked Katherine anxiously.

Her father nodded, 'Yes my dear.'

Telling the nurse to take her daughter and baby Charles inside, Kate waited until the nurse had extricated a reluctant Mall and they were alone before turning impatiently to her father.

'It is over. The King has dissolved Parliament and Bristol is sent to the Tower.'

'Oh praise God! Praise God! My lord is safe then?'

'For the present, yes.'

'For the present? But do you believe there is still some danger?'

Rutland carefully considered his reply. He knew full well that there was still danger: that his son-in-law had only survived because the King had intervened, for there was no doubt that he would have been found guilty of treason. And what would happen now? At some point Charles would be forced to summon Parliament for money to fund the war, and the whole sorry process would begin again. The Earl felt weary and old.

'Buckingham will always have his enemies Kate, that is to be expected, but fear not, he is safe,' he told her gently.

Yes, the Duke would always have his enemies, but now these enemies would never rest or be content until he was toppled and destroyed, even when the King was determined to save him. Despite his dislike of Buckingham, Rutland could not help admiring the younger man's courage, for he had been determined to face his opponents, confident in his ability to defend and explain himself and deeply hurt by being thought of as unpatriotic.

'It will make no difference what you say. They are determined to find you guilty and the outcome is already decided.' Rutland had told the Duke, when he had begged Charles not to dissolve Parliament. Buckingham had not understand this, any more than could Charles understand why his chief minister was being impeached, or indeed, why Parliament could not comprehend the irreparable damage their actions had caused to their relationship with their King in only the first year of his reign. A deputation of peers had besought the King to allow Parliament to sit for a few more days. 'Not another minute,' Charles had snapped. Both Houses had been used to the outbursts of temper from their former master King James, but ah, the anger of Charles! Nothing could match that terrifying icy cold, or the towering rages. The young King had learnt his father's lesson well of his divine right to rule, but had neither that crafty and wily old King's experience, or his cleverness to know how to deal with Parliament.

Nor was it only in Parliament that the Duke was attacked, for now his reputation with the populace was increasingly maligned, and the Earl had himself read several broadsheets criticising and condemning his power and influence, as well as increasing numbers of scurrilous songs and doggerel. It seemed that the mood of the country mirrored that of Parliament, and now the Duke was generally hated and held to be the cause of England's ills.

What was even more worrying was the violence of disaffected sailors who blamed Buckingham for their poverty, for one hundred and fifty sailors who served on board the last fleet in Spain, not having received their arrears, had attacked the Duke's coach with bludgeons while he was sitting in council, smashing and destroying it. Three companies of trained bands had immediately mounted guard at the court and taken the necessary precautions to safeguard the gates of the Duke's mansions.

The rioters were quieted by a little money from the mint, and next day a rigorous proclamation was issued, forbidding sailors and soldiers to quit their commanding officers in bodies or approach London save in small numbers, under pain of death. Rutland knew that they would return, and would only be silenced by money, but there *was* no money, and where could the King find more except by Parliament voting supplies? Despite the warmth of the sun Rutland shivered: he feared for the future; he feared for his family; most of all he feared for Buckingham. He would do all he could to support Kate and her husband, but most of all he would pray.

The Duke of Buckingham rolled off the naked body of Lady Carlisle, sighing contentedly. Lucy stretched languorously and turned to him, her slender fingers running over his smooth, toned chest.

'So have you considered my proposal?' her lover asked lazily, when he had recovered his breath, basking in a delicious torpor.

'I have.'

'And?'

Lucy bent over and lightly kissed Buckingham's lips, and smoothed the curls back over his forehead. 'And I have decided that I would be most honoured to be the King's mistress.'

The Duke grinned. 'Excellent. I will speak to his Majesty then, and inform you of his reply.'

Unlike Charles's failed relationship with Henriette, which had not improved despite the endeavours of the Marquis Francois de Bassompierrre, who had been sent by King Louis to mediate, the rift between Buckingham and Lady Carlisle over his affair with the French Queen had been healed. Although the favourite still dreamed about returning to France and possessing Anne, he was not the man to remain faithful to one woman, nor was Lucy foolish enough to give up her position as the mistress of the most powerful man in the realm, or become his enemy – of course if the King had sacrificed him, then she would have had to reconsider their relationship, but Lucy was astute enough to realise that Charles would never do that; more astute than Parliament.

Aware that his royal master's marriage was cold and unwelcoming, Buckingham had suddenly had the idea of placing his own mistress into the royal bed, guessing that she would be most amenable to an arrangement which could bring her more power, and he had broached the subject to the Earl of Carlisle, who was as obliging as ever. The Duke knew that this would consolidate his supremacy over the Queen, and admitted that he found the thought of himself and Charles swyving the same woman most exciting.

Buckingham reached over and drew Lucy to him. 'Of course,' he murmured, punctuating each word with a kiss all over her neck, 'that arrangement will not alter our own.'

Lucy smiled warmly, and as she responded to the Duke's renewed passion, all thoughts of other arrangements were temporarily forgotten.

Buckingham was disappointed though not particularly surprised that the King refused his offer, while confessing that he had been tempted by the idea, and thanking Steenie for his care of him. The Duke bowed his acceptance.

'Your decision reflects naught but credit upon yourself, your Majesty being renowned for your pure, chaste and temperate conduct and disposition. Yet e'en so virtuous a King has needs, and as your friend I would fain ease my concerns for your Majesty's lack of satisfaction in the marital bed, about which you have done me the great honour of confiding. Therefore, I trust my dear master will not take it amiss that I suggested this, and mayhap you will decide later to reconsider, but may I assure you once more that I am ever entirely your own – body, heart and soul – my greatest happiness being to serve and please you by whatever means whatsoever, as I did for the late king, your father.'

Charles was neither shocked nor displeased by Steenie's suggestion, nor did he think badly of him for his having mistresses, even though he was aware of the Duke's wanton reputation, which in another man he would have severely censured. It never occurred to the King to consider why he accepted his favourite's behaviour with unquestioning equanimity, or that the world looked on at his love for Buckingham and wondered why a man of such moral rectitude would be so in thrall and bestow such power upon one so lascivious and base. Witnesses had looked on with amazement at the king of England walking on foot while the Duke was carried in his box by six men to St. James's to tennis, or consenting to the play at Christmas being started again at the Duke's entering, even though the King had already seen one full act.

Buckingham's veiled offer of serving him by whatever means was not lost upon the King, and had his moral code and principles been less strict, then he might have considered the option, for he could not but be aware of his friend's extreme attractiveness and desire to please him. Charles regarded Steenie as a rare and exquisite being, whose behaviour was beyond the judgment of mere mortals; the most precious of his priceless collection, and one whom he would share with none other, neither would he ever surrender his chiefest jewel whose transcendent beauty was an altar at which Charles worshipped.

The wickedly cruel winter receded but slowly, holding the longed for spring at bay, and both the common populace in the taverns and those at court amused themselves with listening to the latest bawdy or scurrilous verses against the Duke of Buckingham, nor was there any shortage of material. Three fiddlers were brought before the Court of Star Chamber for singing a song to a well-known tune against the Duke:

> *The clean contrary,*
> *O the clean contrary way.*
> *Take him, Devil, take him.*

They were sentenced to pay a fine each and to be whipped and pilloried in Cheapside, Ware and Staines. Their punishment did not detract from the song's popularity. There was also much talk of a book entitled *The Devil and the Duke.*

As the Earl of Rutland had feared, there were other outbursts of violence by mobs of sailors. Three hundred came up for their wages, and smashed open the gate of the house of the Treasurer of the Navy, Sir William Russell, and worse followed when six captains who had served in Ireland, entered forcibly into the Duke's chamber at Whitehall as he sat at dinner, and threateningly demanded pay, only leaving when Buckingham promised them upon his honour that they should be speedily satisfied.

There were rumours of an expedition of ships and infantry; some said it was for the defence of Ireland, but others avowed that the troops and ships were bound for La Rochelle. Even more interesting was the speculation that the expedition would be commanded by none other than the Duke in person, though few believed at first that the hated favourite, who was generally regarded as an effeminate, degenerate fop, good for naught but lechery, dancing and profligacy, would ever seriously place himself at risk. Still less that the King who was so clearly besotted by him would allow him to go, (though the Queen prayed as fervently that he *would* go as the Duke's family prayed that he would not). Many believed it was sheer posturing, taking bets on the outcome, and were sure that he would take to his bed in sickness to prevent his leaving. When it seemed that Buckingham was in truth intending to command, he was further mocked in an outburst of song and rhyme.

> *Rejoice brave English gallants*
> *Whose ancestors won France,*
> *Our Duke of Buckingham is gone*
> *To fight and not to dance.*
> *Believe it; for our ladies*
> *His absence greatly mourn,*
> *And swear they'll have no babies*
> *Until he doth return.*

The Duke was too busy to pay too much attention. The incessant planning and work helping to dull the pain at the death of his only son and heir, the tiny body being buried in the Abbey at Westminster. The alliance betwixt England and France, ever precarious, had deteriorated to such an extent, with anger at the treatment of English Catholics and Louis's sister on the one side, and disgust at the intransigence and deception of the French, who had not only refused to join the anti-Habsburg league but were positively supporting Spain, that although war was not openly declared, the two nations edged slowly towards hostilities.

Each side seized the other's ships, and when the Protestant Huguenots at La Rochelle begged the English King for succour against the attacks of Louis and the Cardinal, both Buckingham and Charles believed it was their duty to come to their aid and at the same time strike a blow at France's ambitions for supremacy at sea, though the commonly believed reason was that the Duke had declared war over his passion for the French Queen.

The favourite had persuaded a reluctant Charles to allow him to command the expedition, saying truthfully that if he did not, his reputation, already much tarnished, would be damaged beyond repair. Buckingham was certain that if God would grant them a victory, then once more he would hailed as the saviour of his country; being more honoured and beloved of the Commons than ever the Earl of Essex had been. Charles had regretfully agreed to his command, and had been irritated at the importuning of both Steenie's wife and mother, who had begged him upon bended knee to prevent Buckingham's leaving. Offended at her familiarity, he had disdainfully withdrawn his hand from the Countess, who would have held it, weeping over it. The Duke's sister Susan, Countess of Denbigh, had likewise entreated her beloved brother to reconsider his decision, and not place himself in such danger, but he told her gently that go he must, though he was as sorry to see her grief as he had been sorry that he had not been able to persuade the youthful Marquis of Hamilton to consummate his marriage to Susan's daughter Mary. The whole affair was shockingly humiliating for the entire family and neither threats nor bribes would move the young man to return from Scotland.

That such a vast fleet should have been assembled in so short a time without recourse to Parliament was wondered at – the money being raised by forced loans, prize money from seized French ships and much from the Duke's own pocket. Buckingham's prodigious energy and organisation were acknowledged by few; more commented upon his ornate military garb, the poor state of the ships and their crews; many press-ganged and mutinous, and the excessive luxury of the favourite's cabin aboard his flagship *Triumph*. Indeed, it was reported that the Duke's cabin was heavily gilded, Persian carpets upon the floor and that there was an altar, upon which stood a portrait of Anne of Austria, with candles burning in front of it; a black and yellow ensign was flown at the main mast; that same queen's colours. People neither knew nor cared about Buckingham's attention to the welfare of his troops, having made much provision for drugs and medicaments, and as many surgeons, doctors and chaplains as could be found to accompany them, and plans were put into place for the care of wounded men upon their return.

Early in June Charles left for Portsmouth, Buckingham being detained at London, and the King inspected the fleet and dined aboard the *Triumph*, writing to Steenie to tell him how much he missed his company already. When Buckingham arrived, on learning that some of his officers had stayed on shore drinking, he took himself ashore and rounded up the culprits, handing them over to be court-martialled. Charles looked upon his beloved friend with pride and admiration, bidding him a passionate and emotional farewell. The great fleet set sail to the accompaniment of cheers and music, the slight form of the King standing in the cool summer breeze, but in the streets and taverns of Portsmouth the Duke's name was cursed by the families of those men forced to sail with him to an undeclared war about which they knew little and cared less. All would have concurred with the anonymous sentiments,

> *And wilt thou go, great Duke, and leave us here,*
> *Lamenting thee and eke thy pupil dear*
> *Great Charles? Alas! Who shall his sceptre sway,*
> *And kingdom rule now thou art gone away?*
> *Are there no whores in court to stay thee? Must*
>
> *Thy hate to France and Spain exceed thy Lust?*
> *Hast thou no Niece to marry? Cannot an Inn*
> *Or bawdy house afford thee any kin*
> *To cuckold Lords withal? Hast thou not a Foe*
> *To poison here at home? And wilt thou go*

And think the kingdom plagu'ed sufficiently?
Most graceless Duke, we thank thy charity,
Wishing the Fleet such speed, as thou but lost,
Though we be conquered, we have quitted cost.

'Here's to the death of the devil Duke, and may his satanic master carry his rotten soul to hell,' spat an elderly man, saved only from being pressed-ganged by his age, unlike his unfortunate son and grandson.

His companions joined him in his toast. 'Here's to his death.'

Chapter Twelve

> *Who rules the kingdom?*   The King
> *Who rules the King?*   The Duke
> *Who rules the Duke?*   The Devil

Katherine Villiers, Duchess of Buckingham lay in her bed, unable to sleep, her hand cradling her great belly protectively. Finally, sighing deeply, she arose, and pulling a warm gown around her against the November chill, she took up paper to write her husband yet another letter.

My Lord,
Since I heard the news of your landing, I have been still every hour looking for you, that I cannot now till I see you, sleep in the nights, for every minute, if I do hear any noise, I think it is a letter from you, to tell me the happy news what day I shall see you, for I confess I long for it with much impatience. I was in great hope that the business you had to do at Portsmouth would 'a been done in a day, then I should 'a seen you here tomorrow, but now I cannot tell when to expect you. My Lord, there has been such ill reports made of the great loss you have had, by the man that came first, as your friends desire you would come to clear all with all speed. You may leave some of the Lords there to see what you give order for done, and you need not stay yourself any longer. Thus beseeching you to come hither on Sunday or Monday without fail, I rest your
    True loving and obedient wife,
        K. Buckingham.

The Duke had neither written nor sent word to his wife since his return. Few awaited him with such eagerness, for of the great fleet of a hundred ships which had gone forth with such hopes, carrying six thousand infantry and a thousand cavalry, only three thousand men had returned, and over half that amount had to be carried ashore. Katherine's heart ached at the pain she knew her lord would feel. 'It was not his fault, it was not his fault,' she told herself over and over, but she knew that he would be blamed. Buckingham had come tantalisingly close to success, but bad judgment, lack of experience and ill luck had snatched that from his hand almost when victory seemed assured. Had the supply ships reached them in time, then mayhap matters might have taken a different turn, and the Duke might even now be the darling of the nation once more as he so longed to be.

Kate rubbed her weary eyes. Her head throbbed, and her child stirred restlessly as though it knew its father's perils were still not over, despite the King's enduring love for him. Kate's anger at her husband had long since gone: he had promised her that he would not command the expedition himself, but would return from Portsmouth after seeing the fleet leave, as she would give him no peace until he so swore, and her wild grief made him fearful for her health, and for the new life she carried, which he prayed would be a son, for after baby Charles's death he had spent more time in his wife's bed, desperate for another heir.

Worn down by Kate's avowals that she would die of grief if he left, Buckingham had sworn that he would not go, but it was impossible for him to keep his promise, and while understanding her fears, he was angered that Katherine would not support him, feeling that her words seemed as black-mail. Kate had believed him, even when he had boarded the *Triumph*; she was sure he would return, and wrote passionately to him, urging him to remember his promise, for if he did not, the grief would kill her. When she finally realised that he had gone, her anger and pain knew no bounds.

My Lord,

Now as I too plainly see you have deceived me, and if I judge you according to your own words I must condemn you not only in this but in your action you so much forswore. For my part I have been a very miserable woman hitherto, that never could have you keep at home, but now I will ever look to be so till some blessed occasion comes to draw you quite from the court, for there is non more miserable than I am, and till you leave this life of a courtier which you have been ever since I knew you, I shall think myself unhappy. I am the unfortunest of all other, that even when I am with child, I must have so much cause of sorrow as to have you go from me, but I never had so great a cause of grief as now. I hope God of his mercy give me patience, and if I were sure my soul would be well I could wish myself to be out of this miserable world, for till then I shall not be happy.

Now I will no more write to hope you do not go, but must betake myself to my prayers for your safe and prosperous journey, which I will not fail to do, and for your quick return; but never, whilst I live, will I trust you again, nor never will put you to your oath for anything again. I pray God never woman may love a man as I have done you that non may feel that which I have done for you. I would to Jesus that there were in any way in the world to fetch you out of the journey with honour; if any prayers or any suffering of mine could do it I were a most happy woman, but you have sent yourself and made me miserable. God forgive you for it.

Your poor grieved and obedient wife,
K. Buckingham.

Katherine's father tried to calm her, for Buckingham had written to him explaining himself, and for once Rutland had agreed with him, but she had an ally with the Countess of Buckingham, who had castigated her son for not only going to war and risking his life, but for his deception towards his wife, telling him that Kate could no longer believe a word he said.

Katherine's eagerness to see the Duke was no greater than the King's, who had spent the months of the expedition in a misery of worry, writing of his love and support, and asking Buckingham's forgiveness at the delays of the supply ships. Charles had been notably unsure of himself without Buckingham by his side, and an ambassador commented that he appeared as an actor on stage without a script. Relations with Henriette had been friendlier in the absence of the favourite and Charles had told Buckingham of this, little realising that his letter had plunged the Duke into a black depression. Worried that victory was slipping away as the time passed and his men died from sickness or their wounds; ravaged as they were by disease, afflicted by agues and rheums, and some polt-footed and shitten-legged with the flux; his eyes ever searching the horizon for the promised supplies, and now believing that the detested French bitch was usurping his position when he was far away; Buckingham truly felt that he would prefer to die there rather than return home to find himself replaced.

He had written to the King, saying that he feared himself and his men forgotten, and Charles, alarmed at the despair from the normally ebullient Buckingham, had been at pains to assure him of his constant love. When he learnt that the fleet had been forced to retreat he had told his friend,

> *With whatever success you shall come to me, you shall be ever welcome, one of my greatest griefs being that I have not been with you in this time of suffering, for I know we would have much eased each other's grief. I cannot stay much longer on this subject, for fear of losing myself in it. To conclude, you cannot come so soon as you are welcome, and unfeignedly in my mind, you have gained as much reputation, with wise and honest men, in this action, as if you*

had performed all your desires. I have no more to say at this time, but conjure thee, for my sake, to have a care for thy health, for every day I find new reasons to confirm me in being,
Your loving, faithful, constant friend,
Charles R.
You cannot come before you are welcome, which I leave to you. The sooner, I think, the better, at least best pleasing to me.

The Duke was met by the Lord Chamberlain with a letter and jewelled bracelet from the King, and by jeers and curses from the assembled crowds, many waiting for men who would never return. Bedecked in jewels, his hair and beard carefully coiffured, he was lean and tanned, though the blue eyes had dark circles beneath them, and the fine cheek bones stood out in the handsome, smiling face. Buckingham was taken straight way to the King, who could scarcely contain his impatience to see him once more, and the two fell into each other's arms.

'Steenie, oh my love,' cried the King. The Duke knelt before his royal master and kissed his hand, then Charles raised him up, and arms entwined about each other, they retired into the seclusion of the King's bedchamber, where they both spent the night. Looking at the Duke's unconcerned gaiety none would have guessed that he sobbed his heart out in Charles's arms, weeping out his sorrow, shame and pain, while the King kissed his tears away, assuring him that none had behaved more nobly and he had naught to reproach himself for. Hearing of his welcome, the Queen retired to her bed for several days.

If the Duke had been detested before, he was now hated and vilified, and his coming home safe caused almost as much sorrow as the loss of all the rest, occasioning a pouring out of derisory rhymes and songs about his Grace and the Isle of Rhé, now called by some the Isle of Rue, in which he was accused of effeminacy and cowardice, even to the degree of saying that he was in league with the French and it was a popish plot.

> *And art return'd again with all thy faults,*
> *Thou great commander of the al – goe-naughts,*
> *And left the isle behind thee; what's the matter?*
> *Did winter make thy teeth begin to chatter?*
> *Could not the surging and distemper'd seas*
> *Thy queasy stomach gorg'd with sweetmeats please?*

The Duke heard these taunts. It was impossible for them to be kept from him, so universal were they. They hurt him, particularly the label of coward, for none of his men could have accused him of that and had acknowledged that he had behaved with uncommon bravery, sharing the same privations and running the same risk of being killed or wounded, even to the extent of insisting he was the last off the island. Buckingham was afire to return – *this* time they would succeed, *this* time they would be prepared and would know what to expect. The news was received with disbelief at first, but then it was confirmed that the King and Duke were resolved to repair the army and the fleet, discussing these matters at meetings of the Privy Council, where his Majesty gave approval that a fleet of one hundred ships be prepared – though where the money was to found was a question none could answer. Buckingham's mother received the news with appalled shock, and for once that redoubtable lady could not speak. Katherine raged.

'No! I cannot believe you would so risk yourself again! Shall I be ever forced to live in grief and despair? You will be killed for certain, and then what of myself and your children?'

The new year had brought the joy of another son, a fine, lusty boy, who was named George, to whom the King stood godfather, and though the Duke was still concerned at the proceedings against Lady Purbeck, he no longer feared that her by-blow would receive his titles had George been a daughter, for to his great relief and gratitude, Charles had declared that if Buckingham died without a male heir, then his daughter Mary would inherit his titles and wealth. After a legal proceeding, Frances had been found guilty of adultery, and sentenced to do public penance, bare-footed, and clad in a white sheet, in the chapel of the Savoy. However, the penance never took place, for she escaped in disguise, aided by the ambassador of Savoy, to Buckingham's great fury, and she later sought refuge in France.

Henriette was surprised to hear that her husband the King intended to recall Parliament.

'I am sure it cannot be true,' she said to her Ladies of her Bedchamber.

'Oh but indeed it is, your Majesty,' replied Lady Carlisle, ignoring the glares of the Countess of Buckingham.

'How so? I did not expect the King to risk Milord Boukinkan to his enemies.'

Lucy smiled at her mistress, despite that Henriette had been forced to accept her services, along with the Buckingham women, the Queen had grown to like her, even become fond of her, enjoying her companionship, gaiety and glamour, and taking her advice on fashion and painting the face. Equally importantly, she had found in Lucy an ally against the Duke's kin who hated her as Buckingham's mistress, and, as in this case, Lucy was privy to much of what went on at court.

'His Grace himself persuaded the King to recall Parliament, though his Majesty was loath so to do.'

'No! But why would the Duke risk himself again?'

Lucy shrugged. 'Why else but for money? The fleet must be equipped, but it is impossible to do this again without recourse to Parliament, and Buckingham and the King are determined that the fleet will return to La Rochelle.'

'But Boukinkan's enemies?'

'The King extracted guarantees that the Duke would not be named during the sessions.'

'Ah! And how do you know this, my dear Lucy?'

Lady Carlisle smiled again, she had heard from her lover, Buckingham himself, but merely replied, 'oh I have my sources.'

Henriette smiled back, knowing full well the name of the source. The Countess of Buckingham could restrain herself no longer.

'Oh yes, we can guess your source, Madam! I wonder what that source would say if he knew of your tittle tattle?'

'My source confides in me fully about *all* aspects of his life, and you might be surprised at what I know about everyone and everything – including his family,' replied Lucy coolly.

Mary opened her mouth to make a crushing retort, but then remembered that she must not name her son, even though everyone in the chamber knew who was being discussed, and were listening intently. Angrily she continued her sewing, accidentally stabbing her finger.

'Why, my lady, I hope you have not injured yourself. Do you wish to withdraw and lie down, for to be sure, you appear most flushed and discomfited?' asked Henriette.

'No, no, your Majesty, though I thank you kindly. I am by no means discomfited, indeed *I* have no need to be discomfited. I thank God that *my* behaviour does not merit censure, nor will you find *me* partaking in idle gossip.'

'I hope your ladyship is not suggesting that the Queen partakes in gossip,' said Lucy archly, one eyebrow raised.

Mary bridled. 'Most certainly not!' she snapped.

'I was sure that you could not have meant that, but do take care with that needle, for at your age the eyes are weak and I would be most grieved for your ladyship to injure your finger again,' replied Lucy silkily, looking at Henriette whose dark eyes were sparkling with amusement.

Mary sat bowed over her embroidery, silently fuming. She would have liked to speak to her son about this, but the last time she had reported some comment of Lady Carlisle's to him, he had just laughed.

'She is most indiscreet, particularly now she has the Queen's ear. You are a fool to trust her George.' She had taxed him, 'before you know it she will even be divulging what you do in bed to all the world.'

'Well, I doubt that she has aught to complain of in that direction,' returned her son.

Really, the Countess muttered to herself, as regards that Carlisle woman, Buckingham undoubtedly suffers from a surfeit of lust.

The Duke of Buckingham's golden coach, pulled by six horses, passed along the Strand; the first man in England to travel thus, and in more grandeur than a king.

'There he goes – his graceless bloody Grace,' spat out one man in the crowd watching him.

Suddenly a thin faced, dishevelled woman sprang forward, hurling mud at the coach. The Duke glanced out of the spattered window in surprise, and the woman looked full into the eyes of the man she regarded as the destroyer of her happiness. It was hard enough to be a widow, but because of this man her two sons had been press-ganged while visiting relatives in Plymouth, and had not returned. Staring up at the blue eyes and proud handsome face, she wondered how it was possible for one so fair to be guilty of such heinous sins. Her face contorting with anger, she spewed forth invective born of her pain and despair.

'Murderer! Monster! Coward! You let my boys die while you ran away!' she screamed.

The captain of the guards nodded at a nearby soldier, who moved forward to restrain and arrest the woman. Once none would have even dared to raise their eyes to the great favourite, let alone their fists, but now he was always accompanied by an armed guard, on the King's orders. She was dragged away roughly, still screaming.

'Coward! Murderer! My sweet boys' bones lie a-mouldering at the bottom of the stinking mud at the Isle of Rue!'

The crowd suddenly surged forward, cursing, throwing mud, stones and any rubbish that came to hand. Temporarily unable to move through the mob, the Duke could clearly hear the insults. He showed no reaction other than to grasp the hilt of his sword firmly and to lift the silver pomander which hung from his belt to his nose to disguise the noisome stench emanating from the sweating, seething rabble.

'Devil Duke! Coward! Satan's whore! Anti-Christ!'

The guards plunged into the crowd, slashing and hacking, dispersing them sufficiently to allow the coach to move on, the footman wiping his bleeding face.

Later in the taverns the incident was discussed, for the Duke was now the main topic of conversation up and down the length of the realm.

'That poor woman isn't the only one – there'll be many suffer who've lost their men-folk, or have husbands and sons who will never be able to work again.'

'True enough, but does his Grace care? Not he.'

'No more does the King. And now it all begins again – there's to be another bloody fleet sent and yet more carnage. God's stones! And for what? All because that degenerate butt firker Buckingham has an itch to swyve the French queen! Though from what I hear he's already occupied her, and she's had his bastard. I tell you, there'll scarcely be a man left alive in the country, and those that do survive will be maimed!'

There was a murmur of agreement, and another added, 'And all this because of a man being favoured because of his face and his arse, a man not nobly born, with no more ability to command than you or I.'

'And is he as handsome as they say? Are his clothes so fine?'

His companion shrugged, wiping his mouth with his hand. 'Never seen the bugger. But I do remember my father telling me not to be taken in by beauty, for even Lucifer himself was once as beautiful as an angel – just like our Steenie boy – another fallen angel.'

'Belike he is buggered by Satan himself,' sniggered another, to general merriment.

'But what hold has he over his Majesty King Charles?'

The tallest man looked at him with raised eyebrows. 'What do you think?'

'Surely not. I know the old King loved young lads, but I hear his Majesty is a chaste, godly young man.'

'Godly or no, he spends all his time with Buckingham – *all* his time, and 'tis said he lives apart from Queen Mary – leastways they've been married three years and no sign of an heir. Nor will there be while the Duke lives, if you ask me.'

'I hear that it is by witchcraft that the Duke binds the King to his will,' whispered another. 'There's talk of one Piers Butler, an Irishman, in the employ of the Duke, who has said that Parliament can do naught to the Duke, nor will he lose the King's favour so long as he keep some type of amulet about his person, which Butler has himself made with the distillation of toads, *and* the Duke's magician Doctor Lambe has made him an aphrodisiac so he can seduce all the women in the land.'

There was nodding of heads. 'There has to be some reason why he is able to rule the King. I only wish his Majesty would heed this jig I heard last week. It goes like this:

> *Charles would ye prevail your foes, thine better Luck*
> *Send forth some Drake and keep at home the Ducke.*

'Well all I know is that we're ruled by a mad-man who's ruled by a useless pox-ridden Ganymede who only knows how to dance, fuck, and spend money. We'll have no peace or prosperity in this country while he lives.'

'Aye,' shouted a woman, 'a plague upon him and his kin! Let him return to the Isle of Rue, and the whole country'll pray that a musket ball will take off his pretty head! And then he can entertain his master the devil with dancing.'

Many others joined in, laughing and agreeing with the sentiment, but some, less drunk, moved away in alarm. One man, an informer, finished his drink and slunk out, and next day most of the group were arrested. It made no difference – those punished were regarded as martyrs, and in Plymouth a gallows upon which mutineering sailors were to be hanged was torn down and thrown into the sea.

Katherine had gradually become aware of the noise outside York House, and had sent a servant to find out what it was. He had rushed back in, his face sweating and fearful.

'It is a vast mob, your Grace, with bludgeons and brickbats. They are swarming around the gates; more sailors I think.'

'Do you think the gates will hold?' she asked, her heart contracting with fear.

There was a tremendous shouting and the sound of shot. William Ward, the steward of the household, hurriedly entered the room.

'They have thrown down the gates, my lady. You must take shelter upstairs.'

Kate picked up a whimpering Mall while baby George's wet nurse carried him, and they and her ladies ran upstairs. Ward directed the other male servants to stand guard in the hall, instructing some to fetch water in case of fires. He and Buckingham's secretary returned outside to face the clamouring mob. There were the sounds of windows being smashed, and chanting.

'Where is he then, our brave admiral? Send him out and let him face us! We want what's due us, or else we'll tear this place down and string him up!'

Katherine stopped on the first floor landing, listening to Ward's attempts to reason with them. 'The Duke is not here. Leave now and I promise in his Grace's name that he will do all he can to ensure you receive your pay.'

'We've heard that before! It's all lies. If we can't have money then we'll take what's in there.' There was a shout of agreement, and more breaking glass.

Kate stood petrified, unable to move or think, Mall clinging to her dress and her ladies weeping in terror. Oh why had her lord decided to reduce the guard at York House? Ward appeared, blood and dung clinging to his face.

'Quickly, your Grace, upstairs to the servants' chambers.'

Katherine turned and ran upstairs in blind obedience. Inside

Ward and the secretary barricaded the door with the heavy bed that the female servants slept in. Katherine fell upon her knees babbling in terror.

'Oh Holy Virgin! O Lady Mary! Protect us! Help us, I beseech you! And save my dear lord.' She feared that her prayers would fall on deaf ears, for how many times had her importuning gone unanswered – were her prayers unheeded because of her sin in choosing her husband before her religion?

Mall stood beside her, her thumb in her mouth, too frightened to make a sound, unlike her brother who was bawling lustily, refusing to be comforted by his nurse's breast. William Ward stood at the door, pistol in hand: not for the intruders whom he feared would shortly be in the house, but for the Duchess and her children, and finally for himself; for he could not allow them to fall into the hands of men so desperate that he doubted not that they would take out their revenge on the Duke's family.

The room slowly darkened as the small group stood in silence, holding hands for comfort, never had time passed so slowly. Even at the top of York House they could still hear the smashing of glass, the assaults upon the doors, the shouting and chanting.

'Oh sweet Jesu! What is happening? Are there even more of them? Are they in the house?' cried Katherine, her eyes huge in her white face.

Ward shook his head. 'I know not, my lady,' he answered but privately he feared the worst, for the rioting and sounds of gun shot outside the house were escalating.

They waited breathlessly, then heard the sound of feet stampeding up the steps. 'Oh God, they are here,' thought Ward. Throughout all the rooms there was a thundering upon the doors. He ordered them back, pistol raised.

'Kate! Kate! Where are you?' cried the voice of the Duke.

'It is my lord!' exclaimed Katherine, bursting into tears.

'God be praised,' said the nurse, faintly.

The bed was flung aside, and then Buckingham was in the room. He swept his wife into his arms, kissing her face and murmuring over and over, 'oh Kate. Oh my sweet Kate. Whatever would I have done if you had been harmed?'

'Daddy?' Buckingham looked down at his six year old daughter, and scooped her up, kissing her tear-stained face. 'All is well, my Mall, be not afeared. Daddy will not allow the naughty men to harm you.'

'Tomorrow you will go to Burley, no, to New Hall, no, to Belvoir; you will be safe there,' he told Katherine.

'No! I will not leave you.' replied Kate, clutching him.

'I cannot risk this happening again. You will be safe with your family.'

Katherine shook her head. 'I shall not be separated from you, and even though I owe you my obedience, I swear that if I am taken there, then I shall return.'

The Duke's tall frame bent over his wife, and he pulled her to him. 'I do not deserve so good a wife.'

The King's anger at hearing of this outrage was terrible to behold. 'They will be hanged, drawn and quartered,' he vowed in icy tones.

At the opening of the King's third Parliament on the 17th March 1628, the atmosphere was as chilly as the cold wind which buffeted Westminster Hall. The chamber was unusually silent, the acrid tension almost palpable; the members quietly seething at the injunction that Buckingham was not to be attacked or even named, and at the sight of the man that was thought the reason and cause of all that ailed the realm, all smiling graciousness, John Eliot gnawed his lips till the blood ran. 'Insufferable!' he muttered.

The King's speech made clear that his Majesty was not willing to compromise, and although his speech impediment was noticeable, it could not disguise his intent.

> *Now is the time for action, and so I will n-not multiply words. Following my example I hope you will decide properly because time presses and we must not waste it upon unnecessary or rather dangerous things, as long discussions*

in the present state of Christendom are almost as hurtful as deciding nothing.

I know that you expect to hear from me the reasons why you have been summoned, but I know also that none of you can suppose there is any other reason besides the common peril, which requires your prompt help. I will not therefore insist upon persuasion because if the support of the true faith, the laws and liberty of this realm, the defence of our friends and allies are not enough to give vigour to your resolutions, I am certain that n-no tongue of man or angel will do so. Let me only remind you that my duty and yours is to maintain this Church and State. God never before urged this duty so strongly. We know that Parliament is the true, ancient and proper way to obtain help for ourselves and our allies and we have therefore convoked it, urging everyone to be ruled by his own conscience. If you should refuse this, which God forbid, which the needs of the realm demand in a time of common peril, I shall be constrained to take other means, which God hath placed in my hands, in order to preserve what others will risk losing for the sake of their private passions.

I ask you not to take this as a protest, as I should disdain to threaten those who are not my equals, but as an admonition from one who naturally has a greater care for your preservation. I hope your decisions will be such that I may have to thank you cordially and meet you frequently in this place. I assure you that I have nothing more at heart than good relations with you.

You may think that I come to this place with great misgivings about your decisions seeing what happened at the last Parliament, but I hope that you and I together shall have reason to forget it totally, as if we proceed in unity of spirit and will, I shall be as ready and glad to forget as you perchance may have occasion to wish me to do so.

However, the members of the Nether House had more anxieties for the threat to their rights and liberties than any threat from abroad, Sir Robert Phelipps saying that he more feared the violation of public rights at home than a foreign army, a sentiment echoed by Sir Edward Coke, who asserted that he feared not foreign enemies, and prayed God would send them peace at home. Endless debates followed upon the subject of grievances, and in particular the great unrest caused by the forcible billeting of soldiers, and despite several interventions sent from the King by Sir John Coke to make an early vote of supply; the House doggedly continued the discussion of grievances.

There had been a deliberate avoidance of the subject of the Duke of Buckingham, though implicit criticism, but now the subject of supply was finally addressed, though in this the House was divided; with some members pressing to show his Majesty goodwill and others reluctant to oblige whilst the King remained so much in thrall to the Duke. It was agreed that five subsidies should be voted in due course, with which Charles was much delighted, but his joy did not long continue, upon the realization that the Commons was engaged in discussions with the Upper House on the subject of preserving the liberties of the subjects, and would not commit to grant the subsidies. With the King pressing for the speedy granting of supply and giving notice that he was resolved to bring the session of Parliament to an end, Sir Edward Coke suggested Parliament should proceed with their grievances by way of a Petition of Right, wherein they could list grievances and ask for confirmation that the same were against the law, the main items being a formal request to the King that he would not order forced loans, arrest without showing cause, the subject of the billeting of soldiers and commissions of martial law.

Charles received the petition, caustically telling the members, 'you will find as much security in his Majesty's royal word and power as in the strength of any law you can make.'

Nonetheless he accepted the petition, but without giving the usual form of assent – the King had reserved the right to change his mind; giving the substance without the form.

Now the floodgates were opened, and Sir John Eliot took up his attack once again upon Buckingham, saying that the King knew not what was happening in his realm, and therefore it was the duty of the House, as the great council of the kingdom, to inform him, by way of a Remonstrance.

'The Duke of Buckingham is the cause of all our miseries,' he thundered to tumultuous applause, 'that man is the grievance of grievances.'

Furious and fearful that once more Steenie was being attacked, Charles reluctantly accepted the petition in the time-honoured form, turning away with curled lip at the news of the celebrations of bonfires and fireworks, the greatest since his return from Madrid, though many of the populace believed the Duke had fallen and were wild with joy. It was reported that a gang of young men had demolished and burnt the old scaffold at Tower Hill in preparation for a new one for the Duke. Yet Parliament still had not finished, and to the King's outraged disbelief, the attack upon the Duke intensified when the Commons presented a Remonstrance listing their grievances which ended by calling upon the King to consider whether it be safe for his Majesty and his kingdom to continue the Duke either in his great offices or in his place of nearness and counsel about his sacred person.

The King listened with barely concealed anger, his face white and tight lipped, his fingers impatiently tapping his cane, and then he spoke coldly of his astonishment that the House should be of such an impertinence as to assume that they knew more of state affairs than he himself. The Duke, also pale-faced and serious, threw himself upon his knees and begged leave to reply to the accusations, but Charles lifted him to his feet, and gave him his hand to kiss, saying, 'I am fully satisfied of your innocency, Steenie.'

Refusing to back down, the House began drawing up another Remonstrance and upon hearing this the King arrived unexpectedly in the Upper House, and sitting upon the throne, sent for the

Lower House, declaring that he would in no wise receive any more remonstrances, and would therefore end this session after giving assent to completed bills which included the granting of five subsidies.

Throughout that hot, fetid, plague-ridden summer of 1628, England seethed and writhed as a beast in pain, desperate to free itself of its sufferings – and none had any doubt as to the cause of that pain – Buckingham. Now there was scarcely any topic of conversation but of the Duke as the national obsession and paranoia grew until it assumed a life of its own. In June Dr. John Lambe was set upon and hacked and beaten to death by a London mob after visiting the Windmill Tavern in Lothbury, calling him the Duke's devil and avowing that if the Duke his master had been there, they would have handled him worse, and would have minced his flesh and have had every one a bit of him.

The next day another tale was told that after dinner, the King and the Duke were at bowls in the Spring garden, and the Duke put on his hat. A Scottish man, named Wilson, seeing it, kissed his hand, and snatched the hat off, saying, 'you must not stand with your hat on before my King.' The Duke turned to kick him, but the King said, 'Let him be, George, he is either mad or a fool.' 'No Sir,' returned Wilson, 'I am a sober man, but this man's health is pledged with as much devotion at Dunkirk, as your Majesty's here.'

The stories grew wilder and more lurid: portents were seen everywhere prophesying the Duke's death. At the same time that Dr. Lambe died, the Duke's picture fell down in the High Commission chamber at Lambeth; the Duke had such a severe nose-bleed that the Lord Keeper's mace was clapped upon his neck to staunch the blood; a self-styled prophetess called Lady Eleanor Davis, foretold he would die in August. It was even claimed that the spirit of his father, Sir George Villiers, had returned from the grave to warn his son of his fate if he did not repent and turn aside from his sinful ways.

One popular rhyme was put to music and sung all over London.

> *There is a man, a Plague upon him*
> *Who hath ta'en many things upon him.*
> *Papists, Protestants, curse and ban him*
> *The Devil his Father scarce can stand him*
> *The Lower House they did thunder it.*
>
> *The Upper House they did grumble it,*
> *His neck from his shoulders they could not sunder it,*
> *And this from his country folks we gather*
> *He came to the court and grew Cup-bearer,*
> *Unto the King he still grew nearer,*
> *In his eye he seemed a Pearl.*
>
> *Sat down a viscount and rose up an Earl,*
> *Indeed he had a very fair face*
> *Which was the cause he came in grace.*
> *Fairly he could trip a Gallyard*
> *And please the ladies with his tallyard*
>
> *I wish when death undoes him*
> *He may rest in the Devil's bosom.*

The King and Buckingham rode in the royal coach to Deptford, to see the ships, where, having seen ten ships ready rigged for Rochelle, Charles told Steenie, 'George, there are some that wish that these and you might both perish. But care not for them; we will both perish together, if you do.'

Now at every corner and in every tavern the portents were discussed, men laying bets on whether Buckingham would outlive the year. Everywhere could be heard the chant:

> *Let Charles and George do what they can,*
> *The Duke shall die like Dr. Lambe.*

Kate could not fail to hear it, even though her father and husband tried to make light of it. At York House she heard it sung raucously or whistled by the wherry men in their incessant journeys up and down the Thames. At the front of the house along the Strand she could hear it still, and as the stinking, rotting stench emanating from the banks of the river stole into the great mansion despite the best efforts of the servants to keep the rooms smelling sweet, the words filled her head during the day and at night they crept into her dreams.

'The Duke shall die, the Duke shall die.'

'Oh do not go!' she begged Buckingham. 'Leave London. Let us go to New Hall, let us go anywhere. Let another take command.'

'I cannot, Kate, it is my duty. Would you have me live without honour?'

'Better that than not live at all,' she wept, her face all blubbed with tears.

'I have no choice Kate! Can you *still* not comprehend that it is only the King's love for me which keeps me from the block?' retorted her husband, gripping her shoulders.

The Duke's family and friends urged him to wear a mail shirt under his doublet, but he refused, saying he would not live in fear of any man. Again, Katherine, his mother and sister besought the King to command him not to depart to La Rochelle, and again the King dismissed their pleas. Yet now, Charles himself was becoming anxious.

'The Countess of Buckingham and the Duchess have had an audience with me beseeching me to forbid you to command the expedition,' he told Buckingham.

'Yes, I know. I beg you will forgive their importuning, it is done for love of me,' the favourite replied.

Charles smiled, and passed his arm through the Duke's. 'I cannot fault them for their affection toward you Steenie, and I will confess that I am uneasy in my own mind about your leaving.'

Buckingham looked at him in surprise, and the King continued, 'No one knows your valour and nobility of heart better than I, sweetheart, but the mission will be fraught with peril, and while I know your stout heart will neither quake at the dangers nor shrink from them, I will speak truth and tell you that my own heart *does* quake.'

Charles turned and cupped his friend's face, feeling the familiar love and pain. 'Steenie, I dare not even begin to think of what my life would be like without you. Please reconsider your decision.'

Buckingham took one of his master's hands and held it tightly. 'If you command me not to go, then I will obey you.'

'I have never commanded you Steenie, nor will I begin to do so now, but as your friend, not as your King, I ask you to appoint another in your place.'

The Duke brought the King's hand to his lips. 'I have as much reason to fear death as any man; I know I am not immortal, but for your honour as well as my own, I must go – matters are too far gone for me to be able to back out now. It is the only possible course open to us, and I love you too well to take any other.'

'Then so be it. You will take my heart as well as my prayers for your safety and the expedition's success.'

On 17th July the King left London for Portsmouth, reluctantly leaving Buckingham behind to complete the final arrangements. He stayed at Southwick House near Southsea in Hampshire, the home of Sir Daniel Norton, spending his time inspecting the fleet, hunting and writing to Steenie. By August 12th the Duke was satisfied that all was ready for the fleet's departure, and had sent a message to the besieged and by now desperate Rochellese, saying, 'hold out but three weeks, and God willing I will be with you either to overcome or to die there.' Buckingham left London accompanied by Katherine who refused to allow him to slip away this time, and his brother Kit's wife.

A week later a small, pock-faced man dressed in a shabby uniform left his drab lodgings in Fleet Street, slowly made his way in the summer heat to Tower Hill, and entered one of the many cutlers' shops. He stood hesitantly as though uncertain of what to do, and the shop owner watched him out of the corner of his eye.

'You buying that knife or not?' he asked him.

'Buying. How much is it?'

'Ten pence.'

He nodded, handing over the money with his good hand, and slipped the knife inside his pocket. Hunched up as though cold, despite the humid weather, he walked to the parish church of St. Dunstan's-in-the-West. He entered the cool, sour smelling building and knelt down, praying long and earnestly, leaving his name to be prayed for as a man much discontented in his mind. Outside it had started to rain, but he scarcely noticed. Intent only on the journey before him, he pulled his hat further over his eyes and turned his grim face toward the long road to Portsmouth.

Epilogue

The glories of our blood and state,
Are shadows, not substantial things,
There is no armour against fate,
Death lays his icy hand on Kings.
Sceptre and Crown,
Must tumble down,
And in the dust be equal made,
With the poor crooked sithe and spade.

The Garlands wither on your brow,
Then boast no more your mighty deeds,
Upon Death's purple Altar now,
See where the Victor-victim bleeds,
Your heads must come,
To the cold Tomb,
Only the actions of the just
Smell sweet, and blossom in their dust.

James Shirley (1596-1666)

Tuesday, 30th January, 1649

The scaffold was draped in black. In the centre stood the block; a mere six inches in height and near it lay the axe. Four heavy iron staples had been driven into the floor in case the accused struggled against his fate and needed to be tied down. A cheap six shilling coffin lay to one side ready to receive the corpse. The area outside the Banqueting House was crowded with those who had come to watch their King die.

Immediately around the scaffold stood a row of pikemen; troops on horseback mingled with the crowds and were positioned at either end of the street. Many clambered upon the roofs of nearby houses to watch the last scene of the great drama played out. The scaffold was crowded with people, their breath steaming in a cold so intense that the Thames was frozen over. Parliamentarians Colonel Tomlinson and Colonel Hacker were there along with several soldiers and two shorthand writers to record the King's last words.

King Charles had given his speech, though few had heard it. He spoke to the two headsmen who were heavily disguised, for the usual axeman had refused to carry out the execution and others had to be found. Then Bishop William Juxon helped him push his long hair under a silken cap.

'I have a good cause, and a gracious God on my side,' the King told him.

'There is but one stage more,' answered the Bishop, 'which though troublesome and turbulent, yet it is a very short one. You may consider that it will carry you a very great way – it will carry you from earth to heaven, and there you shall find to your great joy, the prize you hasten to – a crown of glory.'

'I go from a corruptible to an incorruptible crown, where no disturbance can be, no disturbance in the world,' replied the King calmly.

Charles gave away the last of his possessions. His badge of the Order of St. George and his cane he gave to the Bishop, and his silver and gold watches to the Duke of Richmond, with the order that the gold one was for the Duchess; this had been King James's watch that Mall had played with as a child. Charles had bequeathed his silver striking clock to his personal attendant, Sir Thomas Herbert, who, though a Parliamentarian, had served him faithfully, but was too distressed to witness the execution. Taking off his doublet, the King pulled his cloak around him again, determined that he would not shiver and be thought afraid.

It was then that he saw him, standing behind the block, dressed in the green satin doublet he had worn that day. The air shimmered around him and the bright January sun caught the glint of the jewels. There was the well-remembered, beloved angel face: the lips curved in a warm smile of welcome and love; in his hand a single white rose. The King stood gazing at him for several minutes, drawing strength, his heart pierced once more with the love that was both joy and pain, though most assumed he was praying. No-one else appeared to be able to see him, but Charles Stuart had no doubt that Steenie had kept his promise that not even death itself would separate them.

LIST OF MAIN CHARACTERS

Abbot, George, Archbishop of Canterbury (1562-1633): A strong defender of Protestantism and a member of a faction which advocated an anti-Spanish policy. Abbott actively promoted George Villiers as a counter favourite to topple Robert Carr, Earl of Somerset.

Austria, Anne of (1601-66): The eldest daughter of King Philip III of Spain and his wife Margaret of Austria. She married Louis XIII in 1615 and was the mother of Louis XIV. It was rumoured that she had been involved in an affair with Buckingham in 1625, and that she had borne him a child.

Carr Robert, Viscount Rochester and Earl of Somerset (1587-1645): Scottish favourite of James I. He married Frances Howard after her divorce from the Earl of Essex, but was implicated in the horrific murder of Sir Thomas Overbury in the Tower in 1615 which led to his imprisonment.

Chevreuse, Duchesse de, Marie de Rohan (1600-79): French adventuress and court intriguer. The close friend and confidante of Anne of Austria, and actively promoted the Queen's affair with Buckingham. Marie was the mistress of many aristocrats, including Henry Rich, Earl of Holland, and probably Buckingham.

Coke Frances, Viscountess Purbeck (1603-45): The daughter of Sir Edward Coke and Lady Elizabeth Hatton. She was married to John Villiers in 1617, but found guilty of adultery with Sir Robert Howard whose child she bore. Frances escaped to France, and was later reconciled with her husband.

Compton, Mary, Countess of Buckingham (c1570-1632): The matriarch of the Villiers family. Mary was the second wife of Sir George Villiers of Brooksby and bore him John, Susan, George and Christopher. Six months after Sir George's death in 1606 she married Sir William Reyner, and married Sir Thomas Compton the following year.

Cranfield, Lionel, Earl of Middlesex (1575-1645): Influential politician who held several important roles in service of James I, including Chief

Commissioner of the Navy and Master of the Wardrobe. He was made Lord High Treasurer in 1621, but opposed the war with Spain and was impeached for corruption in 1624. Cranfield was coerced by Buckingham into taking Anne Brett for his second wife.

Denmark, Anne of (1574-1619): The second daughter of King Frederick II of Denmark. She married James VI of Scotland in 1589 at age 14 and bore him at least eight children, three of whom survived infancy.

D'Olivares, Count Gaspar de Guzman (1587-1645): The powerful favourite and most trusted advisor of Philip IV of Spain.

Eliot, Sir John (1592-1632): The son of Richard Eliot and Bridget Carswell. Eliot was a former friend and client of Buckingham, but became one of his most outspoken opponents, demanding the Duke's impeachment. Eliot's opposition to Buckingham incurred the enmity of Charles I, and he was imprisoned in the Tower where he died.

Gondomar, Count Don Diego Sarmiento de Acuna (1567-1626): The highly influential Spanish ambassador to England during the reign of James I.

James Hay, 1st Earl of Carlisle (1580-1636): The son of Sir James Hay and Margaret Murray. Hay was a former favourite of James I and a diplomat. He married Honoria, daughter of Edward, Lord Denny in 1607, and secondly married Lucy Percy in 1617.

Hay, Lucy, Countess of Carlisle (1599-1660): The second daughter of Henry Percy, 9th Earl of Northumberland and Lady Dorothy Devereux. She became the second wife of James Hay in 1617. Famed for her beauty and wit, Lucy was Buckingham's mistress until his death, and became the confidante and Lady of the Bedchamber to Henrietta Maria. Her later lovers included Thomas Wentworth, Ist Earl of Strafford and John Pym. Actively involved in political intrigues, Lucy was imprisoned in the Tower in 1649 where she was threatened with the rack for information about Charles I.

Henrietta Maria (1609-69): The youngest daughter of Henry IV of France and his second wife Marie de Medici. She married Charles I in 1625 and was known as Queen Mary. Their stormy relationship blossomed after Buckingham's assassination, and she bore him seven children. Henrietta's Catholicism and perceived influence over her husband made her unpopular. Throughout the Civil War years she was indefatigable in her efforts to raise funds for the royal cause. The Queen fled to France in 1644, returning to England after the restoration until 1665 when she finally retired to France.

Herbert, William, 3rd Earl of Pembroke (1580-1630): The eldest son of Henry Herbert, 2nd Earl of Pembroke and his third wife Mary Sidney. He was Lord Chamberlain of the Royal Household from 1615-25, and Lord Steward from 1626-30. Pembroke was part of the anti-Spanish faction which brought George Villiers to power, but he later became a strong opponent of Buckingham. He was a patron of Shakespeare, and thought by some to be the 'fair youth' of the sonnets. The first folio of Shakespeare's plays was dedicated to him and his brother Philip Herbert, 1st Earl of Montgomery and later 4th Earl of Pembroke, who was a former favourite of James I. Buckingham's daughter Mary married Montgomery's son Charles in 1635.

Manners, Francis, 6th Earl of Rutland (1578-1632): The second son of John Manners, 4th Earl of Rutland and Elizabeth Charlton. He married firstly Frances Knyvett by whom he had Katherine, and secondly Cecily Tufton who bore him two sons who died in childhood, allegedly by witchcraft.

Manners, Katherine, Duchess of Buckingham (1603-49): The only daughter of Francis Manners, 6th Earl of Rutland and Frances Knyvett. She married George Villiers, then marquis of Buckingham in 1620, and bore him four children: Mary, Charles, George and Francis (born posthumously). After Buckingham's assassination Katherine returned to her Catholic faith, resulting in King Charles removing her children from her care. She married Randal MacDonnell, Viscount Dunluce in 1635, and died in Ireland in 1649.

Maria Anna, Infanta of Spain (1606-46): The youngest daughter of Philip III and Margaret of Austria, and sister to Philip IV and Anne of Austria. Betrothed firstly to Prince Charles, she married her cousin, the future Ferdinand III, Holy Roman Emperor.

Philip IV of Spain (1605-65): The eldest son of Philip III and Margaret of Austria. He married Elisabeth of France in 1615.

Richelieu, Cardinal, Armand Jean du Plessis (1585-1642): The powerful chief minister of Louis XIII of France.

Rich, Henry, Viscount Kensington and 1st Earl of Holland (1590-1649): The son of Robert Rich and Penelope Devereux. He was a friend and client of Buckingham, and the lover of the Duchesse de Chevreuse, by whom it is thought he had a child. Holland was married to Isabel Cope in 1616. He was a Commander of the Royalist forces during the Civil War, and was captured and executed in 1649.

Stuart, Charles (1600-49): The second son of King James VI of Scotland and Anne of Denmark. Physically frail and reserved, Charles became heir apparent after the death of his elder brother Prince Henry in 1612. He initially disliked his father's favourite George Villiers, but became increasingly influenced by him. Charles succeeded his father in 1625 as Charles I, and married Henrietta Maria of France. He lost his crown after embroiling his realm in the English Civil War and was executed in January 1649.

Stuart, Elizabeth (1596-1662): The third child and eldest daughter of James VI and I, King of Scotland, England and Ireland, and his wife Anne of Denmark. Elizabeth married Frederick V, Elector Palatine, and was Electress Palatine and briefly Queen of Bohemia. As her husband's reign in Bohemia lasted merely one winter, Elizabeth is often referred to as The Winter Queen.

Stuart, Henry (1594-1612): The charismatic and popular elder son of King James I and VI and Anne of Denmark. He died of typhoid fever in 1612.

Stuart, James (1566-1625): The son of Mary Queen of Scots and Henry Stuart, Lord Darnley. He succeeded to the Scottish throne at the age of thirteen months as James VI, and succeeded Elizabeth I in 1603 as James I. He married Anne of Denmark in 1589, and produced three surviving children: Henry who died of typhoid in 1612, aged 18; Elizabeth, later queen of Bohemia; and Charles, his successor. Scholarly and peaceable, James's court was dominated by a series of male favourites, of whom the last and most influential was George Villiers.

Williams, John (1582-1650): Bishop of Lincoln and Lord Keeper, later Archbishop of York.

Villiers, George, First Duke of Buckingham (1592-1628): The third surviving son of Sir George Villiers by his second marriage to Mary Beaumont, later created Countess of Buckingham. He was the powerful favourite of King James I and his son Charles I. Buckingham married Lady Katherine Manners in 1620, and was the father of Mary, Charles, George and Francis (born posthumously). He was assassinated at Portsmouth on 23 August 1628 by John Felton.

Feilding, Susan, Countess of Denbigh (1589-1652): The daughter of Sir George Villiers and his second wife Mary Beaumont, later created Countess of Buckingham. She married William Feilding, later 1st Earl of Denbigh in 1607, and was Lady of the Bedchamber to Henrietta Maria. Susan's husband fought for the King during the Civil War, dying from his injuries, and her eldest son Basil supported the Parliamentarian side. She fled to France with the Queen in 1644, where she converted to Catholicism and died in Paris.

Villiers, John, 1st Viscount Purbeck (1591-1652): The eldest surviving son of Sir George Villiers by his second marriage to Mary Beaumont, later created Countess of Buckingham. He married firstly Frances Coke in 1617, whose adultery with Sir Robert Howard caused great scandal, and married secondly Elizabeth, daughter of Sir William Slingsby of Kippax in Yorkshire. John converted to Catholicism, and was prone to depression and fits of madness.

Villiers, Christopher, 1st Earl of Anglesey (1593-1630): The youngest son of Sir George Villiers by his second marriage to Mary Beaumont, later created Countess of Buckingham. He married Elizabeth Sheldon.

Villiers, Mary (1622-85): The only daughter of George Villiers, First Duke of Buckingham, and known as Mall. She was briefly married in 1635 to Lord Herbert, the eldest son of the 4th Earl of Pembroke. In 1637 she married James Stuart, 4th Duke of Lennox, and around 1643 Colonel Thomas Howard. Mall was a leading light at the court of Charles II.

Yelverton, Sir Henry (1566-1629): Lawyer and politician. He was created Attorney-General in 1613 but lost his position for his handling of an attack on monopolies and a subsequent attack on Buckingham.

About the Author

P. J. Womack has had a life-long passion for history, particularly the Stuart period, and has spent several years researching the life of George Villiers, first Duke of Buckingham. A qualified teacher, she lives with her son, her dog and hundreds of books in West Yorkshire.